D1510576

Novels by Lola Irish

THE TOUCH OF JADE
SHADOW MOUNTAIN
TIME OF THE DOLPHINS
AND THE WILD BIRD SING (New English Library)

AND THE WILD BIRDS SING

Lola Irish

NEW ENGLISH LIBRARY

First published in Great Britain in 1983 by New English Library

First NEL Paperback Edition September 1984

NEL Books are published by
New English Library,
Mill Road, Dunton Green,
Sevenoaks, Kent.
Editorial office: 47 Bedford Square, London WC1B 3DP

Made and printed in Great Britain by Richard Clay (The Chaucer Press) Ltd, Bungay, Suffolk

British Library C.I.P.

Irish, Lola
  And the wild birds sing.
  I. Title
823[F]   PR9619.3.I6/

ISBN 0-450-05760-7

For
Andrew James Coble

For the staunch old trees are standing,
And I hear the wild birds sing!
Jennings Carmichael: 'An Old Bush Road'

Author's Note

My thanks to the librarians and staffs of city and country libraries, in particular to those of the New South Wales Public Library, and the Mitchell Library, Sydney, as well as the staffs of city and country newspapers, during my years of research involving biographies, histories, newspapers, journals, diaries, letters, pamphlets, and so on, amounting to hundreds of publications, to compile the period background to my story.

Where applicable I have used the dialects of the time, and I have deliberately retained old spellings such as carrobbery, Jens (gins), as set down in the reminiscences of ordinary settlers able to write but without formal education. A unique and vivid vocabulary has evolved in Australia which has nothing to do with the Oxford graduate or the classical scholar: the pauper immigrant, the convict, or the native-born urchin did not go shepherding, survive the chain gang, or scratch a living from city streets bolstered by a dictionary in his pocket – if he had a pocket!

Some less familiar words and expressions can be found in the Glossary at the end of the book.

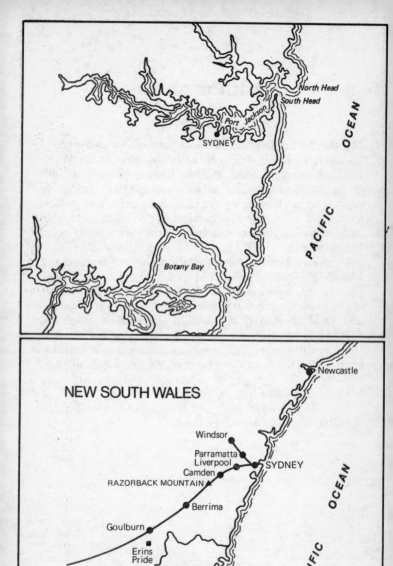

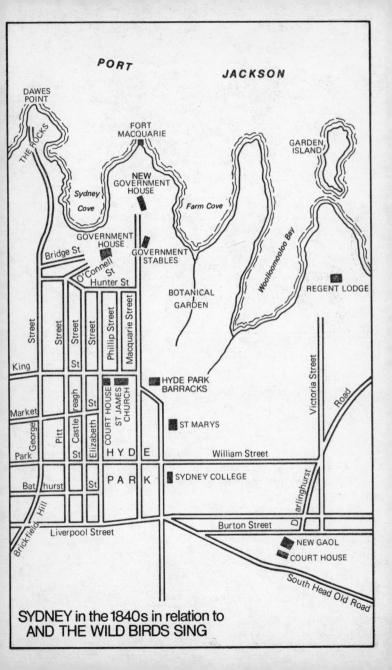

SYDNEY in the 1840s in relation to
AND THE WILD BIRDS SING

Australia, 1841

LAWS DEVISED for gaol and garrison still chained the great sunwashed continent of pastoral estates, feudal communities controlled by British expatriates intent on founding a ruling class. Beyond the nineteen counties of officialdom, Crown land was leased to carry as many sheep and cattle as it would hold without the expense and bother of improvement. Agriculture was an unwanted nuisance. The land remained for the very few . . .

Sydney, a hill and dale metropolis. Melbourne, a scatter of huts. Western Australia, a cluster of disappointed free grantees making the best of their barren land. Adelaide, a chain of pools beside which young gallants sat to champagne repasts while waiting for the promised lower classes to come and do the work. The small island of Tasmania, empty and silent but for the screams of its convicts and the whoops of its bushrangers . . .

The rest of it? A pot-pourri of political and religious refugees. The desperate overflow of the industrial sinks of England and Scotland. The tragic Irish peasant. Half-breeds, hybrid result of loneliness and passion, despised, at the kindest tolerated. Scattered shepherds and lonely wives. Beyond all these, the tribes of resentful aborigines regarded as a species of demon-clown. Beyond again, wilderness . . .

So the first generations of Australians grew to manhood stronger and leaner than their fathers. Vigorous and independent, good tradesmen, fine sailors and, to a man, ashamed, uneasily and fretfully ashamed, of their country's convict beginnings, anxious to dissociate themselves from it somehow . . . anyhow . . .

PART ONE

Chapter One

'LAND . . . *Land* . . .'

The cry beat against the wind then floated gently to the
decks. The *May Queen* seemed to still for a moment before
springing to renewed life. At last it was here, the visible
explanation of those trifles that had tantalised them for so
many expectant hours – the flash of light in a night sky, the
murk of seaweed as it tangled along, the chirruping of a land
bird high on a yard, butterfly wings among the cordage. It
lay before them, a shore dreaming under a summer sun,
indolent and lovely in its hazy distance. The milk-and-meat-
and-butter land. The somewhat frightening but long-awaited
streets-paved-with-gold land. Australia.

The rails were a dark string of pointing men, the 'tween
decks and ladders a flurry of women and children. They
laughed and cried and sang and swore in their released
anxiety as they stared at that floating distant cloud with
eager eyes, impatient for the smell of land, the feel of it
underfoot, the heavy sift of it through the fingers, for most
were of the earth – Kent, Surrey, Essex, stricken West
Countrymen hating city lanes, the outpourings of Ireland
desperate with the struggle in a London tenement. But there
were others too . . . pale waifs from a reeking slum, labourers
who looked the disgraced clerks they really were, haughty
would-be governesses, and the strumpets of the streets, as
one in their joy on this crisp January day as they collected
their children, or discarded transient couplings, or separated
their baggage from the sodden piles on deck. The months on
the death-defined sea road were past – the creaks of the
battered old East Indiaman, nights filled with the urinous
stench of sick and unwashed bodies, starvation rations, and
the despotism of the ship's officers. At last they were here,

at the fabulous land of the sun. Their dreams had become reality.

True, they could not yet land in Sydney Town, for the *May Queen* was a fever ship. The battening down during the Biscay gale had hastened the epidemic and before anyone had clearly grasped the reason six children had been consigned to the sea – but a total of eight adults and twenty-one infants dead was a better record than some ships could boast. A bad thing certainly so many came aboard ill, but they did, and no one seemed to care. The fellow Lorne for instance – there was something about the man that stuck in the mind – had looked half dead when he embarked, his dark petrel of a wife clinging to his arm. A gloomy youth with the arrogant glance of a gentleman coughing out his lungs with a 'delicacy' as the Irish put it, so that no one else could even get near a spitting pot. Why wouldn't he be one of the first to succumb to a fever? As for his wife, one couldn't ignore her either but the reason there was easier to understand. Very easy. Beautiful, if one liked women to be small and graceful with a pert reply to inquisitive questions. Not an easy creature but a lovely one, with a bold appraising glance from eyes that glowed liquidly black, only relieved of their darkness by queer orangey pupils with one jagged streak of green; the colour a dazzled ploughboy with a fanciful turn of mind had likened to 'downland grass in high summer'. Eyes that belied her ladylike dressing and demure ways as if a hussy were trying to be something she was not. And no layer of petticoats could hide a figure as supple and slender as a dryad's for all she was with child – trust women to unearth such facts. The women – the respectable women – could not forgive her her heartlessness, for she'd nursed her husband only when forced to it at the whirl of a rattan, and at his funeral service had stood dry-eyed, strolling on deck that same evening with the woman known as the Duchess. Laughing with the Duchess too. And then of course there was her dancing . . . But stolid male hearts would miss a beat, remembering . . . Perhaps, as their wives insisted, she did possess the evil eye . . . perhaps she was indeed a witch – perhaps she had even cursed the ship. Even so . . . and these busy protectors of families, these worthy pilgrims to an Arcadian dream, could not help a sigh or two as they moved to the bidding of their wide-hipped, capable, so righteous spouses.

Near noon and the *May Queen* – reluctant pilot aboard and flying the fever pennant – was beating her shuddering way in the teeth of a nor'easter towards the rocky mass of the Heads. Down in the foetid crowded Females Apartment Raunie Lorne struggled to dress while guarding her few possessions. She began to feel a mild excitement, a stimulus which she welcomed, for since her husband had died she had been oddly numbed. Not that she hadn't, in one way, welcomed her release from the sickly creature who had almost driven her mad with his railings against fate – the dandy, the splendid young gallant of Courtney House had only too quickly dissolved in the light of maudlin confidences into the drunken weakling of the debtor's prison – but the possibility that he might die and leave her to face a strange raw country alone had never once occurred to her. Others were ill and went on living. But James was dead, rotting somewhere in the depths where the Atlantic and Indian Oceans met, his only bequest to her a degrading exile and a child she did not want. And the swift turmoil of circumstance that had flung them half across the world together had become something of a dream, sweet to the taste, yet bitter . . .

For no son of a peer had she married. Her ignorance as to the domestic interlacings of the family with whom she had risen to the status of a lady's-maid not so much saddened her now as angered her. How greedily she had fed on the scraps of information concerning James dropped by his timid mother and sisters, how she had trembled as she curtsied before him the day he returned from his 'travels abroad', how she had revelled in her triumph as his eyes followed her, sullenly yet persistently. The shock of their sailing . . . Lord Farleigh's disgraced stepson bundled out to the colonies to the elder sister who adored him, to rot if it pleased him to rot. And his wife with him . . .

The barque shuddered. The half-naked women grasped

baggage, bunks, each other in a long-practised effort to steady themselves. Children whimpered, to subside beneath the impatient slaps of their mothers. Moans swelled from the six berths officially termed 'Hospital'. Hospital indeed – almost every bunk had held its sick and dying. The girl who had been in labour since dawn screamed as she rolled against the wall, calling for her husband. She seemed to have forgotten he was dead. Someone stuffed a fold of her bloodstained skirt into her mouth; there was noise enough without such ravings. From the decks floated down the sweet ghost-call of an ocarina. Voices took up the strain. Somewhere the thin tremble of a fiddle tantalised and beckoned. Then, high above all other sounds came a shriek of laughter. A woman's laughter. Chatter subsided and all glanced uneasily at each other. Some flopped into their bunks out of the way. Everyone found something urgent to do. Even the children were quiet. Brushing aside those who blocked her path with her choicest oaths and blows that almost knocked them off their feet, the Duchess fell sprawling on to the shelf at Raunie's feet.

Like an ageing paroquet flaunting ragged and jaded feathers the Duchess might have been forty-five – or twenty. Red matted hair, a face pale beneath its paint, bedraggled skirts dripping scents forever waging war against the reek of her unwashed body. A trunkful of powders and potions and cheap gewgaws. Garish scraps of clothing that she guarded with her life, and a murderous dagger that would slice a girl's cheek at the slightest provocation or pin a man's hand to a post with the dexterity of a Spaniard. Dangerous to her sex and shameless with men, the Duchess was the queen of her kind. Since embarkation she had flattered and coerced the men, subdued the children and dominated the women. As the first terror of the fever took hold she had moulded a crude but swift discipline from the stupefied confusion; she wasn't scared of the fever, not the Duchess, there was only one thing she feared – laughing to mask the terror in her eyes – the hangman's noose. She forced the robust to nurse the sick at the point of her dagger and sobered the vacillating surgeon by dowsing him in a barrel of sea-water and kicking him, spluttering, from patient to patient. It was she who had forced Raunie to tend her dying husband but, despite her bullying, she had from the first made something of a protégé of her, thrusting herself as a shield between the tormentings of the females and the too-amorous attentions of the men. Sometimes she called her 'milady' in a grand mock deference, insisting on sharing the wine she coaxed – or threatened – from the third mate, and leaving the narrow shelf they shared to the girl's restless body, laughing that there was always room elsewhere for a generous-hearted female, fever or no fever. Raunie was grateful to stretch her limbs, yet, in some curious way, reluctant to see her go. She feared the woman but did not know how she would fare without her. Even her ribald humour was better than indifference the morning she found the girl retching out her heart: 'A babe.' And she had rolled about like a drunken Billingsgate fishwife at Raunie's stare of mute terror. 'Lor, as innocent as a lamb, or as stupid. Wait your time and see, gal, wait your time and see.'

But Raunie had retched again, from fright, and cried till her eyes were hot. Nothing had been further from her mind than a child. She had been perhaps five when she had first peeped through a broken window in the reeking alley that was her home to stare at a girl's twitching limbs, striving to understand her gipsy mother's confused explanation of the process of childbirth. Gipsies were lucky, they had babies as gently as animals, but the bearing of life consumed a large slice of a woman's good years and if one could one avoided it. Babes ruined beauty. And it was this threat more than anything else that terrified Raunie. Beauty was all she had. But the eagerly accepted experience of mating, and James's bursts of sexual passion that had roused such an appetite of the body that even now she was tormented by its hot throbbings, had dulled her sense of physical consequence. Now she was to bear that consequence. But she didn't want James's child. Anyone's child. What would she do with a baby? So, while the barque tossed and strained she had beaten her fists against the wood and set her sharp little teeth into the backs of her hands in futile rebellion, wanting to die. She even longed for the fever knowing full well she would escape it. Wasn't she a gipsy – strong, constant, enduring? She brooded and sulked and begged the Duchess for help but the woman only teased her, dragging her on deck to observe the inevitability of her condition in the swelling figures of the other women, coaxing her to dance again, now, before she grew unwieldy. And then the Duchess began to brood. A great pity about the dancing . . .

She had been fascinated by Raunie's dancing since the morning when, bored by James and his coughing, the girl had come on deck lured by the scrape of a fiddle and had tossed off her shoes, hitched up her skirts and with the swollen sails and wide white rollers as background to the awed crowd gathering about her had begun a 'danza', moving only her bare feet. Then a 'bailé'. And when she had finished she had stood panting, complete, all-gipsy, knowing the Irish were blessing themselves and mothers tucking their children behind their skirts and wondering over the token swinging on its chain about her neck before she had time to tuck it away again – and caring nought for any of them. For she was herself when she danced. She was Raunie: the Romany child who, excited and ecstatic, would abandon her rag-clad body and dirty feet to the surging music of a group of travelling Roms and the shouts of 'diba diba' as a dancing bear made absurd attempts to imitate her snapping fingers and tongue, all Romany until her mother dragged her off and locked her away. She was destined for a better fate than the dregs of slum lanes. Wasn't she named 'raunie' and didn't 'raunie' mean what the gorgios called 'a gentlewoman'? She was different. She was singular. Wretched, hating the squalor and stench of the 'tween decks, longing for the clean wind on her limbs, she would turn over to bury her head in the straw that was her mattress. Singular? An almost penniless widow of sixteen with a child on the way and travelling to a country she feared held scant welcome? There was no refuge but in her tears.

But it was her dancing rather than tears that, Raunie sensed, made the Duchess relent. The woman had brought her a mug of evil-tasting fluid and, with a knowing wink at her cronies, had watched the girl drink. This would end the babe, she insisted. All would be well and Raunie could dance forever – never had she, the Duchess, seen such winning ways. But the only effect had been a terrible nausea, a little pain – nothing else at all. A few days more and the Duchess had shrugged, staring at her as she might stare at a freak.

'Too late. Or you've the entrails of a bloody goat. Well, you've got yourself a babe and you'll keep it so make the best o' your trouble. There's lots about to keep you company.' And fat legs apart and hands on hips she had thrown back her head in peals of laughter thick with all the unquenchable spirit of her teeming Riverside.

Now, yelling to the girl moaning in her labour pains, 'Stash it afore you gives yourself a jaw ache, you've hours to labour yet,' she curled up on the bunk and fixed her spiteful dark eyes on her favourite. 'You've been nursing a dead 'un so that dress is for the fire. Give it 'ere.'

'I can't. You know I can't. I've nothing else to wear.'

'Give it 'ere I say. You knows it's the law. Do you want the cap'n down?'

Reluctantly, Raunie handed over her one decent gown, too heavy for this heat certainly, but so very Courtney House. Since dawn the Duchess had been demanding clothes destined to be destroyed and no one dared oppose her even though they knew she would smuggle them ashore to peddle to the highest bidder – and no use complaining to the crew for she would share her profits with them while doing her wiliest to cheat them. She fingered the fine stuff with a grunt of approval then hitched the dress through her belt to dangle like some ludicrous but splendid rag doll. She grinned.

'A reglar prude ain't you, milady? Wear this . . . Too squeezy for me now.'

She dragged something from her own bundle and threw it across. It was the red gown. Bedraggled and dirty now from her strutting about the decks in her particular imitation of the promenading cabin passengers it was gay and bold if nothing more, stolen no doubt from some habitué of Drury

11

Lane, the kind of dress flaunted nightly by the whores of Covent Garden. Ah, she, Raunie Lorne, had thought herself well versed in the ways of back alleys, but that was nought to what she had learned aboard. Why, these pavement strollers here, tossed about in the bowels of an immigrant barque, knew more of the good and the great of England than the good and the great knew of each other! And herself? The great of England were lost with James in her misty bitter-sweet dream, the substance of her life reduced to a dingy cast-off dress . . . But she dragged it over her shift and hitched it about her still-small waist with a length of green ribbon. She was lucky. Some of the others wore only nightgowns.

''Tis an elegant dress.' The Duchess strutted around her, well-pleased. ''Ere! 'Tis milady's,' she shrieked, slamming the fist of a girl daring to finger the hem. 'Clap your dirty mawleys on it and I'll slit your throat from ear to ear.' She jerked a thumb upwards. 'Scurrying up there like rats about an offal pile but nothing to snap their teeth at as yet but cliffs that look like the gates o' hell. The promised land they calls it.' Her laugh shrilled. 'Hear that, you molls? The promised land. And the toffs ashore cussing us for the fever ship we are. Well, one land, one town, 'tis all the same in the end. Pubs and dawgs and lushy laggers – '

'You didn't 'ave to come out,' someone called. The women gasped. A face had been slit for less. The Duchess swung about in fury and fear. 'I did. And you all knows why. Old 'uns can't breathe in Lunnon town. I had to come out, away from Bridewell. I was born in Bridewell. Me muvver died in Bridewell – hanged. And I got to feeling the bloody noose about me own neck – ' Her voice strangled somewhere behind her blackened teeth and they stared at her in horror for she was speaking of things they wanted to forget. They were still, scarcely breathing, till her mood died and she was cheerful again, gloating over the grotesque and bawdy picture Raunie made. 'But I'm daft jawing this way to a gal whats 'usband was the arristoxy itself. A gen'leman if a lushy one. Such an elegant corpse!' She smacked her lips then winked at the women. 'Cotched 'im she did with that innocent look that

12

never once fooled the Duchess. She mayn't know Bridewell but for all her flash airs she knows what makes a lagger's darling . . . don't you, me fancy?'

Faces wrinkled into uneasy grins. A snigger here, another there. Raunie's face burned but she kept her eyes down as she tucked her few things into James's bag – a handful of trinkets, her hairbrush, the bottle of rosewater she had taken from Lady Farleigh's room. The first thing her mother had taught her was to take but never get caught, for the gipsy attitude was simple and not to be argued with; you took what was needed from life or ceased to exist and to cease to exist was unthinkable. She hung her bonnet over her arm. There was little else to pack, for James's clothes, even his greatcoat with its rich fur collar, had disappeared. Indeed, everything unwatched vanished. Through the silk dress she fingered the guineas safe in the little bag pinned to her shift; she had made it of linen to hold the two guineas Lord Farleigh had tossed her and the one gold piece she had found in James's pockets before his body turned cold – there were always lingerers to rifle the corpses. Then her fingers strayed to her precious charm tucked between her breasts . . .

She tried not to shrink as the Duchess's grimy hand fondled her thick black hair and gave a playful pinch to her cheek. 'Such a face and only shepherds to gawp where they'll be taking her.' The woman's hand slid slowly, caressingly, across her shoulder. 'Don't be daft, gal. Stay in Sydney and dance. Stay with the Duchess.'

It was not the first time she had made the suggestion but now, incredibly, Raunie found herself wavering. There was a threat in the woman's interest but there was flattery too. And hope. For this slattern before her was her only friend – if such a creature could be called a friend – while deep within her was mistrust of the strangers waiting to employ her husband, and her husband only for she feared they could not know James Lorne had left England saddled with a wife. If they gave her shelter she would be wanted for the toil of her hands, nothing less, nothing more – James had been mockingly certain on that score. He had known what was expected of them, had James Lorne, as he growled sulky answers to her questions.

'Sydney? What else but a convict hulk ashore? And Witherstone's a righteous cuss. As for his wife . . . a bush hut and kisses and brats, Betsy will take them all from him and ask for more.' But his voice had softened under the bitter grumbling words. 'My sister loves the man, the poor sweet fool. Didn't she set London on its ears to marry a Fenland farmer? And didn't she emigrate? As for this O'Shea who employs them . . .' He shrugged and filled his glass again. 'And the rest of it . . .'

The rest of it . . . Slinking jackal dogs that never barked. Crow-black swans. Willows that were giants to the cringing dwarfs of England. How could he know if such tales were true? And the bottle would rattle against the glass again and he would taunt her with that whining persistency that was all he seemed capable of now. 'You wouldn't have married me if you'd known the truth, would you m'love? Well, you haven't done too badly for a serving-wench.' She shrugged her hated memories of him aside. Should she take a chance on his sister and this man O'Shea? Or would the Duchess be the better bargain?

As if goaded by her silence, the Duchess grasped the chain about Raunie's neck and jerked the charm loose. Terrified, the girl's hand went up to shield it, for her mother had warned her about keeping it hidden while never being without it, her protection against 'malocchio' – evil influences. She had been careless. But the Duchess, she saw, was hiding it as her fingers traced the shape of the boar's tooth with a pig surmounting its base. It was of zinc or copper, perhaps silver – she could not be sure – but she knew it was very old. And when the woman spoke it was so softly no one else could have heard.

'You dance like a Romany. Ah . . . *That's* what you be. A Romany.'

Raunie went cold. 'My parents were Irish,' she whispered.

The Duchess tightened the chain until it stung her flesh. 'I knows a Rom when I finds one.'

And the girl dared not anger her. Yet dared not admit her Romany blood, no, not even to the Duchess, if she wished to be treated as something more than a pariah. She was steeped in the immense pride of blood that was the initiation of all gipsies, and the necessary subtlety to make use of a gipsy's gifts while keeping their characteristics buried deep within her. Her mother had passed on her own knowledge of what was 'mochardi' and what 'taboo', the remedies brewed from herbs and plants, the spells and the tremendous power of Romany magic. The need of amulets and charms and luck-bringers, and the signs and language by which she would recognise 'chabos' – her people – wherever she went. And it lay deep and well-cherished; the scraps and smatterings, the legends and lore, all handed down from Romany generation to generation.

But an Irish pedlar had fathered her. Of that she was certain. Handsome despite his dreadful rags he had come once to their room and fondled her where he ignored her drabs of sisters. Instinctively she had sensed herself in him and though she never saw him again was grateful; the Irish might be unwanted and suspected but a gipsy waif was accursed wherever she went. The Duchess's breath was hot and foul on her cheek.

'But 'tis nought to the Duchess what you be. Come with the Duchess and be what you like. Eh, milady?'

Raunie's throat burned. Suddenly frightened of the woman, but more so of her own indecision, she clawed wildly at the Duchess's hand – and it was then a dull persistent boom, boom began to war with the familiar creaks of the barque. The Duchess released her abruptly and turned to listen. They all listened. And responded. The throbbing of the ship seemed more insistent. It stirred Raunie's blood, reviving her flagging confidence, and she turned from the pale faces and unkempt hair, the never-washed and never-changed petticoats of the Duchess's followers; Thames-side women rotting from disease, running from the shadow of Bridewell Prison, scooped from the London kennels to pack the emigrant ships that must be filled, and quickly, before

15

sailing. She refused to be stifled by them and their world. The protective ambitious harridan of a washerwoman who had mothered her had pushed her through a kitchen doorway into the glitter and sheen of one of London's great houses to take her chance, her preparation the reading and writing of a few short English words, the counting of the few coins that came her way, a smattering of 'gorgio' logic and a mumbo-jumbo of gipsy lore – what would be her mother's choice?

But the Duchess had forgotten all but her fear of falling behind her fellows and was kicking and cursing, weaving a frantic path for herself up the dangerous ladders. Raunie gathered up her things with eager hands. Here . . . now . . . she could not decide. But above, with the wind and the gulls and the breakers booming, she could, perhaps, think? Lugging her carpet-bag, using her elbows and feet as did everyone else she too fought the mob to scramble on deck where all who could walk were scrabbling a place. Children were singing, their fathers whistling, their mothers laughing or pointing or staring out in wide-eyed silence. South Head with its neat buildings and lighthouse soared on their left with giant white-tipped waves pounding the black and cruel rocks to drown voices, all else in their sound. But the children sang louder and more joyously. A paean to the new land.

Battered by gales, foul with the stench of the sick and the dying, pulsating with the sea and the cries of the happy and the quick, the *May Queen*, more by the grace of God than the skill of her captain, sailed through Sydney Heads and into the haven of Port Jackson.

A week later they were beating up the Harbour, a beautiful breathtaking stretch of windflecked water rising in films of spray to tease the cloud-scattered sky. Thick tumbled foliage, piled masses of rock, yellow sand crescents. Bay after little bay with, here and there, a cultivated patch of earth and a small white building amid trees as if afraid to encroach by its civilised shape into such prodigal loveliness.

16

While to starboard the land opened to deeper and still deeper indentations, disappearing into silent wooded mystery.

Balancing by the rails, Raunie was grasped about the waist and soundly kissed. With a clenched fist she freed herself from Jock McPhee, a cheery rogue when sober but an object of ridicule when drunk – and he was drunk too often. But he went off cheerfully enough rubbing a stinging eye. The Duchess could be heard shepherding her women to a higher vantage point to see and be seen so Raunie crept into the crowd, hiding from her as she had avoided her during quarantine while they laboured, roping the berths and fittings together to make crude rafts to be purified by the Harbour water, while the vessel was scrubbed out with lime. At times the woman had sought her out to coax, patiently or angrily according to her mood, while Raunie, miserable and tormented, parried. But she had made up her mind the morning she had strolled round a pile of rocks to see the woman gloating over James's greatcoat. She would bargain it ashore as only she could bargain to some greasy-haired procurer. Then she would bargain her women. And for the women it would be a bad bargain . . .

She, Raunie, would never be . . . used. Never. She was a gipsy. She was proud. If she were beautiful and clever – though cleverness must only be displayed as wit – she could make men dance to her tune. Her own way. Old whispered words ran through her mind . . . 'You have a mind and a body. Waste neither. If one fails you, see that the other does not.' She understood her mother's words now – you used your mind to make the best use of your body, that body to content and enrich your mind. And that part of her concealed in her loins had a marketable value superior to anything else she now possessed or might acquire. So . . . she must do nothing unplanned, nothing hasty or to be regretted. Her favours must be favours of design. Her own design. Whatever she must do, she would survive.

The barque was bearing down upon a tongue of land – Bradley's Head. The points and bays, all the known landmarks were bandied about and clung to as something definite

17

in this space of water and sky and green tangled hills. The sun hung overhead, fierce and cloying, and the children fretted in their heavy clothes. The ship swung round the Head and the whole vivid reach of the lower Harbour opened before them, a tightly packed maze of ships. Barques from London, China, Frisco. Coastal traders, sailing boats, whaleboats with their shouting straining crews. They cleared twisted little islands, one a jagged humpback in mid-Harbour – the Pinchgut – with a sharp splinter of bare rock rearing up from its centre. They pointed out the whalers climbing like black gleeful monkeys to hang from the tops of their vessels, peering between wisps of washing to shout their rough welcome to the Duchess and her friends. And the women screamed and waved and flaunted their hips with all the abandon of the first shipload of women felons to land on these shores. A bawdy welcome but an honest one.

The respectable and timid did their best to ignore such slatterns by pointing out the row of windmills on a rise, the mansions in their shields of trees, a yellow-stoned Fort Macquarie and, on the farther dagger of land, uniformed figures strolling about Lieutenant Dawes's Battery. To the west that arm of the sea called simply 'the River' shimmered in golden light. Tangled masts peeped over the slight hillock that hid the small stretch of water girding the town's heart. But now. . . . And there it lay, nestling in smooth, sheltered, almost secret tranquillity. The birth and breath of Sydney Town – Sydney Cove.

Boats. Large boats, small boats, old boats, bright new boats. They darted from nowhere yet everywhere crammed with whalers and whores, dandies and toughs, top-hatted gentlemen and fashionably dressed dames. Girls and old women – very few of the latter. Children and babies in profusion. Like busy black ants the little boats hovered, clinging to their tired and yielding prey as they bobbed and skimmed, floundering through the churn of clean clear water, strange stuff to those who'd known nothing but the Thames from slime-clogged riverside stairs. The breeze freshened, whipping skirts and bonnet strings and tendrils of hair in a light dancing carelessness while high above the gulls screamed and whirled about the sea-stained canvas.

Like a full-skirted matron teased by her brood of mischievous daughters the *May Queen* slid thankfully, almost with a sigh, towards Phillip's hope and his festering sore: Sydney.

The immigrant barque, as if lulled by the dying sun, had become as a somnolent bird pecked by the wherries darting between the ship's ladders and the wharf. As Raunie followed Robert Witherstone through the crowd on shore, life about the Cove resolved itself into clear if incongruous objects and she longed to dawdle. But there was no escaping the eyes of the dour man who strode ahead so resolutely he was obliged to pause now and then until she should come up with him. Deliberately, insolently, she made him wait. She had wandered the deck striving to lose herself in the shifting groups when she saw the mate walking a stranger towards her – and knew she was trapped. From the moment of meeting those chill storm-grey eyes she had sensed that here was one man proof against obvious wiles. She resented that. She resented him. And had been unable to stop a rush of protests. She was not strong . . . a cabin passenger had offered her a place in Sydney . . . she could not milk or cook . . . she was really very stupid . . . Her useless impulsive excuses had dwindled helplessly away. In a final desperation she had even glanced about for the Duchess. But the man Witherstone had looked long at her strong little hands, twitched his lips at her apology for a garment contrasting so brutally with the demureness of her bonnet, swept up her bag and hauled her along the deck with two iron-hard fingers about her wrist.

'If we cannot have thy husband we must make do with his leavings. We do not travel close on three hundred miles and spend a precious week frying in this hole to take nought back with us to the Pride. Now hurry, and hold thy tongue. Thou art not fit to be seen in other company than this.'

She had kicked out at him but he had simply whipped her off her feet and tossed her anyhow into a wherry where she crouched, shaken. She hated him. She would go on hating him. But she was trapped. Now, sulking, she elbowed her way after him across the quayside. A sailor jostled her, turned and leered. He had one eye in an ugly knife-scarred face. From his shoulder a purple parrot gabbled. She laughed but as the man turned and lurched after her, she ran. Safe in the crowd again she giggled; she could not help it. Earth beneath her feet – she shuffled it, loving the small yellow clouds rising about her ankles – strange new earth but warm and full of promise. Under the brilliant sky, so sharp-blue she could not stare into it long, everything appeared sharper, stronger, the shadows deeper, the black so black, the gold boasting a garish glint. The alley dirt of her childhood had been slimy, maggoty, but here the earth lay dry and bright, ready at the faintest wisp of air to become dust coiling about her limbs, dancing from eyelashes to the manes of horses, from hairtips to a child's fingernail. Her heart lightened. An untidy but exciting place. She skipped here and darted there, dodging the drays and watercarts and champing beasts, the occasional coach plunging headlong to scatter the mob. A barque rested on the beach, workmen toiling on its bottom and sides. Inn doors squeaked open and shut, open and shut. A fight here, one there. Scents rose and clamoured above the fresh harbour breeze to sting her nostrils. And over everyone and everything the powder-fine pall of dust filled the throat and tingled the eyes to water.

The crowd thinned a little, suddenly, as crowds do. Mr Witherstone – as he had bade her call him – waited beside a wagon. Swinging her hips a little she took as long as she safely might to cross the road. He threw her bag into the wagon's maw, lifted her on to the seat then climbed briskly beside her. Jamming his pipe in his mouth his whip stung the bullocks and the wagon lurched over the hot dry road.

The dying sun burned in their faces with a final angry defiance as they swung into a wide street, a better street with neat new buildings, old men stumbling along with baskets on their heads, young men with their cries of 'Fish O' and their breeches strained across their bulging bottom cheeks as they pushed their top-heavy barrows. A mounted police-man, gaudily resplendent with his blue jacket sparkling with silver buttons, a group of officers turning to stare at her as they swaggered along, a carriage swerving by permitting a tantalising glimpse of blue eyes framed by a flowered bonnet . . . She turned to watch the sheltered elegance disappear.

'George Street.' Rob Witherstone spoke for the first time since leaving the waterfront. 'And sulking will not help thee.'

'I'm tired and thirsty,' she said tightly. 'And unused to such heat.'

'The heat will be worse next month,' he said bluntly. 'But 'tis not far now to Old Kate's. Supper will be waiting and then thou'lt rest.'

Perhaps after all . . . She glanced at him. But no . . . oh no. A spare streak of a man, a man who, it was clear, made life a solemn business. She hated and feared and ran from coldness. Warmth was her sustenance. In men, women, life . . . Some-thing dropped in her lap. Half a lemon.

' 'Twill cool thee.' He slid his knife back under his belt. 'And don't waste the juice. 'Tis a precious fruit here.' He sucked his own scrap. 'When any from the Pride come to town we stay with Old Kate. Moll is waiting there. Moll Noakes is by way of being housekeeper to Mr O'Shea and thou wilt be accountable to her for thy work and thy manners. Best mind both where Moll's concerned.' He threw the lemon skin in the gutter and, as if exhausted by his volubility, jammed his pipe between his thin lips and slumped beside her.

Moll Noakes. Another gaoler. But the lemon was tart and cooling. They were plodding through a meaner quarter and soon, an even more squalid one. A huddle of public houses leaned drunkenly one upon another. Here and there a dirty battered door would burst open and a woman with torn shift and wild hair would run screaming into the glare to be dragged back by half-clothed whalers. Street spilled into little street with puddles of noxious ooze seeping from the cottage gutters. Packs of curs fought and goats wandered.

Children . . . a prodigality of little people with straight strong limbs and the rosiest cheeks ever seen. A beggar searched the pockets of a drunken reveller as they both lay in what passed for a gutter, sprawled amid the piles of refuse, all steaming under the blanket of sun. At last they turned a corner to feel a wisp of cool air on their faces and halted before one of a row of hovels that ran in a tipsy line to the water's edge.

A dog bounded at Robert. He teased it. Raunie watched it warily. Dogs were 'mochardi' – unclean. But the hounds of her childhood had been scavenging beasts whereas this dog was brisk and thick-coated. The door opened and a woman, stooping through the low doorway, straightened to shade her eyes with a big gnarled hand. A faded dress, a soiled apron, wisps of grey hair escaping from an aged cap with what had once been lace clinging precariously to its frill. She might have been fifty-five but she strode the tiny path and flung open the rickety gate with the briskness of a girl. A woman obviously of great strength and dominant will.

'The kettle's biled this hour past,' she grumbled. Then as Robert climbed down and sauntered to the back of the wagon, the dog leaping for his ears, she grasped his arm and gestured at Raunie.

'Young Lorne's wife.' He pushed her aside impatiently.

'*Wife?*' she echoed, staring up at Raunie from eyes lost in a network of grimy wrinkles. A scar at the corner of her thin mouth shone whitely. With an arrogant gesture she motioned Raunie to climb down. The girl made two hesitant attempts before she felt herself clasped about the waist and deposited roughly in the dust.

'A fine way o' things, can't even climb from a wagon.' Moll Noakes folded her bony arms. 'What be your name?'

'Raunie.' She picked up her bag and dusted it as carefully as if it were inlaid with mother-of-pearl. She wasn't going to let the woman bully her.

'Raunie . . .' Moll rolled it about her loud and generous tongue. ''Tis queer – nay, more than queer. It has a bad lilt to it. So has this,' she added, fingering the red dress. 'All rags an' jags.'

Raunie snatched it from her hands. ' 'Tis a fine dress. And I'll wear what I please.'

But the woman was pinching and prodding Raunie's flesh as she might knead a lump of dough. 'Thin arms, smooth hands an' a heart chuckfull o' deviltry I'll be bound behind that sly look.'

'She has no liking for work,' Robert called from somewhere inside the wagon.

'She'll learn to like it.' Suddenly alert, she looked about her. 'But your man . . .'

'My husband,' Raunie explained wearily, 'is dead.'

'Dead?' the woman shrieked. '*Dead*?'

'Of fever,' Robert put in. 'But he was half dead already it seems of the consumption, so what matter? 'Tis better that he die at sea than at the Pride with none of us time to be digging graves.'

' 'Tood send a woman crazy,' Moll raved, pacing up and down while a group of toddlers gathered to stare. 'Two fever ships in a month an' naught for our journey down but a saucy gal with a saucy tongue in an even saucier dress.'

'Thou art riled thou hast no such garment. Ask her to lend it thee, the bonnet as well. Thou hast always hankered after a new bonnet and this has fine long streamers,' Robert laughed. It was the first time Raunie had heard him laugh and it did not suit him. There was no laughter in his eyes. He filled Moll's arms with bundles and pushed her towards the cottage. 'Thou shalt have a man tomorrow; a strapping Celt with more brawn than sense. I'll haul him here by the time we leave. I promise thee. Give him the night in which to get drunk and he'll work for half what he now asks, if only to break free of the trouble he's now weaving for himself. Now see to the supper. The girl is hungry.'

Moll lapsed into a murmur of what could only be her pure native dialect but turned and led the way. They made a straggling little procession watched by children, dogs, three blowsy women in doorways with babies on their hips, and the ever-present, imperturbable goats.

The cottage was hot and dim. As Raunie's eyes grew

accustomed to the gloom she saw the parlour boasted nothing more than a few sticks of furniture and an old woman crouched in a corner chair; a witch of an old creature who nodded and grinned and stared at them with red running eyes as she sucked on a foul-smelling pipe.

'Kate,' Moll bellowed, clattering things into corners. 'The boy we come to fetch is dead but this be his wife for what she's worth, which don't promise to be much.' But the crone only stowed her pipe into some fold of her clothing or flesh, picked up a dish of bread and gravy and stuffed her mouth with a sucking enjoyment until juice dribbled down her chin and into the grease-stiffened front of her dress.

'Deaf,' Moll boomed as she flung open a door with the clanging exuberance with which she made her slightest movement. 'An' near blind. Bellar at her, gal, bellar.'

But Raunie ignored them both, loathing them as she loathed all this dinginess and stupidity. But she had no choice but to follow the woman into the tiny box of a room with a window opening on a square of earth and a line of faded washing flapping in what was left of the sea breeze. An old trunk for a chair, a bed of sorts, that was all. But she ached to lie on the uninviting plank. Moll fetched a dish of water and a cloth, remarked that the meal was ready and banged the door after her. Raunie soaked the rag, wiped its blessed coolness over her face till her skin tingled, turned resolutely from the bed, and went out. Robert was eating and without looking up waved her to a chair. Moll broke bread into hunks and filled plates with a steaming mess of dark stew. The smell of it made Raunie's stomach heave. But a plate awash with it, a mug of scalding tea and a lump of bread were dumped before her. She drank eager mouthfuls of tea; it stung her throat but it was good. And soon, though the cooling meat was revolting she would eat it for she was suddenly ravenous. The door opened and a small wizened man limped in and sank into the vacant chair. Moll jerked her head at Raunie as she slid a piled dish before the newcomer.

'Here be all we get for our trouble – Raunie she calls

herself. Her man is dead. Well, she must learn to do the work o' two.'

Raunie met the creature's eyes, surprisingly young eyes in an alert if aged face. But his body was twisted; a crooked right leg and arm, one hand mis-shapen. His greasy hair, or what remained of it, rose in matted tufts all over his large head. He stared at her fixedly and a little foolishly until Moll, leaning across to pour his tea, slapped him over the ears.

'A dull character our Paddy,' she explained, but her fingers brushed his forehead gently. 'Willing an' content but melancholy with the fears of a child in his mind. The hulks an' the irongangs broke his senses along with his limbs.' But as he slobbered the hot stew she sent a blow to his warped shoulder that half lifted him from his chair. 'Spill your vittles, Padraic Harrigan, an' I'll joggle your nose in it, that I will.' She fetched her own plate and sat with a gasp of relief.

There was silence then except for the champing of jaws but Raunie knew each one was watching her and biding time to judge her. Somewhere a baby screamed, a wagon rumbled. The breeze was dead, not even a wisp to creep through the open leaning back door. The hush of night was about them. From close by came the roll of drums and the eerie sweetness of fifes. She looked up.

'Tattoo. The Barracks are in George Street,' Robert murmured. Moll sniffed.

'She'll find the Barracks soon enough. The gals don't like to bake an' wash but they learn bright an' early where the "lobsters" be.'

Robert's lips twitched. 'Hast thou not always hurried to hangings to stare at the guards?'

'Liar. I hate the sodgers an' well you knows it, Rob Witherstone. I went to see the murderers dangle, that's all. Everyone knows Moll Noakes was one for hangings.' She sighed. 'Too peaceable now, the town. When I was a gal they did not pray afore they dangled. They cussed. An' what cusses.' She rolled her eyes. 'They twisted your very bowels, they did.'

'Rhaunie . . . 'tis quare . . . Rhaunie . . .' Paddy rolled it about his tongue in delight as he beamed on her. 'But a jhewel of a name, a jhewel.'

Moll sucked a mess of bread through her teeth with a hideous wheezing sound. 'An' what is Sydney after your mucky London streets, eh? A paradise?'

Raunie pushed her plate aside. Certainly no paradise, Sydney, but who expected or wanted paradise? The place was gusty and alive, above all free, yes free in spite of its legacy of chains, free in the sense that it promised anything and everything. So much could happen to me here, she thought, wonderful changeling things, the things I'm searching for, the things I need. I can't stand still. I must go on . . . and on.

'I like Sydney,' she said, her voice sharp with fright because she knew what she was saying would do her no good. But all her contempt for them came bursting forth . . . 'And I won't go away with you. I never wanted to go with you. Neither did James. Not really. I want to stay here. And I will stay here.'

She gulped. The silence was heavy while they stared at her and at each other. Then Moll half stood and leaned across the table. Her hands struck the wood again and again until the mugs rattled and the plates jumped.

'I'll warr'nt you likes it,' she raved, and for one awful moment Raunie was sure her hands would come curling about her throat. 'All the gals want to stay in Sydney Town. They want an easy place. They want to toddle in the Domain on a Sunday with painted chakes like any shammack's darter – '

'How dost thou expect the girl to understand such words when I barely make sense of them myself?' Robert growled. ' 'Tis time thou forgot the talk of thy county of workhouses.'

'Workhouses!' she screamed. 'Your own place is drowned in quicksand an' fens. An' a Lincolnshire man is no better than his birthplace. He'll drown in a woman's eyes. We have no place for ladies at the Pride. We need willing mawleys an' plenty of 'em. Brick – '

'Even thy precious O'Shea cannot demand labour where

there is nought to be found. 'Tis a bad time now the transports come no more. The girl will work once she gets inland. Leave her alone.'

'I'm no convict slavey.' Raunie's voice shook. 'My husband was a gentleman and I'm a free woman to do as I please.'

'But I'll warr'nt you squealed at your first light o' day in a London kennel. An' Betsy or no Betsy, bless her believing heart in her brother's goodness, I'll swear your marriage to this Lorne was a hasty thing to cover up a wickedness.'

'A lie. I niver let James put a hand abaht me before we wed –'

She broke off, horrified. She had lapsed into her London street jargon. Afraid for herself, furious with them, she sprang at her tormentor and fastened curled fingers deep in the hair rolled at the nape of the woman's neck. She tugged. Moll screamed with shock, then pain, and clawed wildly, twisting and kicking out at the younger woman. Her chair crashed, the table rocked, dishes rolled as the two staggered together about the room. From what seemed a great distance Raunie heard voices, then felt herself gripped at the waist and a stinging pain across her knuckles. Her hold relaxed. She was thrown into a chair.

'Get about thy work,' Robert rasped at Moll, holding Raunie steady. 'The girl's marriage is no concern of thine, nor are her plans for the future. Remember it or I shall complain of thee to thy master. He does not like brawling beneath his roof, even from such as thee.'

Moll tucked her hair under her cap, opened her mouth to argue but instead turned and flounced from the room. Raunie sat trembling. Every inch of her body ached. It would be a long time before she was calm again. Once, long ago, she had done this same thing to a child who had stolen her amulet. She had clung to the brat until she was left with wisps of hair in her clenched hands and her dress spattered with the child's blood. The rage – and fear – at the loss of her possessions had been swift and undeniable. It was always so whenever her safety – or property – was threatened. She had wanted to kill that child long ago. She wanted to kill Moll now. Such ways were Romany ways. Her nails bit into her hands.

'I must see Mr O'Shea. I demand to see Mr O'Shea.'

'He's at Port Phillip, far to the south. For the present I am in charge.' He paused. 'Thou art a foolish girl, Mrs Lorne. Here in New Holland there is nought for a woman of thy class but what is gained by the toil of her hands and the pureness of her heart. Work willingly and thou wilt have wages, with shelter and clothing and all thou canst eat, blessings never enjoyed in England by such as thee – or me. And if thou givst thanks to God each night for such gifts doubtless in time He will reward thee with a second husband.' She fancied she felt his hand brush her bent head. 'Aye, thou art comely. Very comely. Now drink thy tea and take thyself to thy bed. We leave at dawn.'

So that was that. She could see he was in no mood for argument. She drank in silence while Paddy nodded over the table and Old Kate dozed in her chair. This Witherstone had shown her her place, or what he considered was to be her place. But what could a peasant of ridiculous thees and thous know of her place in life? Of her desires . . . Or, indeed, of the great world that lay outside his own narrow one? If marriage to a gentleman did not make her a lady, what did? Power? Money? Was wealth the answer? She must think about it. Paddy stirred. She glanced up to find his eyes blinking on her. He was a leprechaun, a crazy little gnome, but she would need friends. Useful friends. She turned at the door to smile at him.

'The blessed Patrick go with ye,' he mumbled, grinning. And the awful grey tufts went bob-bobbing above his mangled old limbs.

Tired as she was she could not sleep. Cats fought and the dog Matong barked at the moon. Boxes thudded, Robert's slow voice merged with Moll's as the woman bellowed at Paddy. Raunie tossed, tortured by the bites of vermin. Mosquitoes, as if aware of her fresh English blood, bit savagely. She tucked her head under the dirty blanket and gasped for breath. She sat up and rested her head on the sill, fighting the impulse to climb through the tiny window and disappear into the maze of houses that led . . . where? Where could she go? Who would want her, so soon to be slow and awkward in carrying her child? She was trapped and knew it. She lay down and twisted her head restlessly on the hot pillow. She cried a little and, incongruously, longed for James's arms. In a man's arms there was comfort and forgetfulness and James's caresses were all she had to remember. How ready she had been to love James Lorne . . . To trust and cling to him . . . She cried in choking little spasms, longing for rest till, finally, she dozed . . . She was awakened by Moll with orders to dress and come to work. To give point to her orders the woman threw her a garment that hung on her so like a limp sack she tied it at her waist with her precious length of ribbon. The darkness was enlivened by stabs of light, a still, pink dawn. She swallowed tea hurriedly and helped to make ready. The tightly packed dray waited with the wagon, and two fine horses Robert must have brought along in the early hours – she was to ride on the wagon with Paddy, Moll bawled at her. When Robert came at last he brought, of all people, Jock McPhee of the *May Queen*. Raunie ignored him. But Jock laughed as much at her snubs as he laughed at Moll's bullying. An oaf, but a strong one. They needed strength on the road.

The sun was already hot when they moved off, Moll on the dray, the men directing proceedings from their steeds with Matong leaping like a joyful demon from horse to horse. Moll shouted ribald goodbyes to Old Kate, then to passersby as the procession made its way through the sluggishly stirring town, along lower George Street with its tumbledown dwellings and past the long wall of the Barracks on the western side. With the still, livid air heavy with odours from the open sewer of the Tank Stream Raunie stared at the Town Crier on the corner with his bell and his 'Oyez' announcing to a crowd of delighted urchins that one of their number was lost in the scrub and 'God Save the Queen'. Round the standpipes sweaty-faced housewives squabbled over the scanty water and let out at each other with their

29

pitchers while children scooped up the mud to pelt at the vagrants clamped in the stocks at the nearby Police Court. Past the Markets to wind slowly over the Brickfield Hills that sent the torturing dust-laden 'brickfielder' winds to harass the town. Along Parramatta Street Raunie turned to look her last at Sydney: squat shingled buildings under a dust-pall, the aching vividness of green and blue and brown under a blazing summer sky. A golden town. She would always think of it as she saw it then – bathed in light – and watched it disappear with regret. They rolled along the Parramatta Road and out towards the wide lands of the west.

It must have been three hours later when they paused on a stretch of nothingness to drink from the swinging kegs. Raunie stumbled down and hurried behind a tree to be sick. She sensed Moll's eyes following her but she was too ill to care; she had endured the hard seat, the jogging, and the creeping sickness inside her until it was impossible to bear any of it longer. She leaned weakly against the trunk. Then she felt a hand on her arm and Moll Noakes swung her about to meet her narrowed and knowledgeable eyes.

'So it's a babe, is it?' she said.

Raunie nodded.

'When?'

'Late June, I think.'

Moll frowned. 'The sickness should be past by now.'

'It's the heat.' Raunie gasped, leaning against her because she could not help herself. 'I can scarcely breathe.'

'You'll get used to the climate. We all do.' With a firm hand she led her back to the wagon. 'I shall tell the men an' in me own time, for they will not like it much. There's babes enough at the Pride as it is. They can't work so young an' they eat too much. Besides, most of um are gals. You must hope for a boy. A fine strong boy. Now, up with you. An' forget your miseries. No time for sickness. An' – she muttered, as if ashamed of her lapse into sympathy, 'thank any heathen image you're on speakin' terms with that you work for Mr O'Shea. He likes babes. He has plans for em.'

Raunie curled up inside the wagon like a wounded animal

slinking into a hole to lick its wounds. She doubled her fists and fastened her teeth on them to stop their chattering and the tingling of her ragged nerves. How many weeks of this heat and dust and rolling wagon that racked her body with each turn of its squeaking wheels? And when the journey was over, what then? Work. Hard, gruelling work. She closed her eyes, beating back and down her growing despair. Slowly she relaxed, her tongue twisting sleepily about strange words dragged from the recesses of her mind by her sickness and loneliness . . . 'Ut prisca gens mortalium'. A lullaby her mother had often sung to her, only half-remembered now. And 'O Delor Zanal' – God knows what tomorrow will bring.

But tomorrow was a long way off. Enough for today. Thankfully she crept into sleep, the inert empty sleep of exhaustion.

Chapter Two

LIGHTS WERE beginning to glow in the villas above the dusk-calmed bays as Jeremy, with a true Gaelic flourish, turned the carriage into the South Head Road – a reckless devil, Jeremy, but he could do anything with a horse. A second vehicle bowled ahead, a wraith in the twilight. Eleanor, tossing back the laces drifting across her throat peeped out, braving the rush of night air on her bare shoulders. She swung angrily again to her daughter.

'The Clintons.' She was furious. 'By the time we arrive Gilbert will be surrounded by girls all prettier and more amiable than you. The most eligible young man in Sydney. The Clinton heir. And we're late.' She snapped open her fan. 'Are you listening, Barbara?'

'Yes, Mama.' Barbara Merrill's soft brown eyes turned obediently to her mother then back to the dying phantom of shape that was the Regent Lodge she loved. 'I'm sorry I mislaid my brooch.'

'You never mislay anything. You planned a late arrival so there would be little time to talk to people – to Gilbert.'

'I don't care for Gilbert Clinton.' She spoke softly but each word was definite, beautifully concise. Barbara always considered carefully everything she said.

'Why can't you understand that liking – love – have nothing whatever to do with marriage.' Eleanor's plaintive voice shrilled as she fussed with the flowers tucked in her coils of red-gold hair and arranged her shawl for what could be the twentieth time since she had dressed. 'Why must you act so strangely towards men, and eligible men in particular? Why can't you be, at the very least, pleasant? A girl of your looks – and age – simply cannot afford to ignore any man.' She gave an elaborate sigh. 'You're growing more impossible every

32

day and I don't know what's to become of you. If only Gina were older. I could do so much for Gina. She's so . . . so . . . *pliable!*' And she slumped with a series of irritated little rustlings to sulk prettily in her corner.

Major Alister Merrill, H.M. 80th Regiment of Foot (South Staffordshires), Military Secretary to his uncle, His Excellency Major-General Sir Roger Havelock, KCH, Commander of the Forces in New South Wales, ran a finger between his neck and his collar. His face burned but he sweated less from the heat than from his expectation of the coming ordeal. For five hours he must make a pretence of guffawing at third-rate comedians and applauding impossible singers. He must discuss cricket and the weather and the political whims of the land-juggling Gipps when he didn't give a damn for the whole blasted colony – or the Governor. Moreover, he must watch his stubbornly reserved and self-controlled daughter pushed on to the treadmill of the local marriage mart by an ambitious and just as stubbornly determined mother.

He sighed within himself as his eyes slid furtively to his wife. At thirty-six this soft doll-like creature beside him could easily be mistaken for her daughter's elder sister were it not for her consistent falling into flesh. But after intermittent periods of fret and tighter lacing the fact had ceased to bother her; after all, most women grew fat in New Holland. So much rich food, the lazy climate, the wealth of cheap labour – or it had been cheap until now. Now nothing was cheap except the talk of malcontents. He felt the usual gentleness her nearness always roused and knew the usual impatience with himself. And with her. An eternal child, his Eleanor, with an adolescent's appetite for pastries and cream and kisses, for frills and flowers and fun. A soft warmth of approach, a viscid dependency that bemused and thrilled even while it stifled – God, how it stifled. Lately he had found himself brooding on memories of her young stubbornness that had grown over the years to an insistence on the indulgence of her slightest desire. Tears and tempers and hysterics. Unsubtle weapons. Ugly weapons . . .

33

She was intoxicated, over-stimulated by her satisfied ambitions, possessing as she did a definite, and enviable, place in Sydney 'Society', or what passed for Society in Sydney, even if there were the constant wearing effort to conceal their poverty. After all, it was the 'front' that mattered and manage a front she did, having long been determined that her children should make advantageous matches. Now, socially, they would have every opportunity for wasn't she the lady of a powerful military figure and the kinswoman of Sydney's foremost citizen – dear, *dear* Roger. For when you came to consider it, wasn't dear Roger more important by far than any governor since he did control the troops . . . A comforting thought *that*! She was the dame of an imposing villa above the exclusiveness of Woolloomooloo, a rural retreat suitably removed from the taint of the Convict Barracks, dizzy supremacy indeed to the obscure position of a Nottingham clergyman's daughter and the wife of an apparently forgotten lieutenant fretting in the boredom of a Jamaican garrison. She was determined to be the social equal of the Clintons and the Havelocks and the Parkers, mounted securely in their lovely homes above Elizabeth Bay and Potts Point. He – Alister – had never begrudged her these small successes until they began to drain her of all sense of proportion – or all she had ever possessed. In spite of nothing more substantial than their house, her small income, and his inadequate pay bolstered by an occasional win at cards or a lucky flutter at Homebush Racecourse she was absorbed by her tea-parties and dinners, her insistence on imported luxuries, and her swollen, often bizarre, ambitions for Kenneth and the girls. She was making of the Lodge a gaudy salon, of the child Georgina a selfish adolescent, of Barbara a social misfit, and Kenneth – well, what chance had his son to be anything but the idolised weakling he was. And himself? He sighed audibly, not caring who heard. With his wife had he ever been anything but an acquiescent fool?

His weary eyes turned to his daughter, dignified but somehow a little grotesque in her flounces of pink satin looped with overblown roses – he knew she detested pink – her rich brown hair with its glints of red twisted into the bouncing curls she hated. And the brooch she had taken so long to find. He couldn't blame her for that small subterfuge, for it was a vulgar piece. But there was no denying her mother. Wear the brooch Barbara must before they left the house and, because she knew it was important her father appear at the theatre, wear it she did. Ah, he knew. A small gust of benevolence stirred him though there were few spoken confidences between them. He wished there could be more. A long-legged Artemis, this girl of his, laced into a chaste era of shawls and rosebuds and attitudes. She should have been a boy, his son, heir to his stifled ambitions, to resuscitate them and inflate them. To his suddenly critical eyes she looked young and rather pathetically vulnerable . . . how old was she? Eighteen? She'd 'come out' last year, expensively as he remembered, both in money and emotion, for Eleanor had cried for days when her daughter refused to meet any of the men who subsequently called upon her, and the fact they were so few in number made for even angrier scenes. She did not like them, was all Barbara would answer to frantic questions. And the girl meant it. She liked few people, certainly none of the right ones. Well . . . there was time. She would not be nineteen until June.

He could never forget the month for Kenneth had been born in June a year almost to the day before his sister. As if he, Alister, could forget the ravings of his young wife when she had discovered – Kenneth a few months old – that she was nurturing a second child. She hated him, her husband. She hated the baby. Babies were soft playthings that soon grew into squalling burdens so, loathing him even more than she loathed the West Indies, she had sailed for England vowing never to come back to husband or Indies. And she had kept her word. At least, she had stayed away for seven years, years in which there were times he had thought he must go mad for need of her; a strange, moody dreamtime of waiting, for he was young and the taverns filled with shining-limbed exotic creatures. But the centre of his desire had always been Eleanor. And only Eleanor. So he had waited humbly, a little dulled, withdrawn from the throbbing life around him until her father died and her disapproving maiden sisters proved unwilling to house the children longer. And she had come back, bringing offspring he barely noticed and felt he would never understand – except perhaps Barbara. Yes, there were times when Barbara had interested him. But Eleanor was all he really wanted and, wonderfully, she had seemed glad to see him. He had grasped what she offered and made himself content with it for he had long accepted the fact that her love for him was a slight inconstant thing fashioned by conditions and surroundings and her fey, unaccountable nature. But even more incredibly she had seemed happy when Georgina was born, delighting in the child's lush beauty as if it were something she had created alone and unaided; there seemed even now a ghost of that passionate reunion about Georgina in the child's careless enthusiasms, her gaiety, her precocious vivacity.

But they were briefly happy. Inevitably she had tired of their fresh mating and insisted on him angling for an appointment in New South Wales. She couldn't bear the Indies . . . a dangerous pagan region of idolators and filth . . . England was drained by the Peninsular Wars, and after all, could he really expect promotion, or even glory, with a leg that was, in a military sense, next to useless? Roger had helped him before and must help him again – why not? The Havelocks were childless and Roger was fond of his only sister's son, fond enough to have proclaimed him his heir on various memorable if somewhat casual occasions. And he was so beautifully rich . . . he must leave his fortune somewhere . . . Yes, she would devote her time, even to the point of exhaustion or ennui, to fostering affection between themselves and the Havelocks. She would cultivate Janet . . . why not? There were the children to consider . . . and of course, herself . . . Alister clenched and unclenched his sweating hands. A soldier in name, a glorified clerk in reality, waiting as impassively as he might for his kinsman to die. Waiting and rotting. Yes, rotting . . . But there was no answer then as there was none now, and never would be, against the shrewd sense of his wife's demands. She had her way. Eleanor always had her way.

He forced his mind from this always-raw hurt, this inactive isolation from the world of war, back to Barbara. The sight of this daughter was always arresting, even stabilising. He could not tell why. Perhaps because she had always been different from the others, first as a remote child then as a rangy girl with eyes as cool as her voice and a mind sprouting ideas that could stimulate even while they shocked. She was always reading. He glanced from the slim brown hands folded neatly in her lap to her face, which beside the creamy animation of her mother and sister became almost plain. He supposed, compared to some women, she was an assemblage of imperfections but to him, in his flashes of fondness for her, she was angular grace, an attractive voice, pleasing colouring, each attribute in itself satisfying and compelling. Sometimes when memories racked he longed to talk to Barbara, to feel intimacy with her for, in spite of early military discipline necessary to mould daughters to obedience and their ultimate destinies, he felt an unexpected sympathy, recognising himself in this girl in a way that was satisfying even if maddeningly obscure. Dignity, pride, autocracy, and something else she had achieved that as yet he could not completely command – an armour of the mind donned against the demands of the society of which she was a part. A deliberate barrier of unruffled politeness and trained docility. She acquiesced, she complied, in a detachment so complete it was not only unnatural it was awesome, this subtle wall between herself and criticism, disapproval, and the sting of feminine tongues. But it was so flawless he was positive no one, not even he who loved her, could readily detect it or define it let alone besiege it. He had never been able to plumb the depths of this daughter of his. He wondered if anyone ever would.

Now they were on the outskirts of the town, feeling their way cautiously through its badly lighted streets – when *would* they be lighted by gas – following the sound and dim sight of other carriages making for the town proper. With his usual flamboyance Jeremy turned into Pitt Street and bowled towards Sydney's gayest block, and the Royal Victoria. The theatre lights formed a bright oasis as the carriage slackened to a crawl. Jeremy swore then spat. Jeremy was a Leinster fellow and the Major considered Leinster Anglicised enough to be called Saxon and bore with him, heaping the epithets of the barrack-room on his unheading head while aware of his excellence as gardener and groom. Even the Irish, it seemed, had some uses.

Eleanor bowed to passing carriages, staring out at the distant mists of light that marked the hotels and restaurants on the King Street corners. She turned to tap her husband's arm.

'*Do* tell Jeremy to hurry.' Her voice sharpened with impatience. 'Alister!'

He called an order. The carriage jerked to a jogtrot then died as he knew it would do, scarcely moving. Ignoring his wife's complaining he lolled to stare at the passing crowd as he would stare at a dying foundling, a flogged convict – accepting the inevitable, even expecting it, was so much more sensible than pausing to question their existence. That was how he had learned to accept this Sydney, the only way he had steeled himself to endure this panorama of faces that gave the passing scene – the whole place – the bizarre and decadent air of a fallen Babylon, or Rome. Since the frenzy of Waterloo his life had dragged its days behind it against a background of faces – the stifled hatred of Irish faces, the brown fanaticism of Indians, the doggedness of Jamaican faces, the patient docility of the English. But these faces were different. Singly they were recognisable – a Norwegian, a dour and calculating Scot, something of a Spaniard there, here an aborigine muted by two generations of British blood. And the English – ah yes, the English. There was never doubt of the English. But collectively . . . He sought to define them as they drifted slowly past the carriage window. An old face bare of identity and direction . . . The young crowded about, blotting it out. So many young 'cornstalk' faces under their cabbage-tree hats. Purposeful greedy faces with nothing of centuries-old patience or tranquillity. Nothing of the past. These youths, swaggering in their moleskins and checked shirts open at the breast, looked to a future to match their ways – bold and vigorous and tough. Yes, tough. There was no room because no need for the ageing or infirm. There was no room for him. He was here on sufferance as were all of his class and age and at their first obvious weakness the land and this grasping greedy rabble would turn and swallow them. Here in this country they were different. They were vocal. Somehow they learned to read, yes *read*, their People's Charters and National Petitions and every other poison that, despite the utmost vigilance, fell into their hands. They plotted and planned and fought and loved in their own unique way, this verminous flotsam of this rum-sodden village some called a town.

He hated it. God, how he hated it. After four years he still hated it with a detestation that had etched itself into his very soul, that overflowed into his simplest word and deed, that distorted his thought and made vicious his reasoning. For he was as chained to this offshoot of the land of his conceiving as any felon held in the hands of his men. This – after the glory of Waterloo seen through the eager englamoured eyes of an ambitious seventeen-year-old ensign; this after the promise of worlds to conquer and flags to set flying, of a brief young glimpse of the stars. This pottering with jaded officers who knew but a smattering of tactics and strategy, the policing of convict gangs and bullying of the dregs of a military legion, the monotony of dinners and conferences and the senile aimless talk that led to nothing but the signing of documents, and parades that were play-thing substitutes for battle with its ecstasy of drawing blood and the ultimate justification of killing. Nothing to do . . . nothing. And why? Unavoidable, inescapable strangleholds – poverty, a shattered knee, a woman. His eyes watered. He ran his forefinger beneath his collar. Even the post of Commander at Norfolk Island – some form of power at least and certainly well paid – had been denied him, for Eleanor had been appalled at the very idea. A barbaric penal settlement, an island peopled by the most wretched dregs of humanity – how would the girls find husbands there? At least Sydney could boast of some civilised elements. And a house waiting, practically a gift. Roger had been more than generous. And why shouldn't his bounty increase if they dedicated themselves, as a family, to pleasing him? The carriage stopped before the 'Old Vic'.

The Victoria Theatre glowed. The brilliance of uniforms merged with the flower hues, the jewels and gleaming shoulders of the women. Over there three subalterns of the 80th – his own regiment – and a sprinkling of the 28th and 51st. The rest were the steadily increasing 96th. He regarded them, and the scene, with satisfaction, and a suddenly stimulated interest. But the mood did not last. He smiled, bowed, and talked with tight-lipped boredom with one simpering dame after another. All over-painted, large-breasted, as swollen and lax as the flashy fluidity of over-ripe pears – how in God's name had he ever thought there could be seduction in a woman's bosom? And the bland, almost effete faces of his own sex voicing the phrases and opinions he had yawned over for years . . . Bored with them but more sharply with himself he led the women through the handsome iron gates and with practised adroitness up to the 'dress' box that must of course be one of the most prominent in the building. Thank heaven, sighed Eleanor, they were in time. No sign of the vice-regal party yet. There was to be supper with the Governor and his lady and the Havelocks, and new arrivals from England. An important evening. But all such evenings were important to Eleanor, meaning new gowns and adornments. More useless fallals. His eyes skimmed his wife's dress hoping that his luck at cards would hold – it would take more than another of her Sèvres vases to pay for it. She was searching the shifting groups for the Clintons as they jostled their way to their seats, an advance made even more tedious by his limp, slight though it usually was. Indeed, it never did seem apparent to anyone but himself – and his wife when she was angry with him. Then, he was conscious of nothing else. It was too hot. The air was heavy with the brilliance of the argand lamps and the drift of over-lavish perfume. Catcalls and shrieks and obscenity from the pit. Too many people, too much talk. He squeezed irritably past a fat woman in emerald then bowed from habit, uncaring who she was, murmuring some superfluity. Her dress jarred his eyes. He sweated. Clashing tumbles of sound from the orchestra beat at his ears; over-nourished sons of ambitious emancipists, indulging their shallow and nauseous tastes for what they broadly termed 'culture'.

Eleanor rustled in her ritual of 'settling', arranging her skirts and shawl, fluttering her hands about her hair and darting wide over-bright eyes from box to box. She twiddled heavily ringed fingers behind the shield of her fan at tightly-laced old Captain Shore and made exaggerated lip movements to fluffy Mrs Vancourt. Then her body tautened.

'There he is, Alister – there – smiling at one of the Misses Wilmots, though which one I can't possibly tell for they're both equally plain and ungainly. And just as ridiculous.'

'If you insist on holding court to Sydney's bachelors,' he protested wearily, 'spare me, for the time being, young Clinton. I loathe pimpled adolescents.'

Her mouth trembled with indignation behind her wildly fluttering fan. 'Just look at the way she's leaning against him. Really –'

'The lad boasts more advanced physical development than I thought possible if he manages to support eleven – or would it be more – stone of Wilmot.' He yawned, staring down into the steaming, squabbling pit. No use looking for Jeremy. He'd be nursing a bloody nose in the nearest pub. No use trying to replace him either . . .

'Not Gilbert, Alister. Mr O'Shea. Brick O'Shea, as everyone calls him. And the name does seem to suit him, peculiar as it is. There's something – well – stark about it. And about the man, don't you agree?'

Alister started from his hypnotised stare at a woman's

41

blue-veined breast gripped by her baby's greedy jaws –
damn all women for they repelled you while they lured you –
and straightened. Between clumps of gleaming ringlets Brick
O'Shea was briefly visible before being lost again in a group
of twittering women. The entire female population of Sydney
seemed to have lost their hearts – their minds if they had any
– over this upstart of a colonial since he had taken lodgings in
town for the winter season and the hottest of the summer
months to become the hub of Sydney life; the life of the
charlatan, the roisterer – to put it even more bluntly, the
radical and the rebel. Alister ran his finger beneath his collar.
The gesture was beginning to worry him. He was annoyed
that he should even be stirred by this native-born roughneck,
met with and ignored at race-meetings, riding parties and
the like – as much as it was possible to ignore anyone in
Sydney. The only place a gentleman was safe from such
upstarts was Government House, and even that stronghold
was beginning to totter. That such riff-raff as O'Shea had
contrived to cross the path of a Merrill was one of the most
monstrous obscenities of this obscene land, for the man was
an ambitious would-be demagogue, the noisiest of the
currency lads, stalking through drawing-rooms, brothels,
pubs and whaling decks as if he owned them and – if rumour
were correct – many of them he did. Worse, this arrogant
spume of a convict generation was managing to make money
and, even more miraculously, to keep it in a land quickly
being sapped of what currency it could boast. He was
becoming a man to be reckoned with – fast. Too fast. Openly
seeking power through the sly expedient of succouring the
underdog and flattering the no-good and the gullible, he
cultivated the rabble, for though politically incompetent,
they could be embarrassedly noisy – and it was fashionable
these days to be noisy. He would slander a gentleman and
build a ticket-o'-leaver a hut, insult a titled dowager and
toss a slut a new bonnet. Convicts, harpies, murderers,
aborigines, bushrangers, as well as the whole cursed Irish
fraternity, were his champions or his enemies according
to how he saved them, fed them, used them and thrashed

42

them, rewarded them when they did his bidding and gave them his particular brand of hell when they didn't. Only newcomers to his crude and personal justice could claim ignorance of O'Shea. He was a supporter of every seditious scribbler and editor in the place and encouraged most of the radical enterprises mooted openly or behind locked doors. As for the Irish . . . they called their children after him and begged salvation at their Masses for his soul which, according to their priests – and O'Shea himself – could do with all the compassion the Almighty might be induced to grant him. The Irish even worked for him. And he hated the English as virulently as he appeared to love all of Erin's outcasts.

There were sentimentalists, naturally, even among the respectable who, hypnotised by the man's undeniable force, insisted he was wresting his wealth as others had done from a grudging society with no other assets than the toil of their bodies and the manoeuvrings of their minds. Perhaps. But in the first lusty wail of the infant colony even legitimate wealth had been here for the taking, to purloin from shadily acquired or exploited soil, from the whaling and sealing decks piled high with spoils. The snapping up of Illawarra cedar in the twenties, shrewd juggling of the land laws at the beginning of the thirties, and the tossing back and forth of the choicest lots the city could furnish in the land boom of a few years back, had helped a deal. And rum. The country slept and loved and grew fat on it – hot, fiery, East Indian rum at that. It was rumoured that O'Shea owned many of the whalers in the Harbour and that most of the brigs bringing sandalwood from the South Seas moved at his bidding. As for labour – there, his enemies would concede, but jealously, lay his success, for he could bully and flog whalers till his arms gave out and yet keep a crew at full strength. No doubt the fact that he kept the waterfront brothels full of women fresh off the barques won the whalers' allegiance. All the same, he had a knack of picking over an immigrant ship, choosing a man here, a woman there, with a selective abandon that appalled the more discreet, yet with unerring aim. His results were astounding. some swore it was because he was straight with them, paying them well if he considered them worth it – but proving lazy they could starve and be counted well lost. They had their choice.

But how could a man, much less a Merrill, sift fact from the fiction that surrounded O'Shea? One thing was certain, he was behind the seekers after responsible government. And who would doubt the rumour that, last year, petitions to the House of Commons had gone home packed deep in the trunks of Port Phillip settlers farewelled with his fervent encouragement and blessing? And now these rumours of his standing for Council ... Alister rubbed his moist palm along his leg, fighting the urge to loosen his collar. Such degradation could not be endured. He, Major Alister Merrill, Nominee to the Council of Governor Gipps, forced to argue over the country's administration with such carrion? And yet ... the man was shrewd enough to stand upon outwardly irreproachable farming and stock-holding interests, his station near Goulburn being one of the few in the country still unmortgaged while those around him with ten thousand sheep could not get credit for a bag of sugar or a chest of tea. And even now, in the midst of the worst drought the country had suffered he was opening up far reaches of the Maneroo plains, with horse-breeding an added venture. He, Merrill, was sick of the man's very name, appalled by everything about him, yet how to avoid him, how even to dodge discussion of him, for around the billiard tables and deep in the comfortable chairs of the Australian Club and suchlike, the 'pure merinos', priding themselves on their impeccable descent, tore him to shreds when all else palled, as it very soon did. Good, bad or indifferent, O'Shea would leave his mark on the colony – was he not Rory O'Shea's grandson? Few doubted that much for the physical resemblance to the men he claimed as his father and grandfather grew more marked every day; beneath the vitality and assurance that brooding darkness of face and mind. The mark of the O'Sheas.

A wild rapscallion breed. Those citizens ancient enough

loved to tell of wild Rory O'Shea's hanging from a gumtree with his fellow 'croppies' after the rising in '04, leaving his newly-landed wife and son to carry on the weaponless war against authority. They loved to argue, the club élite, over the son, Shawn, and his unheralded and hazy affair with an unknown convict girl and the even hazier and unheralded advent of the present whelp known as 'Brick'. If there were few who lingered over Rory's Castle Hill episode, they loved to recount what they knew of his son Shawn's wayward colonial career, soaked as he was by his parents in the sorrow and passions of his birthland. Rum-runner, shearer, inn-keeper and shepherd between long periods in His Majesty's colonial prisons for his vexing and defiance of His Majesty's troops in assisting runaway convicts and bushrangers – wonder was often voiced as to how he had found time and opportunity to beget a child, much less make money. But he had done both it seemed, getting a start by winning a slice of the north coast in a throw of the dice and remaining sober enough for long enough to collect his stake. But little good it had done him when he stopped a bullet from a trooper's musket in a gaol escape and breathed his last with his head in a ditch – but heaping curses with his final breath on the English soldiers. And still but a youth. As to the woman who had loved him and, most likely, married him – let a man be literal in calling O'Shea a bastard and see what he got – she was anybody's guess. Even fools did not long entertain the idea of O'Shea's convict harpy foster-mother as his natural parent – in any case, it was said, the pair of them had long laughed off that idea. Well, women-hungry First Fleeters and their offspring had only convict transportees and natives to choose between. A convict lass. It was enough. It had to be. So many felons arrived nameless, unidentified, without papers to dictate how long were their convictions or what their crimes. Only the gentry worried what blood flowed in another's veins. Lesser fry couldn't afford to. So they argued, but warily, careful not to take accusations into the open for O'Shea would crack a skull for suggestions he didn't like; for all his controlled coolness he was a touchy man. And a genius at keeping clear of the law. And when all was said and done, concluded the colonists, tempered by good fellowship, gossip and cognac, a man to escape the sheepfold must be something of a wolf, and if one did not approve of the O'Sheas one made the best of them. Alister squirmed in his seat. A Merrill, unfortunately, had never made the best of anything.

The circle of women about Brick O'Shea spread suddenly, gowns billowing and drifting about him like the petals of some heat-withered flower responding to rain. He brushed them aside courteously but, one knew, firmly, and looked about the theatre. His eyes came to rest, finally, on the Merrill box. He was a tall man but not – in an age of over-groomed and attitudinous males – a dandyish one. Broad, with a pronounced width of shoulder, physical strength was his obvious and supreme asset. Watching him move one gained the impression that his mind knew precisely what his body was capable of performing, and, even more precisely, its immediate limitations. A shock of black crinkling hair worn longer than most men wore it, a wide clean-shaven sunburned face. Rather a heavy face; a face one came back to study with a deep curiosity. At least Alister did. A woman placed a hand on Brick's arm and he laughed, the sound loud and hard even above the theatre sounds; one stirred to it involuntarily and without reason. His teeth were straight and very white, his eyes, deep-set beneath heavy brows, would twinkle lazily, or grow chill, or slide from face to face as if searching and watching. He seemed always to be searching and watching. He lifted a hand in greeting to a group of drovers and against the careless splendour of his clothes it was big, gnarled and unattractive. An overstrong hand. But the nails were always well-kept. A contradiction of a man moulded and set by the pioneer cross-currents of a country where strength meant riches and weakness oblivion. Quick oblivion. The entire theatre followed Brick O'Shea, the men with suspicious yet envious eyes, the women with . . . what? Interest? Curiosity? Fear? Desire? Whatever the reason, it was always so.

Small flushes marred Eleanor's pale skin as she saw him turn towards the passage. She rearranged her shawl and unpinned and pinned the coral brooch between her lovely breasts, playing nervously with the lacy folds of her bertha. The she leaned over to pat her daughter's curls and pinch some colour into her cheeks.

'He's coming here,' she whispered urgently. 'I know it. I always sense such things.' She straightened to make excited graceful little patterns with her fan. 'Do you suppose, Alister, it could be because of Barbara?' Her body slumped again. 'But that's really too much to expect when there are so many pretty girls here tonight.'

'Even the renegades of Sydney occasionally pay their respects to authority – if not by reason of good manners then by reason of politics,' he snapped. 'In any case he's still hankering after Donna.'

'Jeremy insists he's the shrewdest judge of horseflesh in the colony,' Barbara put in.

Her father frowned. 'Jeremy talks too much.'

'But he was *most* attentive to Barbara that day in the Domain . . .' Eleanor wriggled to take a long and calculating look at her daughter.

'Eleanor! I have asked you many times to avoid the man's company even if evasion must be carried to the point of rudeness.' He spoke carefully and distinctly as he always spoke to his wife.

'But he sought us out. He did really. And I don't see why I should be unpleasant to him. He can be quite charming. And that's what's so odd . . . he's not at all good-looking and wears clothes so carelessly and never, in any way at all, looks a gentleman, not when one is used to *real* gentlemen, I mean. But he doesn't seem to care about such things.' Her breath quickened. 'There's just something . . .' Baffled, she shook her beautifully coiffured head. 'I wonder what it is.'

'To most people, I suppose, his money,' Barbara said lightly. 'To the rest,' she added slowly, 'vitality. A kind of blended power of body and mind. A rare thing, I think.'

47

Her mother covered her shocked face with her fan. 'Really Barbara, when I was your age I never discussed bodies – blending.'

Barbara's mouth twitched. 'One body, Mama. One mind.'

'That's worse. It's – it's positively pagan.' She shuddered, then allowed herself to become absorbed in the always absorbing O'Shea. 'They say he has a most spectacular future.'

'Dangling from the gallows of the new gaol if he isn't careful,' her husband said coldly.

The fan snapped. 'Really Alister, you must accept the fact that this is not England. It's not, you know. It's Australia. One simply makes . . . allowances. We don't always like the situation but entertain we must and who is available but – well, emancipists and the native-born? I assure you most mothers here tonight would be delighted – and unbearably tedious – for weeks to come if he so much as noticed their marriageable daughters. After all, he's not poor.'

'A typical example of colonial decadence. If a man is rich enough one can conveniently overlook his – to put it mildly – unfortunate choice of antecedents.'

'He is *not* a convict, Alister.'

'Nevertheless, there is bound to be murk in the blood of the grandson of an Irish felon hanged for sedition and the son of a notorious scapegrace and a woman convict – the fact that his mother was a felon seems to be conclusive, does it not?'

'But without proof of all these wild tales about him –'

'The man will never be acknowledged by me or accepted in our home. I expect you both to abide unquestionably by my wishes in this respect.'

Eleanor blinked away her always-ready tears and fidgeted with her brooch. She hated her wishes to be faced with logic and Alister persisted in doing just that. Why had she married a man so forbidding, so disapproving of her tiniest, most harmless, folly? But he had been different then. He had, he *had*. If only he would understand that Barbara was eighteen and still unbetrothed and people were talking.

48

'Mr O'Shea has many enemies,' Barbara said quietly, 'who are, naturally, eager to discredit him. But even if their stories concerning his family are true he should not be penalised for the actions of others. Even convicts deserve to have their mistakes discounted by time.'

Silence. A long and heavy silence in which Eleanor stared at her daughter in amazement. Barbara rarely spoke at such length, even more rarely aired such views. Alister moved sharply.

'Enough of that romantic nonsense,' he snapped. 'It is not seemly for a young woman of your age and class to express such opinions or even ponder on such worldly matters.'

'Do you wish me to ignore the world, Papa?'

'This . . .' he waved an arm, 'is not the world – ' He broke off, sat even straighter in his seat, and composed himself. 'Never let me hear you speak so again. Never. Do you understand me?'

She did not answer, just sat very still and straight, staring ahead. His anger slurred uneasily to alarm. She was, undoubtedly, consuming knowledge at too rapid a pace for her own good. The wrong knowledge. When women began to argue with men, and on such subjects, it was time to put a stop, and ruthlessly, to learning. Worldly knowledge served no better purpose where a woman was concerned than to make her an oddity in society and Barbara, unfortunately, was too much of an oddity already. Where did she absorb these outrageous ideas – even Havelock had remarked on his great-niece's brisk opinions that cut into conversation like the plunge of a knife. That dithering old fool of a Clinton encouraged her of course. For the fun of it. The English squire who had built Regent Lodge had taken himself home in disgust leaving nothing to improve the colony's lamented crudity but a tome or two on horses and agriculture, a Shakespeare, a Bible, and an edition of the *Encyclopaedia Britannica*. There was Eleanor's set of Waverley Novels – no harm there, an orthodox Tory and a good Protestant, Scott. But wasn't there something by Jane Austen? A woman writer.

A hodge-podge of feminine hysteria, what else? And a volume by this fellow Dickens – he had heard him called a dangerous writer, a literate rebel. He frowned. There were too many crackpots wheedling their unsettling, yes, their radical ideas into print for the already disaffected lower classes to pick over and ponder... But Barbara was not the lower classes. Barbara was . . . He ran his finger slowly between his neck and his collar.

Eleanor was greeting Brick O'Shea with her most alluring smile, a smile that not only transformed her face but made voluptuous her whole body. She smiled with each yielding muscle and fold of her drooped shoulders, her white arms, her softly fluttering and beautiful hands. She looked as soft and warm and golden as melted butter – while her daughter sat as straight and unmoving as a stick. With a flash of insight Alister saw why Barbara irritated her mother so – and, at times, himself. He could not take his eyes off his wife. Watching her he felt his blood race and he ached to touch her, a longing so intense it caught at his throat. He swallowed, conquering the impulse with the ruthlessness of long practice. The urge was improbable because Eleanor so seldom bothered to stir him now, certainly never with such tricks of her body. He thought he had long ago ceased to regard her as his wife – the natural receptacle of his passion. But even when passion was gone, because never roused and if so, ignored, something evidently remained of the long association of a man and a woman. The years. And for all one learned to discount women, as he had learned to do, they appeared to be so damnably necessary. A chance look, a touch or a smile and, maddeningly, a man was no longer master of himself. But he – Alister Merrill – must be master of himself. Brick O'Shea bowed before them.

It was the bow of a gentleman, a salutation that, more than anything else about the man, caused Alister to incline his head with the thinly disguised patronage which he regarded as his prerogative yet felt to be increasingly foolish. Even gauche. Damn the man and his insolent social graces when everyone knew the omission of a 'sir' or 'madam' did not spring from ignorance. He, Alister Merrill, had never yet been in his presence without feeling ill-at-ease. An absurd reaction and a degrading one. O'Shea paid Eleanor compliments under which she became even more yielding, then deliberately, slowly, he turned to Barbara. His eyes lingered over her longer than was necessary or polite but she met his glance coolly, and Alister felt a quick pride in her poise and detachment. But as his eyes slid from one to the other his skin pricked with fear. Perhaps . . . But impossible. Unthinkable. Obscene.

'Your sample from the cargo of the *Arabella* suits you well, Miss Merrill,' Brick was saying.

'Then it is true what they say, Mr O'Shea? That you know the contents of the hold of every barque newly anchored from London?'

'All information has some use, I find, even to the number of ladies' gowns for sale in the town.'

'It's nice of you to be polite but I know this shade does not suit me.' Her eyes twinkled above that rare smile that could transform her sombre face into quick and unexpected attractiveness. 'It was cheap, you see,' she added in a hurried little whisper.

'Then promise you'll wear white – or gold – in future and my compliments will rest on a firmer basis. I lie badly. And I prefer to be at ease with your sex.' He leaned forward. 'It gives me the advantage.'

In the words and his voice lay all the age-old lilt of his Irish sires. And the impudence. Here was something more than the knowledge gained by experience allied to the fluidity of an alert mind translated into speech. There were those who sometimes wondered where he had gained his variegated but thorough education, so thorough as to be quite often an embarrassment. Surely not from the harridan who had reared him? Alister pondered the maddening contradiction of the man for when it suited him he could summon the talents of a chameleon. And there was something else about him . . . something . . . Alister dragged his eyes from the man's face

51

to that of his daughter. Both seemed quite unaware of their surroundings. It enraged him.

'I assure you, O'Shea, my daughter's toilette can be safely entrusted to her mother's supervision.'

Brick turned slowly to the older man. 'I haven't noticed you of late at the training ground, Major. I'm still interested in that mare you know.'

'Donna? Lame, with not a chance of running at Home-bush,' he lied.

'Ah! Then you're prepared to sell?'

'Not at all. I make a point of never lightly discarding anything that has served me well.' It was satisfying to be able to refuse the man something he desired, even a mare. How much more satisfying to refuse him his daughter.

'Barbara wants to race Kumara.' Eleanor giggled with the correct amount of genteel embarrassment. She was forever instilling in the minds of her girls the necessity of a pose of feminine reserve and modest ignorance without, of course, appearing the complete simpleton. 'The child is absorbed with horses and has quite an amazing knowledge of their – habits. I know it's not quite nice but . . .' She shrugged delicately.

'A healthy and harmless enough pastime, Mrs Merrill.'

'Why yes, I suppose so.'

She fidgeted with her brooch. In desperation she had scratched at a subject that might possibly rouse this elusive and unpredictable man to interest himself in her seemingly uninteresting daughter. Stimulate Barbara and she would talk; indeed she had been known to become quite animated in the company of gentlemen when the conversation drifted to the finer points of horseflesh. She could grow almost ecstatic over Kumara – a *stallion*! Yes, the girl could, when and if she cared, emerge from her funny infuriating shell of reserve. She sulked of course, but her moods could be dispelled if one cared to take the trouble. She had actually bloomed the day this man had ridden up as they drove through the Domain taking the air after Janet's musty little parlour tea, and the feeling had persisted of some secret

communication between them, for though there was shyness – no, more, a wariness – in her daughter's attitude,
the two conversed as if they had spoken before of animals
and the pros and cons of horse-breeding . . . horrors, what
a brazen girl! Young ladies might go riding and did, but
they did not breed or train racehorses, most certainly did
not ride stallions about the Sydney roads. But Barbara did.
Furthermore, she often expressed the wish to ride Kumara
in a race – a *race* – and went dashing about the sand-hills,
skirts whipped by the wind, no hat, like any hussy. Ah,
how had she, Eleanor Merrill, borne such a strange complicated creature? But she must forgive, she scolded herself.
She must try to understand her child. But, above all, find
her a husband. Preferably a rich and comfortable one, of
course . . . But a husband. She pressed home her small
advantage.

'At weekends she rides the Botany Road. And though
neither will admit it, I'm positive she discards Jeremy. You'll
agree with me, I'm sure, Mr O'Shea, that it's unsafe for a
young lady to ride those hills alone.'

'Let us say, ma'am, indiscreet. Will you ride next Sunday,
Miss Merrill?'

She nodded quickly. Too quickly, Eleanor decided. 'Before
service. Very early.'

'Then perhaps you will allow me to escort you.' His smile
was easy and companionable. 'I've been hearing great things
of this stallion of yours.' Then, as if as an afterthought, he
turned casually to Alister. 'With your permission, sir, of
course.'

Unable from politeness and sheer surprise to do anything
else, Alister nodded. Eleanor beamed and bubbled. Then her
expression changed to one of horror. Her plump fingers
trembled at her throat.

'My brooch.' Her scream became a squeak. 'The coral
brooch. The pin was loose.'

Calmly, O'Shea bent to search the floor. They all moved
their feet, shuffled and searched while the theatre stared; at
least Eleanor prayed people were watching, for tomorrow it

would be all over Sydney that Brick O'Shea had paid marked attention to the Merrill box, and to Miss Merrill in particular. Alister fumed. He had give his wife the brooch and while once she had worn it for that reason, now she wore it because coral was again fashionable. Then, tucked under his foot, he saw the wretched thing. He tried to bend – damn his leg – and felt the hot blood rush to his face as O'Shea straightened, the offending bauble in his hand. Rage made Alister snatch at it. The pin scratched. He dropped the brooch into his wife's lap.

'Evening, O'Shea,' was all he could manage. The man's name almost choked him. Brick bowed to each in turn, then again to Barbara. Her eyes met his, her father noted. Then O'Shea turned and was gone. His gait, Alister noted, irritated that he should deign to further dwell on the man, was peculiarly Australian – head thrown back and step firm. Cocky. Eleanor took a long satisfied breath.

'I do believe Barbara attracts him.'

'It's not like that at all, Mama,' she said quickly.

'What do you mean – it's not like that?'

'Mr O'Shea wants . . . well, he needs assistance.'

'What possible assistance could you, a young unmarried girl, give such a person?' her father asked coldly.

'I don't know. Well, not exactly. But that day at Viola Parker's –'

'So . . . You have met him before. And secretly.'

'Not secretly, Papa. Mama knew of it.'

Eleanor's eyes rounded. 'I? Knew of what?'

'The afternoon tea in honour of Mrs Chisholm. You had a megrim and sent me to accompany Aunt Janet –'

'Chisholm? That . . . lunatic?' Alister's icy voice cut off his wife's bewildered queries.

'Is it lunatic to be philanthropic, Papa?'

'The woman is a nuisance. She plagues the Governor and Lady Gipps with her begging letters, as if she hasn't made herself notorious enough wandering the wharves alone to collect women and take them into her home among her own children. Women of the most depraved and –'

'Alister!' Eleanor's fan snapped a warning.

'But she has nowhere else to take them, Papa. That's why she's trying to establish her Immigrants' Home. Mrs Parker formed a committee and Mr O'Shea introduced Mrs Chisholm and gave her a donation, a large one.'

'Papish plotting between them, I haven't a doubt. The man's a fanatical anglophobe dedicated to destroying law and order, yes, and every other tradition of our civilisation, even to attacking the Throne itself. As to Mrs Chisholm, it seems her idea of immigration is to dump the Irish here—'

'But they must live somewhere, must they not?'

'The Irish? Are you mad?'

'But Papa, can we altogether blame them for the things they do?'

'Enough.' Eleanor jumped as his hands slammed the rail. 'You are meddling in matters you do not understand. Such talk is more than disloyal, it is treasonous. No Irishman can be trusted. Indeed, if there is much more trouble with them in this colony I shall personally take steps to end it.'

'But I do not remember Ireland even being mentioned that afternoon.'

'Of course not. Even the gullible need blindfolding at times. I warn you, if that anarchist O'Shea even attempts to set foot in the Lodge I shall whip him from the place. I am more than surprised that a family such as the Parkers—'

'Mr O'Shea is not likely to come to the Lodge.' Barbara's head was high.

'For his own sake, I hope not. And you will speak no more of riding with the fellow. He knows of course that you will not be permitted to go.'

'But I intend to ride with him, Papa,' she said quietly.

'You *intend* . . . You sit there and defy me?'

'Alister . . .' Eleanor put a desperate hand on his arm. 'Please remember where you are.'

He forced himself to be quiet, to bring calmness at least to his face and hands. His wife seemed actually to be encouraging the girl; why couldn't she realise that one did not offer one's daughter to an O'Shea. This social disintegration must stop: Kenneth in and out of scandal at Chatham, Georgina bringing complaints from her school, Eleanor herself laughed at behind her unheeding back for her frivolous and exaggerated ambitions. Brooding, simmering with his stifled rage, he saw O'Shea greet his party of five, then watched him bend to whisper in the jewel-encrusted ear of a woman with piled golden hair. She laughed and, leaning on him, her gleaming breasts straining, kissed him full on the mouth. Alister's face burned. He ran his finger under his collar as he saw Barbara watching the byplay. But her face was expressionless. Straight from a night spent with some such tart this man would come fawning upon the clean-limbed virginity of his daughter. A Merrill. The man would respect nothing; money and power were his goals and gods, with women only interludes. As Barbara would be. The vision of them together, alone and close, maddened him:

'No.' He wrenched it from his throat. 'By God, no!'

'Father . . .' Barbara folded her slim almost bony hand over his. An old, rarely-used gesture. She had begun lately to call him 'Father' and secretly he preferred it to the infantile 'Papa'. Her hand caressing his roused conflicting emotions – why did there have to be so much of himself in her, why? 'There is nothing to worry about,' she soothed. 'Mr O'Shea is an expert horseman.'

Her eyes pleaded, as much as she would plead with anyone. But now the theatre was rising. Governor and Lady Gipps with their guests were entering their box. The Clintons were properly in theirs. The orchestra was playing. Now, the curtain was rising. Alister sat straight and taut, seeing it all through a blur. Barbara was still, her hands folded in her lap for she rarely bothered to use her fan. Calm again, Eleanor peeped and peered for interesting late-comers; she rarely saw more than half a play and what she did see she garbled. And Alister's eyes turned again to O'Shea as if at the drag of a magnet, devouring the animal strength of him. The overpowering, seemingly invincible strength . . . The arrogance and the surety . . . The cockiness, the conviction that the world was his . . . And with a sag of his rigid self-control Alister Merrill confessed to himself his bitter and lasting need. He coveted that strength and surety and conviction. He craved it all, hungered for it, envied it. He envied the man. He had never been conditioned to endure envy. There had been no need when he was young and full of hope. Then the future held only promise, and completion. Now?

Now he could only hate.

Chapter Three

THE CHILDREN were running after the wagon, fighting exhaustion with excitement, for they loved this coming home best of the long trip to Goulburn with the sun low in the sky, the dust puffing between their hardened toes, and Erins Pride but half a mile away. They called to Paddy as he limped beside the bullocks, bestirring himself now and then to whip their weary rumps. In its niche of sacks the baby woke and began to cry. Betsy opened her shift, picked up her youngest and held it to her breast. The child drank greedily while its mother spread her legs and gave herself, content, to the familiar act of suckling.

'She cries too long. A fretful child. She needs more care than the others did. Well . . .' She smiled cheerfully at Raunie. 'She'll get even less now. I think – no, I'm sure I'm having another baby.' And her soft voice trembled with happiness.

Jolted from her weariness the girl stared at her sister-in-law. There was barely room for them all now in the tiny three-roomed hut – if a minute square jammed with stores could be called one room – and no time or labour to build even a shed. She was suddenly nauseated by this plump pretty Betsy wearing the same dress she had worked in for weeks, her hair that was James's hair uncombed, a harassed cheerful woman revelling in her worship of Robert, her children, Erins Pride – no, Betsy Witherstone did not merely love Brick O'Shea's home, she *was* Erins Pride. Its heart, its growth and its fertility.

She moved her baby to the other breast and cuddled the child. She was always fondling her children; cooing to them or soothing them while the soup boiled over or the hominy burned. And when she had cried her remorse she would dry her tears with laughter as prodigal as her sorrow. Betsy was incapable of half measures, a girl of superlative emotions.

'I shall tell Rob soon,' she murmured. 'Each time he hopes for a son.' Then fiercely, 'It must be a boy. We need sons. Mr O'Shea has promised to help us build our own place on our own land. He'll help anyone willing to work.' She glanced slyly at her companion. 'He'll be here soon. You're anxious to meet him, aren't you?'

Raunie was indeed anxious, eager to complain of Moll's treatment, and her paltry wages, for it would take years to save even a few pounds out of what she was paid. And she was curious about the man himself – but would never admit *that* to Betsy. 'I've seen enough of bullies and rogues,' she said off-handedly.

Betsy bridled. 'He's no bully. As to the rogue – well, perhaps. Most men are rogues out here. There's something about the country that dares them to be even stronger and wilier than it is. To . . . intimidate it perhaps. We all feel that way at times. But just when Brick – Mr O'Shea – irritates you the most you're suddenly quite sure there's something of the saint about him. Oh yes there is,' she persisted at Raunie's laugh. 'You don't know him. Look, if a mother wanted to keep her child he would never let the Factory, or anyone else, take it from her.'

But Raunie looked her scorn. She'd heard too much of O'Shea – his suspect business deals and systematic white-anting of authority, his ruthless insistence on obedience and obeisance to himself – tales that roused her interest, and yet her caution. They paused at the rise. The bullocks always rested here. The soft sucking of the baby and the distant shouts of the little girls were the only sounds that broke the stillness as they stared at the wide familiar reaches. On the slight hill to the right sprawled Erins Pride, the rough-bricked homestead its owner left most of the year to the care of Moll Noakes and his assigned men. Admitted to its inner rooms to scrub and polish under Moll's scrutiny, Raunie had found it tolerably furnished for it was sometimes O'Shea's whim to bring home his friends and his enemies; drovers eager for

Moll's baking, shepherds, runaway ticket-o'-leavers, an officer on the road. And all manner of runaways from the British Isles – doctors, teachers, tradesmen, writers. It was said he made use of them all.

Down the hill a little was the slab and bark hut of the Witherstones, crowded by the addition of Raunie and, most nights, Paddy Harrigan who squeezed on to a pile of rags before the fire or in a corner of the storeroom. Otherwise he bunked at the House. To Raunie's disgust, and continued protests, her bed was a stretcher in a corner of the kitchen-cum-parlour; at least she had managed a sacking curtain before it, braving Moll's teasing. Farther down the soft curve of the hill was the even rougher hut of Ben Hawkes, the youngest of O'Shea's men, and his family. And flung out untidily from these dwellings were the sheds and yards, the chicken-runs and pigstys and cow bails, the vegetable patches, the horse paddocks, and the wheat and grain spreading to the grazing lands merging with the hot trembling distance. Far to the right, farther than the purple smudge of hills on the horizon, was Lake Bathurst. To the left lay the Shoalhaven River. While far south was County Murray and the wide wild reaches of the Maneroo, most of it untouched but being tamed and employed by O'Shea and his ilk.

Raunie stared at it long, with mixed feelings. Earth, holy earth. Absolute, immovable, everlasting – earth was so to all gipsies. But there was something about this earth, this land, that was different from other land. It grappled with you. It did not give, not willingly. So much stillness, so much immensity, stifled by years of drought, the erasing fury of flood, by hot winds and the relentless drying sun. And unceasing work. Woman's work. For none of this cutting into a continent seemingly older than time would function without the toil of women. It fattened and thrived on the ceaseless round of baking, washing, milking and breeding. Rebel tears pricked her eyes and she shrank from the woman beside her. Betsy had become a part of it, and gladly. But she – Raunie Lorne – was no Betsy, no Moll Noakes in the making. Serfdom was for the stupid and the guileless. She was neither. The two little girls scrambled on to the wagon, nestled against their mother and fell asleep. Paddy limped heavily along the road.

The trees were casting long fingers of still shadow as the wagon lurched down the rolling red track with the creek etched nearby, its bed dry and cracked with skeleton shrubs bent low above it. A tendril of smoke near the dark hill to the right marked the Blacks' encampment. There they had come and there they would stay until the white master O'Shea had come and gone. The white master brought, if he brought nothing more, justice. There had been war but now it was over and it was carrobbery, throbbing about the Pride for days, reaching such a pitch of hysteria that the women fainted beating their skin-drums and the men hacked themselves with knives until they bled, and the young girls hung about the kitchen proudly displaying their dripping lumps of human flesh, the torn-off feet and hands and fingers stuffed into their nets. Night after night there was the glow from the ring of leaping fires, the naked painted bodies, the dull beat beat as the Jens thumped their folded opossum cloaks. Raunie, susceptible as always to atmosphere, could not sleep. Her fear of the Blacks had died but she experienced a queer quick response to the monotonous tuneless drums, their pulsation seeming to echo her own rebellion. At the foot of the slope Paddy dumped stores at the Murchisons' boundary and moved on hurriedly; no one cared to meet Clark Murchison or his sons. A cruel breed and God must help their women and their felons for no one else dared. Except Brick O'Shea. More than once Clark's wife had come sobbing to the Pride to find sanctuary until her husband sobered – which was to be expected, grinned the county gossips, for Ida Murchison was still a pretty woman even if her husband had marked her face with a red-hot branding-iron.

They turned in the rough gates and toiled up the barely defined road to the House. Three horses champed outside the kitchen door. Inside, male voices clashed with Moll's abuse. Paddy stiffened and, muttering something about 'constable', limped off towards the trees in the hollow. As if at a signal three assigned men slipped from a barn and followed him. The children scurried after the small procession. Betsy slid to the ground, placed her child on a sack in the shade, and began unloading. Three men stamped from the kitchen followed by Moll bashing a spoon about a basin to force home her insults. Losing what was left of her temper she threw the lot after the magistrates and spat on his horse as he mounted. The little river of saliva ran down the animal's coat.

'There's no work for your kind at the Pride an' never like to be,' she jeered. 'O'Shea does his own bastin', if any. An' does it better 'n you.'

'Hold your tongue, you flat-titted old bigamist.' The policeman, jingling with sword and pistols, poked derisively at her stringy breasts. 'Unless you're looking for a flogging yourself.'

'Clap your claws on Moll Noakes an' you'll answer to the master. Get agoo.' And she shoved the negro-flogger with his cat-o'-nine-tails towards the third beast.

The magistrate, his greedy eyes devouring Raunie's young bosom, jerked a thumb. 'Who might she be?'

'A free woman, so keep your cuffs an' your bussin' for such as have to bear 'em. Not that a touch o' the "cat" across her back wouldn't stir her lazy young bones.'

'I'm thinking she'd do fine for me son. Just taken up thirty acres, he has.'

'Fine son he'd be to take another's brat along with his bride.'

The man shrugged, pulling thoughtfully at his lower lip. 'Woman are scarce and a lad can't afford to be too choosy when he's like to get a lass in the same family way and not know it; a drunken vagabond of a wench beside.' He nodded reflectively. 'If yon pickaninny be a boy he'd come in handy for looking after the pigs.' Raunie picked up the largest stone to hand. She'd stood enough.

'We've pigs here to be tended,' Moll put in hastily, 'so off with you to the Murchisons, they'll keep you hustlin'.' She laughed, but kept a wary eye on the girl beside her. 'Unless you'd like real work to do with a fresh veal pie to charm the dust from your throats after your labours. What do you say to that, lads? The Pride's in need o' strong hands.'

Scoffing, they turned their beasts and were off. Moll turned on Raunie in a fury. 'We don't welcome the law here so don't anger 'em – or make eyes at 'em. Now go tell those rapscallions to come up from their holes.'

'I'll not be married off to anyone, do you hear? Never. *Never.*'

Moll sent a stinging blow to her ears. Raunie's arm swung high. But like a flash Betsy was beside her prising the ugly weapon from her stiff fingers. Moll's arm curled around her throat and held. The girl struggled against them uselessly before her body went limp and the stone dropped harmlessly to the ground.

'As well,' Moll gloated. 'O'Shea don't hold with bastin' without good reason but that would have brought you a whirl o' the "cat" from his own hands that would take the flesh from your back.' She picked up the basin and spoon, dusted them off with her skirt, and swept triumphantly inside.

Dazed by her own anger Raunie did not hear her warning. Her mind was made up. Never would they bully her into accepting their peasant ways, a creature to be bargained for by any stray man – or woman. She must get away from them . . . from this place. And let Betsy summon that back-broken lot from their hideaway. She ignored Betsy's troubled eyes and with head high went in to brave Moll's tongue and temper. She vowed it would not be for long. Somehow she would escape Erins Pride.

May brought rainless days and clear cold nights. The wheat sowing was finished, the maize land broken up, the big white and yellow turnips stored. With scarcely a break in the seven days Raunie toiled from before dawn till late at night. If she shrank on a bitter morning from plunging her hands into icy water Moll would hold her face in it until she shivered. If she complained of the caustic that seared her flesh she was cuffed and sent to bed hungry like a naughty child. There was no end to Moll's malice and no reason for it but that her victim was young and pretty. Under the woman's goading Raunie learned to make candles and boil soap and bake bread and empty slops in a minimum of time. She learned to bear with the huge spiders that darted from crevice to crevice and to grind to a gluey mass the swarms of ants and other insects. She was restless, miserable and quite helpless, fretting for comfort, for the warmth of her own kind about her as only a Romany can fret. Jock McPhee had disappeared after only a month. Moll swore he was gone to the Murchisons where no white-man taboos existed as to what he did with the native women. But Rob merely shrugged and bent himself anew to clearing – felling, splitting and burning – coming home numb from the stinging persistent westerlies.

Raunie's one friend was the near-imbecile Paddy, who took upon his twisted shoulders, where he could, the heaviest of her tasks. So she was kind to him during the long nights when they crouched over the fire with the wind howling like a vengeful thing through every crack, Betsy crooning to her children in the next room, Robert smoking his pipe, and Moll come to gossip and struggle with her hated needle and thread. There were few strangers in winter and little news of the world so there was nothing to discuss but themselves and their memories. Paddy loved to talk, Raunie cross-legged on a rolled-up sack at his feet, ignoring Moll's disgust at the sock she was cobbling. From the beginning Paddy Harrigan had assumed she came from Ireland and his soulful eyes loved to linger on her face; probably he saw her as something from his youth, his wife, perhaps his daughter, for he possessed both, left behind while he served his long exile. When his voice faltered Moll would break in with wild tales of convict hulks and the Factory and men she had known and slept with and betrayed, coming finally to dwell upon her foster-son, her adored Brick. He would be a power in the land one day, would Brick O'Shea. No one could stop him. He would be up there beside the gentlemen for wasn't he as fine a man, as clever, as any gentleman born? And when he came to marry he would wed a lady, nothing less if she, Moll Noakes, had anything to do with it – and she meant to have plenty to do with it! She would kill the chit, white or black, who interfered with Brick's great destiny. And she would begin her reminiscences all over again, this time of poachers and baby-farmers and beggars and men she had known and slept with and betrayed . . . until Rob yawned, and with a terse command to all to get their sleep took himself off to his bed. And his wife.

'As for the rest o' men,' Moll would sneer, her eyes on the Witherstones' closed door, 'eat, sleep an' breed, an' work only when they're made to. An' women must bear with 'em an' hold their tongues, the poor mindless creatures. An' to think I served a sentence for wedding a second husband afore I rid m'self o' me first. Ah . . . but I was a foolish gal with naught but me passions to guide me. Passion!' She would spit into the fire and glower at the spurt of blue flame. 'For a lad 'tis sustenance juicier than meat but for a woman 'tis labour without reward.' But rousing herself from her glooming into the fire she would ruffle Paddy's tufts of hair. 'Stop gawpin', Padraic, an' show us your shiners so we may dream on 'em. A good thing to dream on, gold. A good, good thing.'

And when Raunie smiled her encouragement he would fumble in his trousers for the key, shuffle importantly to the corner, lift a square of the red clay floor and take out the carved sandalwood box he had made for himself so many years before. Inside – and Raunie noted how smoothly and silently the lid opened – was an old cap of forgotten origin, a smudged sketch of his wife when a girl, a bracelet, a rosary, other precious odds and ends. Drunk, he was often careless of the box, leaving it lying about until someone, usually Moll, tucked it beneath his arm; no one else ventured to touch it, it was sacred among the men. Now he pulled out a handful of coins and sifted them through his gnarled fingers. No one knew how many he had but sometimes Raunie counted ten, other times twenty. And there were always more in the box. Brick O'Shea added to them each time he came. It was Paddy's little excitement, his gold.

'There!' Moll would toss a couple in the air and catch them neatly. 'But 'tis a bad habit he has o' hoardin' 'em. Even Brick can't hustle the fellow into keepin' 'em in a bank. Here gal, fondle 'em if you want. You're not like to see so many agin.' And in her generous mood she would trickle a handful on to Raunie's palm and the girl would clink the coins obediently, loving the smooth feel of them, the sound of one against the other. Money was power. Ah, the wonderful splendid things one could do with money . . .

' 'Tis to bring me woif and goil frum Oireland,' Paddy would say as he'd said a hundred times before. 'Mrs Chisholm will find them and send them out. She promised. The master says so.' Poor deluded fool, said Moll's wink. His wife and daughter would be dead by now. Weren't the Irish always dying? 'For a lifer I wuz made, y'see, for the taking of firearms from a constable in a tithe row. The wild madness of a boy.' And he would shake his head, amused at such foolishness as to think he could rebel at life. He was wiser now. Passivity brought gifts. It brought gold. ' 'Twas a bad thing with me Hannah not long wed to me and the goil but a babe. But Hannah's a one, with the tongue she is. When I sez to her loively loike, oi'll bring yez both out when oi've earned your passage money she sez to me jist as loively. "Then oi'll be getting our things together before the sun sets this day for out there in Botany Bay they'll be making ye work for the first toime in your lazy loife." ' He laughed, shaking. 'And they ded in thruth.' Then he would sit quietly, his face twisting and screwing as he remembered and tried to put the thing he remembered into words. 'But they crippled me. 'Twas a hundred lashes for us all, with toime between so as to drag the punishment over an hour. It wuz hot but two scourgers took spell about till they were spattered loike a couple of butchers. And it finished me. I wuz bruised and bent frum a fall the day before . . .'

Raunie's hand clutching the gold would sweat. A hungry thing the law. One must be clever – or good – to escape it. But what did virtue bring? Nothing that she could see but a creeping dullness. So a woman had best be clever. Very clever. She opened her fingers and stared at Paddy's gold till Moll snatched it up to count it – Moll Noakes was proud of the fact that she could count to ten and did so on all possible occasions. But to Raunie the faint click of the little key seemed loud as well as final.

This year O'Shea was late. Inar had been lingering about the Pride for weeks. Moll's manner to the half-breed was a curious one; though she distrusted all natives this one seemed to drive her near-crazy for reasons Raunie sensed were beyond the obvious, for Inar was, in her savage way, attractive. Even Raunie admitted it, if grudgingly. Most of the half-castes about the stations were a dirty yellowish white but only a slight thickening of her lips and a copper tinge to her skin proclaimed Inar's aboriginal blood. But her inclinations were all native. Her hair was entwined with scraps of ribbon and greasy beads. She hoarded a bizarre wardrobe of garments she wore only when forced to dress, wandering naked when the weather was mild. But at her first glimpse of Raunie's red dress – a garment Moll itched to burn as a clear device of the Devil – Inar had offered her new babe in exchange for it; to her primitive mind it represented all the mysterious lure of the white woman, while indicating it would match the reticule of stained red velvet kept screwed up with her other goods and chattels inside the native woman's fish-net in which she seemed always to be rummaging like a curious monkey. Raunie had wondered about the purse until she saw its contents: a mess of silk scraps, bright paper and pasteboard, bonbon wrappings and beads, and a minute wooden box evidently jammed with further odds and ends that comprised its rubbishy content. Junk. Knowledgeable in the ways of waifs Raunie wore her own trinkets beneath her shift or tied about her waist, for Inar believed anything that glistened, had colour and light, must gain attention from the men of her father's race – and Inar craved attention as a prisoner in a cell craves sun. Sometimes pathetic, always sly, she was tolerated among her mother's people by the will of the males who would readily mate with her if they could, while they excused her the rigid tribal laws that were the lot of their women. She could speak English well but angered Moll by using the gesture language peculiar to her tribe, and very little of that, a touch of the ear and a nod of dissent. She wandered about the townships and stations living much as she pleased. And with whom. But at the end of summer she haunted the Pride, refusing to leave until she was ready. She made her own laws of living. There was nothing anyone could do, seemingly, about Inar.

On her marriage the previous year to the full-blood Dgeralli she had been sent with him to work on a western holding but was soon back with a pickaninny, her faithful husband trailing her. She spoke of other children she had borne and conveniently rid herself of – one she had bashed against a tree until it was dead. She ignored her young husband, despising him so much she would be found curled on a bed of sacks on the verandah or on rags beside the kitchen fire. When she tired of Moll's blows she would fasten vicious teeth in her hand, enough to scare off her tormentor, at least for a time. But Moll's endurance was obviously at its end the morning she found Inar in Brick's bed freshly made up for his arrival. Dragging her forth by her hair she had thrashed her with her foster-son's stockwhip. For hours after Inar had huddled moaning, her wailing infant beside her, crouched under Raunie's makeshift couch. The cries of mother and child were ear-splitting but Raunie let the woman be; there was no liking between them, but they bore with each other by reason of their mutual shortcomings. Besides, they were both 'diddikai' – half-caste. And somehow or other Inar interested her. She found herself listening to the woman's muffled complaints.

'He not send me away. He let me stay.'

'Who would let you stay, Inar?'

'The master. He let me stay.'

Raunie laughed. 'He won't like it when he hears you've been sampling his bed.'

'He want me in his bed. He want me, he want me . . .' Raunie was intrigued. O'Shea was not, perhaps, loth to having Inar in his bed whether he occupied it or not? But the woman lapsed once more into her monotonous grumbling, would be goaded no further, and continued to draw herself into a sullen shell whenever O'Shea's name was mentioned.

And the most idle question concerning O'Shea's natural mother brought only snarling evasion. 'No talk. If I talk she pull out my hair and cut off my fingers and men run away because I ugly.' Did she mean Moll Noakes? Seeking to sift fact from fable in the meagre gossip that came her way Raunie would needle her sister-in-law as they prepared breakfast.

'How much gossip about O'Shea is true, Betsy?'

The girl dropped a cup. It did not break but her face was uneasy as she piled the plates carefully on the table. 'What gossip?'

'Oh, you know ... the talk about this Erins Pride, and who his mother was, and Moll's jealousy, and the fact he's rarely seen with a woman about the city ...'

'No one with sense wonders about anything in this country. They can't afford to. In any case, Mr O'Shea won't stand for idle talk. Or questioning. He almost killed a man once –'

'Only once?' Raunie sneered.

Betsy's usually mild blue eyes flashed with anger. 'He has faults, yes, but who hasn't? And he must over-ride men to achieve his ambitions and so he makes enemies.'

'But what are his ambitions?'

'I don't know. No one knows exactly. Unless it's making money to bring immigrants here, the kind of immigrants he thinks we should have. But I never can understand why men act as they do. And I haven't the time to wonder about it. Neither have you. Don't pry, Raunie, I warn you –'

'I don't care what he does.' Raunie shrugged. 'I just get tired of hearing about this wonderful O'Shea as if he's a – well – a god or something instead of just a man.' And she doubled the sugar in her tea not caring if Betsy did notice. She cared not a fig for Betsy, or for Moll – and certainly not for Brick O'Shea.

It was a cold June afternoon when Brick O'Shea came home. At noon one of the tow-headed Rogers boys rode over to say the master had stopped by for a meal but would be at the Pride before dusk, bringing two men. Moll was jubilant, clanging her pots and pans. 'Fine strong country lads for

Rob.' The kitchen was full of steam and food and women and children, with the Blacks encamped in a body at the door and spilling away in a thick stream down the slope – anyone would think the Governor himself was coming, Raunie thought irritably, and found tasks elsewhere. It was late and she was lingering over the milking when she heard the Blacks' jabbering swell to an excited chorus and knew he was here. She wiped her cold hands and straightened her dress then stood hesitant. She longed to run, to hide. A colonial despot. Her master. But no man would ever be her master . . . She was hesitant because he was a man and before all men, for the first time in her life, she felt ugly. No matter how hard she tried, her wide skirts and tightly laced waistline could not hide the almost full-time child she was carrying. There was nothing she could do for her reddened hands and broken nails but cry over them. Even the grease she stole failed to smooth her wind-roughened skin. Her hair refused to shine. It was tired as she was tired. Then she stiffened. She fancied she heard Moll calling her. If she did not hurry the woman would come looking and scold and make a scene. But she rolled down her sleeves and, as she toiled up the slope, whisked off her cap and let her hair fall loose. Moll would complain but she did not care. She might be a drudge but she would not tamely look it!

A horse sweated at the door, its breath clouding the air. Under the trees two more. In the distance men strolled with Robert. Two quite well-dressed men. No labour there, she decided. Moll would be crosser than ever. And, yes . . . she was calling again, her voice shrill as Raunie pushed through the mob of Blacks, sickened even on this cold day by the odours of fish oil and sweat from their closely packed bodies. As she hurried up the steps she noticed the native, Dgeralli, leaning against the wall, apart from the others as always, remote and seemingly diffident. She had never seen him otherwise than in this attitude of brooding intensity, as if he were listening to voices others never heard. She hurried inside.

Coming abruptly from the sun-bright world she could not

see clearly, but felt the blessed enveloping warmth. As her eyes cleared she noticed the man standing near the stove teasing the little girls with a bundle of sweets. A big dark man he was, hairy where his shirt was open at the neck, laughing at the children as they struggled with each other for the spoils, warm thick laughter that sent the blood racing through her chilled body, and she wanted to laugh too for the sake of the unaccustomed sensation. Inar squatted, fondling a string of beads. Her arms were covered in bracelets. Something sparkled in her hair. She had grabbed the baubles brought for the native women and, picking them over, was lazily content. As Raunie stood watching she saw the firelight glint on a necklet of shells – small beautiful cowrie shells – and yearned over them. An amulet. The perfect amulet. But the man O'Shea was looking at her. She tossed her head high and returned his gaze.

She could not have explained exactly what she had expected – a handsome face perhaps, one of suave brutality, or coarseness, nothing certainly that resembled a gentleman as she defined a gentleman. But her first reaction was of shock. He did not look brutal, just weary. He grinned at her and she found it a likeable grin seeming to transform him into a person one might trust – but she must be very tired and weak, she decided in some confusion, to even think of trusting this man. Then, as her eyes met his she felt the full impact of his personality. It clamoured at her, roused in her an excitement such as she had never felt before. Then she knew why he affected her so. He was a most singular, forceful and vital being. By his mere presence he would command attention. Wherever he happened to be would become the focal point for eye and mind – and didn't she possess that gift? For different reasons of course, but she did possess it. It was something she understood . . . Her eyes were the first to turn away but there was not one detail about him that she had not noticed or one distinctive feature she would fail to remember – his crumpled shirt and travel-stained breeches, his stance, his hands thrusting impatiently through his thick black hair.

'So you're the widow Lorne,' he said at last, slowly. 'I

would never have guessed it from Moll's talk. You look harmless enough.' He smiled. 'At the moment anyway.'

'So here you be.' Moll bustled in from the House proper to rake the fire and send sparks flying. 'Pay your respects to Mr O'Shea, your master.'

Raunie bobbed a reluctant curtsy. The children were clamouring about the man again, demanding attention. Moll was at the yard door raining curses on the noisy mob. Raunie moved across to stir the broth, always her evening task, and to keep the fire going. As she passed the native girl her deft and lightning kick sent the necklet of little shells into a corner near the stove. Inar glanced up, perhaps at the faint tinkle, but looked down again, dreamily absorbed. Raunie built up the fire, panting with excitement more than from the weight of the logs or the blaze. Her fingers shook as she piled the wood. A too-large log slipped and would have broken her ankle if O'Shea had not caught it deftly.

'We're not burning witches at the stake,' he said with some amusement. 'At least, not tonight. Haven't you learned yet when enough's enough?'

'She's slow,' Moll boomed, 'but she's learning. I'll see she learns, the lazy young trapes. Haven't I warned you, they'll all laze an' brag if you pay 'em too well. Now I'll hustle Betsy for she'll be maggin' still to that brat o' hers.'

Brick gave a brisk slap to her buttocks as she passed him. She pushed him aside roughly but indulgently. Her voice drifted away, the children squatted beside Inar to eat their sweets, and the kitchen was quiet again. From the corner of her eye Raunie watched Brick tear hunks of bread from a fresh loaf and sensed him perch his large frame on the table edge near by. She knew he was watching her. She stirred furiously, glad of any task that would help her avoid his eyes. His eyes seemed to see too much.

'You look a frail thing,' he said at last. 'But you're young and once you've some colour back in your cheeks you'll find another husband. Plenty of settlers hereabout eager for wives. But take your time in choosing. Fumbling as you are, Moll needs you, she tells me.'

72

'I shall leave here when I please,' she retorted, raising angry clouds of steam about their heads. Her eyes met his defiantly. 'But it won't be to keep house for any miserable shepherd I'm likely to meet in this horrible place.'

'You don't like it here?'

'Like *this*?' she choked. She could feel the sweat dripping down her face. Her eyes began to water and she blinked angrily. 'A drudge for three shillings a week bullied by that . . . that . . .' she swung the ladle in a violent circle to hold it, quivering, at the door, '*harridan*? A bed riddled with fleas? In London I was a lady's-maid –'

'We have no ladies at the Pride. Only women. Learn to be that before you try to be anything else. You might, once you've got used to it, find it satisfying.'

'I was forced to come here. Mr Witherstone –'

'Rob Witherstone didn't expect Lorne's wife any more than I did. Rob went to Sydney to meet his brother-in-law and found instead a girl – and from all I hear a troublesome wench at that. Not that we expected Lorne to be useful but we were resigned to putting up with him. No impoverished – or disgraced – gentlefolk are assets on a property like this, you know. The country's glutted with such fops, and parasites the lot of 'em.'

'You're making good use of me.'

He raised his bushy eyebrows. 'Marriage with a broken-down gent hasn't necessarily made you a lady, Mrs Lorne.'

Outraged, she slammed down the ladle. But, unable to think of an answer stinging enough, she picked it up again and continued stirring, indignation in every line of her heavy quivering body.

'You know . . .' He leaned so close his breath fanned her cheek, 'I could make better use of such energy at my place on the Maneroo. Just a hut. Trees so high you can't see their tops and wild dogs that howl all night and snakes thick as reeds along the river banks. And the river sighs like a wind.' He laughed. 'An ideal spot for taming wilful children.'

'I'm not a child. I'm sixteen.' Talking to her this way when he couldn't be much more than thirty himself. Not young of course but still . . .

He threw back his demon-like head and roared with amusement. She swung from the stove, the ladle dripping fat and scraps. 'I won't be made fun of or bullied or despised by anyone, least of all by you. Somehow I'll get back to Sydney.'

'Will you, now? Then take a word of caution with you. Sydney wharves reek with women; the doxies are getting more numerous and bolder than dockrats with every ship, with most of them only too eager to solace a lonely man. What's more, they're not over-particular about marriage lines. Flaunt your airs before those polls and they'll toss you in the Harbour with a knife in your back. As for the men . . . few are like to be bothered with you at present, or with your young child.' Sick at heart, she was silent, fighting her dangerous desire to slam the poker across his face as his eyes drifted over her face and body. 'You're Irish I hear.'

'I am.'

'There's a Cockney twang to your speech.'

'I was born in London.' Well . . . I think so, she reflected ruefully. But who here to say nay to her explanations, true or false?

He turned and, striding to the corner by the stove, bent and – yes, picked up the cowrie shells. Inar slithered to him and reached for the prize. He swore at her, holding her off with his foot, and snapped the string to send the shells clattering. The native girl crawled about gathering them up. But Raunie noticed he had kept back the largest and most perfect shell. He tossed it high, caught it, then hiding it from Inar held it out on his palm.

'You want it, don't you,' he murmured. She moved to take it but his hand closed abruptly. His other hand grasped the chain about her throat and pulled her charm free. She struck out but he brushed her hands aside. His grip was compelling, and somehow she did not want to fight it. She was still, waiting.

'So . . .' He ran exploring fingers over the carving. 'My mother left me some strange books. There's one about a

74

devilishly odd wench, a gipsy I should think.' He let the chain slip slowly beneath her collar again as he released her. She found her heart beating strangely and knew she would always remember his hands on her. He laughed. 'No need to be scared. Inar doesn't know the meaning of the word "gipsy".'

She gulped. 'Moll . . .'

He made a quick gesture. 'Moll never looks too deeply into things, just pleases to see all young women as the Devil's spawn. And few others are like to guess it of you for there are few of your race here.'

'My father was Irish,' she persisted.

'Then give thanks for that much.'

Then she abandoned all pretence. She grasped his sleeve urgently. 'You – you won't tell – promise you'll never tell. Please.' Hating herself for her pleading. But she was helpless before him.

''Tis nothing to me if you want to trick the world – unless of course such trickery should cause me trouble. But you'll be well advised to veil those eyes when you lie,' he added softly. 'They're wonderful eyes, quite wonderful. Indeed, you're as well equipped in looks to make your way as you doubtless are in cunning – Egypt.'

But the word was more of a caress than an insult. She took a few steps, swayed a little, leaning towards him because she could not help it. It was so long since any man . . .

'One more thing.' His voice was softer still as his hand folded round her arm and steadied her. But his eyes were mocking. 'Learn to be more careful of yourself in future. Most of the pretties searching for easy fortunes take care they do not burden themselves with brats. You'd best find a way of doing the same.'

She struck him with the grease-coated spoon; a savage impulsive blow that took him by surprise. He staggered slightly. Inar leaped, snarling, to her feet. Moll, hurrying in with Betsy and the children, sprang to slap Raunie's ears. The baby screamed. For confused moments it was pandemonium dying abruptly to horrified silence. Raunie began to cry. Her child-heavy body drooped and she put out her hands to cling to the nearest solid object. It happened to be the roaring stove. She screamed and sucked her burned palms. On the point of collapse she felt herself swept off her feet. With great shocked gasps that broke into the ravings of hysteria she clung to Brick O'Shea.

He carried her through the House and laid her none too gently on a bed. Through a blur of misery she recognised the room – his room, his bed. Then she caught her breath in a choking gulp as he slapped her face, hard, and stood over her till her sobs died to whimpers. He turned to the women and children in the doorway:

'I'll have no driving on the Pride and well you know it. The girl is exhausted. Leave her to rest and make my bed by the fire. And call my guests indoors. Hurry now, all of you.'

Horrified, Moll began to argue but he was adamant. Alone with Raunie he unfolded her scorched hand and placed the little shell on her palm. Her fingers curled over it lovingly. Somehow it soothed, even a little, her pain, her sense of outrage. He stood watching her. With half-closed weary eyes she stretched her body then let her limbs fall limply. She wanted him to stay so urgently it was with a cutting disappointment she saw him turn abruptly and go out. She heard his boots stamping through the House, his long loud halloo, the frantic barking of dogs, the neighing of horses. Somewhere Moll's voice mingled with Betsy's. Footsteps, the closing of doors, silence. Sweet heavy merciful silence. She lay still, nothing clear or close just then but the smart of her burned palms. She snuggled under the clothes and clasped the comforting little shell tightly to her breast. He had given her the shell. And she loved him for it.

She woke. His voice – Brick O'Shea's voice – had woken her, of that she was certain, that more than the clink of tankards, the scrape of boots on a rough floor. Light seeped through a crack in one wall. Lamplight from the kitchen . . . She scrambled out of bed, wrapped herself in a blanket and put her eyes to a crack. The men were gathered about a barrel of home-brewed beer gnawing at chicken legs and hard hunks of bread and slices of cold pie. Ben Hawkes sprawled in a drunken sleep while Paddy, nodding, looked about to slip to the floor. Rob was filling tankards for the strangers.

As she watched, Brick drained his beer and hurled the mug through the doorway in a fury. What was he saying . . . something about another blasted Tory out from England to take his place beside the Clintons and Havelocks and Merrills and all the other imperialists who knew not a stick of cedar from sandalwood or an honest immigrant from a prison-hardened murderer, pottering as so many fussy dowagers with liquor licences, postage, naturalisation of aliens . . . *Aliens* mark you, when the place throbbed with Australian-born still stifling under penal laws, ignored but to provide cheap – nay, slave – labour for the toffs . . .

'If we must take the outpourings of Britain let us mould them to the shape we need, our way – '

'Don't you mean *your* way, Mr O'Shea?' his youngest visitor burst out.

Raunie looked at him with interest. Tom, someone had called him. Tom Wells. She decided he must be drunk. And Brick was filling another tankard for himself. He drained it without seeming to draw breath, and slammed it down.

'Those who know the country and do its work and take the risks should fashion the country's laws. What fairer? North America has governed itself for two years now. Why shouldn't we? First, let us get our two-thirds elected into Council and make a great rattle in shaping things – ' his eyes flickered briefly – 'our way. A better way. No more felons, never again, not even to Norfolk or Van Diemen's Land, to waste their strength in gaol or under the "cat". Free immigrants. And no more cramming of them into ratholes of ships to die on the way out – if not of fever then of starvation – and the rest to land sick or useless to be a drain on us all. As it is, the agents don't care. Why should they? They get their money.' He laughed thickly. 'Why, even I can get nothing better than a quarrelsome brat from a London kennel who threatens to shuttle off, taking half the Pride with her when she goes.'

Raunie shivered more from indignation than the cold.

Drunken sot. They were all drunk. The whole country ranted and raved. Wasted talk, wasted time. Things were, so you let them be, and made the most of what was before you. 'Cut your coat according to your cloth.' Now she knew what it meant. If you couldn't move obstacles you accepted them and twisted them to your purpose. But she wrapped the blanket closer about her and rested her forehead against the wood to listen. Drunk or not, ranting or not, she liked the sound of his voice. And what if he did despise her? At least he knew she was alive . . .

'I say this . . . If what we get are worn hopeless their children need not be –'

'That's it, Mr O'Shea, that's the answer.' Tom was leaning forward, his smooth boy's face alight with enthusiasm. 'Man's character is made for him, not by him. The predominance of virtue or vice lies in the hands of men themselves.' His voice had a sing-song rhythm, as if quoting from a book. 'Inequality and misery can be wiped out –'

'Balderdash.' Brick wiped the back of his hand across his mouth. 'Merely controlled, like vice. Only vice and misery can prevent the world from being over-peopled, so we must have a dash of both.'

'But the evils plaguing mankind will change when men and women change.'

'What makes you think they will change?'

'Mr Owen –'

'*That* for Robert Owen's high-faluting experiments.' And Brick threw the chicken bones at Matong's nose sniffing about at the door. 'What use are theories? A man needs answers to work on. Well, I already have one answer. A mob feels, and before it feels anything more it feels cold and hunger and hate. Mostly hate. So give a mob shelter and food along with sustenance for its hate and that mob belongs to you.'

'But people feel love too. Mr Owen –'

'Your precious mode-making Owen has persistently over-rated human nature and will continue to do so. So he must fail in his aims. He deals in dreams, you young fool.'

'But he has not failed. He has sown seeds. His school saved me from child-slavery. It taught me . . . dignity. It taught me so many things I resolved, I swore, others must be made to see too. That is why I am here – '

'You are mistaken.' Brick stood over him, swaying only a little, his voice dangerously cold. 'You are here because I was interested enough in you and your ability to wield a pen to pay your fare to Sydney. So you are in my debt – and I collect my debts.' His voice softened only slightly. 'Forget your far-off Utopias, Wells. I've one close by for you to serve – the opening up of Crown lands in small lots for cultivation. We must have food. And keep your nagging free of your prejudices – I understand you also nourish Malthusian theories, so none of your birth-control chatter or those confounded pamphlets advocating sexual restraint tucked under the doors of the unsuspecting. Understood?'

The boy flushed. 'Too many children are born to starvation.'

'Not here. No one need starve. Those who settle Australia must people it and I happen to see it peopled a certain way. Native-born children have never known any restraint but the garrison. Mingle them with the Irish to whom squire and parson are invader and heretic, and those English who have suffered under both, and we raise a new race with a new way of looking at life; a nation of rebels I well know how to handle.' He filled his mug again while the boy watched in silence. 'So teach as I tell you to teach, write as I command you to write or return to what you are – a refugee from radical riots. British justice, I shouldn't need to point out to you, is anything but sentimental.'

'Are you threatening me, Mr O'Shea?' Tom asked quietly.

'If that's the way it sounds.'

He sprang to his feet. 'You'll never make me return to the Old World.'

'Then stay here and starve. You talk too much and too wildly. Boys of nineteen who are breaking my bread don't decide what they'll do. I decide.'

'Not for me. I'm not afraid of you. This isn't your kingdom

79

yet. What I was taught was for the glory of mankind not the glory of one power-mad human being. I'll be no party to your selfish personal ambitions – '

Brick's ring sparkled in the firelight as he struck the youth across the mouth. Wells did not move or even flinch while the blood dripped down his chin. In a drunken fury Brick swept the table clear, food and plates and tankards clattering about the room. Ben Hawkes did not even stir, but Paddy mumbled and turned over. 'Are you mad? Do you think I'm like to let one gangling stripling stop me in what I mean to do? Get out,' he bawled. 'Go walk off your insolence. Get out before I take the "cat" to you. Get *out*!'

But Tom took his time in straightening his coat. 'I am not deaf. And I'm quite clear-headed. I should say you were in greater need of a sobering breeze than I.'

They stared at each other, breathing heavily. The other men were still, the room quiet but for the dogs rooting in the spilled food, growling at each other. Suddenly Brick threw back his head and laughed. '*Touché*. I might even join you outside in a moment.'

But the boy did not laugh. He wiped his chin carefully, settled his collar and went out slowly into the darkness. O'Shea, as everyone knew, had made another enemy. But friend or enemy, it seemed all the same to him as he slopped beer into tankards and kicked those asleep till they roused and joined him.

Raunie yawned and, half-frozen, climbed into bed. The man was a bully, eaten up by prejudices, pride and ambition, most of all by hates that surely were beyond the understanding of ordinary men. A strange, unpredictable devil of a man. She remembered Tom's pale but resolute face . . . he had seemed a harmless enough, almost gentle individual. But now? Yes, O'Shea changed people. And in changing them seemed, in some inexplicable way, to destroy them. Well . . . she stretched luxuriously in Brick O'Shea's bed . . . he would never change her. Not Raunie Lorne. Or harm Raunie Lorne. She was a match for him, for she understood hate. She understood ambition. And pride. She tucked the blankets warmly about her; what a fool he was to prefer an argument or making an enemy to . . . making love. But he did give me the little shell, she consoled herself, kissing it. Smiling, she fell asleep.

Moll woke her the next morning by dragging off the bed-covers in one determined sweep. 'An' don't get the idea Mr O'Shea is soft,' she boomed. 'He lives hard an' expects others to do the same. He treats women easy to get the best from 'em, that be all.'

Raunie did not doubt it. 'He's a beast,' she said cheerfully, wiggling her toes at the outraged Moll. 'But you must be easier on me. He said so. Betsy heard him say it and whatever he says is Betsy's law.' And she lay laughing as Moll flounced out, her posterior and cap waggling her disgust. For the first time in months Raunie felt rested. In spite of her burns she had slept long and deeply. Now she would go to Betsy. Betsy would mend her feelings as well as her raw hands. But she dressed slowly, savouring the room, lingering in the hope of seeing its owner again, and went to her tasks reluctantly. But dawdle about the House as she might she saw nothing more of Brick O'Shea. He left early and returned late, said Betsy, spending his time at neighbouring stations, attending to the grievances of settlers, his men, and the Blacks. And three days later he was gone, taking his guests on to the Maneroo, with the Pride left to manage as best it may. Raunie went about her work with reluctance, strangely depressed. It would have been better if he had not come into her life at all to leave it again so quickly. Then she was angry with herself. She disliked him, didn't she? Unpolished, rough and quarrelsome. A cruel man, of no real consequence to those of position and importance. He was nothing more than a challenge – yes, that was it. Challenge had always stimulated her. But there was no time to dwell on Brick O'Shea, no time for anything but her struggle with her thick and cumbersome body and the ceaseless round of labour.

It was a raw June morning when she woke from uneasy sleep to feel the bed sodden beneath her. As she lay half awake she heard the wind curling viciously about the hut then felt the moisture gushing from between her legs. It was her time. Fully awake now, she called for Betsy who came softly so as not to waken the children, in her old washed-out wrapper with her bright hair braided to her waist, a Betsy growing even prettier as she grew more rounded. It would be hours yet, she pronounced, and coaxed Raunie to her feet. The men must be got to work. The girl moved with difficulty for there was a growing heaviness in her legs and across her back. Food choked her. When the sky lightened and the men were gone she tried to work but the pains were coming at regular intervals, and at their sharpest point she could only stand gripping a chair, the table, anything solid till they had racked her and passed. Moll came down from the House and took the little girls away while Willa Hawkes cared for Betsy's youngest. So the raw wind-filled morning dragged on.

By midday she lay on her bed shaken by long heavy pains that left her, during their brief respite, sweating, waiting in terror for the next. A gipsy woman bore her baby as simply as an animal . . . but this was not simple. Gipsies of the country lanes perhaps, tumbling unclothed and free-limbed from childhood – yes – but her young years had been spent in the confines of a lodging-house room. She was frightened. Demoralised by pain and the unknown, her teeth bit into her lower lip until it bled, her moans broke into screams which she tried to stifle in the pillow. But tormented by pain and fear she went on screaming. Betsy held her down and she clung to the woman, gibbering. Her ravings broke into prayers, 'O Deloro . . . O Deloro . . .' so she called to the Good Spirit, the Great. She tossed in despair. The prayers helped not at all. The pain was worse. In brief moments of clarity, as she lay exhausted, she saw Willa hurrying in and out and the children standing impassive but curious in the doorway until shooed away. Betsy fastened ropes to the bed and she pulled on them obediently, dragging, tearing her hands . . . Gone now was all her summoned dignity, all reason. She was a drooling primitive creature of squirming limbs, her mouth formless, her eyes glazed. At intervals she dropped into a haze of wispy dreams . . .

One dream became definite . . . one place . . . a terrible place . . . fading, mercifully, just when it became terrifying and unbearable. A sky of rich purple tinged with red above a mountain of black rock with no vegetation of any kind to cover its nakedness. It was dark and smooth and gleaming, that rock. There were no trees, nothing but a honeycomb of black caves connected in crazy ways by slithery footholds. And if one slipped it was into a yawning cavern stretching far into nothingness. She knew that space. The world of the dead. The hole at the end of the setting sun through which she was descending to the underworld . . .

But she wasn't dying . . . was she? No, no, she must not die. Fiercely she clung to the rocks, clutching and straining as she fell, to hang, fighting a rushing wind intent on hurling her into eternity. It swelled to a gale, that wind, whisking her backwards and forwards, hurling her against the point of the pit that stretched ever deeper below her. And the torment of her body was drawn out, sharp, clear, a pain so terrible as to be almost exquisite. She wandered that dreadful mountain again and again seeking something, calling someone, never finding what she was looking for. Now there were faces peering at her from the caverns – the faces of the bad fairies . . . the Earth Dwarfs. She was trying to scream and there was no sound . . .

From this terror and confusion she would emerge to sense rather than see shadowy figures cross the room, feel fingers moistening her lips with water. And hands . . . torturing cruel hands tearing at her entrails. She could not fight them off. They were everywhere those hands. Voices merged to form jarring puffs of sound. She slipped into the dream again but now, somewhere around the misty jagged corners, far in distance, was the cry of a child. It came nearer to her . . . nearer . . . she put out her hands towards it . . . threw wide her arms . . . her head rolled . . . her eyes opened . . . flickered . . . dimness still . . . she moistened her cracked lips with her tongue as she stared slowly about her . . .

Light beat at her eyeballs. The room was bright with the spasmodic rays of afternoon sun. A woman – Moll – stood at the corner table wrapping something in an old blanket. Betsy was beside her, smiling. Raunie sighed. She felt weak but wonderfully without pain. It was like the blessed hush after the buffeting of a storm.

'It'll die if she don't feed it.' Moll shook a doleful head. 'A long time for such a tetchy mite.'

'She stood it well.' Betsy looked anxiously across at the bed. Raunie closed her eyes. She did not want to talk, not yet. 'Willa made more of a fuss at her fourth, you know she did.' Then softly. 'There's some . . . some . . .' She struggled with words, 'fineness about Raunie —'

'Balderdash! Too many bouncing ways to come to any good. The poor must work an' suffer an' be cheerful about it. 'Taint their place to be putting on airs. Now give her the brat an' run an' feed your own. The lads'll be in soon.' Moll wiped her hands briskly and without even a glance at the bed went out, banging the door behind her.

Betsy smiled at the child in her arms. 'A boy,' she breathed, almost with reverence, her tear-swollen eyes beginning to sparkle. 'Oh, Raunie, you have a son.'

She placed the baby carefully in its mother's reluctant arms. Raunie stared at the wee puckered face and the tight flailing hands and, incongruously she supposed, felt hungry. But since Betsy demanded interest she took an earnest look at her child. It was white-skinned with long black hair. Soon its skin would darken. She knew it. It would grow a true gipsy. Well, at least he would not be reminding her of James. That was something. Now she would sleep, heavily and for a long time, as long as they would let her. The baby was still, slack in her hold. She stirred restlessly.

'Take him. He's heavy.'

Eagerly Betsy picked up the baby and cuddled him. 'He's really quite small and thin. You'll call him James of course.'

'James?' Raunie yawned and moved her legs gingerly. Her body was tightly bound. She rubbed her hands over her stomach glorying in its flatness. It was quite numb. Nothing existed between her neck and her feet. It was wonderful. Quite, quite wonderful. She yawned again, her lids heavy.

'Oh Raunie – please.' Betsy's blue eyes grew misty again, yearning over the now-sleeping child as she tucked him securely in his place. 'You know how I loved his father.'

'Oh, call him anything you like.'

She turned over in the bed, away from the woman's sentimentality, and away from her child. She closed her eyes, snuggled her cheek into the damp pillow and listened to Betsy's footsteps going softly from the room. She sighed with relief. She had borne the child and it was over and she was alone with herself. Never, she swore, would she endure that torment again. She was certain, remembering snatches of her dream, that she had struggled for life, wanting life and everything in life to enjoy and remember and keep. And she had endured that agony for what? For a scrap of bone and skin and thin wrinkled flesh. Alien flesh. James Lorne's flesh. There was nothing there she could love. Whether that was right or wrong she did not know or care. It was true and that was enough. She hated the very memory of James Lorne – why should she not? And because this child was his, she felt nothing for it.

She ignored it, and fell asleep

PART TWO

Chapter Four

RAUNIE CROUCHED under the tiny gunyah – sheets of bark supported by pronged sticks – that Inar had found for them for it was very cold. There was no moon so she could only guess it was two to three hours since the woman had left her and it must be, at the very least, one o'clock. She was hungry and tired but even in the shelter was afraid to sleep for the night was full of sounds; small rustlings, tiny squeaks and grunts, all springing from unknown and hidden sources. She thought of the wild cattle – once on a ramble with Inar she had watched the shaggy beasts from a safe distance – and hostile Blacks, and wild dogs that could swallow a sheep whole, a woman too if she were small so swore the men solemnly. And the dreadful Bunyip, the Blacks' 'devil-devil' with a body striped like a tiger and a calf's head that bellowed out of the unknown . . . But Rob always laughed off the Bunyip. Even this slight consolation was dispelled by the terror that Inar would leave without her or worse, from spite or hate would betray her to Rob Witherstone, that even now she was at the Pride – *No*, down that way of thought lay panic . . .

For the first time since creeping from the sleeping Witherstone hut to join Inar she was frightened and her fingers closed over the revolver at her waist, savouring the cool strength of it. Rob Witherstone's revolver. Paddy's old pistol was too big to hide easily so she had stolen the revolver for nothing must go wrong now that her goal was within reach. For over a year she had coaxed Paddy into teaching her to use a gun, finding she had a knack with firearms that delighted the old man so much she had trouble wheedling him to secrecy. Now she believed herself competent with any gun, certainly she had no qualms about using this one, for she had known from the beginning that the utmost self-protection would be necessary on the long journey down to Sydney Town. Just as Paddy's old clothes were necessary. And the money. Taking the gold had been almost too simple . . . soothing Paddy asleep before the hut fire, taking the key when all were asleep, prising up the flooring, unlocking the box to clutch a handful of coins, replacing the box then the key back in his pocket. Eight golden guineas. She wished she had taken more for five were already paid to Inar.

Her hand closed on the little bag pinned to the underside of Paddy's shirt, which she wore, sleeves rolled to her elbows and tucked into a pair of his old trousers secured about her waist with string. Her feet looked twisted and immense in his old boots. The guineas tinkled against her little shell – three guineas added to the three she had kept from the *May Queen*. Six pounds and a few shillings, all she had in the world for her pitiful wages and the odd coins collected here and there had gone to buy blankets and provisions for the trip down – Inar was striking a hard bargain. In her carpet-bag was her only dress, Betsy's shawl, a kerchief (Paddy's) and the red gown. It was the latter that had finally won Inar's help. Promised to her when they reached Sydney Raunie had flaunted it as the ultimate bribe. Inar could never resist the red gown.

She shivered. A tremulous wilful spring. Perhaps it meant, at last, the breaking of the drought. Travellers had brought desolate tales of a land lying perched and gasping, of Blacks fighting the cattle for the slime-covered pools, of glutted buzzards thick on the trees, and the wild dogs tearing off the living flesh and the crows picking out the eyes of the dying stock. Even so, the weather must not break. Not yet. She even prayed to her 'O Deloro' that it would last, for with fine weather and a measure of luck she could coax McPhee and the bullocks and the sulky Inar to haste, why, they might even make Sydney in under a fortnight on a firm road. Excitement made her stir and move her cramped limbs, longing to be on the move. Not that she was disturbed at the possibility of Paddy opening his box and sifting his money; he could not count, and even if someone did point out the fact that some coins were missing, there was always the master O'Shea to make good his losses. It would be a small matter to Paddy. And as for the others . . . Moll would count herself well rid of a nuisance, Rob probably visit a doleful curse upon her head, but Betsy wouldn't care. Betsy Witherstone might even be glad.

Betsy had been a changed woman since the Christmas Eve on which her newborn son had died after a few hours spent wailing in his box. She had lain staring fixedly at the wall, so still that there were moments when they had feared she was dead herself. But after a few days she had turned over and smiled and begged for the tiny Jamie. She had cuddled the dark little man-child with a terrible urgency and cried with relief as he sucked the first milk running from her breasts. And Raunie had watched them, scarcely believing her luck. To be done with suckling and the monotony of baby caring – here was her chance. After all, she must leave Jamie somewhere and Betsy would love him. It was best. Children belonged to the Betsys of this world; what chance would she, Raunie Lorne, ever have in life with a baby clinging to her skirts? So the small James nestled to his foster mother while Raunie bound her breasts and spent her few spare moments primping before the scrap of mirror, brushing her hair, smoothing her hands, and crouching over the fire at night watching Paddy gloat over his wealth – an eager Paddy Harrigan soon off to Sydney and the O'Shea stables – scheming by what miracle she might herself cover the robber-infested miles that separated her from Sydney, from life, from Brick O'Shea.

Along with the chance of escape she lived for news of the man, cherishing each scrap of gossip that sifted through distance to settle on the barren existence she detested more fiercely every day. There were slightly better conditions on the immigrant ships due to agitation by himself and Mrs Chisholm. On a wild south coast beach he was building fast strong boats of native timbers to bring his horses, bred on the Maneroo Plateau from stallions of the best English breeds, Clydesdales and Clevelands, as well as Arab, up the coast to his stables – he asked and got fifty pounds a beast in Sydney. He was establishing a crèche, and a school for foundling children – while philanthropists talked approvingly of compassion. Compassion? Raunie would laugh to herself. As if Brick O'Shea really cared about a child's empty belly. All he ever sought was the fawning of the mob.

But from Moll's boastful accounts of his activities one name began to surface – a girl's name. It appeared that he went riding openly and frequently about the sand-hills of Sydney with a certain Miss Merrill, a lady, Moll would emphasise proudly, daughter to Major Merrill. 'Toffs!' she would exclaim, running the Merrill name about her lips as if it were honey until Rob cut short her gossip with orders to mind her own business and set about her work. But Raunie would lie awake wondering how much of what Moll told was truth and how much mere wishful thinking. She longed to pump Betsy yet hesitated for she was chided enough over her questions. But the girl's name nagged at her to become a spur and she would wait even more impatiently for Brick O'Shea's next visit. It was for him she wore the dress Betsy gave her, worked hard, even forced herself to be pliant under Moll's scolding. But his only response was to call her Egypt – mercifully when no one was within hearing – and toss her some trinket which she cherished fiercely, ignoring the fact that he brought gifts for all the women. He was kind to the small Jamie, why she could never understand, for her child irritated her. She refused to believe he was entirely uninterested in her even though, when he might have her for the taking, he went hurrying back to Sydney. To Council. What had Council to do with him? She would shrug exasperated shoulders. Some day all would be different. With the return of her good looks came confidence and an almost overpowering vitality. Increasingly, in her thoughts and plans, Brick O'Shea's life became coupled with her own. If his work and activities were in Sydney then she must be in Sydney. She must be near him. He must see her, and see her often, as he saw the silken cherished women who fêted and chased and lured him – as the Merrill girl lured him . . . She would sink to sleep at night dreaming extravagant dreams of the future. Their future. In those months after her son's birth, revelling in her precious new freedom of body and mind, she was almost happy.

Her resolve to leave Erins Pride was sealed finally by Moll's taunts that her master meant to take her farther inland and leave her there forever. Never would she go to the Maneroo, she screamed in defiance, never would she go anywhere it did not please her to go. But how to reach Sydney? A coach went from Goulburn but how to reach Goulburn without help, for she would surely be questioned, perhaps even dragged back to captivity. And so she grew desperate, so desperate she accepted the one course possible to her – Inar.

The woman had drifted into a spasmodic affair with Jock, Moll gleefully predicting they would be certain 'to be murdering each other' or the long-suffering Dgeralli would turn on them. It was but a matter of time. But Jock was going down with the Murchison clips and Raunie felt certain Inar would go, so she set about pleasing the woman, stealing food for her, giving her little presents, scrambling through the countryside with her on long often frightening rambles. But, a creature of caprice, Inar held off until one day she admitted she was going on a long journey and Raunie offered her money (which she didn't have) to be taken along and nothing said about it. The woman's eyes glittered but still she was hesitant, fingering the red dress, waiting. Raunie, beaten, had agreed to her price. Inar could have the dress, yes, but only when they set her down safely in Sydney, terms she was well aware would be almost impossible to enforce. All the same, she must enforce them. In the crude shelter of the gunyah she fingered the revolver and felt comforted. So far she had managed well.

A sudden soft rustling and snapping twigs. Inar slithered close, naked save for the opossum skin wrapped about her middle. Her almost bare body was still that of a girl, lithe and fluid. She thrust a slice of bread into Raunie's hands. As she ate, Raunie watched the movement of the copper limbs, the smooth thighs and the high-pointed breasts the woman guarded as gems from the jaws of the babies she was continually bearing – and killing. Killing was simplicity itself to Inar. She – Raunie – would be alone with her and the probably drunken Jock for weeks to come.

'Is he alone?' she asked, sharply because of her sudden fear.

'There's a boy. Along the road a little. Jock sleeping.'

'Drunk you mean,' she moaned, but roused and groped for her bag and Paddy's water-bottle. Drunk or not they must be moving, at least strive to put a few miles between themselves and habitation; she meant to pass through settlements at night when possible. Not that she expected anyone to come after her but why not lessen risks where she could? She kept up with her cat-footed guide for she had come to know the country well, even to be at one with it, not because of its association with the Pride but because of the gifts it held. In her time at the Pride she had let herself drift back, quite simply, even a little humbly, to nature – the running streams and the richness of trees and the expanse of stars. On such a night, like this, she was all gipsy. Even so, in spite of such acceptance, there would always remain something about this country that daunted her, as it seemed to daunt all men. All except Brick O'Shea. He not only subdued it he turned it to his will.

They followed the swollen stream to the curve of the hill then across the paddock to the road. A dray loomed before them. Farther along was the wagon, a four-wheeled, eight-bullocked unwieldy thing – they wouldn't make much time with that. A youth was busy with the horses. She eyed the beasts with suspicion, for she didn't take kindly to riding, as she went seeking Jock. Snores came from beneath the wagon, always the sleeping quarters of men on the road. He was sprawled on a bed of sacking. A note for a year's wages in his pocket, a giant thirst and a string of inns all the way to Sydney – they'd be lucky if they made the trip in a month! She kicked out at him. He mumbled, turned over on to his back to sprawl and snore and snore again. Inar came from somewhere out of the blackness, dragged an iron bar from the wagon and dropped it with faultless aim on his half-protruding stomach.

'Up. Up!' She began kicking her lover with bush-hardened vicious feet.

Gasping and swearing he scrambled from under and up. A sleepy drunk, a lout any woman could do with as she pleased if she were young and possessed of any brains at all. But jealousy was Inar's sharpest motive for violence and she was jealous of all women, white or coloured, younger than herself. Force to force she – Raunie – would have little chance against the pair of them if they carried firearms and they surely would have at least a musket. Her poor little attempts at protection seemed suddenly ludicrous. It was going to be a cat and mouse game. Money would be the deciding factor – or finery. She must play the subtle teasing game, luring Inar on with the promise of the gown she craved.

'Jock . . .' She stepped close, then backed hastily from his breath. He peered at her, wiped his face with a hairy hand, hitched up his trousers then slapped her heartily across her bottom.

' 'Tis auld hornie hisself creeping up in the night ye look, ye wee black-haired crittur.' He boomed his delight. 'And from whut micht ye be runnin' in your borrowed pants an' all?'

'It's time to start. You can sleep later.'

He yawned then belched. 'I'm more than content where I be till daylight.'

She left him to Inar and climbed on to the wagon. She scrabbled a place for herself with her bag for a pillow and an odorous blanket as covering and waited for them to argue it out. At last she heard Inar clamber up and Jock's morose orders to the boy, Matt. They moved off slowly to animal sounds and the creaking and crunching of wood and iron while she lay half asleep, staring up at the black that was the sky, fascinated as always by the wink of stars in the great void of roof to this land that was now her torment and her destiny.

The dawn was cold, cloud-packed and heavy. Inar was

sleepy and lazy, yet watched Jock with such brooding intensity that Raunie decided never to let herself be alone with him, for the slightest move on his part towards her made the woman taut as a bird of prey. Matt was a strong young puppet, scared or half stupid, it mattered not for he was so much her unquestioning slave she felt safe enough with him by to sleep a little. But Jock insisted on stopping at every inn and by the time they reached Paddy's River she was tired with the effort of being amiable, the constant vigilance and the broken sleep from which she always expected to stir minus revolver, bag and money. She worried so much over the red dress she wound it tightly about her body next to her skin. There it could stay until she was ready to part with it.

Hard travelling now. Hilly country, the road bad, the bullocks tiring quickly. Jock was iron-strong and a fine bullock-driver drunk or sober, but they sorely needed another man so he took up anyone along the road who would work for the ride and a meal. Jock went off with a shepherd to roister at Gray's Inn, was still absent at dawn and Raunie despaired of ever reaching Berrima – how could she have thought they would make twenty miles a day? The light was already strong and they were packed and waiting when he staggered into camp bellowing:

'Oh, the shearing all is over and the wool is coming down
And I will get a wife boys when I go up to town –'

And filling the bullock-bells with rum and forcing the stuff down Matt's throat till Inar knocked her lover senseless with the convenient bar of iron. They tossed him into the wagon and forgot him for a blissful hour or two. The miles stretched too slowly behind them.

They camped by the tree-fringed Wingecarribee to replenish stores and repair a damaged wheel. Teamsters sang and fought and swore round their fires dotting the river banks. While Matt worked, Jock made his round of the inns and camps and the women wandered the tiny settlement of Berrima. Though bone tired Raunie could not rest. Every hour on the road seemed an eternity. Two bearded teamsters carried Jock into camp but, incredibly, he was sober if bleary-eyed at dawn. The track through the Bargo brush was the worst yet, such a terror they did little more than crawl. Then more hours to ford the river and pitch camp under trees black from past fires, with a long gaunt skyline and a cold wind sighing through the twisted bush. A gloomy sullen place. The dullness of it depressed them and they longed for the sun. Bored, Jock bullied Matt who seemed to be continually nursing boxed ears, while Inar teased and taunted her lover or crouched, rummaging through her old purse for a piece of comb or a string of beads. Raunie did her best to hide the dwindling stock of food from their greedy fingers. She was tired of cooking and carting water. She was sick and tired of them both. Toying with the idea of begging a lift from another team, on impulse she sawed off her hair with the rusty knife. There . . . with luck she could pass for a boy. Her tanned wind-roughened skin would help. But a few days more and she thought better of it – even Inar and Jock were preferable to some teams they met on the road.

A day's rest to prepare them for the climb over the intimidating Razorback Mountain. They moved off in a chill dawn with an indecisive drizzle falling from a thick sky. If the rain sharpened, the wheelruts would soon be cloying ooze. With sacking cloaks over their shoulders they trudged on and up, gained their second wind by taking turns to ride a while beside the rocking springless dray before setting to again to push the wagon, urging, shouting at the bullocks, unloading and loading till their arms ached, their hands bled, and their boots were heavy with caked mud. The dray overturned and almost took them with it down the mountainside and even with the help of passing teamsters it was an hour before it was back on the road. The tired horses stumbled. Raunie suffered from a bruised leg. Intent on the task in hand, they spoke only to shout orders or answer necessary questions. Few cared to spend the night atop the Razorback.

The descent, if possible, was worse, the road a quagmire. The constant grating of the wet chains that locked the wheels, the shuddering of the 'frying-pan' dray and the cumbersome wagon that portended its possible overturning, shook their nerves and worried their senses. The bullocks, necks scalded by the friction and weight of the yokes, stumbled and sprawled, weaving a pattern of giant interlocking prints in the mud and slush. They cut down small trees and fastened them behind the vehicles and the descent became safer if slower. They stopped but once to brew tea and gnaw lumps of sodden damper but even so it was long after sunset when they camped, exhausted, at the base of the mountain. But they were over the worst of it. Nothing to come compared to what was behind them. Indeed, they had been lucky. No one had tried to rob them.

Matt slept beneath the dray. In the wagon Inar's sodden hair fell across Jock's chest as they slept together – their almost nightly squirmings bored Raunie so much she tried to sleep as far from them as possible. Matt's threadbare coat about her shoulders, she crouched by the fire rubbing her jagged hair with a scrap of sacking, shivering with tiredness and the pain in her leg. Only the thought of a simpler tomorrow kept her going – Camden, Liverpool, then not much more than a step to Sydney. She sniffled with the chill in her very bones. She took a chance – she unwound the red dress, dried it before the fire and replaced it around her body. Its brief warmth soothed her a little. She made a bed of sorts under the shelter of a tree, curled up in her misery and shivered herself to sleep.

Passing Camden, Jock insisted on taking the old Cow-pasture Road. Matt's protest that it was seldom used these days and would be almost impassable in rain gained him a slap across the jaw for his trouble. Raunie decided that one road was as good or bad as another. The first few miles were bearable but soon their progress became so jolting as to be wellnigh impossible and they moved at little more than a crawl. But to go back would be as bad as to go on. This aged and desolate stock-route of a bygone heyday rose and dipped to its beginnings, skirting the Prospect waters, the only relief in its wilderness smudged homesteads far in distance, so indeterminate and forlorn she began to feel uneasy. Somewhere to the right would be Liverpool, but it was all bush and tall trees with an occasional scrubby track branching off to nowhere in particular. Ten miles or so from Camden they camped on a slight rise with the sky clearing a little and the new moon through scudding clouds. Her heart lightened. It would be a fine day tomorrow, surely. But under the tremulous beams the dense hills seemed peopled with ghosts of the old road's important past and for comfort she dragged the mattress of dried leaves Matt had made for her close to the fire – a fire to a gipsy was a friend. She gazed absorbed, possessed by the thin spiral of uncurling smoke, forgetting if briefly her cold and hunger and fears, lost in dim avenues of the mind . . .

She woke suddenly and sharply to a sense of danger. Her hand clutched the revolver tucked in her waistband. But she was looking up into Matt's eyes and his warning finger. As she attempted to rise he put his hand over her mouth. They poised, listening.

'They be goin' to rob ye,' he whispered, 'an' leave ye. Me too maybe. An' if ye give trouble they'll leave the wagon so they can say we ran off with it. An' should ye keep fussin' they'll not hesitate to murder ye . . . Shhhh!' he hissed as she let out a gasp. 'I heard them plannin' it for the first dry day.' He jerked his head. ''Twill be fine tomorrow.'

'What do they expect to get from me?'

'Money. An' a dress o' some kind.'

'Why didn't they do this before . . .'

He chuckled softly. 'They must 'ave liked your cookin'. Besides . . . you've got two hands.'

'What can I do?'

'There's a crosstrack farther on.' He pointed to the north-east. 'Once on it ye'll stay there easy enough. 'Twill take ye to Liverpool. Ye can get along the road now an' hide till it's light. Take me coat.'

'And you?' Stuffing her things into her bag and peering to where Inar and Jock slept. All was still and quiet.

'I'm off too. To the west. Got a sister works on a farm out there – or she did. But she's somewheres about. An' whatever

99

she finds for me can't be worse than gettin' a bashin' mornin', night an' in between. I hope they get up to their bloody necks in mud,' he hissed savagely. 'They never meant to go back, y'see. They have to get money. Planned to dump me I suppose or slit me throat along with yours. Ye'd best get goin'.'

As he led her carefully on to the road she pressed a coin into his hand. He shoved her forward. She slithered rather than walked the slushy road, creeping her way but not pausing till the vague shapes of the wagon and dray had disappeared. Then she began to run, or rather stumble, sliding, wandering blindly off the road to feel her way back again. But there was no sound behind her. She thanked her 'O Deloro' for Matt! Wrapping his jacket tightly about her she sat for a moment to get her breath with the grey-black mist of dawn spreading over the crisp cold desolated bush. To the west was a thickly covered bank of hills beyond which stretched the smudge of the Dividing Range. To her right the land was flat, bathed in indeterminate shades to the distant sun-lightened horizon where lay Sydney, her Mecca. All she had to do was to walk into the sun.

The day was gaining strength, coming to vivid life. Magpies chattered. A kookaburra sang his song that is without melody. The derelict road slumbered in a dim drifting mist. She screwed what remained of her hair under Paddy's kerchief and did up the one button of the coat. Could she . . . Yes, somehow she must pass for a boy. A roadside waif.

Here at last was the track, narrow, muddy, with prickly growth leaning to hide it. Spots of rain fell. Now, a powder-fine drizzle. She trudged on, a small shapeless shuffling figure in a lost grey wasteland.

She opened her eyes to the glare of the sun, blinking in yellow light. All she could see was light, all she felt was warmth. Blessed, blessed warmth . . . She lay enjoying the glow through her still-weary body, staring up through trees at the clear morning sky. She felt for her carpet-bag, always her pillow on the road. Her pistol was in its place. She struggled up, groaning, for her body ached from the gruelling labour demanded of her since being picked up by a team of bullockies just outside Liverpool . . .

She coughed. Her chest hurt. She leaned against a tree struggling for breath. She had been forced to stifle her cough as she had stifled her speech, keeping her face averted as she moved to the whims of the drunken rum-soaked louts who had loaded her and the two young boys with tasks so heavy the work had almost killed her. She stayed only for food and water and a ride on the wagon now and then – anything to cover the miles to Sydney. Another team fell in with them and she felt safer for they were all too interested in drinking and wasting time to care about the mud-coated boy she appeared to be; indeed, it was their befuddled eyes and minds that saved her from rape for nothing could have done so if they had been clear-headed and curious enough to snatch off her kerchief, unbutton her jacket and rub the mud from her hands and face. She huddled beyond the camp fire's glow to gnaw at her hunk of stale bread and listen through a half-sleep while they drank and argued and fought each other . . .

Too many immigrant ships dumping their human cargoes on the depressed colony . . . Too many people tramping the roads begging work . . . Too many whores – hadn't they enough already? Never enough, one roared, and they downed more rum and made jokes about women while she brooded on Sydney – not far now, surely? And whatever Sydney was, it would be hers; she had left it with reluctance almost two years before and she had not survived these dreadful weeks on the road to be scared off by talk of depression. But a sullen young bullocky took to following her with his eyes so she decided on escape, tramping the night road till she passed cottages warm with candlelight, roads and tracks branching to right and left, and inns with lanterns glowing. Despite the sickness in her chest and limbs she fell asleep in the bracken with something almost like contentment.

Now, the rumble of a cart. She must be close to the road. The Parramatta Road. She crept from the bush to see a cottage with chickens pecking about its door and cows in a field. A cart with a man and woman bounced along the track to the house. But no more begging for help. And no more bullockies. She would walk the road when it was deserted and take to the bush when people were about until she lost herself in the anonymity of the town. The day was fine and grew warmer. She drank from the waterbutt of a deserted house, keeping the last of her bread till she could no longer bear hunger. More cottages. Market gardens in the distance. To her left, well back from the road, was a country mansion amid rich and sheltering trees. Rows of little houses now. Stalls and public-houses and shops. The sun fell behind her as the road curved north to slope down the Brickfield Hill to the town proper.

Carts and coaches, wagons and horse-riders stood lined up at the toll-gate. Drabs of women wandered, begging. She paused. Her feet smarted in the battered mud-caked boots. She was very hungry. She needed rest. She turned off along a side road that ran behind the stores and houses into the lanes of this haphazard squalid approach to the town. Cottages leaned above patchy gardens. Dogs rooted in pools of muddy water and the inevitable chickens scattered before her. She flopped in the shade of a lean-to shed to finish her bread and massage her feet. She slipped the pistol into her carpet-bag while she loosened her shirt stiff with dried mud. Her fingers closed over her amulet, then her money-bag. The little shell clinked on the gold. Money enough for board and lodging till she decided what to do. She let the coins spill into her palm, loving their shine.

She froze. A woman's hand with broken dirty finger-nails was groping from inside the shed, round the partly open door towards her carpet-bag. She saw the hem of a skirt. A second hand groped, a slightly younger hand. Hands seemed everywhere, their owners obviously unaware she was watching them. She snatched up the carpet-bag and sprang to her feet as in a flash they confronted her, legs spread and arms blocking her way. Two grotesque women in dirty clothing and painted bloated faces under battered feathered hats.

Public women. Fancy women. Women who preyed on travellers forced to stop at the toll-bar. Shrewd crafty grasping women adept at thieving and running from the police. Raunie swung the carpet-bag in a great arc to thud it against the younger and send her sprawling. But her companion sprang at Raunie and they fell struggling in the dust. The second joined in and all struggled for the bag, scratching, pounding, kicking and hitting out, tearing at each other's hair and clothes and eyes and skin.

Raunie fought like a mad thing. But the coins went spinning. With shrieks, and a savage blow that swept her violently aside, the strangers fell on the gold and fought each other.

'Whores! *Whores!*' Raunie screamed, her voice cracking. As the women ran with their loot she shouted after them, cursing them, cursing the empty lane, the empty world. Too weak even to crawl, sick and beaten, she lay in the dust, lips to her precious charm, mouthing a violent terrible gibberish of despair.

Chapter Five

'MAXIM . . . MAX . . .'

The young voice crackling with eagerness rose above the clamour of the Barracks – the medley of clattering boots, doors banging, voices hoarsely outshouting each other. A door crashed open and the handsome young subaltern smoothing his perfumed hair before the mirror swung about in delighted surprise.

'Merrill!'

'Max!'

With laughter, playful jabs, slaps on back and buttocks Ensigns Maxim Werner and Kenneth Merrill of Her Majesty's 99th Regiment of the Line greeted each other. Fellow officers milled about the door till Maxim kicked it shut on their grinning faces. Kenneth straddled a chair, rested his arms on its back and smiled at his friend.

'I've found lodgings. Squalid of course but cheap. Mama's raising hell but I can't stand the Lodge when the Major's there. But the crowd – I can't find Holt. And what's happened to old Berwick?'

Maxim Werner smoothed his tunic with soft plump hands and turned back to the mirror to survey the result. Life had always dropped into those hands the easiest detachments, the best and oldest liquor, the prettiest women. Particularly the prettiest women, Kenneth thought enviously as he watched him as always, admiringly.

'Both at Port Macquarie. But from what I hear it's deadlier than this Windsor you're forever complaining about. Trumping up a list of floggings for the sake of something to do – and see.'

'Nothing could be as bad as Windsor. A bunch of rotten shanties with nary a canary to kick or a pretty girl to kiss. Had visions of toasting in '45 with the dregs of a barrel of old stringy. But –' he stood and stretched his long limbs, 'I'm here and aching for fun. You promised me fun – remember?'

He grinned, his light skin glowing, his thin hands nervously ruffling his crisp reddish hair. His father's slim loose frame, his mother's vivid colouring for which he never ceased to curse her in a jocular yet half-resentful way. Sensitive, fastidious, idealistic in a sentimental, at times even maudlin way, Kenneth Merrill moved with a feline almost feminine grace that he struggled to offset by a hearty good-fellowship towards his fellows and a studied casualness towards women that he sincerely believed concealed his innate repulsion of matrimonial entanglement. Marriage was a duty. Like penitence and family visits. Like education. Like war. Like faith in the invincibility of England. Marriage, like duty, was dull. And damnably inconvenient. He sighed. But an inevitable duty to be avoided as long and as expertly as one could. He considered himself something of an expert at avoiding it. And every other responsibility under the sun.

Maxim examined his chin. 'You had Parramatta longer than most of us. Girls in abundance.'

'All too respectable.' Kenneth studied his friend carefully then added with a considered airiness: 'Any news yet of New Zealand? Aren't the "Nines" to get a poke at a Maori pah while there's one left standing?'

'Why the hurry? They build their silly houses up again as quickly as we knock 'em down.'

'But I want to know what's in the wind.'

'Then pump your Major.'

'My venerable papa is more secretive and humourless than ever since the 80th sailed. Dripping vitriol in every word. Says I look better for my spell of country air. He can never stomach the fact that I'm unable – through no fault of my own – to flaunt even one scar of combat. Takes my intactness as a personal affront. Feels he's failed somewhere. I tell you, he'll sacrifice me to his lust for blood-letting at the first opportunity. And to impress Havelock. If he doesn't snazzle the old buzzard's money he'll go under, nothing more certain.' He tapped an impatient foot, biting his underlip like a small boy. 'Can't get sense out of Mama either. Now that she's roped in a possible husband for Barbara she's busy fattening Gina for a kill – '

'She's a beauty,' Max murmured.

'Gina's a brat. If she weren't my sister I'd call her a tart. Caught her in Parramatta riding with some noisome toff. Swore he was her dancing master. Stuck to the tale too all through the fuss. She's only fourteen.'

'Looks more.'

'That's the trouble. Too developed. And I'll admit she'll make an admirable bait to retrieve the family fortunes – what there have ever been of them. I swore I'd tell the family about that do in Parramatta but . . .' He frowned and ruffled his hair. 'When she snares the heir to a dukedom or, more likely, the son of a local brewer I'll settle with her for a thousand.' He chuckled. 'Anyway, a hundred.' Resting his chin on his hands he gazed thoughtfully at his friend. 'Is there a wench left in Sydney Town you haven't studied?'

Max shaped his already perfectly shaped moustache. 'I doubt it. But I shall be leaving them in your hands, or arms if you care to have them there. At least for a time.' His pause was impressive. 'I'm going to be married.'

Kenneth's eyes widened. 'Why?'

'Any one of the reasons a fellow embraces matrimony – or allows matrimony to embrace him. Boredom, the need of physical release, money, love.'

'You're never bored, you've never stifled your emotions one iota, and you never fall in love. So it's money.'

'The lack of the stuff to be precise. The irritating lack of it.' He flattened an infinitesimal wisp of hair. 'Gentlemen are forced to be calculating in their choice of a wife.' And sighed.

'While clerks and saddlers choose where they please.' Kenneth sighed with him. 'Well, who's the lucky lady?'

'Miss Carver.' Max grinned a little foolishly at his imma-culate reflection. 'Jenny's a charming thing but alarmingly over-maternal. I suspect I shall be obliged to provide her immediately – and probably continually – with a succession of bouncing young Werners. Fortunately she will be well able to support her children. And buy me out without the usual fuss.'

'Carver?' Kenneth frowned. 'Isn't there – ' He broke off uneasily. 'I mean . . .'

Maxim turned to face him. 'There is,' he said coolly. 'Mrs Carver is the daughter of an emancipist – ex-convict if you want it more plainly. One on every street corner now you know. The quickest way, in fact the only way to a fortune in Sydney these days, is to turn publican.' He struck an exaggerated pose. 'How will I look as a barman?'

Kenneth coloured, then began to pace nervously, flinging the inoffensive chair violently out of his way. 'How on earth can you even think – '

Maxim laughed. 'Easily, my dear fellow. I hereby invite you to down your sensibilities in true colonial gluttony washed down with wines that are the cream of the old man's pubs – all four of 'em. Snub emancipists on the street if it makes you feel proud but don't scorn their dinner tables. After all, you're not marrying the girl.'

'But it's New Year.'

'It's early yet. And I'm free till dawn. Have I ever been stumped for an excuse when I wanted to escape? Hang it all Ken, I believe you've forgotten Chatham.'

Kenneth laughed, his outraged proprieties forgotten for the moment, or rather, put resolutely aside. They shook hands solemnly on their memories and went out.

The Carver house was in fashionable Lyons Terrace facing Hyde Park. The Park itself was crowded and would be more so towards midnight. There was something new in the air . . . nothing definite, nothing even tangible, yet all about them was a sense of elusive yet quivering excitement. As if this new year of eighteen hundred and forty-five would bring something of hope, of the promise of full bellies, of work, of goods to buy and money with which to buy them. The end, to be hoped, of the crippling depression. Progress . . . *progress* . . . one heard little else these days, bedazzled as were the citizens by catch-cries – agriculture, education, representative

107

government, cessation of transportation . . . practical decisive aims, goals into which to set their teeth. And the sense of well-being, of hope, transmitted itself to the swaggering young officers, causing them to joke with coachmen and housewives, brush the harlots of the town from their path less firmly than was required of them and hurry up the imposing Carver steps.

Adam Carver – Brother Carver to his fellow Freemasons for upwards of twenty years – was a fat anxious little man with a thin anxious little wife. He gave the impression that he was nourished on beer which promptly turned sour in his stomach. He puffed. His belly gurgled through silences so that one found oneself talking of nothings at a feverish pace. His two Kings School sons were smug and pimply, his Jennifer damply pink and cloyingly sweet. Kenneth longed for the taste of vinegar or tart apple as he watched her fawning on Maxim, hanging limply on his words, indicating his glass to be refilled before it was half empty, suggesting this and passing that to pile his already heaped dinner plate. But there was no doubt about the Carver money. It shrieked from the profusion of potted palms to the richness of the piled furnishings, the overdressed women, the aggressive snobbery of the Carver whelps. Kenneth beamed on them all while creeping inwardly from the taint of trade and felony, uncertain just then which was the worst. A few years of marriage plumpened by child-bearing and contentment and Jenny Carver would look the very mother of a barmaid. Poor Max.

But Ensign Werner was engrossed in his performance of the continental gallant, fanning the merriment with subtly shaded anecdotes spiced with French blasphemy he was confident only Kenneth would understand – and be damned to the pimply sons. But even they contrived to justify their wasted school fees as they laughed in all the wrong places and glanced knowingly at each other. Their mama, bemoaning the Maori trouble along with the audacity of the Australian aborigine, beamed her delight when the young ensigns vowed constant vigilance and protection against both. The dinner was lavish if heavy and Kenneth felt mellow enough to applaud Jenny's last hollow discord as she raised her fat little hands from the pianoforte in triumph. He was even considering a mild flirtation when there came sounds of a disturbance in the street. Or the Park. Maxim was out of the doors in a flash and across the road to mingle importantly and officially with the crowd. He returned with a long penitent face and the news that all officers were recalled to Barracks. Immediately. He gazed sadly on his disappointed Jenny while removing her clinging fingers, bade her parents a regretful adieu and, with a puzzled Kenneth at his side, walked sedately down the street and around the corner. Then, gasping with laughter, he broke into a run.

'What the devil . . .' Kenneth panted, trying to keep up.

Maxim eased to a walk. He was always lazy. 'Haven't the slightest idea. A drunken brawl I suppose. But a lucky one. Come on.'

Now for the fun of the evening. It was early, not long after ten o'clock. Parties at all the hotels, halls, many private residences; they could take their choice as could any officer on leave tonight. Brick O'Shea would be holding open house at the Royal . . . Of course, one never quite knew with O'Shea, one would like as not drink with scum tonight whom one would be obliged to question, or have flogged, next week. And there was that confounded arrogance and insolence about the man one could never quite pin down or safely object to . . . But he provided the best of wine to soothe and the worst of women to satiate lonely young officers down from the aridity of upcountry irongangs. And champagne to toast the midnight. So . . . It would be the Royal and be damned to opinion. Champagne was expensive stuff.

All Sydney seemed bent in the same direction. George Street was a sluggishly moving tide of jostling bodies. The ugly pile of the Royal Hotel was hugged by beggary and thievery. Toughs and idlers mingled with respectable family folk in from the suburbs to see the lights and discuss the gowns and admire the carriages. Entertaining and cheap and gayer than a fine Saturday night – if one did not have one's pockets picked. Yokels from out of town stood gawping at the brightly lit balconies, craning their necks to see each vehicle draw up and new arrivals force a path to the entrance with fist or stick or whip. Maxim, heavier than his friend and with the added gift of forcing lesser fry to make way before him, forged ahead, but Kenneth found himself halted by a barrage of citizens pointing and shrieking at a carriage. O'Shea's carriage. All Sydney knew it. A jingling ornate thing seized in settlement of a debt from an unlucky restaurant owner and drawn by four magnificent greys with the O'Shea mark distinct against their pale coats. He rode with two bearded men and a fair woman flashing jewels – a Mrs Lakey who sang at the Victoria. Her name was flung from tongue to tongue. A woman of the people – they liked her and shouted their approval. O'Shea was a man of the people was he not? The rabble were pleased to couple them if they could, for there had been too many rumours of late about O'Shea and the Merrill girl and no one knew what to make of it. Only one thing was certain . . . little good a lady born would do O'Shea, filling his head with fancy ideas. Still, lady or not, there were those who swore Miss Merrill helped at his school and his crèche and at Mrs Chisholm's Immigrants' Home. But there was no telling what would come of it all. Perhaps, O'Shea being O'Shea, nothing would come of it. So many women . . . such brief episodes . . .

Kenneth saw Maxim dart from the crowd to greet the party and made an exasperated plunge to join them, using elbows, knees and clenched fists as did everyone else. But he was held stubbornly. Damn Max for a selfish sot. And blast this verminous rabble. A filthy scurfy mob. Besotted most of them. And the rest would be drunk before the night was out. Not that one could blame them entirely when the police worked such traffic in rum. And, for that matter, most other things. As he pushed he became aware of the soft but determined resistance of a girl who had turned about and was struggling to pass him. As the crowd swerved and swayed they became so tightly wedged together neither could move more than a finger and his sense of the ridiculous became

110

throttled in fury at such female stupidity. Petulantly, then viciously he barred her way; even if she could pass him he would stop her. His hand, vague and flailing, found her wrist and held it.

'You can't get out,' he snapped. 'Not this way. The crowd's too thick.'

'Let me go,' she gasped. He felt her breath hot on his cheek as she dragged at her arm and squirmed her body in a desperate bid for freedom. He sweated in his heavy uniform. The crowd was becoming unruly. A rotten way the populace was policed. He began to wish he'd never left the Carver house. Then, managing to raise her free hand the girl struck him savagely across the mouth. The sting was sharp. He felt a dribble of blood – something, a ring perhaps, had cut his lip. 'Let me go!' she hissed.

He had been drinking. His head swam. He swept his tongue round his mouth and the blood tasted warm and horrible. He loathed the taste of blood; didn't much like the sight of it either. He lost his temper, then his head. 'Slut,' he bellowed and grasped her wrists and wrenched cruelly at her arms. She screamed with pain.

Women murmured threats. A youth knocked against him, swearing. Someone tugged at his tunic. He felt sick. A redcoat was never safe in a rabble and if he didn't get out, and quickly, he'd have a brawl to contend with. The girl was whimpering. She kicked at him awkwardly and then, with a sudden frantic twist of her body that was like the sinuous movement of a trapped animal, she bent and fastened her teeth in his hand.

His fingers loosened. Half bent she wriggled past him. With an oath he turned and pushed after her. A blow here, one there and he managed to keep up with her. At last they were free of the dangerous crowd and running along George Street, stumbling on the rough surface, dodging strolling groups and slithering round obstacles. People turned to stare at them, one or two called derisively. With a final lunge he caught her. He heard the soft tear of lace. Dragging her roughly into the comparative seclusion of a doorway he swung her about and held her until she was still. They stood, furious with each other, gasping for breath.

'Vixen,' he breathed and shook her violently until her hair came loose. 'What do you mean by setting your teeth into one of Her Majesty's officers? You can finish up in a cell for less. You know that, don't you? In a prison cell.' And in the glare of a street lamp he watched her eyes, close to his own, widen with terror. He gloried in it.

'I had to get away,' she whispered. 'From the lights and the crowd and –'

'Well?' he prodded. She was silent. He shook her again. 'Well? From what were you running? Or whom.' Then sarcastically. 'Your mama?'

Her face was impassive. 'It doesn't matter. Not now.' She leaned towards him. 'Please – you're hurting my arm.'

She said it so gently, so softly, he felt the anger seep from him like blood from his veins and his grip loosened. He was ashamed of his roughness, perhaps more sharply of his lack of dignity. But he was intrigued as to the reason for her fear, for she had been frightened, back there in the crowd, of something . . . someone? As he still held her, but loosely and awkwardly now, she straightened her gown, arranged her hair and tucked the torn length of lace bertha between her breasts: neat tight little breasts he noted with eyes long starved of the least intimacy and enjoyment of a woman. His eyes slid up to her face then down over her body, slowly, with the trained judgement of a connoisseur. She would be twenty, perhaps less. Her dress under the light glowed a deep red slashed with dark lace. She wore flowers in her hair. Not even a shawl to cover her showiness, or perhaps it had been lost somewhere back there . . . no, he couldn't remember any covering. Here and there about her an ornament sparkled. He saw a ring on her finger. A cheap thing of course. A slut, but a ravishing one. People jostled them. Still angry but curiously attracted he stared around him. They were near Market Street. A cab stood nearby, its driver asleep, his legs stretched out like thin sticks, his paunch rising and falling with each snore. Kenneth let out his breath with what was

112

almost a sigh; it was months and seemed years since he had been able to follow his slightest impulse, indulge his smallest whim. The girl, and the waiting cab with its inviting dimness, were irresistible. He dragged her across and lifted her inside. If she had resisted he knew he would have hit her. She did not resist.

''Ere . . .' The cabby stirred indignantly as her skirts fell across his face. Kenneth hauled him forth, set him on his spindly legs and held him swaying like a drunken clown. Then he pushed him up on his perch and tossed a coin on to what passed for his lap. The fellow's protests faded to bleats.

'There'll be more when you've done what you're told.' And he clambered inside. The girl sat quietly. The look of her there made him feel more than ever master of the situation. He revelled in the sensation.

'Well, seein' as 'ow it's New Year . . .' the man called down. 'But I'm to be back 'ere by midnight. Brought a party to town and promised to take 'em 'ome.'

'Plenty of time. Drive towards the Quay then round by the Domain. Slowly.'

The cab creaked as the man squirmed in his place. 'Them's dark parts.'

'Get along.'

He got along. Kenneth leaned back. As if suddenly conscious of their solitary state they sat silent and a little apart until they were jogging through a dim stretch of George Street. From the corner of his eye he watched her cooling herself with a fan she had miraculously produced from some fold of her garments, leaning gracefully, seeming to be half-smiling at the passing groups. She appeared supremely restful and he was grateful for the period of quietude. It meant he could study her covertly and decide on his actions. But he didn't really want to make decisions, he wanted to go on being swept along by this blessed, long-awaited sense of release, of freedom. But as the quiet became almost heavy he began to wonder what she was thinking. Then what she thought of him. He leaned across in the hot leathery dimness:

'Why were you running away?'

The fan paused, then resumed its gentle rhythm. 'I've forgotten.'

He slid his arm along the back of the carriage and touched her shoulder. She didn't draw away. 'You were running from a man, weren't you.'

'What makes you think so?'

He stretched his long legs, easing himself deeply and comfortably into the seat, pressing himself against her thigh. 'Every woman in town is running from a man tonight, or running after one. Would you run from me?' he added, watching her through half-closed eyes.

'I did, didn't I?'

'But now?'

She turned her head slowly, deliberately, and seemed to study him. Then she turned back to watch the street. 'No,' she said. 'Not now. You don't frighten me at all.'

He felt out of his depth. She wasn't acting like a tart. She wasn't doing anything but sitting there answering his questions. Tarts always talked, flaunting themselves at you, at the world. This girl was composed, outwardly controlled, the antithesis of the scared little creature of a short time before. But despite his puzzlement his eyes could do nothing less than approve her. She looked very lovely leaning back with the sparsely spaced lights casting jagged golden shadows across her face and shoulders. Lulled by the churn of the wheels, the soft sway, comfortable and at ease, he let the cabman have his way. Through the Quay and along Macquarie Street, slowly, because of the bad lighting and the shocking roads. Bursts of laughter and the tinkle of pianofortes filtered through the curtains of the dignified residences beginning to line it in spite of the proximity of the Convict Barracks. Occasionally the girl leaned forward to look out. He spoke to her at intervals because he wanted to hear her voice; there was something odd but pleasant about her voice, compelling yet soothing. He was becoming more sure of himself, more certain of her. He moved his arm round her waist. Gently and slowly he slid his hand up and around one breast. His fingers closed and he felt the nipple, soft then hardening beneath his touch. He heard the sharp intake of her breath as she stirred. He scarcely noticed her movement, concerned as he was with his own reaction. God, he must be in a worst state than he had realised. He was in pain. Aching . . .

'What do they call you?' he whispered against her and shivered at the perfume of her skin. It was intoxicating. He had not savoured perfume for a long time. It was far too long since he had savoured a woman.

'Raunie.'

'Just – Raunie?'

'Isn't it enough?'

He laughed. 'I suppose so.' A pause, then he added: 'Would it be French?'

'Irish.'

He laughed again. 'Only the Irish would be fey enough for it.' He frowned. 'Irish, eh?'

Her eyes flicked him with a glance almost of disdain. Damned insolent, the Irish, you never knew where you were with the breed. He agreed with his father on that point – about the only point he ever did – but every sane Britisher agreed that the Irish were trouble. They bowled smartly past the Barracks and along College Street where all was dim and solitary. Dangerously so. The Park crowds kept to the brighter side near Elizabeth Street. Past the incomplete pile of St Mary's then the black bulk of the Sydney College. Just as they reached the South Head Road Kenneth heard Jeremy's whistle. One always heard Jeremy before one sighted the Merrill carriage; there was no mistaking the whimsical little air born of his native land. Kenneth felt his heart thud. His father, on his way home from some stuffy club gathering. Or a dinner with Havelock. His heart thudded again. Deciding between them when and where to send him to be butchered. A deep primeval fear combined with an even deeper resentment set him on the defensive. What if his father did see him with this girl? He did not care. He simply did not care. The only trouble was, it would mean a pause, small talk, delay – and his father's eyes. Those eyes never told – damn them – what they thought they had found. They mocked. And condemned. He crouched back in his corner.

But he reckoned without Jeremy. There didn't seem to be a coachman, groom or cabman in Sydney that Jeremy didn't hate – or love. And evidently the shapeless one outside was one he loved to distraction. They shouted at each other in cracked voices and the carriages swung together for an alarming few moments. Alister leaned out and stared directly into his son's face. Then the vehicles passed to pull up eight or ten yards apart, the Merrill carriage under a light. Kenneth placed his hand on Raunie's as a warning and climbed down; better to go to his father than his father come to him. He hoped the girl was discreet, indeed he began to wish he'd taken her directly to Madame Julie's despite the woman's foul champagne and grasping ways. Alister leaned out.

'I didn't expect you to stop. It appears you're not in your usual frantic hurry.'

'A few moments, sir, are neither here nor there.' He swallowed and forced himself, as he always did, to be at least polite. 'I hope your dinner was worth your time?'

'As all dinners.' Alister's eyes flickered past his son to rest on the waiting cab. 'It seems you've found a more interesting way in which to spend the evening than taking supper with your family.'

'I sent my excuses to Mama this morning.'

'Your mother, foolishly, continues to make the mistake of expecting consideration from her children. I had not expected to see you for days. Not, as is your usual practice, until you needed something.'

There! He could feel his flesh shrivel under the lash of his father's eyes and words, both as cold and dry and brittle as old parchment. It had always been the same; a scourge of critical destructive observation.

'I take this opportunity to remind you,' his father went on, 'of the tightening up of leave.'

'And I, sir, to remind you that my uncle deems me in need of recreation. A military commander who happens to be a

116

relative is an asset, a circumstance I intend to put to good use.'

'You may not find your Uncle Roger quite so tolerant in future.'

'Then I must devote myself to keeping his good will. Goodnight, sir, and a pleasant New Year. I shall pay my respects to Mama and the girls tomorrow.'

He bowed correctly, turned, and without a backward glance strode to the cab. A tiny pulse beat in his throat, his hands were hot and moist, his limbs weak. He felt as sodden and inadequate as an old old codfish. Why must he meet his father tonight? Why must he be made to feel a fumbling and futile adolescent? And why had he fallen back on mundane and caustic inanities, for whatever backchat he used to fortify himself he always knew he must obey his father and humour his uncle – at least in a military sense. Could they send him to New Zealand for insolence? Damn it, he didn't want to kill Maoris. He didn't want to kill anyone. He turned restlessly to the girl, Raunie, forcing himself to be conscious of her again. And only her. She was the centre of his need tonight . . .

'The address?'

She did not answer. His hand tightened on hers and she gasped. It gave him a perverse pleasure to know he had hurt her. If he must hurt her to gain response, then it must be so. Response was what he must have. 'Alfred Terrace,' she said quickly. 'Number five.'

Well, what had he expected – Point Piper? Anyway, even the best of Sydney seemed to swarm with bugs. The cab sped recklessly along the dark road. Alfred Terrace, though obviously cheap, was clean. Or cleaner than most. Her room was small and airless with the usual rickety furnishings of such places but with exotic touches making it different and rather lovely – a bowl of peaches and plums, red blooms like patches of freshly dripped blood tossed carelessly into a green bowl, a gay scarf on her dressing-table, a bright cover that might have draped a Marquesan belle thrown across the bed. She lighted candles. It became a room of exotic sensuous colour that enveloped them until he began to feel warm with

117

colour, drunk with colour. Drunk with her. The house and the lane outside were quiet, the house occupants doubtless revelling in town or sleeping off the drunkenness of the day. He sank gingerly on to the bed. It was soft. He turned to Raunie.

She had wandered on to the tiny balcony and in spite of his eagerness he could not help but appreciate the dim shape of her there with the flickering light playing on the flounces of her skirt. He was becoming increasingly pleased with himself. He had been wise not to let her go. One might search all night and not find another such, even though, to be honest, she was not the kind of girl he usually noticed, or wanted; for some unexplained reason his eyes and his subsequent desires followed the gay, the yellow-haired, the plump. He had never known or stopped to consider why. Not until now. Perhaps because their looks and allure were in some half-defined way those of the mother who had been his sole need and repose all his life; their breasts like the soft bosom he had counted all-important in his first wavering years. He even liked women to be a little brazen and quick-feeling. It made lovemaking simpler and he had ever been an indolent man, even at the game of love. Indolence was a kind of safety, a protection. One could become too quickly and dangerously involved with women if you didn't goad them into taking the initiative.

But there had been a nagging sensation inside him ever since he had met this girl. It was the conviction that she was different from the others. What was it exactly? He leaned back against the piled bed cushions. He decided it was her eyes. Her dark heart-shaped face bejewelled with those strange eyes entangled his senses in a cloying persistent attraction. A dangerous attraction perhaps. She was exciting and so she was dangerous. Ridiculous as it seemed, in spite of her showy dress and obvious calling there was about her – well – a certain rarity. That was the only way he could define it. She did not look or even act as the females who cluttered the streets and the public-houses. They were always too eager, too crafty, or bored you with their demands and ambitions. They were too openly voluptuous. As he lay

118

watching her he felt vaguely uneasy, then tormented by doubts. He had never felt like this before. He had the sudden crazy impulse to run from the room and lock the door after him and so escape from her, all of which was baffling and quite ridiculous. But he was puzzled. And when he was puzzled he became angry. Anger turned to truculence. He scrambled off the bed. And because he was young and so strangely unsure his voice broke as he called to her: 'Raunie.' Then because he liked the sound of her name he repeated it roughly. 'Raunie . . . come here.'

Slowly she walked back into the room, put down her fan and smoothed the flowers in her hair. She patted them then decided to take them out and shake her hair loose. She turned to face him. Raunie Lorne had no idea what she was going to do when he moved to take her. The situation had marched ahead and enveloped her for she had thought no further than a drive, supper together, plans for future meetings. He would be attracted to her and insist upon seeing her again, but beyond that she didn't want to think. Not yet. At first, in a way, she had been a little bored. He was so eager. Subalterns were to be had on any street corner, gay young blades who lived to a pattern and loved to a formula. A coin tossed at daybreak and they were gone. But an incident had occurred to stimulate her interest. Peeping from the cab to watch him in close conversation with the bemedalled official to whom he bore an indefinable but undoubted resemblance she had thought quickly and hard. A distinguished man. An important man, surely? Perhaps they were both important. When he had demanded her address she had given it – to avoid argument, to gain time, to keep him by her until he told her who he was and who were his friends. Even an ensign could have connections.

'Aren't you going to tell me your name?' she queried.

He grinned at her. Well, what did it matter? 'Kenneth,' he murmured. He had never known black hair so rich and beautiful. Clinging. Like sleep. He felt an almost intolerable need to sink his face in it, deep . . . deeper. He moved restlessly.

'Just Kenneth?'

'Just Raunie?' he mocked. He unbuttoned his tunic and held out his hand.

'Tell me . . .' she stepped back slightly, 'the name of the officer you spoke with. The one in the carriage. I seem to have seen him somewhere before.'

He paused, surprised at the question, even more so by the fact that she had not recognised his father even in the semi-dark. Could it be that she did not know his father? He was so certain, with the perverse pride that made him despise his father as a parent and a man but revere him as a personage, that all Australia knew Major Merrill. Perhaps she was an immigrant, perhaps a runaway from some country property . . . but she was too fragile to have come from a bush hut. Then who was she? What was she? The mystery of her enthralled him . . . spurred him. He lunged for her and grasped her wrist, hard.

'Well?' She stiffened.

'I thought everyone knew Major Merrill,' he snapped. Her persistence was irritating him. With a savage gesture he drew her close.

'Merrill?' she panted. 'He's important – isn't he?' Her heart was pounding. That name . . . that family . . . that girl who gnawed away at her . . .

'He thinks he's important.' His arms tightened.

'Don't you like him?'

She had small, even, white teeth that gleamed between moist lips. Perfectly shaped lips. Mobile lips. Tender lips. Impatient with this ridiculous bargaining, and the deliberately conjured up image of a father of whom he didn't wish to be reminded, he held her against him, pressing her close. But with unsuspected strength she forced herself back, her hands flat and firm against his chest. She was resisting him. The conviction pricked at his mind and body with sharp horrible little stabs.

'Don't you like him?' she persisted.

'I don't have to like him.' It burst from him angrily. 'He's my father.'

Her eyes widened. 'Your father? Wait . . . no, *wait* . . .'

He was kissing her deliberately and savagely. His mouth pressed into hers, his tongue explored . . . She closed her lips against him and with an effort so violent and intense it made her dizzy she arched her back and pushed from him. With all her strength. And she was strong.

Kenneth felt her struggle and a small pulse hammered in his head. The room, the candlelight, all merged to become obscured by the feel of her in his arms. It was so long since he had even held a woman – too damned long. Abstinence was bad, deadly, and if he kept on kissing her she would lie still and unresisting. They always did. But he was shocked to feel her wrench herself free and a length of her hair brush his face to snap and leave a coil of it tangled in his tunic buttons. He stared at her incredulously as she clung to the dressing-table, panting and dishevelled, her eyes wild and frightened. Frightened? Yes . . . frightened. He had the curious, dreadful feeling that if he so much as moved a hand towards her she would turn and hurl herself over the balcony. Like a threatened virgin. Like a . . . lady. God! He stood staring at her, sweating, his face contorted. Then he turned, lunged for the door, whipped it open and clattered down the stairs.

He was on the small landing when she called him. He stopped and turned. She was leaning over the stair rail. 'Come back. Kenneth . . . come back.'

He had never heard anything as beautiful as her voice with its faintly sing-song lilt, seducing him. It was what he wanted. He could not help himself. He smoothed his collar and buttoned his tunic while a tiny pulse throbbed in his throat. He walked up the stairs towards her.

Chapter Six

'YOU'LL SWELTER in church this morning.'

Brick flicked the horses till they ambled away to nuzzle the scrub on the hillock where Jeremy sprawled beneath a mimosa tree picking his teeth. Though it was not yet eight o'clock the sun was ablaze with all the fury of a January morning in the Antipodes.

'Mama and Gina are too lazy to dress when it's so hot, and Papa expects at least one of us to accompany him. In any case,' Barbara added rather primly, 'I like church.' She moved her hand in an arch across the distant shimmering blue that was Botany Bay. 'I like it almost as much as I like the view from this hill.' A tiny smile flickered. 'But not quite.'

'A filthy swamp. Can't understand why you always want to ride these wretched sand-hills.'

'To most people it's desolate, even ugly. But I'm happy here because – well – perhaps because it's so alone.'

'You're the most solitary creature I know. Maddeningly so.'

She moved to sit in the small shadow of a clump of ti-tree, took off her hat and twisted the veil carefully about the high crown. Her habit was neat but shabby, as were all her clothes. Yet she wore everything as if she didn't care – or know.

'Surely you find a few humans in this world bearable?' Brick persisted, throwing himself down beside her.

'Children. I like to be with children.'

'Only children? Surely after four years I've managed to penetrate, even slightly, the tough shell of your regard?' he teased, brushing the fine dust of sand from his tousled hair. They had ridden hard and long.

122

She smiled. 'Every week you ask me that question – casually – and every week I answer in the affirmative, not at all casually, knowing well that the suspicion even one female in Australia walked the ground unheeding of your presence would nibble at your vanity.'

He threw a spray of sand at her. She dodged and they laughed, he with his rare deep enjoyment, she with her chuckle that was little more than an audible smile.

'You're always honest, sometimes damnably so. But frankness in a woman is so rare as to be valuable. And when something is valuable it's deucedly attractive. Anyway, to me. I think that's the reason I spend so much of my leisure with you.'

'Perhaps. But riding with a woman who promises to be more accomplished at it than yourself is a challenge. You can't resist a challenge, you know.'

'I can't resist watching you point Kumara at a fence. You take an obstacle as if Paradise itself beckoned on the other side.'

'It does.' Her breath quickened. 'Again, you delight in the fact that even being seen with you infuriates my father. Poor Papa, he would have sent me back to England long ago if any of our relatives could have been induced to have me.'

'So, instead, he plans to dispose of you in marriage.'

She stiffened slightly. 'It will be years before Godfrey – Mr Selwyn – is in a position to marry anyone.'

'And years before you whip yourself into regard for the man, let alone love him.' He crashed his whip into the sand. 'Love that – that –'

'Love was never a part of my education.' She flushed slightly. 'Only duty. And that has always been clearly defined. Indeed, I have every reason to be satisfied, for Uncle Roger is interesting himself in Godfrey's future. Uncle Roger –'

'Is expected to leave your father his money. Common gossip.'

' – has placed Godfrey in the Surveying Department,' she finished, folding her hands tightly over her hat.

123

'And what would Selwyn know about surveying? Or any-thing else about Australia? Haven't we enough parasites –'

'I cannot have you speak so. I respect Mr Selwyn highly.'

'Certainly. You also admire Mr Selwyn, for Mr Selwyn is proper and correct with his scraps of rhyme and his dancing pumps and his platitudes. Mr Selwyn is a church- and throne-revering gentleman presently financially embarrassed but rich in county family, a petty nabob fresh from India where he did nothing but soak himself in whisky and avoid the worst smells while kicking the natives for causing them – the enfeebled ones only, by the look of Mr Selwyn – while he waits for his father to die. And whether he admits it or not he finds this a far less odorous place in which to wait for his money. And you accept this monstrosity of an arrangement as any miss straight from the nursery. And I thought, of late, you were beginning to think a little.'

'There are things required of a woman –'

'Of other women, certainly. Why not? For them it's simplicity itself. It's all they crave because it's all they're capable of – docility, fertility in abundance. To compete, as it were, against the output of their dear papa's mills and work-shops with the human output of their bridal four-posters –'

'You're horrible.' Her face flamed. 'Horrible.'

'I'm honest. I'm taking a leaf from your own book. Wait . . .' he commanded as she made a violent movement of protest. 'You shall hear me out. I hoped you would shy from the accepted ritual of husband snaring: the hypocritical smiles and attitudes and niceties, in particular the large persistent hypocrisy of simply not seeing the . . . well . . . the fleshly cavorting to which your respectable and fashionable Godfrey – rather particularly I think husband Godfrey in his cups – is likely to drift from time to time –'

'Stop. Oh, *do* stop.' Her lips were white as she stared ahead.

'Because, my dear Barbara, you could never submit to masculine superiority or cling to masculine support. Not simply because the man happens to be your husband. You could not because you're learning new ways to live.'

124

She turned her head and stared at him, her face colourless, her eyes wide. 'There are times when I loathe you for having made my acquaintance, let alone making use of me . . .' Her hands sank back into the soft grey sand and she leaned on her wrists, rigid.

'Making use of you?'

'From the beginning you've used me . . . to persuade women whom you would not ordinarily meet to help Mrs Chisholm. To persuade my mother's friends to take your more hopeless Irish girls into their homes. To teach your waifs and strays. To collect clothing and medicines you couldn't otherwise get your hands on. Oh, and money. Particularly money. You've used me to wheedle contributions to schemes that wouldn't rate a farthing if the donors knew you were involved, certain through it all that I would never break my promise of secrecy – ' Her voice shattered. She could not control it. Her throat hurt. She was talking wildly and knew it. If only he wouldn't just sit there watching her like that.

'No one can use another unless that other is a fool or willing to be used. You're not a fool, Barbara. You were very willing. You were ready. And if you're useful to me I'm useful to you. You see, you use me too.'

She straightened. 'I – use you?'

'Exactly. Even though I'm everything you've been taught to despise I'm the expression, shall we say, of some need within you that is – well, ambition . . . fulfilment . . . oh, call it any name you like. You won't admit this because you don't clearly know it, but it's true. Even though you're a little afraid of the world I show you, you're enamoured of it. It's as if my dreams were becoming yours.'

'Dreams . . .' she scorned. 'Confused and exaggerated visions. You want a country, you want a kingdom, you want a world.'

'Why shouldn't I have all three? Given the chance I can build a world here free from the mine and the ragged school and the famine. England holds more than two hundred million acres of Australian aristo-exploited, idle land; why shouldn't it be used for those who need its fruits?'

'Not even you can build a world from poverty and weakness.'

'There speaks your father.'

'It's the way I see it too – yes I do. You ignore the force of old beliefs, of traditions. How can they be overcome?'

'I'll overcome them. I'll teach my immigrants what they want, then help them to get it. I'll teach them to defy every Gipps, every Clinton, every Merrill.'

'You have no reason to hate the Governor or Colonel Clinton. Or my father.'

'I have reason to hate tyranny.'

'But you see all law and order as tyranny.'

Yes, she was beginning to see . . . His philanthropy, his apparent kindnesses, his devious plans had but one aim – power. Personal power. Her first romantic conception of him and his work was giving way to disillusionment, a slow but certain yielding to the truth. And the worst of it was, she could do nothing. She had no weapons with which to protect herself.

'This law and order that means so much to you is so often injustice and it is an injustice that breeds agitators. I can't touch such systems yet. But I can touch a Gipps and a Clinton and a –'

'Merrill?'

He turned impatiently. 'Exactly what I am doing, is it not?'

She stared at him and his eyes met hers frankly. Dark cool eyes now, eyes that were even a little . . . menacing? Gone was the banter, touched with ice though it always was, that lightened her heart while twisting it. She went cold, there under the hot sun, and wanted to scramble up and run from him. But she did not move. She could not. It was too late. But . . . did the motive really matter? Were not results all-important? And knew she was vindicating herself; indeed, she seemed always to be making excuses.

'What use,' he went on, 'is a war-loving tyrant fidgeting behind a desk with laws he can only understand by imposing to the letter? England's laws. Penal laws.'

'My father does not belong here,' she said carefully. 'He's a soldier with a soldier's mind and habits and needs. No one knows better than I what's happening to him. He's – ill – with boredom and inaction and disgust. Yes, disgust. And I, who love him, do less than help. Once he detested a pack of cards. And drinking was a pleasant weakness. Once, he would rather ride with me than sit watching a horse race. Once. But now . . . now I ride with you.'

She stopped with a familiar sinking of her heart. He was staring out into the heat haze, a slight frown over his eyes, lost in some introspective bitterness. He had not been listening, she was sure of that. Familiarly too her resentment against him swelled and then, just as familiarly, died. What was the use? In spite of their jarring disunity he had only to expect a favour of her and she acquiesced. He never begged. He took. At first, when her father forbade these rides, she defied him and he locked her in her room. Joey, the stable-boy, had released her and he had beaten Joey as he would beat a dog and she had stood by her window listening to the crop descending, trying not to scream. And Joey came to release her again and again until in disgust her father left her alone. Though her throat hurt and the tears burned behind her eyes she did not know how to explain to him for she could not understand herself. Brick invited her to visit his crèche, then asked her advice on matters of organisation, of teaching, and so it had all begun. She became expert at parrying her mother's questions. At first she gave a day each week, then two, helping to select nurses, pay wages, order food and equipment, seeking help and advice of Mrs Chisholm at her Bent Street office and giving what assistance she could in return. Her former friends, almost to a woman, snubbed her but she did not even notice, intent as she was on this other world, the existence of which she had not even suspected much less expected to become part of. Her revulsion that fine babies should be born to squalor, that their mothers should die in want, that children should be hungry and emaciated, was dissipated in the only way she could, through her busy hands. And gradually she came to know, or to believe she knew, the man who was Brick O'Shea: the hater of the England to which she was considered as belonging, worshipper from afar of a martyred Ireland, the little-better-than-atheist with his vast confused hodge-podge of knowledge from which he took that which suited his purpose at the time, his energy and vanity and persistency that seemed impervious to reason or argument. And his restlessness, his fanatical feverish ambition that she had come to sense was centred finally only in himself. He was more than a little mad no doubt, but incredibly gloriously mad, a hurricane beating at the trees. But as yet, mercifully, he had not snapped her in two.

He turned to her at last and spoke slowly, thoughtfully, as if coming back from a great distance. 'Children . . . yes. You understand children as much as you like them. That's unusual and very important. It means I can trust them to you while I'm abroad.'

'You've been talking about going for a year now,' she said a little impatiently.

'Well, I'm off. Mrs Chisholm sails early next year. I want to be in England before the good lady arrives for I mean to have a hand in any sound migration scheme and she and I might, at least in some directions, help each other. But I can do nothing on second-hand views and opinions. I have friends in England and Europe. And of course, Ireland. And there's no time to waste – too many here are importing coolies.'

'She trusts you.'

'Mrs Chisholm? I think perhaps she does. Despite my heresy . . .'

'You sound almost proud of it. Why wear your unbelief in God as you wear a cloak, showing it off?'

'Unbelief? Let us say, scepticism. And I see no reason to hide my views.'

'But you must. It's a terrible thing not to believe in God.'

'Why not admit I find it well-nigh impossible to accept the Thing, or Being, you call God. I'll grant it's a comfortable idea for your class but something quite impractical for others – it's almost impossible to be humble when you're hungry. To the starving, God can so easily become a mockery.'

'I should think he would be their only refuge.'

'Where is His hand of mercy in hunger? Where is this God of yours in the wasted bodies of starving children, in the whipped flesh of desperate men.'

'It is blasphemy to talk so,' she throbbed. 'Wicked blasphemy.'

'I . . . well . . . I beg your pardon.' He said it stiffly, grudgingly. But he had said it. And because it was unusual for him to apologise about anything she went all the way to meet him.

'You will go to Ireland?'

'Of course.'

'Mama has letters from a relative who lately travelled there. An unhappy country, he says, the inns so bad and the climate uncongenial . . .' Her voice trailed off. She felt at a loss. Was she a fool or simply ignorant? Were they one and the same? 'I can't do it,' she hurried on. 'I can't manage your affairs here when you're so far away. You make the decisions and give the orders. I only try to carry them out. I can't do it alone. There's too much.'

He thudded his fist into the sand. 'But there's no one else I can trust. No one. Don't you understand?'

The heat danced a fiendish reel above the dry and sandy scrub. She closed her eyes against the glare. Against him . . . But she could hear him breathing and was more conscious of him than if she were actually touching him. And so they sat, silently resenting their unexpected, unwanted, but deep-rooted dependency one upon the other. Every morning when she woke she vowed . . . Today will be the last day. I give no more of my time, my life, myself to him to use as he wills – yet each time she gave a little more. But now, gradually, their resentment died from lack of immediate impetus, leaving them listless and spent. He roused and pulled her to her feet, his violence gone. When they railed against each other, which was often and thoroughly, she knew his anger was not directed at her, only at what she represented.

'When do you sail?' she asked quietly.

'September.'

She sighed with relief. 'Then you've some months.'

'With a great deal to do.' He picked up her things and turned to where Jeremy stood with the horses. 'If you're set on church-going we had better get back.'

They started a jog-trot with the intense unspoken pleasure they felt when riding together; the one thing in their relationship entirely uncomplicated. Like many lonely women Barbara often felt this perverse hungry longing for space, to breathe deeply, for the open world, for movement, and to satisfy her desire with Brick beside her brought her closer than she had ever been in her life to ecstasy. The Botany Road was desolate with only an occasional urchin wandering the hills and, here and there, cottages with vegetable plots struggling in the swampy loam. Along these ridges and sprawling down the slopes to the Bay were the camps of the Blacks. And graveyards . . . in this windswept scrub Sydney chose to bury its dead. Native women and a cluster of children gathered firewood. With sudden violence Brick broke into a canter and a herd of deer fanned out over the dunes. Kumara quivered and tossed up his head, striving to fling his splendid limbs through the bright morning. 'Release me!' She sensed the stallion's desire. 'See me pit my vigour against the vigour of others. Watch me hurl my power against the power of this day.'

'Have your way then,' she breathed, half-laughing with joy. Her delight matched his as she gently pressed to him. And she forgot everything, even Brick there in front, in the rhythm of the hoof-beats, the rush of air that caught her hair, her burning cheeks. And it was a long time before they eased, side by side. Turning near the imposing new Court House and on to the road that led out to the seacliffs they mingled with basket-laden parents and befrilled children and a stream of vehicles carrying picnic parties to the sheltered sparkling bays that bit into the Harbour all the way to South Head. Colts and fillies worried their riders – and the strollers – as they meandered arrogantly to and from the training grounds. Brick liked to watch her control her finely-bred mount so she let Kumara mince a little beside his bay hack. Carriages passed, conveying to town or church gloved and bonneted women who stared over the heads of the cheery pleasure-seeking heathens with a haughty superiority. They followed the gaol wall, soldiers in white jackets with muskets on their shoulders guarding the parapet, then turned off at the track that led to the Lodge, pausing now and then to stare for enchanted moments at glimpses of the Bay and the curve of the Domain on its far shore. A whispering swirl in the tree-tops heralded the nor'easter. It touched their burning cheeks. And the bells of St Mary's pealed lazily across the valley.

Brick took a deep breath. 'Wish I could carry sea air enough to last me the next few months. It can be damnably hot inland you know.' He looked at her. 'Erins Pride means a lot to me – it was the beginning – but no doubt you'd find it rough. No use for gaslight or dancing floors. But the best horseflesh in Australia and some of the most enlightening books. They were my grandfather's. He was, I believe, some kind of a god. At least Moll and my mother thought so.' But as always when a mood prompted him to speak of his mother he leapt to other matters. 'A sum of money in lieu of wages has been set aside for you.'

'But I couldn't . . .' Almost stammering in her surprise and confusion. 'I wouldn't dream –'

'Oh yes you will. I pay for services rendered. But I pay what I think they're worth, no more, no less. And I see what I pay is earned. I'll write as often as I can.' And before she could speak further he had touched her hands with his as lightly as a breath, turned his bay and was off with a flick of his hand. And so they parted. As they always parted, decisively and with no looking over their shoulders. But today her disturbance lingered. As she poised, considering all he had said, admiring his horsemanship, irritated by the odd sense of escape mingling with loss which she so often experienced when he left her, she saw him draw rein and speak to a rider who approached him from the town. They talked earnestly. Brick glanced back, seemed to hesitate but, motioning to his companion the two broke into a gallop towards the city.

She watched them out of sight. There was something almost frightening about such urgency on this calm summer morning. But she remembered she must change for service. She turned Kumara and rode on till she glimpsed the Lodge square and white and green-shuttered, serene against its framework of English trees. The pillared verandah enclosed by Venetian blinds was hugged by peppertrees and clustered orange vine. Down each side glowed Joey's beloved geraniums. More geraniums meandered to the coach-house and stables and kitchen garden. A beautiful house in a perfect setting. Or it was to Barbara. The dignity of Regent Lodge, its outward serenity, its cool solitariness had always been her delight. Indeed, the sight of it, like this, sheltered from the blaze of sunlight brushed aside its inner turbulence. Alone in the Lodge she was invariably content and at rest. But she was rarely alone anywhere. The sound of a cantering horse behind her made her pull up. It was her brother, his hair blazing, his golden lashes gleaming in the sun.

'Just passed O'Shea riding like a madman.' He mopped his burning skin. 'Someone must have broken the news. They've been searching the city for him since a boy rode in this morning with news of his station – Erins Pride isn't it? Up in smoke. At least, most of it.'

'Not his home?' she gasped.

'There! I'd expect you to be upset. Most people are glad he's lost something at last when everyone else seems bordering on the pauper.' His face grew sullen. 'And while we're on the subject of O'Shea . . . what do you think it's like for me, for Mama, to hear of you wandering the city streets with the man? The suggestions this morning when they couldn't locate him were enough to try the patience of a saint.'

'I hope you didn't come to blows on my account,' she retorted, a little too flippantly.

He flushed with anger. 'Don't you know people are coupling your names, even betting on the outcome of this – this absurd association? Don't you realise our friends only accept you in their homes for Papa's sake? If you don't care for your own

132

reputation what kind of an example do you think you're setting Gina?'

He caught her amused glance and felt the pompous platitudinous fool he knew he must sound. Barbara's mind had always been uncannily astute. Pugnacious intelligence was unnatural and unnerving in a woman. It was wrong. Thank God all women weren't like Barbara.

'You know only too well more brazen ideas are born behind Georgina's seemingly innocent eyes than anywhere else we know.'

'All right, she's a piece. A proper little baggage. But we're all rotten if it comes to that,' he raved. 'The supreme example of decayed gentility. The upper crust coating the slime. Scratch it and bare the stink. And why wouldn't there be a stink? This place is enough to pollute anyone. What is it at best but a dumping ground for those without a niche anywhere else? I hear the Major owes that Marchant trickster fifty pounds, and all the time he's shovelling out sermons about my miserable little wagers – '

'Not only wagers, I'm sure.'

He made a gesture of distaste. 'Well . . . what can one do about the Hebrews? They're the only jewellers who've got decent trinkets. And my order was only for ten pounds – brushes and toothpicks and such. Trouble is, this Solomon hounds so.'

'I have no money to pay him,' she said coolly.

He shot her a look of hatred. 'And I'll bet Papa's in the hands of the Jews – that swine Goltby seems to have his talons into all Sydney. So much for our Major's sedate little card games in his sedate mansions. Give me a gambling hell any time. You know where you are there. At least I'm not a hypocrite . . .'

He raved on in fury, so bitterly that she glanced at him with interest and a concern that she had never expected to feel. They were almost strangers, seeing little of each other and caring less, but now, even though conditioned to his outbursts that were so like their mother's, she felt uneasy. There was something wrong. Not that there wasn't always something wrong with Kenneth – moody, peevish, dependent on their mother for affection and funds – what could anyone do with him or for him? They rode on towards the Lodge. As she drew Kumara to a halt Jeremy cantered up and Joey scampered from the stables. She ruffled the boy's hair – an eager urchin who had followed Jeremy home, begged a meal and stayed to work and adore. His heaven was his Lodge garden, his horses, and Miss Barbara. Georgina came yawning from the end of the verandah in crumpled muslin, her red-gold curls bound carelessly with a green ribbon, a tawny rounded girl with pale petulant lips and white even teeth that bit squeezily into a preserved fig. She flung herself upon her brother.

'No wonder your teeth ache,' Barbara observed a little vaguely as she went inside, wondering if Jeremy knew anything about the Pride fire. She'd go through to the stables and enquire. If he didn't know now he would certainly know after church . . .

Georgina watched her sister disappear. There'd be the usual row when she found Ada drunk and the roast thrown to the dogs – still, she supposed if it weren't for Barbara they'd never sit down to a decent meal. The prospect of semi-starvation haunted her; food was her current passion. But she drew her mind resolutely off food and her sister to cling to her adored Kenneth.

'Have you come to see me? Or Papa . . .'

'Neither. I'm creeping upstairs without even meeting the Major if I can.' But he brushed indulgent lips over the bows on top of her hair and snatched an edge of the squashy fig.

'Then persuade Mama to let me come home. I *loathe* Summerdale House. And Miss Cooley. I detest milk puddings. *And* castor oil. Tell Mama if she wants me to have any stomach left – '

'Milk puddings?'

'The *oil*, silly.' She giggled.

'Excellent I understand for wilful children,' he teased while his wary eyes watched the doorway. He couldn't face his father. Not now. Not yet.

'I'm not a child,' she pouted and prepared to wheedle. 'I'm fourteen. I swear if Mama doesn't bring me home soon I'll run away. I shall. I shall!'

'With your dancing master?' He grinned at the alarm in her lovely eyes, dipped a hand into her lumpy pocket and eased out the figs screwed stickily into a handkerchief. He eyed the mess with distaste, slipped it back in her pocket and licked his fingers.

'You're an untidy wench. Like Mama. You both leave ends dragging, bless your hearts.'

'You promised never to tell about – him. Remember?' Her big eyes implored, her hands caressed his sleeves.

'I remember the reason you wangled this extra week home. All because Max will be at the Clinton dance Saturday. You're a conniving little flirt and I know all your tricks, and you'd best remember it.' He called off-handedly as he went inside. 'He's going back to Parramatta – did you know? Moreover, he's hankering after an heiress. An heiress, just think of that, my poverty-stricken beauty.'

She stood frowning for a moment but brightened again. Gossip. Maxim was so often the centre of gossip . . . one reason she loved him. He was amusing himself, as young men did, just as her own little flirtations were fun. Oh everything about Maxim was exciting and she craved excitement – another of her hungers – but Barbara could do nothing about *that* one. She giggled and popped the last of the figs into her mouth and sidled to the couch, a mangled swollen old thing half hidden by the clematis vine, and sprawled again, propping cushions about her. She opened the dog-eared novel she had slipped from her mother's glove drawer and, just in case, tucked a corner beneath a cushion before she peeked. The ravishing Julia had already swooned twenty-seven times and now it appeared as if . . . yes . . . 'One of the sweetest smiles that ever animated the face of mortal now diffused itself over the countenance of Lord St Orville as he fell at the feet of his Julia in a deathlike swoon . . .'

She rolled over on her back and sighed. Love was delicious but was it always so exhausting? The sun burned through her gown and she stretched lazily. The house was quiet now, almost lonely. She didn't really mind church with Mama and all the people to admire her best clothes, but Barbara scolded when she peeped through her fingers. And on hot days the convicts smelled awful. Did all wicked people smell? She could ask the curate though she doubted if he knew anything much, even about wicked people. She sighed again, heavily. Things were just *awful* at fourteen; a neuter existence shadowed by the backboard and boiled mutton and the ignominy of having to chew green peaches and feign head-colds to coax a bedtime glass of wine – she loved wine as much as Mama did – but worst of all, shadowed by a prim old maid of a sister who would stay prim even if that odious Mr Selwyn did marry her one day . . .

She licked her fingers, giggling. She would *adore* to run sticky hands down Mr Selwyn's frock-coat. But they must be nice to Mr Selwyn because it was so hard to find husbands for girls as queer as Barbara. She didn't know what that queerness was exactly, unless it was reading too many books and riding over the hills without her gloves with that demon-like Mr O'Shea – though she rather suspected something exciting about that too. But shocking. Quite shocking. Mama said so. And the girls at Miss Cooley's whispered together and laughed and insisted that Barbara and Mr O'Shea were great friends. *Close* friends. Infuriating prigs. And what would they know about anything? Stupid gossiping creatures always talking nonsense like the time Lucy Owens swore babies came out of your body fat and rosy and hurt you worse than the tortures of the Inquisition – Lucy boasted three married sisters and swore she *knew* – and you lay with your legs spread apart while people peeped and prodded and poked at your inside. Doctors too. Men. So *silly*. How could a woman stretch to expel a baby? Babies came small as a pinhead and flat then swelled up like a balloon when they were fed. How else? But sometimes her hands sweated at such monstrous possibilities. In any case, how did babies get inside you? Exactly what was inside you? Once, frantic with curiosity, she had asked Mama. Mama had dropped her scissors and

136

stared then dabbed at her eyes and said in a resigned sort of way: 'God sends babies, Georgina. It is a woman's fate and you have to put up with it. There's absolutely nothing you can do about it except . . . well, except . . .' And she had dabbed at her eyes again and would say no more. Georgina's impatience had flowed over. 'Well, it's a wonder God doesn't get tired of sending them just to get head-colds and measles and to cause trouble all the time and die some day after all.' But Mama had packed her off to bed for impudence which was unfair when Miss Cooley was always saying alertness of mind was a virtue to be encouraged. Perhaps she'd better ask Miss Cooley about babies. Or the curate . . . If babies came from God he should know all there was to know on that subject!

Laughter, thickened by distance and the heat, drifted up from the Bay. The tide was coming in and soon the sand and mud would be covered and boys would be diving off the old hulk. How lovely to climb down the 'steps' and run barefoot over the cool squashy sand and feel the water curling about your ankles . . . How wonderful to be a boy, loose and free and bold. Yes – bold. Boldness in a girl was a tragedy. Mama said so. Barbara for instance, though Barbara didn't actually look bold she just was. Under the blanket of heat Georgina's eyes wavered and half closed and she saw the world as black spiced with dancing needles of red. She turned over lazily. The silence, like gentle little wavelets, lapped her about. Sunday. She must think piously for a while. She would think of the Bible . . . 'my beloved is mine, I am his . . . thy lips are like a thread of scarlet . . .' She didn't mind reading the Book if she could read that and think of Maxim. A flush made her bury her face against the cushions. But her thoughts were her own, were they not? Safe and untouchable. And God, oh God understood all about love. God understood all. Snuggled deep into the warm flaky blackness her thoughts dreamily, ecstatically, encompassed Maxim . . .

At her 'coming-out' at Government House he would lead her from the crowd of men about her and pluck a rose in the arbour where they would conceal themselves and he would

137

present it on bended knee and then . . . then he would kiss her. With passion. He might even faint like Lord St Orville. A little thrill ran up her body from her toes. In her mother's novels she read of this passion that burned and seared, and obviously to experience it was the ultimate, the wonder of wonders, the very sin of sinning. She held shaking hands to her cheeks. How wonderful to be a man and permitted to know passion. For only men were permitted it. Women must only know love, and love seemed . . . well . . . dull. But she wouldn't let anything be dull for herself and Maxim. All must be forever splendid. Because Maxim was splendid. He would take her on a honeymoon tour of Europe for despite his grumbling he was rich. All gentlemen were rich, just as all gentlemen grumbled; it was simply the thing never to be quite satisfied, for weren't people satisfied with their lot ignorant fools? Mama said so. And one must have money or how did one live? Mama was definite on that point too. One must have money. Lots and lots of money. And Maxim lived wonderfully. Excitingly.

Meanwhile, he would be in Parramatta again. Miss Cooley and her horrible Establishment for Young Ladies might not be so unendurable after all. Georgina yawned, breathless and thirsty in her corner, but dared not go inside. Not yet. She must wait until Barbara and Papa appeared and got into the carriage – Barbara so neat and quiet, Papa tall and splendid and severe, the Papa of all Papas. She remembered as a little thing, terrified, wanting to run from the rattle of his sword and the tramp of his boots when he had attempted to play her games with her and watched his face grow cold each time she managed to slide from his grasp. But how could she play with Papa? She never even answered his questions now without the old familiar tremble of her limbs, and it had all been worse since he had grown furious with Barbara. Angry tears of impatience pricked behind her eyes. Oh, the worst of being only fourteen was being too young to marry Maxim. The days, months, of waiting spread endlessly before her . . . But here in her corner, her safe shiny gentle corner, she and her dreams were safe; safe from all Papas, from

Mamas and Barbaras too. She turned on her back again and raised her arms to the dancing sunbeams then twined her fingers behind her neck. Yearning, she raised her face . . .

Eyes closed, inert, she gave herself happily, a little fearfully, but passionately and with great hope to the sun's touch. For the embrace of the sun was as warm, as complete, as exciting as Maxim's embrace would surely be . . .

Kenneth caught up with Barbara at the top of the stairs. She paused with her hand on her doorknob. 'I came to see Mama,' he said. 'How is she?'

Barbara opened her door and his nose twitched at the scent of musk. He loathed musk. 'She hates to be bothered before midday, you know.'

'Is she ill?'

'In a way,' she said thoughtfully. 'But it's no bodily illness.'

'Are you trying to tell me there's something wrong with her – her mind?' His voice broke with dismay.

'Her mind is perfectly clear. She's merely discovered that a deliberate inertia is an effective way of gaining and keeping the attention of her family and friends.'

'Nonsense.' His voice rose, thickened. 'What utter blithering nonsense.'

She shrugged. 'Doctor Barclay's diagnosis, if not exactly in those words. He finds her an interesting case – or she believes he does. After all, she's too valuable a patient for him to lose. Anyway, he drives over every week and Mama makes quite an occasion of his visits. Has tea sent up. And special cakes. There's a pile of his bills on Papa's desk. To say nothing of those from the apothecary. Oh – ' she stopped him as he moved off impatiently, 'agree with everything she says, then, when she becomes exhausted by the subject, change it. That's your only chance. And don't give her wine. Well, no more than a drop. Doctor Barclay's orders.'

'Gad, you're as cold as a – a damned codfish,' he blurted, stumbling over his words as he always did when angry. She shut the door on him. Sometimes he loathed Barbara. He did now. But even so he wanted to go on talking to her, to someone, to postpone what was to come. In the quiet of the hall he felt desolate and terribly alone. His father had not emerged from his study, nevertheless he wished he might talk to his father about – well – women. But such a conversation would of course be ludicrous. What would his father know of women? – a sire impatient of all frailty and whose name was rarely mentioned outside the pompous gatherings of male authority. Impossible to associate his father with silken hair and moist cloying limbs. There seemed even something indecent in his possession of their mother. As for her, she must understand his position for if she didn't . . . New Zealand was becoming a higher and shinier beacon. Almost a refuge. War was to be preferred to many things, which he supposed was the reason for it. War was escape, and the chance of plunder and prize-money – the soldier's reward. In his case it might mean promotion. He needed money too, and anything else life could be induced to give him. There seemed sense after all in beating Maoris into extinction. He might even return with a scar, a small neat scar of course. And a decoration. He was beginning to like the idea of both. And Auckland they said was gay. Still . . . Oh God, was anything ever easy and clearcut before him? Everything was a mess. A bloody mess. And his mother could make it worse . . . He turned miserably to her bedroom, tried to straighten his shoulders, and knocked. At her faint 'come in' he opened the door to hesitate at the shock of the dark, completely airless room.

'Darling. Oh *darling* boy.'

Her voice came drowsily from the mound of cushions on the huge bed. As everything else, she was dim and shapeless, each object a shadowy sponge in a sea of half-light. It depressed him further. He strode across, pulled aside the window drapes and flung the windows wide with a defiant clang.

'But it's so *hot*,' she wailed as she struggled upright, blinking. Her hair hung loose and tangled under her nightcap, that vivid rebellious hair that she had bequeathed in varying degrees to her children. Then she smiled and held out her hands.

He sat on the curtained bed and kissed her again and again, loving and needing her, devouring her as he had always done, soothed by her ruffled femininity. It was an instinctive reaction to her as a mother and as a woman. He enjoyed her scented kisses and maudlin attentions for, with his mother there was no need to spur himself to an effort of thinking or talking or doing. He simply was. He revelled in the comforting sense of her as he revelled always along the path that required the least effort – damnably easy to be indolent in this land of indolent people and ways. The place only too truly carried its curse. Then, mingling with the faint perfume of powders and medicinal scents about her was another odour – the sickly sweet smell of wine. She waved a languid hand at the jars and boxes among the lotions and creams that littered her small table, and pressed his fingers. She said in her invalid's voice:

'You may give me my powders. Doctor Barclay's new prescription. He's such a dear sympathetic man. The only one who is sympathetic, except you, of course – but then you're seldom here. As for Barbara, she's quite brutal. Does her best to starve me. If only she would marry.' She sighed. 'I'm terrified poor Godfrey will lose patience with her – but I mustn't even *think* of such a thing. It would kill me I'm sure. That's why I'm so nice to Godfrey. You will be nice to him too, won't you dearest boy. No – ' she stopped him as he picked up a decanter of water, 'not that. That other . . . there. You know, sometimes I think Barbara brings fevers and such into the house but she just laughs in that infuriating way of hers when I tell her to be careful of her surroundings. And your father is almost unbearable to live with these days. Of course he never did care for anything but Army life . . .'

She watched closely as he poured wine into a tumbler. Did his father know he wondered, as she swallowed the bitter powder and gulped the liquid. She ran the tip of her tongue round her lips.

'For my nerves,' she explained. She sank back on the pillows, smoothed the bedclothes contentedly and pouted at him. 'Why you bother with lodgings when we've room here is more than I can understand. You haven't been near me for weeks. If only I could get you out of the Army.'

'You know . . . I might even like it with a lieutenancy.'

She blinked. 'But you've always insisted you hated –'

'Mama.' He was beginning to perspire. 'I'll get orders from New Zealand, nothing surer; the Major and Havelock have their heads together over me. Well, I'm beginning to see that confounded country as my one chance of promotion. In fact I'm certain of it. So, if I must go, I'm going with grace.'

'The Wars?' She sat up with a tiny bleat of despair. 'But I won't let you go. Oh why did I marry into Army? First your father and now you. The dreadful climates and the worry and the insecurity have ruined my health and no one cares how I suffer. You just don't *know* what it's been like. If anything happened to you I'd die. Do you want me to die? You're the only creature in the world I love. If Roger and your father do this to me I shall find some way to defy them even if it means losing – well, the money. But then . . .' A tiny frown creased her pale forehead. 'I don't know what we shall do if we lose the money. But I can't let you go to the Wars. I simply can't.'

He patted her plump shoulder awkwardly but desperately. 'I can't stand garrison duty. None of us can. One of the men put lime in his eyes yesterday to get his discharge. We get desperate. And nothing will happen to me over there, you see. All we need is to swell our numbers and we'll finish off those savages in a few days.'

He waited while her sobs died and she lay quiet. But the silence was oppressive. It worried at him. She turned over and lay languid and pathetic, sniffling a little in her delicate way. Now then, Merrill, he told himself, out with it. *Out* with it.

'And there's another thing . . .' He gulped and stopped dead. The words would not come. But they had to come. 'I've something to tell you. To ask –'

'Oh darling boy, not *money*?' She sat up straight. Her face took on a guarded look. He knew that look only too well. 'It's impossible. Your father does nothing but rage over my poor little household accounts and it's so unfair when I *do* try.

I simply don't know what happens to all the things we buy. They disappear. I suspect Barbara of taking food for those spoiled urchins of hers – why, she would bring them home if I permitted it, I know she would. And my funny little income scarcely pays my milliner's bills and how can I object when Madame Clare overcharges me, she's quite the smartest in town. And there's Gina's 'coming-out'. And what is to pay for Barbara's wedding I cannot imagine. Your father will just have to borrow again. And when I think of Roger there . . . I mean . . .'

'Being so deucedly inconsiderate as to go on living, eh?"

'Now dearest boy, you know I never wish poor dear Roger harm but it *is* aggravating when he's been ailing so long and gets these nasty turns and then gets over them and gets promotions and depends on your father so much and leaves him practically everything to do and has that tremendous fortune and no children. But I did think he looked worse than ever he's looked last Friday . . .' She pondered a while then threw up her hands with impatience. 'So you can see that we're desperate.'

'And elegantly useless. Nary a barrister or sawbones to impress Society. Nor can I really bother to tell the ewes from the rams because, I suppose, I don't care. We might try going into trade,' he teased, 'even if shop-keepers swarm and publicans are two a penny. Saving that, we'd best concentrate on Gina. A minx with nothing in her head but romantic drivel and already a toast in Barracks. You should be toting her about the countryside showing her off.'

'Your sister is still a child.' Her voice was sing-song prim. 'Still . . . to bring her home would be a saving.'

'Do it then. She'll learn more at one of your teas than she will in a year at that flea-bitten seminary.' He took her hand in his and turned it over slowly, playing with her fingers. 'Stop fussing Mama. I'm not here for money – though I did lose ten pounds on that cocking match.' He pressed her fingers gently, fondled her wrists and waited.

'Well . . .' She pouted. 'I might manage five.' Then her voice hardened slightly. 'But no more than five.'

'Wonderful.' He hugged her, then took the plunge, pursuing his advantage. 'It's – well, there's a girl.'

She patted his cheek. 'There are always girls.'

'But this time I – a few days ago I – married her.'

Accustomed as he was to her extreme and lavish moods he was not prepared for this reaction. She stared at him then shot up suddenly from the pillows, opened her mouth wide and screamed; a piercing shriek he feared would bring the servants running. Startled and blundering, he backed against the door. He didn't know what else to do. Fool! He should not have blurted it out that way. But the house remained quiet – Regent Lodge was accustomed to such outbursts from its mistress and tolerant of them for the reason that she seldom interfered in household tasks. So few of them interested her. She lay back and rolled from side to side. She held her lace handkerchief spread dramatically over her eyes. She turned over on to her stomach and squirmed, gasping. He stared at her, embarrassed. He had never seen her so before. In despair, whispering pacifying endearments, he took her glass, poured more wine and held it before her. She turned gulping, but her sobbing gradually ceased and she drank. She lay back and looked at him with piteous eyes, murmuring recriminations, asking questions. He tried to explain, breaking off his rush of words to begin all over again. But now she had a new pose. She was injured in spirit. She was martyred. She moaned softly: 'You can't. You simply can't marry anyone.'

'But Mama, I have.'

'But why? So suddenly, without warning. Oh, how *could* you?'

'It had to be this way. Papa would have stirred up a hurricane, turned me out then and there – you know what he's like. As it is – well, it's done and if you break it to him, smooth things over a little, he might not take it so badly. I had to marry her, don't you see? It was the only way I could get her.'

He ruffled his hair miserably. How to make her see what he couldn't see clearly himself? Leaving Raunie that first night

144

of their meeting he had been curiously ashamed and humble. He had misjudged her. She was gentle and innocent, a victim of cruel circumstance. She let him kiss her but nothing more, always that maddening withdrawal from his caresses, that wordless censure of his persuasions, driving him insane with irritation and desire so that time after time he stormed from her room swearing he had done with her — only to come creeping back. Sometimes he was sure it was her eyes more than anything that drew him; never before had he looked into such eyes, the changing colours fascinated him. At other times it was the faint sense of mystery about her, even though under his continued pressure she told him small things . . . She was a widow recovering from a long illness caused by the death of her husband and her helplessness in a heartless world. She was quite alone. Her savings almost gone, it was necessary that she support herself. She counted herself lucky to have had some early training as a lady's-maid. She was too proud to throw herself on the mercy of her husband's family; she would make her own way. Somehow. Just as soon as she was strong enough . . .

He had picked up her small hand, a lady's hand, watched her beautiful strange little face and felt all the maleness, the latent sympathy in him, surge forth. He was surprised at himself and vaguely annoyed, for deep within him he bitterly resented this pursuit of her. He had tried to get over it. He had gone sailing, to theatres, to balls. He had wallowed in the blowsy replica of the London 'shades' deep in the Royal cellars. He had got roaring drunk. But after a few days, sober, he was back knocking on her door. He must see her, kiss her, possess her if he could. But how could a man possess such a girl? He was terrified of his persistent desire and the fact that he was concerning himself with the sensibilities and hesitations of a woman. She was entangling his senses, undermining his resolutions . . . such a thing could not happen, must not happen. Why, Blayney had married a girl without family background and ruined his chances for life; finished up scratching a living on a poor little farm along Cook's River. A married ensign was a social prodigy.

Marriage? Good God, what was the matter with him? Marriage on his debts and a subaltern's pay? The family would kick him out. His father . . . well, his father would have a right to kick him out. But he wanted her, damn it. He wanted this girl.

And so he lost his head. There was nothing one could not buy in Sydney if one wanted it badly enough – even marriage. He had borrowed from Maxim and spirited her off to a bottle-mad old clergyman in a mean back street. Or was it some church? He supposed Max had been there – yes, he vaguely remembered Max arguing with him. But argument had been useless, all he was conscious of was Raunie. He supposed he must have been more than a little drunk with rum and desire for her and never would get that night clearly in his head – actually he didn't want to. But it was legal – she was always reminding him of that. They were man and wife. Raunie would remember everything that happened. In the light of day it seemed almost a degrading business and often made him feel more than a little sick. But he had succumbed to feeling that night, not reason. He had lost himself in Raunie. But now he knew, uneasily, he must do something about their life; he must find some way out of the mess. For one thing Max, for all his affability, didn't like lending money. And what to do with his wife now that he had her? Oh, to hell with everything! The Wars? That would take care of him. But Raunie wouldn't come to Auckland even if she could. And so before he went it all had to be told, explained, endured, lived out. Damn it all, lived out.

'She's pretty, naturally.' His mother gulped the last of her tears. Thank God she was a little quieter. His face softened as he thought of Raunie. He trembled.

'Lovely. Clever too.'

'Clever women make me nervous. I can't tell what they're thinking. And they're always thinking.' She sighed. 'Well, I must pray for the strength to bear this catastrophe. Tell me her name.'

'Raunie.'

'Hmmmm. Is that all?'

'I don't – yes I do. Raunie Lorne. She's – she was a widow.'

He even felt queer admitting it. She'd said little about her first marriage and, according to the class into which Almighty God had seen fit to bestow him, Kenneth Merrill, women filled their separate niches. Gentlewomen were sheltered, destined from birth for marriage and motherhood and gentle teas in the best parlour. A female worked. And a whore – well, her place was as necessary but always unchangeable. One never combined all three. Or did they? The way Raunie . . . responded was . . . He sweated. He fidgeted. But he must not torture himself. Raunie was simply not quite like other women. Raunie was . . . oh, whatever she was she was his delight and his torment. But he cursed silently, as he secretly often did at the strange macabre chance that had thrown them together, for now he could do nothing about the spell she had on him. Nothing.

'Any children?'

'Heavens no. At least . . .'

God, he must stop these awkward questions. Besides, he sensed, grimly, his mother was beginning to enjoy his discomfiture. There were more important things to settle. As his wife, Raunie could not go on living in that horrible room in that horrible part of town. He refused to go there any longer. It wasn't decent. She was making a devil of a fuss about staying there too. But he hadn't a penny. There was only Regent Lodge, his home.

'She's a lady – of course.' But his mother's eyes were sharp.

'In many ways – oh yes. Yes certainly.' He floundered. 'Do try to understand, Mama. Can't you see I'm at my wits' end?'

'And you want me to take her in. She's making you bring her here to your family, to be provided for. But really dear boy, you must realise how things are with us. Another mouth to feed is impossible. Quite impossible.'

She didn't really mean it. And she knew he knew she didn't mean it. Her curiosity was taking possession of her. He refilled her glass and she drank. Soon she wouldn't be able to talk clearly let alone reason about anything. Certainly not

147

with him. And when that happened he would be able to do anything with her. He spoke hurriedly and urgently.

'Her – Raunie's first husband was Lord Farleigh's stepson. I've checked, Mama, and it's true. Nick Watling knows everyone in London.'

All Nick had said had been irritatingly vague and most of it derogatory but connections with a baron would impress his mother; they'd all been soothing her this way all their lives, making rash promises, telling lies, weaving excuses. She had stopped whimpering. She was listening to him. Yes, she was impressed and avid for details. He fabricated some. She pushed herself up and he propped up her pillows. She bit her lip thoughtfully. This of course was better than she had expected, a doubtful balm certainly, but nevertheless balm. Her daughter-in-law related to the peerage – it sounded well. And she could make more of it. It might even compensate with the Havelocks, with the rest of Sydney, for Barbara's deplorable deficiencies. And how wonderful to boast to Charlotte, who could be maddeningly superior at times. Why, the stories she could weave about the girl's former life! With a loving gesture she held out her hands and Kenneth clasped them tightly.

'You see, Mama,' gently persuasive, 'I want to leave Sydney knowing Raunie's in your care, certain that for my sake you'll try to like her even if you can't love her. But you will love her for herself once you know her. And she'll be an asset, you'll see. She'll do wonders for Gina. London fashions, modes and manners, the latest ideas – things like that. You know what I mean.' He racked his brains for arguments as her glance wandered fretfully.

'I shudder to think what your father will say and do.' Her voice slurred. Her eyes began to droop.

'Why consider Papa before you must? I never do.' And he laughed, his spirits soaring. Yes, she was almost won over. And with his little presents and personal attentions – that parasol he'd noticed yesterday? She adored parasols. He'd get it for her. And he'd visit the Lodge daily – well, at least for a time. She hiccuped, then chuckled, and with a small languid sigh drew him close. Her wonderful, wonderful plans for this adored son to be smashed like this – it was too bad. A lewd little social climber, what else? A grasping, undoubtedly vulgar little piece fighting her way back up the slippery ladder of Society. She'd planned for someone like Viola Parker, a simple girl, and rich enough to buy him a lieutenancy, perhaps a captaincy. Oh, all she had ever wanted for her children were the things they deserved; the valued, important, worthwhile things of life.

Still, men being what they were a mother must expect headstrong episodes. But men being what they were they could wriggle out of impulsive mistakes. The girl might be but a temporary hindrance. After all, women did die in childbirth. Or she might get lonely and take herself off. Or New Zealand would help Kenneth forget her. Many things could happen. She felt a little easier at the consideration of such possibilities. Yes, perhaps it was working out for the best. Keeping the girl under her nose meant she could watch her, even make use of her. Meanwhile . . .

She shuddered, revolted. Still, it had to be done. An insertion in the *Herald*, all right and proper. Her head dropped. She felt quite deliciously drowsy and didn't want to be bothered thinking with Kenneth here beside her, alone with her, her own dearest boy. Her first-born. Her wanted child. Her son. Ah, she would never let him become the tool of some painted fortune-hunter, for naturally the girl believed they had money. She felt more content. There was always tomorrow. Something would turn up! She laughed softly. Her laughter strangled in hiccups and she gasped for breath. Her beautiful rounded breasts shook with merriment as she watched her son pour wine for them both. There was something almost funny somewhere in the situation . . . Or it had seemed amusing just now . . .

'After all . . .' Her words slurred between giggles and hiccups. 'Why *should* you let your father bother you? You're not in the least like him, you know. Thank heaven.'

And they did their best to imagine the Major wedding a dusky siren on impulse, at the midnight hour, and failed. Her faintly tipsy laughter rippled. Holding each other close they rocked together and his laughter rose to join hers in happy peals of release.

Barbara stood at her window smoothing her gloves. It was a big room facing south; sunless in winter and breezeless in summer. A neat room almost bare of furniture, permeated with that scent of musk she loved because it was a fresh clean scent, no more. No fripperies, nothing even remotely out of place. On her desk a pile of letters and a neat stack of books. The chintz curtains about the big old-fashioned bed were sadly faded. A valise, boxes and trunks, relics of the family's earlier travels, were piled precisely atop the big wardrobe. A calm remote room, and her own. The carriage had not yet come round and she wanted to avoid waiting below with her father, for she knew he would be reluctant too. She picked up a letter and read it slowly. She folded it neatly and opened a book to slip it inside as was her habit when she wished to keep correspondence close by. The printed page made her pause.

'Her brow was overhung with coins of gold, that sparkled o'er the auburn of her hair . . . her dress was many-colour'd, finely spun . . .'

Haidée had been all of beauty to her when she, Barbara was a thin intense eight-year-old. With a bitter-sweet stab that was almost a physical pain she relived the moment when she had torn at her stiff curls and flung aside the party dress and pantaloons that pricked so horribly when she moved and had stood naked demanding a veil of lace. Like Haidée. To be beautiful as Haidée was beautiful. To be loved as Haidée must have been loved. Nurse had thrown a towel about her and the Aunts had come running to stare horrified then look away in shame. She hated the Aunts as she had never hated them before and felt guilty but could not help herself. She hated them for the sparing charity with which they sheltered Mama. She hated them for the way they never understood. Never. Then Mama had come to shriek and wail and ask questions against which she closed her lips and folded her

150

hands firmly and stared at the circle of women with wide puzzled eyes. They did not know Byron. They had not heard his words. They had eyes but they could not read him. Yes, that was it. Poor, poor things, they did not know Byron.

They found *Don Juan* tucked under her glove-box, the first and only book soft foolish Aunt Adelaide had ever been coaxed to read to her. Nurse had been dismissed, poor Aunt Addy had shed floods of repentant tears in ignorance as to the precise reason for her penance, and the offending book had been carried between Aunt Hortense's bony thumb and forefinger and thrown in the fire. Barbara had stood watching it burn, repeating over and over until they thought her hysterical or mad, 'But it's beautiful, Mama, truly beautiful.' She asked if the book suffered from leprosy. Or cholera perhaps? It surely must have attracted some terrible disease, for the Aunts were constantly and volubly aware of the world's maladies. In fact, disease was all they ever seemed to discuss; disease both physical and moral.

She had never put anything beneath her glove-box again. She tucked what treasures came her way into a discarded sachet and buried all in her old dress-basket. As she buried her ideas and wishes and dreams. She moved through her childhood with withdrawn eyes, withdrawn heart. So much emotion about her frightened her, and so she knew she must avoid emotion. She must have no part in it, ever, for it was a dangerous wayward thing to be avoided and struggled against forever. It damaged. She had known that long ago. She knew it now. Mr Kempt had found her this copy of Byron after a deal of time and trouble – he often found books for her, secretly and discreetly. No one knew she had it. No one would ever know. It would be hidden with her other precious volumes and Brick's letters and her blue-covered diaries that were her only true confidants and knew her very soul, all stored in the basket that no one wanted now because it was broken and so disreputable even the key could not be depended upon.

For how could anyone rob her of the things she loved if she never, by word or deed or emotion, showed what she valued?

Enthusiasm, anger, impulse, impatience – her mother was enslaved by such drives. So her own feelings must be stifled where they could do no harm – inside herself. Or in her dress-basket, to put it another way. You only remained untouched, unhurt and therefore safe if you hid your needs and desires, your very loves, where no one could see them or even suspect their presence. You kept the thing that was you, hidden in the close secret places of the world. And in your heart.

She looked up. Laughter. Warm and tingling laughter. A woman's laughter. A man's. Kenneth and their mother laughing together, shutting her out. She closed the book gently and replaced it on the pile. A vagrant wisp of breeze ruffled the window curtains and for some reason she shivered. For an instant, standing there in the dark cool room, panic possessed her and she floundered in the void, that deep dark aloneness that had been and always would be hers.

The carriage, Jeremy's whistle, Joey's voice. She took up her Bible. Gloved, bonneted, properly dignified, even a little demure, she closed her door softly behind her and went down to join her father.

Chapter Seven

IT WAS a beautiful morning, a hush of a March day between the summer gone and the winter to come. High above Woolloomooloo Bay the Merrill carriage bowled smartly along. Raunie folded her hands in their new French kid gloves atop her new parasol and rubbed one foot against the other, savouring her new boots. Her rich and rustling skirt, her tight jacket, and her bonnet lavish with ribbons were the height of fashion. She knew she looked lovely and hoped she looked confident (without of course appearing in the least brazen) for this was the day the young, newly wed Mrs Kenneth Merrill drove to meet her husband's family, and to be made welcome in the Merrill household. She let out her breath in a long satisfied sigh. Her last twinge of trepidation died under the strength of her inner excitement, familiar, and always there whenever life snatched her up and spun her along to meet yet another fresh and exciting experience.

Her husband cantered slightly ahead. At times he would glance back but she avoided his eyes. She knew his every mood and was bored by them all. She understood him only too well. So little really to understand – ardent, indulged, all that a young ensign conscious of his position in a garrisoned town was required to be, a mere boy of whinings and complainings, of suprisingly clumsy but always demanding caresses. He was also a coward. She could do no more than despise Kenneth Merrill yet value him as a means to an end, for she had known well what she was about when she married him. She had planned it from the beginning. She saw her marriage to a Merrill as her ultimate safety, her one sure way of becoming an indisputable part of Regent Lodge and so making of herself what she must become – a lady. Only a lady could demand respect and subsistence as her right; respect bothered her not at all but the comforting sustaining entities of life were sweet to her taste. But beyond all other reasons was the one of all importance: only her acceptance as a lady in the life of Sydney could help gain for her her secret and most cherished aim and end – Brick O'Shea.

There had been other reasons too, dimly understood and only half acknowledged but always urging and driving her – damaged pride, resentment, the need of revenge. Why should not this proud and established family be the one to repay her for her years of menial toil and the degradation of her life since she had run from Erins Pride. Why should not the substantial props of the Merrill household wipe out the memory of the illness induced by her trip and her exhaustion and confusion in a Sydney she did not recognise or under-stand; a ribald city crowded with humanity bitter with the knowledge that it had fled across the world from misery only to find it a bedfellow once more. Bewildered immigrants landed to deep depression . . . The banks failed and there was nothing but paper money . . . No pay but food for braving the inland . . . Huge useless mansions waited vainly for purchasers . . . Auction marts were glutted with sellers instead of buyers . . . Insolvents chafed in the hands of rapacious money-lenders . . . But they were too occupied in trying to fill their empty bellies to ponder the conditions or causes proffered by the glib tongues of authority and the gossips of the streets. They robbed and cheated and battened on to each other for what sustenance they could find or, starving, lived off the garbage piles. With puzzled eyes, Raunie watched the shiploads of emigrants sailing down harbour to seek work in South America, passing vessels sweeping through the Heads with more mouths to feed. And still they came, the wooden hookers, from a teeming homeland that did not know or care where they landed so long as their embarrassing appetites could be eased in some less clamouring quarter of the globe.

Then came the women. A glut of women with only what covered them and their hearts full of hope. And greed. But along with its surplus population the Mother Country sent its surplus disease and they died as flies. Still they came, spilling on to the wharves to sleep under the Domain trees, to spend days in aimless search for the work that didn't exist, or dawdle on street corners begging the women-satiated bullockies to take them, no matter where, in return for their food. The gaols were full and the brothels bulging. The Hospital overflowed with despair. The one rock in this sea of great need was Caroline Chisholm, gathering those she could from the lanes and courts and beaches and jolting with them in her creaking tied-together drays over the dreadful roads of the interior to find, at least for some of them, a future.

Raunie had been not only weak and shabby but lacked those necessary adjuncts to respectable employment – references. In any case there were fifty girls for any place offering. It was useless to beg, for too many were at it. She sold the revolver. She sold her one decent dress. Then she drifted, demoralised by the gipsy's two fears, loneliness and sickness. The hag who sheltered her one night tossed her out the next morning and kept her carpet-bag. In her incongruous outfit of man's shirt and trousers she was forced to sleep in yards and doorways terrified of the battles between local gangs and Yankee whalers clashing with flensing knives and harpoons, and the wandering packs of starving dogs that attacked children and would easily pull a horse to the ground by its throat. Or she huddled for warmth behind the piles of junk on the new road the convicts were cutting through the Rocks, her fitful sleep tormented by the dream of the black mountain with the cave and the rushing wind and the wild sweet cry of the child. She brooded on Jamie. She even dwelt nostalgically on the Pride's harsh security, hearing again the crackle of the big fires, staring into the purple distances, tasting Moll's baking and enjoying Betsy's sympathy. And she longed for Brick yet would die rather than face him as the helpless creature she had become; despairing as she was, she would not seek charity for fear of contact with his menials, or even himself. But she was hungry . . . hungry. The last food she had eaten she had stolen. It seemed that unless there was succour somewhere, and soon, she would surely die.

One despairing night in late summer hardly knowing what she was about she wandered down to the water. It was black and subdued, lapping softly against the deserted wharf. She stretched herself on the wood, sank her hands over the side, then held their wetness to her face. Down in these oily-looking depths there would be no hunger or fear, only peace . . . But as she lay, too weak and despairing even to want to move a man spoke nearby, a woman laughed, and from the far shore came the quick high bark of a dog. Life, harsh as it was, was around her. She looked up to rest her tired eyes against the peaceful purity of the stars. Gipsies never wilfully altered the course of nature, they merely allowed themselves to avoid where possible the starkly unpleasant aspects of it. It was then she remembered the Duchess. Indeed, she had often thought of the Duchess these past weeks, yet shrank from the idea of her. Yet . . . The Duchess existed. The Duchess would always exist. And where else but here? She scrambled to her feet. She did not want to die.

> 'Kitty was a young thing
> and lately left her mammy ho . . .

As she heard the rough singing of approaching men she called to them. They paused in a faint glow of light. Sailors of course, one tall, the other short and bearded. 'The Duchess?' They laughed at her question, then at each other. Was the girl drunk or mad? Of course they knew the Duchess. Everyone knew the Duchess. But if she wanted the Hulk she'd best come along with them, they'd get her in easy as pie. The Thames Hulk . . . She had heard much of the place and had kept well away from it. A tavern and lodging-house catering to the needs of sailors ashore, the most notorious pot-house of this most notorious quarter of Sydney Town. Afraid, but desperate for food and shelter, she joined them.

They were noisy, and evidently pleased with her, for the small one, a Portuguese or a Spaniard, grasped her arm as they led her along an alley. Sounds of revelry drifted – the bellowing of male voices, the shrieks and excited laughter of women. The tall sailor thudded on a door and eyes peered through a slit. The heavy door swung open and the men shoved her ahead of them. The door banged behind them. She stood, her head spinning from the heady fumes of hot food and tobacco, of rum and sweating human bodies. It was a big sparsely lighted room jammed with rickety tables and stools. Rough benches were fixed round the walls behind greasy tables fringed by wooden forms. Through its scant sawdust the floor was caked with liquor and spittle and food scraps ground into slimy blobs. The tables were filled with card-playing sailors and men in old soldier's jackets and one ludicrous would-be dandy sporting a battered top hat. But most were whalers – Portuguese, Lascars, Chinese, Americans from Nantucket up from Van Diemen's Land. Wretched frantic bacchantes of women lolled in drunken half-clothed communion anywhere it was possible to rest their bodies. More wandered the tortuous little stairway and in and out of the rooms high up under the ceiling. Screams and drunken laughter drifted down, sometimes cutting off abruptly. Raunie found herself shivering.

Her sailor jerked her towards a table of men but she wrenched herself free. 'Gitana,' he hissed and, terrified, she searched the crowd for the Duchess just as the woman swept in to slither mugs on tables, part a brawling couple and thump a quarrelsome whaler over the head with a tankard, ale and all. Her hair was as beautiful and grimy as of old, her ears and fingers gleamed with what appeared to be gems but were doubtless glass. She slumped at a corner table beside a girl sipping raw black tea from a plate. There was something so familiar, so reassuring about her bombastic presence that Raunie stumbled forward to fall against the table with a sob of relief. The woman looked up angrily then her eyes widened and she stared at the weary pinched little face, the stained garments, and the hair that hadn't been brushed in weeks. She pushed her into a seat.

''Pon me sammy, 'tis the widder Lorne. Bleaky!' she yelled. 'Vittles. And hurry about it or I tips a walloper across your snout.' She wiped a mug with the hem of her skirt and indicated the painfully thin girl beside her. 'This 'ere's Mary. Should be in hospital.' Again her eyes travelled over Raunie. 'And by the look o' yourself you should be there with her.'

'No.' Mary crouched over her tea. 'I've been to the Hospital. I've watched them dragging the bodies off the beds when they're scarce dead and covering them with rags. Such rags. And the dead-house is horrible.' Her lovely, too-large eyes implored. 'I want to die here. You promised I might die here.'

The Duchess patted her skeleton fingers. 'And you'll die at the Hulk no matter what Halfred says. Just be quick and quiet about it, that's all. Halfred likes fings done right. A finicky lad, Halfred. But 'ere comes tea so stash your jawing and clap it down your necks afore someone else nabs it.'

Raunie gulped the tea and the bread and meat, unable to speak or even think coherently till her terrible hunger was eased. But at last she rested back, satiated, aware that both women were watching her intently. Here around her was sanctuary of a kind. The thought of the black and lonely night outside was not to be borne and she answered the Duchess's questions with something almost like eagerness. Yes, she'd left Mr O'Shea's station and found her own way to Sydney . . . She was a free woman to do as she pleased, was she not? Her child? Ah, the poor mite, it had died soon after birth . . . a girl too . . .

The Duchess yawned and studied Raunie behind the shield of her hand. Only the Devil, and perhaps O'Shea, knew under what circumstances this hussy had run away, no doubt thieving what she could in the process. All the same, it was true she was no convict woman. And though there was little of the beauty about her now, with rest and some bright clothing men would pay well for her. She, the Duchess, had always known the wench to be a valuable prize; even while they infuriated her she recognised the girl's high-faluting airs and proud ways as assets to bargain with. She would be a fool to let the chit slip away a second time, since she was clearly desperate and would be much more amenable. And if O'Shea did happen to be looking for her he came but rarely to the

158

Hulk. And even if he should come . . . She patted Raunie's cheeks.

'There now, you looks better.'

'I've nowhere to go. I thought perhaps . . .'

The Duchess picked her blackened teeth and sucked through them with gusto. 'The doxies come a' banging on the door day and night willing to do the doocedest things for a crib. But seeing as 'ow we're old cronies . . . Look, I'll send you to a place I keep for special gals till you get some flesh on your bones, then, well I keeps a reglar two in a flash house in George Street. And o' course there's Julie's – though we've but five rooms there and more gals than we can use.'

Raunie squirmed – with food, a little of her resilience came flowing back. But if she went out into that loneliness again . . . And though wary of the Duchess there were women worse on the Rocks; she'd suffered them as they tried to force her into their dens of drink and drugs and thuggery. With this woman she might, just might, strike a bargain. But all she had to bargain with except her body was her dancing – well, why not? A few months here, a measure of good luck, and she might escape with enough money to take a room of her own.

'Let me dance. For my food. And a little money if you will. You could let me try.'

The Duchess pondered. The minx was playing for time, planning for higher stakes. She had always been the leary one. Still and all . . . dancing? It would be something new. At least, the way this girl danced. And if she gave trouble she could always be handed over to the women who had their own ways, and not always pretty ways, of curing flashness. She gave one of her raucous indulgent laughs.

'Still playing the toff, eh, milady? But this 'ere dancing now . . . Laggers get gals for a crust or a kind word and little they waste of either since they're glutted with the bawds. So we might use your dancing to loosen their moneybags. If you please 'em they'll toss you their wages, if you anger 'em you'll be left to handle 'em alone. And in a temper they're like to slit your throat.' She tossed back her wild hair. 'You gives me two-thirds o' your takings and if you cheat . . . well, *I'm*

159

like to slit your throat. You can doss with Mary.' She poked a derisive finger at Raunie's trousers. 'And rid yourself o' them.'

'I've only the dress you gave me – remember? – and that's in my bag. A woman named Sarah Bird kept my things.'

'Sarah? My lads'll soon settle that pot-house bitch,' she raged. She stretched her long arms, almost knocking the featherweight girl beside her off her seat, and got to her feet. 'The gals'll larn you what to do. Just follow the rules and we'll git along fine. Now you will do m' bidding wivout trouble, won't you, milady?' There was a threat in the words but she pinched Raunie's cheek playfully, hitched up her skirts and sauntered off into the quarrelling mass around her. Raunie slid what food scraps were left on the table into her lap for later, avoided the stares of the men, and endured as best she could the sad beseeching eyes of the doomed Mary.

She soon discovered that though in many ways the Thames Hulk was the worst tavern in Sydney Town it was one that knew the unseen hands of discipline. Within a month of landing the Duchess had married Alf Burleigh, captain of one of O'Shea's brigs and, due to his carelessness with his money while sleeping off his drunken orgies, his wife had been able to buy herself the disreputable and run-down Hulk. She was proud of her investment and under its patched-up roof had accumulated the dregs of the port, fighting for the queenship of its tide of cut-throats, pimps and gamblers with fists and teeth and a collection of murderous knives. Her slightest whim was law – or had been until the day O'Shea kicked open her doors and proceeded to clear the overcrowded rooms, search closets and cupboards and rasp out his questions, the answers to which he gave her before she could invent suitable lies. Sampling her hidden store of cognac he pointed out that fires began easily in this run-down quarter of the town and she'd best come to terms with him before the Hulk should be razed to the ground.

The place was to be cleaned up from cellar to roof. As much to drink as the men wanted as long as they could pay for it. And the women must be willing. On this point she began to argue; he knew as well as she did that her girls were irreclaimables, fit for nothing more than the life she gave them. But he was adamant and insisted on being informed of their comings and goings. Old Milly the baby-farmer, who filled her lean-to in the next lane with unwanted offspring and fed them gin to kill them without sound or fuss, was forbidden the Hulk altogether – the Duchess really screamed her fury at this. But he wanted the children, healthy or sick it mattered not, delivered to his crèche with no questions asked. The Duchess, certain he was barmy, was further convinced of it when he insisted the girls be better paid – it was madness to treat these harpies as human beings, she stormed. As for herself she was to receive a fixed sum – a nice enough sum certainly – to send his men back to their ships in good time instead of leaving him as other owners, with nothing but a long list of deserters. Even more important, she would be paid extra for keeping his name out of all her activities. And she would be protected from the police, her rivals, and her enemies.

It didn't take the Duchess long to decide that his demands were more eccentric than excessive and, considered in the light of losing the Hulk, distinctly to her advantage – after all, he might have come demanding tribute. And in any case, if she never saw what the girls did with their brats how could she be blamed for their disappearance? And who of her women dared insist on money? – yes, there were ways to outwit even an O'Shea. But though she flaunted her hips at the man downing her precious brandy he seemed so completely unaware of her body that she decided to move warily; he was not only the most desirable man she had ever seen, he was also the only one she had ever been afraid of. All in all, they understood each other very well. She decided on which side her bread was buttered and even found life surprisingly simple when the threat of his name was enough to make a customer sober into obedience; he'd whipped a drunken sailor along the wharves many a time, and raised the victim's pay when he took it well. It was conceded about the wharves that O'Shea's generosity could often be worth a good flogging.

And so the Duchess proceeded to coat her butter generously with jam, strolling in the Domain of a Sunday or clip-clopping up to watch the hangings at the new gaol in her most colourful clothes and a basket of veal pies made with her own hands to share with her friends. And she was cultivating some quite respectable friends. Mrs Alf Burleigh was at least outwardly respectable, while she saved for the day when she might settle in some more acceptable lodging-house or invest in a place in a more affluent district. But she was only too well aware of her overpowering weakness – rum laced with sugar and tobacco and a dash of vitriol. O'Shea had forbidden her women to supply it so she was forced to get it through outside channels for she went raving mad these days without its bite – but she went mad with it. Her 'spells' grew more frequent and more violent and the glint of her dagger sent the room scattering and her girls to hide in terror, for she played with a knife as easily and carelessly as a child might play with a favourite toy. When they heard the dull thud on wood and the cursing and crying and stumbling about her room at the top of the stairs the Hulk must fend for itself and the girls hide from her till it was all over and she was fit to come down again. They had not even the heart or the courage to run away. Indeed, they would not have known where to run. Terror paralysed them. And habit. It was as if the Thames Hulk lay accursed.

Raunie fought with a savagery born of desperation for her share of the Hulk spoils and hid her slowly mounting pile of coins in a corner of the rat-ridden shed that was now hers alone, for Mary was dead. The Duchess had given the girl a bang-up funeral, almost as fine as the one she gave Sarah Bird. Sarah's funeral had been the talk of the Rocks, the mystery of her death forgotten in the excitement of watching her carried to her grave by a group of suitably sober whalers followed by the Duchess's girls garbed in their best, scattering wilted flowers over her coffin. And Raunie's carpet-bag arrived intact.

She refused to doss with any of the foul-mouthed jades continually bearing children who were whisked somehow into a mysterious oblivion, but she minded her business about the babes as she did about all else. And she became adept at passing on the demands of the men; to a tipsy sailor, starved of women by many months at sea, his woman became the one closest to hand. And any woman would do. Instead, Raunie danced. And in spite of the fire her dancing aroused in herself, as well as in others, she went on dancing for it was her refuge – while she danced she was safe. And as they soon came from all parts of the country and the seven seas to watch her dance, pickings became so good the Duchess let her do much as she pleased. The people of the Thames Hulk forgave Raunie much when she danced for them.

Most of the men were from Brick's ships, and so she encouraged their talk. Even so it took long coaxing and patient eavesdropping to learn that O'Shea went riding over the hills with a Miss Merrill; a lady, even if she did teach at his school and was sometimes seen with Mrs Chisholm and others down back lanes where ladies were not supposed to be. So there was truth in Moll's ramblings . . . Driven by jealousy, hating the Merrill girl and obsessed by her, Raunie asked questions. Surely, scoffed the men, she knew of the Merrills? Where had she been cribbing? All Sydney knew the Major was the despot behind the General, looking down his long-beaked nose at those he kept to heel. The son was a strutting cockerel, the mother as pink and white and frivolous as a party cake, and the young miss still in the schoolroom – but Miss Merrill? They grew confused. A strange pair this girl and O'Shea, though perhaps not so strange when you watched them on horseback. But one man's bet was as good as his neighbour's as to how it would all end . . .

Raunie would creep away to count her money once more. The little pile of coins grew too slowly and she lived in fear that even this bit of treasure would be stolen. So Brick wanted a lady . . . his own words, and those of Moll Noakes came back to taunt her. She, Raunie Lorne, would never make a lady of herself in this sink for, as time dragged by, alone and losing heart, she felt drawn and bound by the steamy hopeless life about her. But what escape from it but the streets? The Hulk terrified her, but she was even more afraid of the demands of her hungry young body. There was no escape from herself. All the erotic tricks of sex she was forced to watch fascinated her then tormented her. She began to wallow in luxurious longings. Her breasts strained against her bodice, her lips could not stay still, her hands sweated. Her every movement was accentuated and she knew male eyes lingered on her as they never had before. She began to seek relief in small furtive ways. Still it was not enough. She longed for limbs against her limbs, mouth to her mouth. Above all she longed for Brick O'Shea. So it was that, at last, with a fierce and sobbing despair, she succumbed to Feli.

Thin and lean and dark, with a brooding intensity about him, the moment he walked in the door Raunie knew him for what he was – a Romany. Her heart took up a new beat, strong and so persistent that she found it impossible to ignore him. She was constantly and terribly aware of him. She watched him as he sprawled in a corner with a crowd gawping about him, playing his flute made of willow, or of aspenwood. He wooed the room, she felt he wooed her too with his music and though he appeared quite unconcerned she knew he was supremely conscious of the power he held over them all. And why not? She knew the same elation of spirit when she held power. It was what she was born for; only then did she live to the fullest. When he tired of the flute he played the fiddle, and how he played it, conjuring from strings that seemed bewitched rhythms that changed from a wild orgy of screaming strings to the softest, most tender melancholy. Fire, agony, passion, yearning, all were flung upon the ears in an ecstatic blend of European folk-tunes and Oriental rhythm. And he changed with his music, gay and smiling one minute, dark moods gone, tragic and desolate the next. He intoxicated himself with his own creation. Eager and awed, his emotion-drugged audience laughed with an excitement they did not understand or cried with the maudlin sentiment of the Cockney and the Latin. They stamped and shouted and wheedled their seducer on to greater feats of speed and virtuosity until he became an acrobat, wielding the bow with his teeth, gesturing in grotesque patterns, tossing his fiddle into the air, capering with slim feline legs, or twisting his supple body like a serpent mad or in ecstasy. And at the height of the excitement, drunk with sound and rhythm, the crowd would yell for Raunie and Feli would play his tambourine and she would give herself wholly to the passion of movement, lost in herself. Lost in Feli.

He came every night for weeks but they rarely spoke. There was no need of speech. They felt, trembling to each other with the expectation of what was to come. He called her 'chi' and a dozen little endearments in Romany that she had never heard before yet instinctively understood. He was her kind. For the first time in her life and perhaps the last she was all gipsy and it was impossible for her to resist him. Moody, whimsical, mischievous, wholly passionate, the essence of all the raggle-taggle vagabonds of history, he was all she would have been but for her alien father. Their weeks together were a torment yet a delight, nights when she lay on the old couch in the shed in his arms, his hands fondling the charm about her neck, as she fondled it herself freely now, loving it and needing it, as she needed him. He understood it. He understood her. He seemed to understand everything. Then, unable to do without him longer, she would turn over into his arms with a sigh. She was enamoured even of his cruelty that aroused in her a bizarre exultation of the body. No man had beaten her before. Feli beat her, and viciously. She was often afraid of him, at times hated him, yet was spurred by his thin strong demanding hands into giving herself to him with a primitive savagery. He gave her nothing, neither money nor gifts, and she did not care. She was entirely possessed.

June. A chill wet night. The sodden little lanes about the Hulk were deserted and there were more people than usual in the tavern with the sealed warm place giving off a worse stench than usual as it rang to ribald slang and cant and the tortured squeaks of a cornet. They were tired of comic songs and choruses so Feli was called to play and Raunie to dance while the customers thumped their tankards and pushed the pot-boys out of their way and clapped and laughed and

165

shouted for more. They even cried in their tipsiness and threw coins with a reckless generosity. But sharp as a blow silence fell, a silence that whirled Raunie to a dead stop to stare into the impassive face of Brick O'Shea.

She stood trembling, panting and sweating, looking her fill of him. Two sailors blocked the door, resting their powerful frames against the doorposts. All three were in sailor's garb, boots oozing moisture, rain glistening on hair and shoulders and beards. Brick looked . . . well . . . different. Yes, different. But he was still Brick O'Shea, and she stood struggling with her urge to run, to hide herself, yet her longing to stay. There was no sound but the childish whimper of a drunk. Then Brick moved. Brushing her aside he pounced on a man crouched under a table. He lifted him cleanly and tossed him into the arms of the men at the door. He dragged forth a seaman attempting to hide under a woman's skirts. Then he paused beside Feli.

'You're a better fiddler than a cook but I've a brig sailing with the tide. At least you can soak ship's biscuit in rum. Get along with the others.'

The youth plucked defiantly at his fiddle. 'I like it here,' he said. The room gasped. Brick snatched the fiddle and broke it cleanly across his knees. With an animal wail Feli threw himself at his persecutor and the two men locked together, swaying. But Feli hadn't a chance. Brick knocked him senseless and dragged him across the floor to the guards.

'Sober them up in the Harbour,' he ordered. Then, feet apart and firmly planted, he stood dead centre of the room. 'Any more would-be deserters?' No answer. Not a sound. 'Then don't overstay your leave for next time it'll be the "cat", a tester at least. I know where to strike so you'll be of little use to wine or woman for weeks to come.'

Someone whistled nervously. A guitar was plucked. Talk began and swelled. Without a word to her Brick grasped Raunie's arm, hauled her into the tiny solitary pantry and kicked shut the door. She wrenched herself from his grasp.

'Save your bullying for your men.' Then with a childish

violent petulance, 'Your beard . . . *that's* it. That's the difference. I don't like it.'

'Can't say I found your dancing as exciting as rumour has it,' he drawled.

'I'll not go back to the Pride,' she flared. 'Do you hear? I will not go back.'

'You're not wanted at the Pride, Raunie. Moll would take herself off if you came within a mile of it. You were never conducive to peace about the place, you know.'

'Peace! Who wants peace?'

He laughed. 'Neither you nor I, it seems. But you weren't very considerate in your flight from my board and shelter. Paddy valued his boots even more than his trousers. And how much money did you take?'

'Money?' She tossed her head. 'What money?'

'You'd never leave anywhere with empty hands. Paddy didn't miss his gold, but I did. Hard too on Rob losing his revolver. It was a good one. I hope you drove a hard bargain in the selling of it.' He came closer. 'And out of all dives on the Rocks, why choose the Hulk?'

'The Duchess came out on the *May Queen*,' she explained sullenly. 'It's hateful, I know it, but I don't starve.' She shivered. 'I never mean to be hungry again.'

'You didn't starve at the Pride.'

'Oh, I starved,' she said bitterly. 'And not just from lack of food.'

'And your runaway friends? I want the truth. What happened to Inar?'

'I don't know and I don't care. All I know is that if I hadn't escaped from her and Jock they'd have robbed me, even killed me. They needed money so they could stay in Sydney.'

'Well, Jock's stay was brief enough. He was dead when I turned him over, hurled off the bridge with a knife in his back in a gang war.' He laughed shortly. 'But Murchison's still looking for his wagon.'

'Why do you search for Inar?' Then jealously. 'Are you in love with her?'

'She has a husband interested in her whereabouts.' He

pulled her close and held up her face. 'Does she come here? Answer me.'

'I haven't set eyes on her since I left her with Jock on the road. Let me go. You're hurting me.'

'You're lying.' He shook her violently. 'You're always lying, you gipsy bitch. A lying half-breed.'

She clawed free of him. 'If you want Inar find her yourself. And keep away from me. I hate you. *Hate* you . . .' They faced each other, he with furious eyes, she with hurt despair. But it was more than she could stand as he turned to open the door. 'I didn't mean that,' she said miserably. 'Stay. Please . . .'

'Leave here, Raunie,' he said quietly. 'The place is vile.'

'Well, isn't that something of your doing? Anyway,' she shrugged. 'I do no worse than dance for them.'

'You'll not fob them off with that for long. Get away from here. Make some other life for yourself.'

'There's no work in Sydney.'

'I need girls for my crèche. Nurses.'

'Tending brats?'

'You'll be no more useless at it than most who come to take it on. And you'll be well paid. And housed. Go down to Millers Point and ask for Miss Merrill. Everyone knows her. She'll look after you.'

'Merrill?' She turned on him with all her stored-up resentment. 'I've heard about her. And I won't be *her* servant. Nor yours, ever again. I'll make my own way in my own time –'

'And make it steadily downwards by the look of things.' He opened the door.

'Brick . . .' With a swift movement she banged the door shut and leaned against it, looking up at him. She put out a hand. 'I mean . . . Mr O'Shea . . .'

'Well?' He was impatient and unyielding. Her body slumped.

'Oh, what's the use.'

'For a moment I thought you might be going to ask about the son you deserted.'

Yes, she had been wondering about Jamie. He was as

shrewdly perceptive as ever where she was concerned. 'Betsy always wanted a boy,' she defended herself.

'He's an engaging lad.' His eyes rested on her thoughtfully. 'By the way, one gipsy is trouble enough, two are impossible. You won't see Feli again, I'll take good care of that. And think about the crèche. And think hard.'

And he was gone, so briskly her mouth still trembled with arguments. She wanted to run after him and beg for his love if she couldn't get it any other way . . . but she stayed. She, Raunie Lorne, begging for the love of a man? One day he would give her what she wanted, freely and gladly . . . but first she must escape this terrible world that was beating her down. If Brick O'Shea would only look twice at a lady, she must become a lady, or as close to one as it was possible for her to be. She went off to count her money.

It was a warm spring evening when it happened. The Duchess had taken to her room and in three days had only appeared in her doorway to bellow down for food and spirits. The Hulk feared for itself with an over-all watchfulness that could not be dispelled even with a forced and feverish gaiety. Upstairs it was bedlam, with the participants unknown and unseen, for leading off the Duchess's bedroom – and place of business – was a balcony with narrow steps leading down into a narrow lane, and anyone could come and go unnoticed. The half-daft little waif, Bleaky, was nominated to do her mistress's unpredictable bidding and, whimper and complain and wipe her button of a nose on her skirt as she might, she was driven up the tortuous stairs to leave a tray or a pitcher just inside the woman's partly-open door then scurry down as if all the fiends of Hell were after her. The Duchess's door was always slightly ajar – to keep her eyes and ears on things, she insisted – and she had already sliced the ear of a girl who had dared to close it. She was yelling for more rum. Raunie, bored with the woman, the Hulk, and everyone in it, even more so with the urchin cowering on a stair, tucked the jug of spirit under the child's match-thin arm and pushed her upward.

'Don't be a ninny, she's not caught you yet, has she?'

'She'll be killin' me if she does,' the girl whimpered. 'She's near crazy up there with things broke, and ripped to pieces, and money spilled all over the place and –'

'Money?' Raunie paused. She turned back to Bleaky. 'Whose money?'

'Hers, I suppose. She likes to be countin' her money when she's this way. Knows every hog she's got too. Did they tell ye what she did to poor Meg the night Meggy slipped a handful down her shift?'

Raunie tried to ease the girl's fears whle her mind raced. Would one peep inside the Duchess's bedroom be worth the risk of a sliced cheek? The whole place was watching them, hushed and curious, and in the quiet Raunie heard the Duchess's slurred yet still strident tones break in on another voice, a woman's voice, in argument . . . She took the pitcher from Bleaky.

'Go down then if you're frightened. I'll take it.'

'Ye will?' The girl quivered, scurried downstairs and out into the night. The crowd watched, awed. Flat against the wall and moving in that soundless cat-like manner that was so natural to her Raunie moved up a few steps, a couple more, to listen by the partly open door.

'Give it 'ere, y' thieving slut.' The brittle sound of a bottle against a cup. 'And don't take so long about your next visit.' The Duchess's laugh cracked in answer to a murmur from her visitor. 'And come quiet. O'Shea don't like niggers about the Hulk. He don't like 'em about these parts at all. So if y' don't do as I says you'll be back on the streets where I found y', starving for certain. You be getting on, and plenty o' young 'uns these days.' She laughed shrilly while Raunie listened for the soft halting other voice. 'How many niggers git a chance anywheres, let alone at Julie's, even as maids, eh? None. But I says what's done at Julie's. And I'll see y' stays there nice and cosy if y' brings me this reglar. And I means reglar.' And the bottle rattled against the cup again. 'Along with some good pickings now and then.' Her voice grew even harsher. 'What fallals this time, eh?'

The conversation blurred, the Duchess's voice slurring

between drunken threats and hiccups. There was the sound of a scuffle and her voice rising in anger. 'A miniature? A blooming silly miniature of a blooming la-de-da lidy?' She was furious. 'And this 'ere ring, a bit o' glass no more. A toothpick? 'Ere, gimme the rest o' the stuff, y' swindler.'

'There's nothing else, I tell you.'

'For three weeks' work? And you the flashest I ever seen at filching? And Julie's giving y' the chance o' gold pins and studs? Watches too. For why do y' think I put y' there, eh? Cause I likes the colour of y' bloody skin? You're a lying thieving Jen. 'Ere . . . that fancy purse o' yours . . . Turn it out.'

'It's mine. There's nothing in it worth –'

'Open it.' A scuffle. 'Open it or I'll –'

'No. *No.*'

Raunie pressed back to the wall. How well she knew that other voice – yes, it was Inar right enough. Then Inar screamed, a harsh and terrible sound above the Duchess's tipsy oaths. A thud, then another scream as Inar stumbled through the doorway, staggered on the landing and threw herself forward, away from the Duchess's wicked knife. The Duchess had gone quite mad, that was plain. Raunie had a moment to recognise Inar's terrified face before she put out her foot, slightly, but enough to trip the native woman. Inar staggered, then with a terrible scream crashed, rolling over in a scatter of tawdry finery to the base of the stairs, her bonnet loose, her head striking the wood with sickening thuds. Even so she staggered up, the wild-haired raging Duchess after her and they rolled together about the room. The knife flashed, blood spurted and Inar lay still, the blood from her slit face mingling with the filth on the dark greasy floor.

Pandemonium. The mob, conditioned by fear, saw the Duchess on the rampage and it was enough. A woman lay apparently dead – only an Indian of course – but it could mean trouble. They all knew O'Shea's orders. So, you ran from trouble, most certainly you ran from O'Shea when he was bent on vengeance and justice. They were running mad, fighting at the exits or scrambling up the stairs to drop to

171

the street from the tiny windows. The women fought and shrieked and bit into each other as they struggled to escape the demented Duchess and her dagger. The men knocked the women down and walked over them, then turned to fight each other, terrified of O'Shea's men who would come, nothing more certain. They ran to scramble over fences and through little houses, to hide in yards and sheds and boats till time made it safe to slink back conveniently lacking in recent memory, to the Hulk or their ships. An overturned lamp burst into flames to lick a discarded coat, feeding on grease and spilled spirits. At the tables, heads on their hands, were those so drunk they did not know or care. And through it all Inar lay, her face unrecognisable from the blood that oozed like tiny ripples of water over sand.

Raunie hesitated in the Duchess's doorway. She would never get through that chaos below. She slipped into the bedroom and shot the heavy bolt in the heavy door. The shambles was incredible; spilled food, broken bottles, clothes ripped and torn. But scattered over the floor were golden sovereigns and guineas. She scooped handfuls into a fold of her skirt and ran on to the balcony. But she hesitated, something dragging her back.

On the floor, spilled open in the struggle, was Inar's old reticule. Gleaming in its scattered rubbish were coins, a silver bracelet, a gentleman's watch. She examined the watch hurriedly – yes, it was certainly gold. So the Duchess had been right, Inar was cheating her. She scooped up the bag with its contents, filled it with the money and ran on to the balcony again, coughing. Smoke . . . she scrambled down the steps and into the lane, deserted except for a few cautious figures far at the end. Her carpet-bag! It held her savings. She slipped in the gate ignoring and ignored by the scattering demented figures, snatched her bag from under the loose shed boards and tore with the speed of necessity through the back lanes she knew as well as she knew her own hands. People were running with brimming buckets. Others, in a desperate bid to save what they could, ran with blankets, bundles of clothing and knick-knacks. But she kept running while the sky deepened from yellow to red and the shouts of the trapped grew fainter. Finally they died on the still air. For her at least it was the end of the Hulk. It surely was the last of Inar. She dropped to rest in a doorway, exhausted, but free at last. Free. *Free!*

She found a room in an offshoot of George Street south. Alfred Terrace though murky was cheap, and cleaner than some. It would do for a beginning. She paid her rent for two months and hid herself to repair the ravages to her appearance, to mend and adorn her only decent dress, and count her money. Twenty-two pounds. The bracelet was a poor thing but she tucked the watch carefully away. She threw Inar's purse with its rubbish into her carpet-bag and forgot it. As she forgot Inar. The gutting of the Thames Hulk, the worst dive on the Rocks, provided Alfred Terrace with gossip for weeks but she kept to herself, creeping out only to buy food or oddments to brighten her dingy room. She made herself clothing. She slept long. But towards Christmas-time her solitude became quite suddenly unendurable. She felt heady with the urgency of her own returning vitality. She needed comfort and warmth. Desperate for life and laughter, drawn by the lights and the sounds of the town, on the eve of the New Year she had put on the red dress and gone down into the thoroughfares to lose herself and her loneliness in the bright world about her. But when Brick had drawn up before the Royal so suddenly, so unexpectedly, she remembered the money, the stolen watch, and panicked. She was standing exactly where he must pass . . . Shock, then fear had set her on the run, spun her about and into the arms of Kenneth Merrill. And opportunity . . .

Now, in the Merrill carriage she stirred, rousing herself from the past, back to the most satisfactory present. They were turning in through imposing gates and bowling along a neat drive to stop before the most beautiful house she had yet seen in the colony. How important – and rich – the family must be. And now she was one of them. As her young husband helped her down his grip on her hand tightened. He was begging something of her. He was always begging.

'Mama seldom comes down before midday. She's not very

strong, you see. But I've explained all that, haven't I. Gina's at school of course but the others will be waiting. With Mama. I've prepared them.'

So — she was not to be welcomed, servants lining the hall, properly and formally in the withdrawing-room. But Kenneth's eyes softened as they travelled over her. 'You look so beautiful this morning they can't help but love you. But . . . well, don't expect too much at first. You'll have to be patient, you know. We must both be patient . . .' His voice trailed away in his discomfort.

She was accustomed to his indecision and confusion. Deliberately she held her gloved hand to his cheek. He loved the gesture. Indeed, any gesture that brought contact. 'It won't be my fault if they don't like me. You are proud of me, aren't you, dearest?'

'You're always wonderful.'

'Then . . . even if they don't like me very much at first, I won't let it matter. You're the one who is important.' And she smiled her most generous, her most limpid smile.

He shifted awkwardly. His eyes evaded. 'Matter of fact I'm not important at all. At least, not here. Damned if I seem to be important anywhere, really . . . Well, let's go in. Might as well get it over with.'

As they followed the housemaid through the dim cool hall her eyes missed nothing. A door on the left stood slightly open, left so no doubt by the same housemaid — the drab looked as if she might forget such commonplace tasks as shutting doors. There was a certain laxity about the girl as there was, now she was inside it, about the whole house. There was dust on the bench there, on the picture-frames and window ledges. And the floors should boast a higher polish. She had just time to glance inside the withdrawing-room; thick carpet and footstools like fat queer-shaped mushrooms and dark curtains drawn against the sun. And she visualised a party there, with massed flowers, subdued laughter, and handsome men clustered about the pianoforte gleaming with golden candles. And how elegantly she might descend this graceful stairway with lights playing over her shoulders and painting her hair with darting shadows ... She sighed and patted her ribbons and spread her skirts wide as they were announced, her husband's hand, sweating she knew, under her elbow. Her mother-in-law's boudoir door closed softly behind them.

She was, first of all, acutely conscious of the room; Mrs Merrill's room, surely the best and largest in the house. Untidy, heavily perfumed and, as the rest of the place, dusty. But there was a cloying femininity about it that gave it a slatternly distinction. A tall man and a girl stood near the windows. But Kenneth was leading her to the woman reclining on a couch robed in a frilled white morning-gown, made even more starkly white by the flaming colour of her hair – Kenneth's mother. The hair was Kenneth's hair, darkened only slightly by age. Raunie had no doubt they were alike in other ways too. If so, everything would be so much easier. Kenneth was murmuring, stammering slightly. She curtsied, then straightened to watch with a silent amused fascination the pale soft face of the woman before her crinkle then dissolve under noisy tears.

The man by the window stirred; a movement of impatience Raunie felt. The girl took a plain white linen handkerchief from her pocket and passed it without a word to the sobbing woman. Raunie felt the girl's eyes on her. Kenneth was fussing, patting his mother's shoulders, rubbing her hands, making an abject ass of himself. Raunie decided they were both quite as silly as each other. As she waited politely for the hysteria to pass her eyes rose to meet those of Barbara Merrill – and she knew that here was one of the most urgent reasons she had contrived to join the Merrill household, this moment one she had anticipated for a long time. She had fretted to meet this girl, a girl entangled, in some manner, with Brick O'Shea and who, because of it, must be fought and vanquished. Kenneth was making introductions.

Barbara saw a small beautifully formed young woman with strange greenish eyes and incredibly golden skin, the composite impression of her, one to stir the blood. Raunie took careful note of the tall, almost-too-thin girl in a frock of

175

brown merino, its only softening a bertha of fine lace. There was a darn on one arm, and the lace was yellow as if it had been used often – she looked as careful as she might be parsimonious – but her hair with its centre parting and drawn across her forehead to coil softly over her ears flattered her where the style was too severe on others. Even so she was not beautiful, or even pretty. She looked every inch a blue-stocking, supercilious, proud and studious. It was ludicrous, quite impossible surely that Brick O'Shea could find her attractive. Then what was it about this girl that held his attention . . .? Mrs Eleanor Merrill sniffed loudly into the handkerchief then fluttered her lashes and her richly ringed hands at her daughter-in-law – the perennial performance of the perennial coquette, Raunie decided.

'You must forgive my mother – Mrs Merrill.' Barbara spoke for the first time. 'I'm sure you can understand what a shock your marriage has been.'

'I don't see why it should shock,' she answered cheerfully. 'And you may call me Raunie, you know.' And delighted in watching the girl stiffen.

'Thank you,' Barbara said quietly, 'but I prefer to wait until we know each other a little better.'

'Well, I shall call you Barbara. After all, I am one of the family, am I not?'

'You're young.' Eleanor's light eyes fixed themselves on Raunie so steadily anyone else would have been disconcerted. 'Very young.'

'I'm turned twenty, ma'am.' Stressing the 'ma'am'. No servile 'madams' here. She had no intention of being patronised.

'Kenneth was three and Barbara a year younger when I turned twenty. How did you manage to come through a marriage without – ' She dabbed at her still tearful eyes. 'Your clothes are quite . . . elegant.' She had been about to say 'extravagant' but remembered the girl was a clever seamstress, or so she had gathered from Kenneth's garbled explanations. She, Eleanor, would be needing a new dress-maker, for the hitherto decently servile Miss Hartley was

176

pressing for her money. Quite the nuisance, for Gina would need so much . . .

'I owe my former mother-in-law a great deal,' Raunie explained. 'Lady Farleigh always insisted that in the gradual assemblage of minor perfections lay the perfect whole.' At last the brief hated marriage was serving her.

'Ah yes . . . Lady Farleigh . . .' Eleanor's eyes glittered, but not with tears. 'You must tell me all about her.'

'I'll be glad to, ma'am.'

Perhaps, Eleanor considered, studying the girl closely, it could be much worse. The girl had certainly married into the aristocracy even if she had married an obscure stepson. Most certainly, she was forced to concede, it was not to be wondered at that any man would want the girl, men being the fools they were. Even poor darling Kenneth . . . But she refused to let any designing female ruin his life. Since this girl had made use of him she must be used in return. And she might be very useful, at that. Now, if only Barbara . . . But there, Barbara would try the patience of a saint, and this girl, she hadn't any doubt at all, was far from being a saint. She, Eleanor Merrill, knew a hussy when she saw one.

'My father, Major Merrill.'

Raunie swung about to curtsy with her most demure smile. She caught the faintest glimmer of response about the mouth of the man before her – the soldier of the carriage, Major Alister Merrill. Handsome in a finely drawn way, wearing his uniform as only an aristocrat could wear it – why, Kenneth looked a browbeaten private in contrast. A long thin nose, cold eyes, a fundamentally harsh and undeviating face. But she thought it a tired face. Or bored. Perhaps both. But whatever else he was he was everything that was important in the colony. She knew that much. Dignity, prestige, power, wealth, everything to be revered and cultivated. She meant to cultivate it. She smiled at him again. She was not afraid.

Kenneth came to stand beside her. She saw his hand clenching and unclenching nervously at his side. He hated all this. He was uncomfortable, even a little scared, and so there

177

was an edge to his voice, a faint undertone of defiance. Well, let him suffer. The important thing was that she was here. This house and all it had to offer was now hers. Some chance had crossed her path with the Merrills and she intended that each of them, in a unique way, should serve her ends.

Her steady eyes met those of Alister Merrill and she knew that if he did not entirely approve of her he was certainly aware of her. To Raunie, awareness of her, the acknowledgement of her existence in the world, had always been more significant, more important by far than mere approval. So far she was well content.

PART THREE

Chapter Eight

DGERALLI WAS born a Katungal, the 'fishermen' of the Yuin tribes who claimed the eastern coast of Australia from Cape Howe north to the Shoalhaven River, so that the foaming curves of beaches, the streams that crawled down the tangled brush to merge with the rivers, the cliffs soaring above the jewel-coloured Pacific – all this that stretched east and north and south from the high flat rock where he lay still and waiting – this was the land of his fathers.

He lay on his side, one motionless hand clutching a scrap of dried fish, his only movement the narrowing of his eyes against the sun. The fiery ball was not yet overhead and it burned his forehead as he stared out to the far specks that were native canoes dotting the lakes where they meandered their flat jagged way into the sea. In the calms and among the sifting sand-banks his people were fishing. They would be lying across their rough canoes, faces in the cool water and fishing spears immersed ready to strike, brown smooth bodies glistening in the summer sunlight, while in the boats the women and children would fish with lines, squatting patiently hour after hour until they had caught enough to cook over their tiny fires laid on sand and, in turn, raised on wet seaweed on the boat bottoms. And at the thought of the touch of the sea on his feet and the sea wind on his temples Dgeralli felt his eyes sting and his thighs quiver with the urge to run and keep running until he had joined his fellows; to replace the strange unhappy years away from them with the sounds and scents and ways of this, his lost and long regretted homeland. For such had always been the white man's world to him – strangeness – and he had hated the white masters while suffering them for the sake of the only creature to make their way of life bearable: Inar.

But it was almost two years since he had seen Inar and, perhaps because their marriage belonged to the world of the white man, he knew he would never see her again, wife though he regarded her. At first, patiently as always, he had searched for her as far as the lands where her people roamed but nowhere had he even heard her name. She had not passed by. So he had come back to work for the Murchison masters, for the Murchisons hated the white master O'Shea and he would work only for the Murchisons if he must work for anyone, clinging to one final hope. Inar had disappeared before, to return to Erins Pride when the white master O'Shea was due to appear. So he would wait. But the Murchison men drove him mad with their talk. Inar was not dead. Inar was not with other men – hadn't one or other of the Murchisons looked for her each time they went down to Sydney, and never a breath of her? Inar was with the white master O'Shea. And wherever O'Shea went she would follow; had she not, despite her running off with this man or that, always followed O'Shea? Even if she did come back to the Pride it would not be to take him, Dgeralli, as her love again. Dgeralli had lost his wife.

And so they had hinted and taunted him and given him rum and the rum became a sharper poison to a mind already full of venom and he dared not speak much for fear of his misery flowing over and engulfing him – and them. And as he drank, suspicion against the white master O'Shea oozed to the surface, and all the hate too that had simmered there since that day long ago when he had seen his wife and . . . It pained deep down, twisting his bowels to think of it, and so he tried not to think of it. He drank. But when he drank much he remembered even more sharply and wanted to kill the master O'Shea or at least wound him, hurt him, do him some damage. Great damage. So when the master O'Shea did come he could not even look at him or go near him for the loathing that he felt quivering at his eyes and mouth and hands like blood stored and ready to gush from a wound. And then the white master had gone again. Back to Inar, the men laughed, sniggering behind their hands.

Filled with loneliness and misery and rum he had gone with Wayandi and Maddu the night they planned to rob Erins Pride. A few chickens, perhaps a sack of flour, a box of tea – spite-roused raids fanned by a drunken Murchison bent on neighbourly spite, for Wayandi and Maddu had been flogged many times by O'Shea for stealing. But the other two had made a fine big careless fire to cook the chickens and they had drunk more rum and when they were so drunk with rum and their triumph that they could not think, they had run in frenzy with burning brushes to fire the stacks of wood under the House, and the dry tinder huts, the stables and the bails and everything else that would burn. And everything did burn. Men came rushing to fight with them but they had knocked them down and scurried off into the bush and hid and watched the figures running from hut to hut, listened to the neighing of horses and the agonising bleat of burning animals, heard the screams of children and the cries of women. And watched the night turn to fire that licked and consumed all before it. And when the sun rose they nursed their own burns and peeped at the scarred remains of the Pride and heard and saw men and women riding up the road then away again, a day of smoke and pain and great sorrow it seemed for the white people. And Dgeralli had crouched sick and stupefied with rum yet exultant because he had found a way to hurt the master O'Shea. He had been afraid to kill the master O'Shea but he had done the next best thing – he had killed his home. Near him Wayandi and Maddu still drank and fought over scraps of clothing and food and a sandalwood box full of money they had stolen from the House. Then they began to argue, then to fight each other and Maddu lay with his throat cut and Wayandi rushed into the bush dripping blood from a deep wound. And Dgeralli was glad to be rid of them both. After two days of hiding, with Maddu congealing beside him, he bound his burned and stinging leg with a scrap of dirty rag. With a spear, a cloth about his middle, a throwing stick to serve as a knife he set off towards the gloomy forests of stringy bark that fell from the coast range to the sea. Engulfed by them he would be lost to the white man. Above all, he would be lost to the master O'Shea. He would be safe. He was as sure of that as he was sure of a prayer or his own name. He would find his tribe. And so find safety.

His hand jerked. With a squirm of his sinuous body he caught the bird and killed it. He squatted and held his fire stick with its tiny gouged hole firmly between his toes and inserted a second stick vertically in that hole. Then he twirled the second stick between his hands. Faster, then faster still twirled the tiny stick and the palms of his hands, still soft, tingled with a fine exquisite hurt. But he went even faster, loving the pain of it. Fine dust from the cup fluttered about his eyes. The hole grew larger and the stick twirled faster . . . faster . . . until at last there was smoke. Then a spark. More sparks. He brushed tinder of grass and teased bark across the beginning of the flame and sprang to his feet and swung the tinder around in the air as fast as he could twirl himself. He had made fire. He laughed aloud in the exultation of creation and squatted contentedly to build up his fire and cook his food. And he decided, with a deep satisfaction, that when he had eaten he would send a smoke signal far up into the clear sky . . .

From high on the tortured convulsion of rock that was the Pigeon House Mountain Brick O'Shea swung his concentrated gaze north over the tangled country to the barren tableland bounded by the white line of sand that was the beach within Jervis Bay. Thirty miles as the crow flies, and nothing on the sea but a speck of a vessel. Then his eyes swung slowly south over the inland ocean of deep green woodland, wild and dim and seemingly impenetrable that stretched for so many miles into distance. To most men it was impassable but he could traverse it by day or night with little trouble. Long ago, Blacks had shown him how to exist on gum, and the tops of young plants, where to find the water vine and the varied native fruits. And wild berries were everywhere. The Blacks had taught him other things too.

Over the years, on this wealth of native lore, he had learned to travel his land with something akin to comfort.

His body stiffened. Far below him was a wisp of white. It was so fine, so ethereal as to seem almost a part of the haze, a dream thread conjured up by his weariness and his half-closed eyes. But he decided to believe in it, to accept it exactly as it was. Smoke. Smoke from the fire of a wandering bushman, a tribe of Blacks. Or the smoke signal of a lone native searching for his fellows – Dgeralli. Mentally he could see the Black, deep in that mass of foliage, holding high a rolled sheet of bark stuffed with burning bark and dry leaves. Dgeralli . . .

He rested his strained eyes. Two weeks – or was it three – since he had left Sydney, for time had become a succession of sunsets and stolid tramping and persistent questioning; the careful sifting of truth from the scared lies of natives, of the mute testimony of a stolen sandalwood box, and then the planning of his journey when he knew, finally, the one he was seeking. Maddu and Wayandi had both been found dead in the bush; now he must hunt Dgeralli, Inar's husband.

Inar and Dgeralli . . . They were there linked in his mind as they had been linked, he admitted now, since that time with the girl beside the creek where it swished into a soft little pool curling and frothing before it flowed on, at ease once more. Inar had followed him there, as she followed him everywhere, a lush dark scent and sense at his heels. He had even married her off to Dgeralli and sent them away, but still she came back tantalising and teasing. The blinding overpowering urge that rushed them together there in the still afternoon against the background of curdling water had been satisfied and spent. Well spent. He had left her lying with her savage hair spread around her and come up through the trees to sense eyes on him. On them both.

Dgeralli . . . The native had stood quite still, merging with the dusky trees and the shadows that were lengthening into some hazard that seemed to him, quite suddenly, chill and ominous. He did not take gladly to being silently threatened. They had stared at each other but had not spoken, for there was nothing to say. He had not looked back at Inar, the half-breed who had been his childhood playmate. He loathed Inar. A half-breed's a half-breed, hadn't he always insisted it? He loathed Dgeralli. But more sharply, more terribly, he loathed himself for he could not understand what he had just done. Or why. It had not been simply an act of fornication. Something . . . primitive . . . had gained mastery. Mastery over himself. Sorcery? He knew there were strange intangible forces in the native lore and he had always resisted such enchantments, had revolted against all superstition no matter its source that might block the independent will by which he lived.

But all that was long ago, a flimsy cord knotted into his memory. Now his pursuit was clear and uncomplicated, his thought and energy and action concentrated upon avenging his home. Dgeralli would seek his tribe, he was certain of that. And due west of the ridge of the Pigeon House Range he found his first clue. A 'cornstalk' had given a native with a bad leg burn a meal. But the scoundrel had been more active than appeared possible for next morning the kitchen was ransacked and the Black missing. Paddocking his horse Brick made his way on foot. Difficult going now, but he took little rest. He could not rest. Dgeralli had destroyed life of value to him. Dgeralli had destroyed the Pride, the home he and Moll had shaped by their sweat and cunning and abiding love of their land. Both had given it shape and substance but it was his mother, that shadowy creature of his babyhood who had given it its heart. Moll swore it. Moll had instilled it into him. Maddy, his mother, had planned from its beginning to give her son the Pride. So, warned Moll, no matter how he built it up again he could not make it complete. Not quite. There would always be something missing.

Its beginning . . . But what exactly was its beginning? All he knew was what Moll had told him and even that he had not known until the death of the Pride's former owner, Tal Bellamy. He had been about fifteen when, Tal but an hour in his grave, Moll had coolly, almost brutally, made him aware that she was not his mother. A woman named Maddy, long dead but never forgotten by her friend Moll Noakes, had given him birth. These facts had scarcely ruffled his serenity, for Moll had catered to his needs for as long as he could remember. He needed no other. But Moll went on to speak of other things that were significant, indeed important. His father had been one Shawn O'Shea, and of course he knew of the O'Sheas. Everyone knew of the O'Sheas. And Moll could swear till her death (and beyond if she had anything to do with it) to his legitimacy. So, with the fabulous Shawn, for whom Moll seemed to have precious little time, began his questions.

A puling brat astride Moll's hip, his child-mother under Moll's protection, they had gone out with elderly Tal Bellamy to his virgin acres granted him after years over an inland irongang, one of the first ticket-o'-leavers to obtain a grant in the county. They were, so far as they knew, the first white women to sight Argyle and had battled the land, the hard-drinking Tal and twenty odd of the most mutinous convicts ever to growl at the lash of Moll's tongue – but laugh at it too. Tal had found limestone and good brick clay on his land, started a kiln and set his men to making bricks for his house, the first brick house in the County of Argyle. He had put up a shearing shed and pens for his shearers and had the first paddocks marked out and cleared while Maddy moved between her cooking pots and her trunk of moulding books that for months served as their only table.

Books . . . there was the link. His one tangible link with this Maddy who had borne him. Somewhere in his memory there lingered a soft voice and a gentle hand upon him but this was as vague and insubstantial as a dream. She had written her name in some of the books, in others quotations, favourite little phrases, all redolent of that Ireland already woven into his life and mind, all in a hand that anywhere, in any walk of life, would be distinctive. Through her handwriting he had amused himself by conjuring up a personality – warm, intense yet gentle. Reckless too. Yes, she must have been that. She wrote backhand, with a dramatic quirk to letters, particularly the M and R. And the S. Maddy O'Shea. He liked the name. But why, he asked Moll, the lies and the long secrecy? No lies. But secrecy . . . yes. Because of reasons important to women, reasons he could scarcely understand at fifteen. For one thing, the old days had been bad days, particularly for women such as themselves – and their offspring. Maddy had feared for herself, more so for her child. Bellamy, a spiteful man, unpredictable at best, often violent, had been vindictive towards her, even more than towards others, not only because she was Irish born but because of other traits . . . Her pride. Her spirit. Her child was safer with another. Both she and Moll knew it. And so, to the little world that was suddenly their own, the child was Moll's.

Brick shrugged such explanations aside as the imaginative fears of women. In any case, what did it matter? He had survived, he had grown, to lie under the trees staring at Maddy's strangely written words, never knowing, then, they were written by his mother, or simply brooding or dreaming, turning the pages of her absorbing books. He had done his man's work of shepherding and ring-barking with a volume stuffed up his shirt. And many a sodden tome he rescued as it washed from his belt as he waded swollen streams when he took the teams to Sydney. He ached to ask about many things in those books but Moll was a busy ignoramus, and as for Bellamy . . . he never even spoke with Tal Bellamy if he could help it. Despising him, he ignored him. He had learned to read and write and speak connected English from the fly-spattered pages but the most he learned he learned from life. He learned cunning to hide in a hastily scratched hole wincing at the screams from the 'flogging tree' gloated over by the drunken Bellamy. He learned strength to stand the floggings he couldn't escape. And he learned his own failings, even more bitterly the vulnerability of his man's body that was a challenge and a danger. He learned the love of the Pride and all this virgin land, as he learned distrust of its overlords who, so far as he was concerned, were a flash of scarlet and buff, questions and orders. Overlords forever hunting.

But they would never hunt him, Brick O'Shea. He would take care. He would hug to himself his flaring spirit and profit by the weaknesses of his fellow men. And women. He would not stand dominance by man or woman. Particularly woman. He would harness the failing of others to nourish and support his desires. All this he swore as he nursed a back laced by the 'cat' and nourished his pride, his immense invulnerable pride smarting from the added lash of Tal Bellamy's tongue. He would crouch, safe in the bush, staring through the brittle lacy fronds at the lovely sweeping acres before him. Some day all would be different. Someday, somehow, he would make all this his own. He had already named it Erins Pride. His own.

Then Tal Bellamy was no more. Brick carried the pile of bottles from under the man's bed and buried them deep in the creek. No doubt they were there still. Moll had been inexorable; Talbot Bellamy had been a vile man and fit only to die unlamented and now the place could forget for all time its polluted birth. What if she had fired Tal's temper with brandy and his ailing mind and heart with rum . . . 'Let him take who has the power and let him keep who can.' It was enough too for Brick. He was a man now, a man to accept his parentage, avenge it too if need be. And Moll had one more thing of importance to impart. His father had left a piece of land somewhere along the north coast, the deeds in the keeping of an innkeeper at Newcastle; if he wanted his rightful heritage, he'd best seek it out, and quickly. They must not lose the Pride. Ah, but he would have paid twice, thrice, ten times what the sale of that coastal land brought to get the Pride, even run-down and shunned as the place had become. But in his own way, his unique and devious way, the Pride was his.

They annexed the wasteland adjoining the grant. They rid themselves of what assigned men remained from Bellamy's day and replaced them with fresh. They burned the 'cat' and used their fists, or a brick, in place of it – a man had a chance to dodge stones. And the lame ducks always got a start. So Brick's odd name clung to him until he knew no other. Here at last was his land and it must learn to accept him if not willingly then by force. He would reshape the land and build it into a world. His world. And suddenly, all things were possible. Intoxicated, he began to look beyond his horizons. He would go on building, but a world he could understand, for he could not understand this one; the great contradictory world that lay outside his own boundaries. His mother despised as an Irish convict girl, his father wilfully shot, one grandfather hanged, another done to death. Why? Sedition, rebellion, escaping and defying justice, he had been told. Sedition against whom? Against what? Shame surrounded his forebears . . . he had been told that too. But he, Brick O'Shea, understood no shame. He, Brick O'Shea, was no convict. He, Brick O'Shea, was a free man, free and able to pit himself against laws that were terrible and unjust. What had English law, penal law, to do with him? Distrust grew to hate. Hate to an iron resolve. He would fight these overlords and he would fight them with weapons of his own devising, devious secret weapons they would not recognise or know how to overcome. Their law would never touch him. Never. He would be too strong for them. One day he stood and looked about him; at Moll's handiwork, his own, at the small compact world they had built together and knew it was time he knew the world outside. Moll stood firmly on the home ground. Brick O'Shea went a-roving.

He learned from all he met and he met many: a broken-down schoolmaster bestowed a varied but surprisingly thorough education on finding his petty gambling debts settled. A disgraced wizard of finance taught him about money. Another built up his body with boxing lessons. He learned the use of firearms from a former duellist, among others. He learned a good deal of law and what passed for politics. He learned mainly from trial and error, thrusting a finger in all pies, not hesitating to manipulate the human flotsam and jetsam that stumbled within his orbit. He fought insults and insinuations by cracking skulls and flinging rum – regretting the rum – in the faces of foppish lieutenants and gentlemen settlers alike. He learned to stifle feeling where it was dangerous to feel, killing softness and sentimentality, never knowing love other than the casual though wary affection he felt for Moll. And wanting no more. Passion

190

of course was undeniable, a real thing, but it was, after all, a thing of moods, and so he went to those designed by nature and the rules of Society to cater for such needs, for with them a man was safe – no emotion, no ties, no loyalties. One took and one discarded. In place of love he put the pursuit of money and the possession of the Pride and the fulfilment of his large and growing ambitions, both for himself and . . . perhaps one day, in circumstances that suited him, his son. Another O'Shea. But this time an O'Shea too important even to touch, much less despoil. Meanwhile he sneered at claims made upon him on the score of offspring – as if he would not know his own son. As for women . . .

He had been tired of fools when he first saw Barbara Merrill and, opportunist as he had learned to be, proceeded to exploit. Now? Coolly and ruthlessly he blocked all consideration of Barbara. Inar? It had taken a surprisingly heavy pile of coin to get at anything like the truth of the gutting of the Hulk. An Indian was the cause of it all. No, never been seen around the Hulk before. Her name? Did Indians . . . niggers . . . have names? Finally, he'd stood beside his man Mick Bannon, staring down at Inar, still bleeding, dying surely and raving mad, and recognised the Duchess's handiwork. A crone held out a withered hand for money. As he pacified her his first horror at the sight of the woman tossing on the broken-down cot turned to a relief so intense it left him weak. Inar was at last subdued. Never again that lush dark scent, that sense of her always at his heels. More gold and she was placed secretly with a derelict family out on the sand-hills, alive, but in a remote half-world of her own. As for the Duchess . . . He'd finally dragged her from hiding, snivelling and blustering, scared of answering questions or asking them. She remembered nothing . . . could she be blamed for what she did when she was lushy? She would sign the pledge, she would do anything he wanted if only he'd rebuild the Hulk and set her up again. He had little doubt she was feigning ignorance. He might have told her the girl was dead and tightened the hangman's rope about her neck. He might have done many things. Instead he sent her back to what was left of her beloved Hulk with Inar a silence between them, a weapon at her head forever.

Raunie . . . Ah, Raunie was passion itself. Even in rags she was the shine and the glitter, the depth and the power of it. She was feeling and odour and depth and breath of all that was female. And because she was this he feared her as he had never feared a woman. Raunie was . . . He sweated, but not only from the high summer day. In remembering Raunie, in dwelling upon her too long, and too deeply, there could be the end of what peace lay within him. He had learned bitterly and terribly to keep his guard over himself, against beast, against man, against woman, and to confront life with the inborn instinctive caution of the wild animal. So, he would not swerve from his chosen path. Not even for Raunie. But there was still something of her he could have with safety – her son. Here in the solitude, along with the natural world about him, he could admit it, bring it out into the blazing light of day. The boy Jamie would permit him to possess Raunie without her controlling him. He could enjoy her without loss to himself. Yes . . . there was Jamie Lorne.

He got to his feet. Erect, feet planted firmly apart, he stared down at the vast sea of trees and a sense of power born of his physical elevation and imagination, and assurance in this world he knew, enveloped him until his head spun. He let the mood take hold and waft him where it would. He was only really at ease when alone like this. With others, no matter how many or how few he always knew a nagging sense of pressure. And so he resisted pressure, set himself to dissemble it and fight it, to overcome then destroy it in the only way he knew, by going out and confronting it. Why was this so? He did not know. He shook his head clear. You made up your mind what you wanted for yourself and those you considered the important of this earth and let nothing halt you. Nothing. So he must use others, despoil others as they would despoil him if they could. The weak, the foolish, the useless and the vain, all those unfit to bargain with, must be submerged, used and manoeuvred to suit his ends. None, from the highest born of a Merrill to an aborigine named

Dgeralli would stop him. He stared at the tendril of fine, almost illusory smoke for a long time, turned his back on the sun and descended into the jungle.

A few miles from the settlement of Moruya there is a wide flat ledge of rock that juts over the river slinking far below. The natives call it the Nogoroo – the Nose. Like the Pigeon House it is a landmark. Brick tramped towards it steadily and silently, keeping his direction by the stars – the native River of the Sky. To the east was a faint but strengthening yellow light. The moon would be rising over the rim of the sea. In another hour or so it would be hanging above, penetrating and cleansing these black motionless woods. For days he had shadowed Dgeralli, losing him for a time then locating him again. Patiently, tediously, he had gathered scraps of information from Blacks with whom he had made friends at Bateman's Bay. On a beach farther south where a tribe clambered about the rotting carcass of a washed-up whale, he had learned more. Now it was night and he would always find Dgeralli after sundown. Night is the aborigine's weakness. Dgeralli's fear of night was awful and all-powerful so he would not travel by night. To ward off evil spirits he would make a small fire long before the set of sun and keep it burning until the sun rose. And he would not move far from it without a firestick, for the night was as much to be dreaded as thunder and lightning and the beautiful but awesome drop of a shooting star. The moon glow on the horizon became brighter, then brighter still as Brick climbed the hill behind the river. But he was in no hurry or need now for the glare of the moon, because down on the bank was a faint but quite unmistakable glow . . .

Dgeralli sat up with a jerk then crouched back against the rock, staring directly before him. He had not been asleep. Fear did not let him sleep at night. Not soundly. It was only a doze from which he stirred now and then to feed his fire and reassure himself with its light and warmth. But now fear wrapped him about and held him until he crouched shaking, not daring to move. He had been waiting, longing for the moon. The moon was his friend. The moon exuded light and friendship. But there was a long time of darkness yet before the moon would blaze into his face. He slithered back hard against the bank. He could not move quickly because of his leg. It pained. By day he could move but slowly and at night curl into tree trunks, under bushes, into caves, tired, nay exhausted, anywhere at all to crouch from the spirit-haunted darkness. And he was still far from his tribe. He had sent many fire signals into the sky and walked many miles, so many he had lost the thread and sense of them, but he was far, far from his tribe . . .

He stared about him, big-eyed and terrified. A sound had disturbed him, a soft and alien noise. He slithered close to the fire but he could see nothing outside the ring of pink mist and he knew deeper, more poignant fear of what he could not see. The unknown was out there. His head moved from side to side and his eyes rolled. He heard the crack of a twig. Then he saw a shape. It was indeterminate, a dark edgeless thing of a shape. He groped for his spear. The feel of it gave him courage. He threw his only weapon. It disappeared with a harmless clang. And the thing was still there. He cried out in his terror, harsh and formless sounds. He had only one defence left, his strength. He sprang.

Brick and Dgeralli locked together, struggling, Dgeralli's legs twisting and squirming, his long bony hands clawing at the other's neck, as a savage. But he felt a stronger, more savage hand tighten about his throat. A second hand gripped his throat and his breath strangled. He fought for breath but the hands pressed tighter. Then the thumbs came down . . .

Dgeralli's eyes swelled and distended and stared up unblinking into the still face of the man bending over him. With every ounce of his strength Dgeralli fought back. He was very strong. He would have subdued any other man. But the white master was stronger. He had forgotten it. The rum had made him forget it. His senses blurred as he saw the blackness below and sensed the river rising towards him. He knew then that he was dying. He ached to cry out his misery yet could not. A curve of silver flashed by. Darkness . . . the shock of cold . . . a shivering cold . . . silken smothering drowning water . . . a roaring in his ears . . . a roar . . . roar . . .

Long after the water was still, Brick O'Shea crouched above the black river. It was done. He was alone, as he needed to be alone. There was nothing around him, nothing human to know the thoughts struggling at the back of his mind, clouded thoughts springing from an emotion that had always been little more than a taste, a vague flavour. The closest definition would be . . . perhaps . . . fear? But no need any longer for fear. Both were gone – Inar with her bastard lure, the Black who had watched them together. He was free of them both. He was safe. For in annihilating this man stirring about somewhere in the black water below he had, in some curious manner, annihilated the woman – it was as if she too were dead. He had snapped the thread that had bound them over the years. He had severed a cord. Yet . . . in some odd way he regretted his action. A curious sadness enveloped him and his limbs began to shake. His ears hummed. He breathed in great gasps. His hands gripped the rock behind him and he fell against it, leaning, exhausted.

Had he severed a cord? Or had he tied frayed ends together . . .

Chapter Nine

BRICK O'SHEA's stables and foundling home – school as he insisted it be called – on the waterfront had been convict-built in Governor Macquarie's time. The place had changed hands many times before Brick pounced on it, planning to acquire the dilapidated building adjoining and renovate it as living quarters. For the present however, the small army of urchins had to be squeezed into two inadequate floors, for the stable section, above which Brick sometimes roomed, housed his yearlings bred on his Maneroo lands and made up for market as only he knew how. Though other breeders were following suit there was no lessening in the demand for O'Shea's chargers – in India they brought as much as one hundred and fifty pounds apiece.

The school was in the eastern wing, its overflow taking lessons in the open or in part of the next building, over whose purchase price its owner haggled, striking a shrewd bargain in leasing, patched as it was against the weather as best as could be done. To teach the girls and the smallest boys was one Emmaline Banner, deserted bride of a cardsharp. She did her best to translate Mr O'Shea's somewhat startling orders into practical lessons which her ignorant charges might assimilate. As for the older boys, they struggled under male masters who came and went with monotonous regularity. Mr Milbank for instance. Brick had come upon the man sweating his class one hot morning over the verse:

> I thank the goodness and the grace
> That on my birth have smiled
> And made me in these Christian days,
> A happy English child.

'Few, if any, have smiled on their birth, Milbank. Furthermore, they are not English children.'

Mr Milbank's jaw dropped. 'Not English?'

'Oh, Cockney if you must. Cockney, a dribble of Scot, and more than a dash of the Irish, is forming the Australian race. A new race. As for this rubbish . . .' He ripped a book and flung the pieces in the man's startled face. 'What use are Latin roots to lads who must wrest a living from soil not yet turned by human hands?'

'But – but it is right and proper that the culture of the most advanced and civilised areas of the United Kingdom should be carried to its more savage regions –'

'I want nothing carried to this region but commonsense.' Brick shook another book an inch from the unfortunate man's perspiring nose. 'Is this your idea of knowledge? . . . "beaver hats . . . gunpowder . . . snuff . . . the places of origin of nutmegs . . ." What do they want with stuff of that kidney? These boys are learning to build a life. A new life. They must learn new things.'

'New things?' The teacher's eyes widened. 'But what new things?'

'Wriggle yourself into a pair of riding breeches and I'll show you, you fool.'

Mr Milbank resigned. And so it went on, the boys hanging on the angry episodes hoping for a fight or, even better, a half-holiday. Or wriggling in their seats wondering what they'd get for supper; the certainty of a meal was too recent a wonder to be lightly accepted. Came an impoverished gentleman who declaimed in impassioned accents his teachings in hedge-schools through Ireland as Brick scrawled angry lines through his carefully prepared curriculum:

'Navigation . . . fluxions . . . classics . . . meditations of the Grecians . . . a small taste of Hebrew based upon the Masoretic text . . . Can't I find just one of you with sense? Masoretic text! We have no time to waste on absurdities. I don't expect a master to be a walking oracle but I do expect him to be a useful human being. Teach them to read and write – then ask me what they are to read. Geography – yes, agriculture – yes. But who's to teach them hygiene? Doc Peter hasn't the time or the patience. Carpentry? The trades?'

One day Hugh Whaley sauntered in, street boys at his heels, with what was left of a battered Irish head-piece clinging to incredibly puckish curls, his old-fashioned clothes stained and faded, and a battered box held together by scraps of rope whose contents, as long as anyone knew him, remained a mystery. He drew a mutton bone, a well-padded and cleanly wrapped mutton bone, from one of his deep pockets and nibbled away at it unruffled while Brick swooped upon him as a thirsty soul pounces on water found in a suspicious but still capacious well – his experience as one of the pioneers of the Irish National Schools was invaluable.

Whaley was not young, his face was grizzled with an old Gaelic wisdom beneath his incredible hair, but he displayed a logical well-balanced mind that was not at all Gaelic, coupled with spontaneous affection for children. He appeared to have at least a smattering of knowledge of every subject under the sun but he parried personal questions with a string of irrelevant anecdotes, amusing ones at that. Pretty women – all women for that matter – Hugh Whaley could not leave alone, and Emmaline Banner lived in a state of excitement and not a little of wonderment as she set herself to protect her chastity. Barbara liked him enough to let him linger, a touch of amusement in his eyes, while she pondered over Tom Paine's *Rights of Man*, Godwin's philosophy, the works of Brougham. She was even encouraged sometimes to talk over her reading with him. Hugh Whaley it was who introduced her to Southey and Coleridge. And Hugh Whaley it was, his narrowed eyes staring out over the glittering water, who answered in his soft educated voice her wondering questions: 'You ask of Ireland, Miss Merrill . . . It is true there is peace, but it is no more than the quiet of deep weariness. A despair and a loathing grip the once merry man and his household. I could not stand the sadness longer . . .'

Despite the way he thrashed them, his charges loved him. It was not the birch a boy – or a man – resented, he would say, it was injustice. Most of his pupils were pinch-faced Irish bratlings picked up from the streets, snatched from swamp huts and bawdy houses and pubs. Tall and slight and thin,

198

they were quick to quarrel but equally quick to learn, laughing at icy winds with a joke on their lips. They came in a steady stream from Mrs Chisholm, from harassed clerics, from the watch-house, from Doctor Peter Mahafy. But even so they constituted but a fraction of the thousands of abandoned and illegitimate children in Sydney. Almost everyone shied from these waifs: Protestant quarters cluck-clucked of popery while the Roman Catholic hierarchy sulked at Brick's refusal to allow priests at his flock, with the exception of course of Father Hamill, whom O'Shea, the Devil, or Her Majesty's Forces could never keep away from anything. So Brick O'Shea maintained his school with only occasional donations from wealthy philanthropists and business associates intent on a little buttering-up, or sometimes a bazaar or benefit arranged by the committee of which Barbara was the one consistently active member – a paper committee, a sop to philanthropic fashion. A list of names, no more.

Babes and toddlers were housed at the crèche at Millers Point, in the old cottage known as Kate's, the overflow in the rundown places each side, all tended by tough but healthy slum nurses. Old enough to hold a slate-pencil they were wedged in at the school. Both places were overcrowded, noisy and hilarious, blots, most citizens agreed, on respectable society. The girls were taught to sew and mend and cook, how to care for babies, the rudiments of cleanliness, to read and write (but not too cleverly) and how to manage money even though they might never acquire any of their own. At nine or ten the boys were taken on the ever-shifting caravan of drays and wagons to commence life on O'Shea's stations or those of his friends and protégés, or the farm schools he was building as quickly as the barques landed tradesmen or farmers to erect and teach. To offset the toil he demanded, there was food in abundance, help and advice. There was a deal of confusion, many mistakes, but there were results; less sickness and brawling, animal good spirits and enthusiasm, and a rough, self-conscious, but always insistent loyalty. There was a semblance of security, most certainly a future. Fronting all this Brick continued on the move, making plans, explaining and complaining, combing new chums to find assistants, riding here and there, spending money as fast as he made it. At times, faster. A chill trafficker in human bodies and souls, the scoffers and his enemies called him. He had many names: a nabob. A petty monarch. A Nero.

All this Barbara followed through his letters, acting only on his comments and commands. He would write to her from beside the campfire of a shepherd, or a valley stream, and send the letters down by woolclip, a lone wagoner, an ensign galloping to a city assignation. It was another life, this strenuous responsible world she entered two or three days a week, more frequently if her mother were not demanding of her presence. At her sometimes tired protest Brick laughed, over-rode her every excuse, and loaded her with so many extra duties she found herself too busy to argue. His dependency upon her was constant and so deep she knew he didn't realise the extent of it. If she failed to appear on a promised morning a hired carriage would arrive to wait until it pleased her to appear for there was always some new and urgent task; to accompany him to see a batch of new babies, to choose nurses to replace those who absconded, to collect clothing or beg donations, to confer with Banner or Hugh or Margret Magouran, the matron. Or hasten to an urgent call from Doc Peter for help in his clinic or on his rounds. Viola Parker or Lucy Vine, on the pretext of taking a music lesson or dressmaker's fitting, seldom joined her now – in any case they would have held up their hands in horror at Doc Peter's clinic – but she mourned them not at all for they were silly romantics brushed by the glamour of the O'Shea name and her own defiance. They were spurred by the adventure of it while she was driven by . . . what? By all the rigid standards of her upbringing this underworld habited by a pariah caste and ruled by O'Shea was something to shake one's head over and hurriedly put aside. Instead, it was engulfing her and she could do nothing to block its rising tide.

The bedroom shared unwillingly by Banner and the matron looked south, its doors invariably open to cover the stairs and dormitories. Old Paddy tended the furnaces and

stoves and helped the girls wait on table. Hugh dossed in
the other wing with the hands. From her pigeonhole of a
downstairs office Barbara answered letters, wrote her lists
and read snatches of the books someone was always thrusting
into her hands, planned the lessons and, to the best of her
ability, solved the children's problems. Assistant teachers
came and went and she substituted where necessary, having
determinedly overcome her early sense of inadequacy before
so many pairs of juvenile eyes – now the children were
respectful of her if not always awed. Or, in a moment of
respite stared out at the sunlit stable yard touching the
Harbour, breathing in the tang of hay and listening to the
neighing of beasts; how could she blame the boys for peeping
at the men leading the horses across the courtyard, hoofs
prancing and jingling on the stone, these beasts that con-
tributed so much to their support. Oddly, she loved this
strange, this so different world. It frightened her sometimes
how much she had come to love it, without reason or sense or
clear understanding. The love and need of it came from deep
within her, but on such evenings, contrariwise, she would go
home to the Lodge with a headache. She suffered from
headaches lately, she who had never known an ache or pain
in her life. It was queer. But no stranger than the many
things she strove to understand yet could not. She would
decide to ask Doc Peter to prescribe powders – then hesitate.
She was always hesitant with Doctor Peter Mahafy, even a
little afraid of him. She found a flask of eau-de-cologne,
borrowed her mother's smelling-salts and did her best to
ignore her aching head.

Even so, her hours in the doctor's poor little clinic and on
his rounds if depressing were sharply memorable. Intense,
bluntly honest, it was impossible to imagine Doctor Peter
Mahafy taking orders even from a Brick O'Shea. But actually,
if to the tune of criticism and even abuse, he carried out
O'Shea's instructions to the letter. Brick had financed the
clinic in his neglected, falling-down house in return for the
man's skills, and the arrangement, loose though it was,
appeared to work. He gathered as many admirers as he

gathered enemies for, unorthodox as were his methods, they did get his patients on their feet – from sheer terror, Hugh always said. The doctor's first act on entering a sickroom was to fling open the window, or if jammed, smash it with his stick. 'Let in the air, woman. The *air*!' Then leave a few shillings for a new pane if they must have it. As for his clinic . . . often too sick at heart to talk, Barbara obeyed his brusque concise orders like some kind of puppet. The pale-faced girls, the mothers with their whimpering children, the coughs, the careless lassitude, more than anything the dull-eyed result of hunger, left her trembling with surprise and disgust. The doctor would send her to feed them broth before he would examine them. 'The women can't think clearly to answer my questions if they're starving.' And holding the basin while a girl no more than fifteen, with something of Georgina's fair prettiness about her, haemorrhaged, and Doc Peter mumbled over the lost baby: 'No matter what I say she'll fret; her fine mistress turned her out. You can't face hurt like this with reason. Do what you can for the child.' And Barbara felt a swift and searing anger against she knew not what as she held the girl close in her arms and let her sob her heart out.

In his dingy parlour again he would unscrew a flask and drink long, and she would feel the incredible desire to drink the stuff too. She had never tasted brandy but there must be some merit in it – Doc Peter appeared to drink it by the gallon. He caught her glance, slopped some into none-too-clean a cup and pushed it across.

'Drink it. And if you mean to be so squeamish all the time don't come.'

'It's not the . . . girl exactly. I have a megrim. I suffer them a lot of late.'

'Women!' He snorted. 'Fools, the lot of you. Always lacing yourselves. Let in the air, girl. Let in the *air*!'

Baffled and miserable, she sipped the brandy. And though she loathed the fiery taste of it, finished it. She had always sensed he did not like her and now, almost fiercely, wondered why. It mattered. Because she was weak? Or because she was, simply, Barbara Merrill? She must make an effort to reach him.

'You come from Dublin, I understand?'

'I have that honour – doubtful though I personally consider it to be.'

'But I have heard it is an elegant city. Such balls and fine houses and dinners, quite as fine as any in London.'

He poured brandy into his cup, spattering it. 'Indeed? I knew nothing of that, Miss Merrill. Most of my time there was spent in the Liberties.'

'Oh?' She murmured politely. 'And what are the Liberties?'

'A collection of beggars, fevers and dirt so vile that to describe them minutely would not only prolong your megrim but cause you to heave your breakfast egg down the front of that fine lace collar. And that would be a pity. Eggs are hard to come by here, even for your kind of household at times I understand.' He was bitter. 'Such a neat gown, untouched I'm sure by filth of any kind.'

She recoiled. Ridiculously she wanted to cry. She bit her lip but met his eyes without flinching. 'I have a strong stomach, Doctor Mahafy.'

'Have you now?' He finished his drink at a gulp, and seemed to unbend a little. 'Oh, forget the Liberties. Neither of us can change them. I graduated to the Foundling Hospital and . . . well . . . spoke out of turn.'

'It seems to be a habit of yours,' she retorted, and was instantly sorry for her sharpness. He was a good doctor. And his shirt was so frayed she wondered how it hung together. Moreover, she knew he would not let that girl in there leave empty-handed. 'To be outspoken is not a crime, surely.'

'Enough of a crime for the Hospital Committee to boot me to the colonies. One should not protest, it seems, when children are kept like animals.' He slammed down the flask. 'Consider yourself free to be off to your parlour teas. I can manage for the rest of the day.'

'I have no intention of leaving.'

He shrugged. 'As you please. Far be it from me to foil Good Works. In your world, as I understand it, philanthropy is considered excellent for the soul and the more sordid the task the greater the celestial rewards. Well, someone must hold the basin and who does so matters not as long as they hold it steady.' His gaze became intent on her face, uncomfortably so. But his own face, if a little pale above the whiskers, was expressionless. 'Understand one thing, Miss Merrill, I have no time to be at pampering. In any case your kind is pampered enough. But in any walk of life a woman can overdo her martyrdom. Get more rest. And while you're doing so, give thanks you have a soft bed to rest upon.'

But the next morning he sent her some physic. And there were days when a mood, soft and almost tender, took hold of him and he would talk to her without bitterness. And other days when he bubbled with enthusiasm and a crisp humour that set her laughing with him. And he would glance from her bright eyes to the colour in her usually pale cheeks and nod and say: 'Laughter's a stronger tonic than any. Even better than fresh air. Let it out, girl. Let it *out*!'

Making the most of such moods she would question him closely; she wanted to know more of these people, the Irish. Dirty? Oh yes. Shiftless? She supposed so. But so pitifully, childishly lost. And some so strangely, incredibly innocent. They troubled her in their amazing ignorance.

'I find it difficult to talk to them on some matters; they turn aside from my questions. They don't seem able to answer them. They're so . . . innocent, yet they tell me they come from "shielings" of one room all huddled together.'

He nodded briskly. 'A fall from grace is met with great severity. But it is something else too. Years of meagre living and hard work have worn at them, spirit and body, until day's end means tiredness instead of an eagerness for each other. But six months here and O'Shea will be building more and more crèches . . .' And doubtless he was right, for the conversation she overheard one morning in his clinic was even more illuminating.

'But doctor,' came a young male voice, 'the shyness would be upon me.'

'Shyness?' Bang went the familiar brandy flask, or bottle of some kind, and the doctor's voice was nothing if not Gaelic as it boomed in anger. 'The big gangling clod that ye be, acting the sheepish young fool and yeself with a pretty bouncing young bride to be holding and herself wondering what she's done to displease ye. The likes of it I say, with your immigrant ship and all in together never learning the natural way of a man with a maid.' The bottle clinked against cups. 'Here man here, if it's help ye need. A starting point as it were . . .'

The struggle between church interests for the souls of his flock often sent Brick into rages. The Nonconformists at least were clean, he conceded. But praying Tories he called the clerics of the Establishment, fiddlers and fishers the Catholic priests, which was nothing to what he called Father Hamill. For the sly and subtle Father worked in ways that Brick found harder to contend with. What a fiddler and jumper he was – Father Hamill never believed in letting the 'Divil' steal all the merriment. First the 'Irish Washerwoman', then some gentle southern air to woo the exile, and as he played, his sensitive face shining and alight, there'd come with the keening of the fiddle the smell of new-mown hay across the boreen and the larks singing again in the Irish sky and the blackbirds in the whitehorn, and the women would draw their shawls over their heads and hope their tears went unnoticed. Oh, Brick O'Shea knew what he was up against; the good Father fought back in his own way, and he fought all the time. But he and O'Shea talked together often and long and Brick would pour a whiskey – his best – and become confidential. 'I'd prefer to scare the wits out of them with a hell than with a flogging – the threat of Hell seems to have more lasting effects – so give them your blessing and ab- solution and all the rest of it if it keeps them in order. But no superstition. It makes them too stubborn . . .'

But of all who crossed her path Barbara was drawn to the Reverend Simon Westman who sometimes brought a child to Brick, then stayed more for the talk than the meal set before him before departing with one of Margret's boxes of clothing and food for his congregation.

'I would have given up long ago, Mr O'Shea, but for my belief in the latent goodness of men – '

'Goodness?' Brick's tone was dry. 'How can you base your life upon goodness? How can you even define it?'

The Reverend's eyes, kindly, so confident they seemed to hold a smile in them, would linger on Barbara. 'Difficult I agree, for it is not something that is always an act, not something one can always see, a tangible thing one can put one's finger upon and say – this is goodness. It is perhaps more of words than of deeds, a response, a sympathy, an understanding, a thing that prompts the person in great need to look into another face and say trustingly . . . this one does not avoid me or judge me or call me a fool. This one is giving of himself. Perhaps, Mr O'Shea, goodness is simply another word for . . . compassion?'

Yes, there was an offhand intimacy in the relationship of all these men, at surface odds though they were, that was new to Barbara. And she wondered about the ones not yet met with: Rob Witherstone, Moll Noakes, the clever youth Wells who countered every pamphlet of O'Shea's with one of his own, a thorn in O'Shea's side but a thorn hidden beneath many leaves. It seemed one must either hate O'Shea, or love him. No half measures. So here it was, her other world, a world she loved and feared and resented yet could never for a moment ignore.

This morning she was restless as she waited for Brick. He had been back in Sydney two days, telling her little of his trip but that he hoped to have the Pride rebuilt within six months. He'd brought a child down to the school; a woman had died in the Pride fire and it was her son he'd taken under his wing, a boy by the name of Jamie. Doubtless he felt some responsibility for the boy's motherless state, even so he seemed more interested than was necessary. Today he was bringing Jamie to begin lessons, but she was anxious to discuss her own pressing affairs; she could not be at his call like this, day or evening, any hour of the week he demanded it. It was too much. It was now almost two months since Kenneth had literally dumped his wife in the bosom of his family, left them

all to an uncomfortable adjustment and, in a restless indecision as to the Wars, gone his usual way about the theatres
and race-tracks. On his visits to the Lodge he avoided his
father yet seemed even more uncomfortable in the company
of his womenfolk. In his presence Raunie was sweetness
itself, but once he disappeared down the Lodge drive the
wilfulness that was always there in her dealings with the
household asserted itself. She had found her mother-in-law's
little weaknesses and proceeded to use them; when Barbara
caught her taking up wine and forbade it on Doctor Barclay's
orders, Eleanor defended the girl. Georgina, home from
school, was clearly enamoured of her new relative and they
talked and laughed together for hours, adding bows and frills
to Georgina's already over-decorated gowns, Raunie even
being permitted to make over the younger girl's discarded
clothes for herself. She ordered the servants about till quarrels
were commonplace. She even seemed to placate the Major,
for his only answer to complaints was a weary: 'She's your
brother's wife so try and get along with her. It falls to the rest
of us to maintain dignity in this business since your brother
goes about his affairs with such stupidity. As, I might add, do
you. You are in no position to criticise Raunie's lack of
decorum, Barbara. So don't come to me with your women's
quarrels. Leave me to what little peace I have left.'

So the disorder grew. And the expenditure. It was, Barbara
knew, only their connections with Roger Havelock and their
expectations of his legacy that gained them the credit it did.
Sometimes, as she watched her father frowning over piles of
accounts or listened to him pacing his study at night she
ached to join him, to feel at one with him, perhaps to find
with him some emergence from this whole horrible mess;
at least to help him cast off his lethargy, his attitude almost
of passivity to their financial crises. She yearned for their
old closeness. She loved him but he ignored her overtures,
never speaking to her except through necessity. Sometimes
she felt he hated her – as she felt sure she had incurred
Raunie's dislike. For the girl watched her, and constantly.
She even sought her out to ask questions about Brick

O'Shea's movements – why? There were many things about Kenneth's wife she did not understand. Those strange beautiful brooding eyes following her about the Lodge disturbed her more than she cared to admit.

Finally, there was Godfrey. Her father had brought him home to dinner one evening and in his brisk impersonal way that always left her shivering inside had explained that Uncle Roger considered the young man a deserving and proper husband for his great-niece, when the boy was in the position to support a wife. It was essential they please Uncle Roger. In any case marriage must put an end to this nonsense of hers, mould her to ways respectable and discreet. There was to be no snivelling or argument for she would have time in plenty to become properly acquainted with Mr Selwyn – the young man felt it a duty to wait until his father died to marry. In fact, his father insisted on it, an eccentric no doubt but an old man, and the pair of them still young enough to wait. Meanwhile Mr Selwyn had been placed in a government department and introduced into the proper clubs. To certain women, Barbara supposed, Godfrey would not be unattractive, and wondered why he agreed to such a match, for, apart from a scrupulous respect, he showed little affection for her. Meanwhile she clung to the certainty of an old but hearty parent whiling away his declining years by the weeding out of prospective fortune-hunting daughters-in-law. Lulled by her imagery she gave Godfrey tea once a week, listened to his latest pastoral poem, and sympathised with his ailments. She was gentle with him as mute apology for her inability to sit sewing samplers, contrive watercolours and mouth weary nothings over wearier afternoon teas. She had battled all that out long ago, and went on with her life in the only way she could – by compromise. But a precarious, delicately balanced compromise. It was that disharmony, that fragile poise of balance that constantly, wretchedly, terrified her.

The door opened. Brick pushed a small boy towards her and stood waiting, watching them. The child was quite tall but his face was that of a baby. He *was* a baby, and she felt an unexpected tenderness for the delicately chiselled little face beneath a mass of black hair curling about a perfectly shaped head. Enormous liquid dark eyes. Smooth slim golden-brown hands. He moved with a natural grace, so attractive she found herself following his every move, not only because he fascinated her, but out of curiosity; there was something about him that was familiar, as if she had seen him before . . .

'This is Miss Merrill, Jamie,' Brick was explaining. 'I've told you about her, remember?'

The child stood regarding her solemnly until something in his steady, faintly disconcerting gaze propelled her to hurried speech. 'He's younger than I expected.'

'But strong for his age. Smart too, I think. There's a keenness . . . a sharpness . . . I have plans for him.'

'Merrill,' the boy repeated slowly and distinctly. 'Miss Merrill.'

'I've told you a little of what your life is to be here,' Brick went on briskly. 'Rules are few but I insist upon those that exist. Miss Merrill is always here to help you. Now run along to Mrs Magouran.'

The child faced him squarely. 'You come too.' It was a command.

Brick laughed. 'You must learn to get along without me now. And you will – once you're accustomed to the other boys.'

'Oh . . . *them!*' The amused scorn was immense. There was nothing of the babe about him now.

'You must get along with them willingly or they'll set about forcing you. And you'd best wait a few years before you try to cross them in a fight.'

'I'll fight 'em when I want to.' The black head tossed in defiance above the clenched hands and firmly planted legs.

'You already have, as I heard it, in your first hour among them – but came off a bad second. Better double up on your breakfast oatmeal, son. You're a light-weight.'

'I'm not your son,' the child retorted in his solemn distinct way. Man and boy stared long at each other until Brick's face showed an angry flush.

'Who told you that?'

'Boys.'

'Boys don't know everything. Don't listen to them.'

'I listen to Sammy. Sammy's going to be a whaler.'

'Is he, now?'

'I want to be a cedar-cutter. Like Matt. Matt wants to cut trees.'

'Matt will have the muscles for it. You must use your brains.'

'What's "brains"?'

'Brains are what you think with.'

'What's "think"?' The black eyes glittered with humour before he dissolved into bubbling laughter. Brick laughed and ruffled the child's hair indulgently. Jamie said nothing more but his grin showed the edges of fine white teeth as he slipped from under Brick's hand and without even a glance at Barbara was gone, swiftly and sinuously, banging the door behind him. The room seemed strangely quiet.

'Get to know him well. Though you're not likely to find it a quick or easy task. There's a deal of independence there. And defiance . . .' He shuffled the letters on her desk, his thoughts obviously still on the boy. She stirred, unable to hide her impatience. She needed to talk of other urgent matters.

'Brick . . . please listen.'

'Mmmmm?'

'What is to happen when you're away? Here at the school, I mean.'

He looked up sharply. At last she had his complete attention. 'Happen? Why, you're in charge, you know that. Everyone knows it – in charge, that is, of all things affecting the children and their teaching. But I hope you'll be able to manage the crèche as well. Hugh and the others will give you every help. You know the routine, every move, every rule.'

'But you make the decisions, give orders. I only try to carry them out. I can't carry on alone. I can't do it.'

'Can't do it?' he repeated incredulously. Then sharply. 'What do you mean, you can't do it? What's happened to you? If you doubt Hugh –'

'It's nothing to do with Hugh. Or with anyone else. It's just that I have my home, my duties there, my own life to consider.'

'Your life? What life are you talking about? This is your life. Well, isn't it?' As she fumbled for words he grasped her by both arms and shook her. 'Don't you see that the only way I can stay abroad so long is to know I can depend on you to carry out my wishes? To be absolutely certain, when I'm thirteen thousand miles away that you will be here, doing the things we've planned together. To know there's at least one person I can trust . . . Don't you see?'

'I didn't . . . realise – '

'Then it's time you did.' He released her abruptly. 'If anyone should realise the difficulties I face, it's you. My interests and activities are scattered over the length and breadth of this country; so many things to be done and so few to do them.'

'It's not the work,' she said miserably. 'Not really. It's – something else.'

'What then?'

She hesitated. She couldn't find the words to express her perplexity. He turned aside impatiently to open letters, and shuffle through a pile of papers as if suddenly conscious of the liberty he had taken with her. He moved to the light to read, apparently absorbed, which made it even more difficult to answer him; even when she had his attention part of him was always off somewhere, reading or writing or watching or talking. Planning . . . But she must answer him. And now.

'My brother is going to New Zealand.'

'Well . . . he's supposed to be a soldier isn't he?'

'There is his wife. She . . .'

He turned. 'And what has your brother's wife to do with you?'

'It's rather difficult to explain a girl like Raunie.'

The papers in his hand slipped to the floor with a whisper. He stared at her. 'Raunie?'

'It is a strange name, isn't it. I've never heard it before.'

211

'Raunie. There would scarcely be more than one to answer to it. So Raunie married your brother, did she?' He smiled faintly. 'And why not? Why not indeed.'

'You know her?'

'Our paths have crossed,' he said dryly. 'The woman who died in the fire at the Pride was Elizabeth Witherstone. She adored a scapegrace brother by the name of James Lorne whom I brought out some years ago in order to give him a new start – as his sister rather whimsically planned it. But he died at sea and all we collected for our trouble was his widow – Raunie. She didn't stay long at the Pride, I might add. She ran off, leaving – ' He glanced at her quickly. 'But no doubt she's told you all about herself?'

'Very little. She's not much given to confidences.'

'No? She was, as I remember, quite inordinately proud of her connection with the nobility, even if that husband of hers was clinging there by the skin of his teeth.'

'She seems to have confided in Mama, but then Mama magnifies most things. In Raunie's case I think she feels it will excuse . . . traits in her she doesn't like.' She paused. 'I doubt if even Kenneth himself knows much more about Raunie. They married quite suddenly, you see. But my younger sister adores her while Papa, naturally enough I suppose, will not let Mama send her away.'

'And you?'

She frowned. 'I have the feeling she dislikes me.'

'She dislikes all women.'

'You speak of her as if you know her well.'

He laughed. "Probably better than anyone else in this world, man or woman, knows her. Take my advice and leave Raunie well alone while praying she'll leave you in the same solitary state. That's the most you can hope for. Now!' He was sorting the books he had brought, piling them before her open at certain pages – he often did this when pressed for time. 'I'll send you fresh stuff by every ship. And regular letters. You'll know my every move.'

She stared at the books in despair. There was another pile as yet unopened on her desk. And another barque in the

Harbour. More pamphlets, more newspapers, more confusion. It was all too much. She brushed her hand across the
back of her neck. Pain . . . there. Not harsh, not intense . . . but
uncomfortable. And there was still something she must say.
She frowned, striving through the wisp of pain, to remember.
Ah, yes.

'There's Mr Selwyn – Godfrey.'

Books thudded on to the desk. 'Selwyn? Why do you let
that puny poet bother you.'

'It's my duty to consider my future husband's wishes.'

'He'll never be your husband.' He scattered letters. 'You
know that as well as I do. For one thing, how could you live in
England? You'd die in England. You belong in the sun, out
along your sand-hills, here in this school, working with these
children – '

'I shall have children of my own I hope,' she burst out. He
was making her very angry.

'Then if you're wise you won't depend upon Selwyn's
ability to father them,' he sneered.

She felt the hot blood rush to her face, and was angry with
herself for being so vulnerable. And for speaking of Godfrey;
Brick, it seemed, could not leave him alone.

'How, for that matter, could you live anywhere with that
sniffling purveyor of words.'

'Godfrey has other talents.'

'If slipping a toe inside an open door and keeping it there is
one, I agree. Get rid of the fop. Send him packing. You'll do it
sooner or later so why not now?'

'I – '

'In any case, I haven't the time or the stomach to discuss
Selwyn. We must go over the school.'

'Brick – '

'What now?' And he swept everything aside in a fury. In
the silence the murmurs of the children droning their lessons
drifted in. They would soon be out of classes, clamouring at
her, at him. There was never time for the things she wanted
to say, for the balm of a solution found. He moved to the door.
He did not mean to listen. He would not listen. His hand on

the knob, he said abruptly. 'The boy Jamie is important to me. Whatever else must lapse you must take great care of him. Doc Peter and Hugh understand. You can depend on them. I trust you in this as in everything else. You know that, don't you?'

She nodded. She could not speak.

'Then, will you give me your promise to stand by me?'

She swallowed hard. He had expected, demanded, coaxed, but this was the first time he had ever begged of her. Yes, begged, for that was what he was doing. But however he asked, whatever he asked, she knew she could not refuse. She put out her hands to him, then let them fall in a helpless, futile, but dedicated gesture.

'I promise.'

On the morning of May the seventeenth of that year, 1845 – a Saturday – eight officers, fifteen non-commissioned officers, five drummers and one hundred and sixty privates of the 'Nines', a captain of the Royal Engineers, two privates (prisoners) of the Royal Marines and the rest comprising the 96th Regiment – two hundred and one men in all – were drawn up in open column in the Barracks Square and inspected by His Excellency, and the Commander of the Forces accompanied by his Staff. Then, headed by the band playing the 'British Grenadiers', and dogged by most of Sydney, they marched off the ground in Companies to the Commissariat Wharf to board the barque *British Sovereign* bound for Auckland and the Wars. Sydney bade them a spirited adieu then straggled home to forget them, miss them, curse them or hope for them according to their sex and age and station in life. Those who cared neither one way nor the other found the departure an excuse for a holiday and proceeded to get, as usual, drunk.

Raunie collected Eleanor's muff, her shawl and reticule, her little boxes of comfits and lozenges, her tiny bottles of pills and packets of powders, her smelling salts, her crumpled handkerchiefs, a brooch and two trampled posies, all scooped

214

up from the carriage seat and floor, then hurried up the Lodge stairs. Major Merrill was, of course, still about his duties, and so Eleanor, languid on Barbara's arm, had led the procession indoors. A tearful Georgina, home for the occasion, hovered about Ensign Werner. Carriages would soon arrive to spill into the flower-heavy withdrawing-room stiffly gowned women and their subdued husbands to drink tea and nibble at sandwiches and Ada's over-sweet puffed up little pastries. It was a grand and stately display for today all must be subjugated to Eleanor's love of the dramatic. And what better reason for an emotional performance than her adored son's sailing for possible fame and glory. If not fame, most certainly, most undoubtedly, glory.

Raunie moved briskly about Eleanor's dishevelled bedroom, smoothing the bed curtains and counterpane, hanging her clothes in her wardrobe – so many clothes – and in the kitchen they scratched about for the ingredients of a fruit cake. How the gentry clung to their petty, personal economies! She tidied the dressing-table, folded stays, paired shoes and slippers, and tucked from sight wisps of lace and muslin, for the ladies were coming up and there was no one else to spare to right the room. But at last it was tidy and there was nothing further to do for the moment so she removed her bonnet and smoothed her hair. She moved to lean against the window-sill, pleased with the luxury about her, with the Lodge itself, pleased most of all with her new place in its domestic scheme of things. She had played her roles of submissive obedient daughter-in-law and dutiful little wife for the last time. No longer would she be ordered about, or made use of behind her husband's back. Kenneth was gone, and this was the last time she would act the servant in his house. Instead . . . she would bargain.

The day was cold now. People would be drifting home from the little bays all the way to South Head where they had picnicked to watch the *British Sovereign* disappear. Kenneth would soon be on the high seas. And all she felt was relief and a rising excitement at the thought of the crowded rooms downstairs, the important guests, the elegance of her skilfully made-over gown. Her husband was gone, but Regent Lodge was left to her . . . But she must be wary. She must not hasten things. No. In a moment she would go down to take her place still unobtrusively, still tactfully, among the guests. Why of course she would miss her dear devoted husband, but her loneliness would be tempered by the knowledge that he had sailed to his duty, to uphold the glory and safety of his Country and his Queen. And Eleanor would agree – if pushed a little – that it was indeed comforting to have the support of such a courageous young daughter-in-law, such a helpful young daughter-in-law. They would bear their anxiety together . . .

She straightened and almost savagely, as if to shut out an unwanted episode, drew the window curtains tight. There was something of the rite about the gesture. A final rite. She was here and she would stay until she chose to go – and then only on terms of her own making.

Kenneth Merrill had served his purpose. Now he could be forgotten. Indeed, she had already forgotten him.

Chapter Ten

RAUNIE PICKED her way round a pile of rotting fruit routed by hungry children, lifted her skirts from a mongrel pack snarling over putrid meat and climbed into the cabriolet. As Joey heaped her purchases at her feet she took up the reins with determination and aplomb. Even though her shopping was done she had no intention of driving home. Not yet. She was more than willing these days to drive to town for she was clever at managing family errands to leave time for herself; to avoid even for a short while her mother-in-law's patronage, the niggardliness from carriage to kitchen that lay behind the Merrills' pointed extravagance. It was all rather . . . well, puzzling. Surely it was meanness and not . . . but that of course was nonsense. Poverty? Major Merrill? She brushed the idea impatiently aside. Mean they were, a mealy-mouthed stingy breed. Mean at least towards unwanted daughters-in-law.

She swung expertly through a gap in the traffic without so much as scraping the varnish, making a great show of cracking her whip and sending Jane so smartly along that Joey, acting Tiger, swayed alarmingly on his perch. People turned to look after her, and the jaunty little conveyance. It was an elegant vehicle certainly, but somewhat outdated, nothing at all compared to a phaeton, or even a curricle. But use it she would after all the trouble it had been to coax it from hiding – Eleanor was terrified of horseflesh and after one abortive attempt long ago to drive the thing had given up in despair. Eleanor . . .

She kicked the parcels heaped at her feet. It relieved her feelings a little. Hours of matching this and checking that with nothing at the end of it all for herself. Never a thing for herself but what she could manage to scrounge by her wits.

They never seemed to think she should want better than castoffs, in return for which she was expected to run errands, entertain the pimply curate, be polite to elderly guests and refuse cakes when there wasn't enough to go round – and there never were enough. And most tiresome of all, take the Doulton plates and pieces of old silver down to Isaac Goltby's funny little house in Bridge Street with its back rooms crammed with junk and, almost suffocated by the stuffy odours of furniture polish and aged upholstery, flatter and coerce the Jew into a sale, or at least a loan.

Eleanor Merrill was a chicken-hearted fool! Catch her, Raunie, sneaking off to bargain away such fine pieces for a paltry few pounds simply because she was too afraid of her husband to ask for pin money. Well, she was making these little excursions serve a useful purpose; she had wheedled more from Goltby for the watch than she had hoped for, with no questions asked. And the money tucked safely away. Yes, she had learned to bargain until she could pocket the extra or buy something for herself such as the bonnet and parasol beside her to match her green velvet cloak remade from one of Georgina's. She knew she looked dashing for she wore it as she wore all garments, with flair. And by Eleanor's jealous glances she knew others admired her too.

Everything she did seemed to rile Eleanor. At the afternoon tea reluctantly given to present her to Merrill friends and acquaintances all had succumbed if, here and there, somewhat uneasily. But no one, she knew, had been able to take their eyes from her for long. Eleanor had taken refuge in headache powders and wine, with spiteful, scarcely veiled jibes at her daughter-in-law's still neat waistline. But Raunie was accustomed to her probing and ignored it – let her wonder. If she ever thought about the matter she felt certain she would not become pregnant again. And if by any chance . . . well, she'd learned a thing or two.

So she and her mother-in-law sparred neatly with each other, for as Raunie clung to the Lodge so Eleanor Merrill was learning Raunie's worth – a cross between a lady's-maid, a governess and a servant. A witch who could make or remake a dress in a twinkling of an eye, who could spirit away a headache or heartburn, advise a rebellious Georgina on what was correct for a young lady not yet 'out', and lace Eleanor into the correct notch of her stays without winding her unduly. She could be allowed with safety to dust what remained of the Chelsea and Derby ware. And Raunie accepted all tasks that allowed her to move about the house with some measure of authority; she delighted in scaring the wits out of the lazy superstitious servants.

The carefree Jeremy mocked her, Joey silently did her bidding or kept well out of her way, but the others lived in awe of her. Ada the cook-housekeeper who, when sober, insisted on being addressed as Mrs Jollipy but, tipsy, kept her false teeth displayed in a saucer on the dresser to spite that ''aughty Miss Barby'. Or, staggering drunk, lay on her bed 'blowing a cloud' from a yard of clay pipe while all waited for her bed to go up in flames, and drinking concoctions the ingredients of which were known only to herself and the Devil. The half-blind housemaid Bess. Tilly, the adenoidal scullery girl who bore with monotonous regularity pale and sickly babies and, when reasoned with, shrugged, hoisted her apron over her distended stomach and opened wide bewildered eyes: 'But t'aint nothin' else to do, ma'am. And 'tis nicer even than watchin' a floggin'.' The babies just as regularly died and after a brief interval in which her energy was spent on seeing the child tearfully buried, she took up with her familiar pursuits. The women were underpaid when paid at all, but remained because they were too inefficient to be tolerated elsewhere. Even so, Ada was always giving notice, or being dismissed by Eleanor to be placated by Barbara who scolded them in her detached austere way then soothed their toothaches and wrote their letters, sometimes even trusting Ada with the household keys to dangle importantly at her waist. So, while Barbara calmed, Eleanor fussed and fretted and the young Georgina dazzled, Raunie terrified. They scuttled from her shadow. And she revelled in it – it was power. If they would not love her they could hate her. It was all the same.

219

With her father-in-law she was respectful, even a little submissive. Usually he would pass the time of day with her, enquire as to her health, then spur his horse down the path or slam his study door before she need answer. But there were times she noticed him staring after her in a way she had long ago recognised and knew how to encourage. She felt confident with him. Indeed, confident with the entire household – except Barbara. Barbara Merrill was the irritating enigma of her days. Her manner was as polite as her father's but even more remote and Raunie sensed the girl took pains to avoid her even more than she avoided other people. Resenting Barbara Merrill, yes, hating her, she took to watching her, tormented by curiosity as she visualised the girl in solitude behind her locked door reading the letters that arrived so regularly for her. Brick O'Shea's letters.

Raunie had soon come to know when Brick was away from Sydney for instead of the young boys who refused to deliver them into the hands of anyone but Miss Merrill herself, the letters became as travel-stained as the messengers who delivered them. How many times she had stood gazing at his hand-writing, so well remembered from her days at the Pride, coveting the knowledge the man or boy's grimy hands kept from her. Were they love letters? Did they ever discuss herself, Raunie? Had Brick told Barbara of her son? Of her sojourn at the Thames Hulk? Worse, of her gipsy blood? Barbara vouchsafed nothing. But might not the girl hug such knowledge to herself, perhaps to use some day against her brother's wife? She tormented herself with doubts and possibilities and resolved that soon she would wipe Brick's dingy memories of her, yes his contempt for her, from his mind. Somehow she would face him as Barbara faced him – sheltered, cosseted, deferred to, respected, no longer ridiculed and despised as the slum wench who was all he had to remember. She was a Merrill, a woman whose word would be respected far more than his own. Because she was a Merrill. A lady. She would ram the fact down his arrogant throat and make him pay her the homage that was her due.

It was three o'clock on a sunny June day. The streets were lined with stages, gigs, four-in-hands, drays, and the long lines of barrowmen in George Street and upper Bridge Street. She closed her eyes against the sun – skin wrinkled early in this climate. She widened them quickly, startled that she should even be brooding on age. It was then she saw Brick O'Shea. Jane stumbled with the sudden jerk of the reins, and slowed.

He was standing in the porch of a small house – yes, of all places in the world it was Goltby's house in whose rooms she had spent two hours that morning arguing over the purchase price of Eleanor's silver teapot. And beside Brick talking with a great gesticulation of hands was the Jew himself. They stood in a patch of shade but there was no mistaking their earnestness. As she stared a small boy ran from the end of the pocket garden and clung to Brick's coat. He smiled at the youngster, took his hand and led him to the gate. As Jane jogged down into the little dip in Bridge Street Raunie made up her mind; if she stopped to greet him now he might, just might, ignore her for there were people about. No carriage waited before Isaac Goltby's house. No horses were tethered. Incredible as it seemed he must be out walking the child, perhaps to stroll through the Domain or about the foreshores of the Harbour. As she let the mare walk up the slope she glanced back. Yes, they were following. At the top of the hill, facing Government House stables, she stopped and waited.

The Harbour and its shipping lay like a clear bright painting below her. A nurse-girl marshalled her charges under the tall gums on the vacant land to her right. Otherwise it was quite solitary. Raunie whisked out the new bonnet and tied it under her chin, smoothed her black rolls of hair and fluttered her handkerchief reeking of Eleanor's perfume about her shoulders. She opened the silk parasol and rested it over her shoulder at the fashionable angle. Listening for their voices it seemed an age before they came up with her. She peeped through the fringe of her parasol. Brick was talking to the boy, looking very much as if he were enjoying his company, so much so that he did not even glance at the waiting vehicle. She had not expected to be pointedly ignored. It maddened her. She leaned forward.

'Mr O'Shea. Brick . . .'

He stopped and turned towards her. He did not seem startled, or even greatly surprised – but then he never showed confusion about anything. He glanced from the parasol to the neat little equipage then back to the bonnet that made a perfect frame for her glowing face. He grinned at her in the old way. With the child at his heels he sauntered across and made a mocking little bow. And her heart seemed to turn right over.

'Mrs Merrill. It is Mrs Merrill now, I believe?'

'You know very well it is. You know everything.' The words flashed with her eyes but she was sorry for her sharpness; she had not meant to act like a shrew. Hers was to be a different role now. But he was just as impossible, as infuriating, as of old.

'Tell me,' he teased, leaning against the cab, 'do you always mean to marry men you don't love and love men you can't marry?'

She decided to ignore such provocative questions. 'Where are you going?'

'Through the Domain. At least, that's where my young companion here is taking me.'

'Down to the water,' the child piped up. 'I want to see the ships.' His eyes moved from Raunie's face to Brick's, then back to Raunie. But she had eyes only for Brick.

'I'll drive you. I have plenty of time.'

'Fortunate woman. I can seldom find even an hour to promenade with Jamie.'

'Jamie?' A spring snapped in her mind. For the first time her eyes lingered on the boy. Yes, he would be about four years old, if tall for that age and with an assurance of manner and speech beyond his years. Dark, finely-featured, serious as he studied one then the other. Yet she fancied the trace of a smile about his mouth and eyes, as if he would see humour where others did not. But there was no mistaking his hands.

For the first time in her life she felt she was going to faint. But she didn't faint. She just went on staring at the child's hands. They were as golden-brown as her own but otherwise they were James's thin bony hands curving ghostlike in the candlelight, grasping at her like a drowning man while he dreamed his crazy dreams and she stroked his head, heavy on her breasts. 'Jamie . . .' she repeated slowly, and let out her breath in a long gasp. She smiled at him. He returned her smile, slowly, as if he had thought it over carefully and decided to capitulate. 'You'd like to ride down to see the ships wouldn't you, Jamie?'

'Yes. With you.'

She laughed. The child tried to clamber up. Brick lifted him in then sprawled beside her, stretching his legs and scattering her boxes and parcels. He gestured helplessly.

'If you expect me to ride in such a nonsensical thing something's bound to be upset. Here, let me drive. I don't care to be just an ornament.' She quivered at the touch of his thigh against her own, his hands brushing hers as he took the reins. As they moved off he laughed. 'It *is* amusing, you know.'

'What?'

'Contemplating what Major Merrill would say if he could sée me, trying to look at my ease in his cab alongside his daughter-in-law, with one of my . . . well, bastards as he would doubtless delicately refer to the boy.'

'Major Merrill would never comment on my pastimes,' she retorted with a measure of satisfaction. 'He certainly never interferes with them.'

'So I hear,' he murmured and she glanced at him uneasily. Had Barbara . . . But his expression told her nothing. He thumped the side of the cab. 'Not a bad little runabout at that. He got it for a song you know. It belonged to old Tom Saxton. But I'm boring you with facts you already know –'

'I know nothing of my father-in-law's affairs.'

'No? You surprise me. From all I hear –'

'What do you hear?'

'What you yourself implied; a mutual state of confidence and trust. Sentimental enough to be nauseating, if I may say so. As to you knowing nothing . . . come now, you make a point of knowing everything there is to know about everybody.'

She gave a warning nod towards Jamie then Joey, and he had the decency to be quiet until they were through the Domain. Little patches of new grass about the trees were bathed in the delicate tracery of light and shade. What morning wind there had been was dead and in the stillness the sun warmed and soothed all it touched to a state of near somnolence. The sails of harbour craft hung limp and unresponsive. Lazy little waves slurred against the rocks. But Jamie was all energy, eager to scramble about the rock pools so Brick let Joey take charge of him with orders to watch the child well and both keep within their sight. Raunie felt resentment, then anger at his concern. Her child – for of course this was her child – made so much of when she was by his side. She swung about petulantly as Brick stood staring after the boys. Eager for his notice she spread her skirts and seated herself on a small hillock beneath a tree.

'Do stop fussing so,' she burst out. 'Joey is older than he looks and more capable than his years. And isn't it a little odd for you to be interested in a child of mine? For Jamie is my child, isn't he?'

'Oh yes, he's yours. Or rather – was. There's much of you about him. And much that isn't. The maddening part of it is I never quite know whether it's you or his father in him that annoys me the most. Or interests me.'

'Why is he with you?'

'I've adopted him.'

'You've – what?'

'Adopted him, Raunie. Legally. The boy is mine; a situation entirely of my choosing and distinctly to my liking. I have plans for him.'

'Oh . . . you and your plans. You can't put my son in a box and make him stay there till you're ready to take off the lid and let him out. He's my son. I left him with his aunt. She promised to care for him.'

'His Aunt Betsy is dead.'

'Dead? I . . . didn't know.'

'It's over five months since the Pride was burned to a cinder – salvage amounted to little more than Moll's cooking pots and a trunkful of books.' His voice grew harsh. 'Wasn't it the talk of Sydney at the time?'

'I did hear talk of a woman dying – yes. But I never thought of Betsy.' Fair, slovenly, pretty Betsy . . . It was hard to believe her dead. Betsy Witherstone had been so consistent, so seemingly indestructible.

'She died saving Jamie's life. It was Moll's habit to take him up to the House to sleep for he was forever running off to the Blacks. Betsy ran back for him, smothered him in blankets and threw him from a window. He suffered a broken leg, a few burns, but he survived. He seems to have inherited that determination of yours. As for Mrs Witherstone, she was the finest and bravest of ladies, and for her sake – along with a few other good reasons – I decided to provide for the lad. It seems I'm already dubbed the father of most of Sydney's bastards so it makes little difference if I father one in practice.'

'And Rob Witherstone?'

'Manages my station on the Maneroo. Nicely settled with a new wife and another child on the way. Perhaps a son of his own at last.'

'I trusted the Witherstones.'

'As you never trust me.'

'Does anyone trust you?'

'Jamie. I even think he's growing fond of me.'

Her anger flared again, illogically and terribly. Jamie was not of great importance to her. He had never been more than the son of a man she despised; a child she had never wanted. But that Brick O'Shea should claim him as coolly and readily as he claimed everything else from life was unbearable. The knowledge that she might have the right and the power to deprive him of something he wanted fired her to recklessness.

'You can never pretend you're his father. Too many know otherwise.'

'I don't pretend I am his natural father. And the world can make what they like of us. I teach the boy to look upon me as his father – and to call me so. He shows no undue curiosity about it; I even think the situation titillates his strong sense of the dramatic. When he's old enough he will be told of his adoption, with a parent or parents conveniently deceased, whatever I consider best at the time. Those who know otherwise will keep still tongues in their heads, I'll see to it.'

'What do you mean by that?'

'You don't come into it, Raunie. Not now. Not ever.'

'You shan't bully me. Or Jamie,' she blazed. 'I won't let you have your way with my child as you have it with everyone else –'

'This sudden attachment for your unwanted offspring would be touching if I didn't know it was born of spite. You've a vicious streak in you. I accept that. But I won't stand your pretence. Not in your dealings with me. You've never wanted your son. You've never mentioned him to your husband and you never intend to for you know full well he would be unwelcome in the Merrill household when you only just manage to keep your grip there yourself – isn't that so? Be glad I'm willing to have him. Why recklessly add to your problems?'

'Why should I have problems?'

'The same old reasons. You may be a little cleaner – at least to the naked eye – than when I last saw you but soap notwithstanding, you're the same girl. Still a Romany even if civilised a little by bows and bonnets and the probable removal of lice. Furthermore you know what you are and it scares hell out of you. A gipsy wench will always over-ride the trappings of a lady.'

She sprang to her feet in fury. 'And what else has my dear sister-in-law told you about me?'

'Barbara doesn't gossip.'

'No?' she sneered. 'You knew I was married to her brother.'

'As you remarked – with your usual exaggeration – I know everything. The fact is, military alliances, legal or otherwise, soon become the gossip of Sydney. Barbara's only mention of you, quite casually, was that her brother had wed a girl by the name of Raunie. That was enough for me.'

'She said nothing else?'

'Nothing that you haven't told me yourself.' And, strangely, she believed him.

'And what have you told her about me?'

He gave a half smile. 'I've been expecting that question since we met.'

She trembled as she moved to him and grasped his coat. 'I must know . . . Did you tell her?'

'Tell her what?'

'That Jamie is my son? That I lived at the Hulk? About Feli? Oh . . . you know very well what I'm getting at. That I'm part gipsy? Did you tell her? *Did* you?'

He was unsmiling and serious as he looked into her eyes. 'No,' he said slowly, loosening her hands on his lapels. 'I have never told her, or anyone else, those things.'

'Why not?' Suspicion made her persist.

He shrugged. 'So that I might bargain with you perhaps. Yes . . . that's it. As a matter of fact I aim to strike a bargain with you here and now over Jamie.'

'Jamie?'

'You're free to lie your head off about your past as long as you keep your mischievous fingers out of my pies. I'll have none of your maternal meddling or whispering or dropping of hints about Jamie while I'm away. So far as you're concerned he doesn't exist. Is that understood?'

'Away? But where are you going?' she wailed. 'Can't you stay in the one place long enough – '

'I'm going to England.'

'England?' Her eyes were wild. 'You can't go to England. You can't go so far away.'

'I sail in September. I'll be away most probably, a couple of years.'

227

'Years?' She grasped his coat lapels, clinging to him. 'But you might not come back.'

'Of course I'll come back.'

'Take me with you,' she begged frantically. 'I'll do as you say, always. I'll not be any trouble. I promise – '

'Don't talk like a fool.' He freed himself roughly.

'But it's not *fair*, when I've been trying so hard to be what you want.'

'How could you possibly know what I want?'

'A lady. That's what you want. Moll said so. Other people say so. I only married Kenneth to be part of a family like the Merrills; people with money and position. And privileges. So that I'd have a chance to be like – well, like Barbara, in a way. So that you wouldn't go on despising me for being nothing, having nothing.'

'I have never despised you for having nothing.'

'You have. Oh yes you have.' She was near tears. 'And I don't want you to despise me. I want . . . oh, I want you to love me.' Her words strangled in a great sob as she reached up and flung her arms around his neck. She clung to him, kissing him, demanding his response. She kissed his face; quick, demanding little kisses. She kissed his mouth, hard and long. Like the pagan she was she lifted his hands and kissed them. But he did not return her caresses. He clasped her wrists and held her firmly away from him. 'If you don't take me with you I'll die,' she moaned. 'I'll kill myself.'

'You'll do nothing of the kind. You'll shrug your lovely shoulders and take a look about you and prepare quite happily to enjoy what's to hand. You've married yourself into a sweet cushiony corner of the colony but if you don't keep your head and your tongue you can talk yourself out of it just as easily. So be content with what you can get and stop reaching for the moon.'

The shouts of the two boys came closer. Weary from emotion and sobered by his cool detachment she was silent as he straightened her bonnet and wiped her eyes and handed her her parasol. 'By the way,' he went on quietly, 'an apology for a cook by the name of Feli deserted in the Fiji Islands. Another of your bridges safely burned behind you.' He called to the boys and they came running. 'Jamie . . . we're walking back to town after we see Mrs Merrill to her carriage.'

'Merrill,' the child repeated, slowly, his eyes clinging to her amulet necklace that had somehow loosened and hung glittering at her throat. Brick must have noted his glance for he reached out and covered the amulet with her collar. But Jamie's eyes followed his every movement. 'Mrs Merrill,' he persisted. Then, with a kind of chant. 'Merrill. Merrill.' Delighted with himself. And with her, it seemed.

'Mrs Kenneth Merrill,' Brick explained. 'You see, there are a number of ladies, each charming in her way, in the Merrill family.'

The child nodded solemnly. Raunie loathed her husband's very name as Brick handed her into the cab and dropped a kiss on her moist palm; she wanted to snatch her hand away yet longed to feel closer contact with him. She put out her hands to him, grasping eager hands, but he ignored them as he leaned close.

'I'll tell you something more. I knew it could only be you there in Bridge Street – oh yes, I saw the cab waiting – for no one else would flaunt a parasol exactly this shade of green. Don't play over-hard at the game of being a lady, Raunie. You'll find it tiring and rather thankless. Other paths have been scratched for such as you.'

'Brick . . .' She yearned to him. 'Oh Brick . . .'

He straightened. 'Now go home and write to your husband. And you may give him my regards. Furthermore, if you have a line to spare, deliver my congratulations on his acquisition of a beautiful, shrewd and calculating young wife. I wish him joy of you.'

He flicked the horse and she was off. She wound the reins tightly around her hand and sank back, watching the road through blurred eyes. He'd never get rid of her with his carefully chosen words of reason. Somehow, if it took her all her life, she'd awaken in him a lasting desire, a need of her. Whatever submission and selfless yearning lay within her for a man was centred in Brick O'Shea; all that was within her of love. But it seemed always so. When you loved you were not always loved in return. And you were capable of hate for those you loved. And for those who loved you. Well then, what of love? All she craved in the end was his unguarded response. His capitulation. Let him hate her if he must but let him possess her. It was all that mattered really – that Brick O'Shea should possess her. And she him.

Then she began to cry, with disappointment and rage and her love for him that was so tangled with her hate, and she tore Eleanor's handkerchief to fine lacy shreds that fluttered off on the afternoon air like her dreams.

The day had been without rain. There were even beams of wintery sunshine and the men eagerly, almost pathetically, saw in the wavering yellow streaks an omen for good after weeks of torrential downpours and bitter cold, of swampy tracks and bubbling overflowing creeks all the way from the Bay of Islands. Now they were tired unto death of leaky bell-tents pitched in liquid mud, of beds of sodden fern, with the sacred towering pah looming before them on the hill and the stillness of the night hours pricked by the stentorian challenge of the rebel sentinels. 'Come on soldiers and avenge your dead, *whai mai, whai mai.*' And the maddening spasmodic firing from the pah guns and the fear of surprise assaults and their own feeble replies from the four, six, and twelve-pounders that flung forty-year-old shells to embed themselves unburst into the stolid unshaken timbers of the palisade. But today the sun was shining and a naval thirty-two-pounder was mounted and waiting. They were more than ready. The sight of a captured Union Jack floating from the staff within the pah beneath the native flag, half-mast and upside down, had roused the anger to strike the fuse . . . They would storm the pah of Ohaeawai and raze it to the ground.

It was after three o'clock and cold, even for a New Zealand July. The attacking parties were standing-to facing the north-west angle of the front face of the pah; the advance, the 'forlorn hope' ready in front, the assaulting body in the centre and the supporting parties to right and to left. The silence was thick and awful, broken only by the occasional report of the cannon from the hill to the right, defended by their native ally, Tamati Waaka Nene. Nothing had been explained, it seemed, to anyone. At the advance perhaps two hundred seamen, with volunteers from Auckland, and the redcoats in their stained red tunics and white crossbelts and wearing the old-fashioned leather stock and burdened with full knapsack; ragged, barefoot or with battered boots tied with strips of flax-leaves, they were to rush the pah and force an entrance somehow, anyhow, armed with nothing better than muskets, effective enough at close range yet useless at a distance – and old and ill-tempered muskets into the bargain – bayonets, that inadequacy of a weapon, the officers' 'regulation' sword, a few hatchets and ropes and bill-hooks and ladders, anything in fact they could lay hands on in an attempt to destroy Hone Heke Pokai's 'plaything', the bastion that had excited their laughter and contempt but now commanded their silent if suspicious admiration.

Kenneth moved slightly and his arm brushed his tunic. To his over-sensitive ears even that slight sound, that was actually no sound at all but a sensation, was fierce and somehow vulgar in this pregnant man-made hush. He found himself wishing they would hurry for he did not like waiting. Anything would be better than this waiting. Or – would it? But waiting like this, in such silence, one thought of things one had no business to dwell upon, things like . . . well, this struggle over a filthy scrap of earth that, once won, would surely be of little use. Or, if useful for anything, no one will know what that thing is . . .

There! Another sound. But he could not be certain from which direction it had come. A tiny wave of apprehension passed through him. God help me but I'm scared . . . yes, I must be scared . . . like a child. But we're all scared aren't we? Crowthers there, and Watson . . . I know they're scared too. It's there on each face . . . well, isn't it? But it will be an easy victory. Of course it will be easy . . . One hundred and fifty filthy ignorant savages crouching behind a laughable structure of puriri logs . . . we'll bowl them down like ninepins . . . we must bowl them down for they're the enemy. An enemy to be despised, the Maori. But the Maoris could so easily have cut off our supplies and they haven't done so – why not? They've let cattle through . . . they say beef will make us all the stronger to fight them. Is that a bad enemy? Ignorant savages? Heathens? But . . . this way of thought is . . . treason. I could be shot for treason. I must push on. Distinguish myself. It's my only hope. But God in heaven I'm scared. Will some of us die today? But of course there will be death today. Someone always dies . . . to join the history books and the official despatches and the graves of their fallen comrades. Death . . .

Oh God, death . . . here I am thinking of death and I never think it . . . I dare not think of death. And there's no reason to be scared. No reason at all. I must think of life . . life. Raunie is life. I'll think of Raunie . . . the times I've kissed to warmth that body of hers. Still . . . it's strange that I feel like a child and want, not Raunie, but Mama. Mama would not talk of the glories of war. She never did. When shall I see her again? Shall I ever see her again? Enough. Enough of that. And enough of Mama. God . . . how the chaps would roar if they knew I longed for Mama, but damn it all, I do. And if I could only see into their minds at this moment I'd know they're all thinking much the same thing. None of us look at each other. But . . . do we ever really look at each other? And why, with all the glory of England behind me, do I think I'm scared? For there, of course, is the meaning of all this. This is for England . . .

England!

The bugle blared the 'advance'. A pepper of orders. Bayonet at the charge Ensign Merrill advanced with his men at a steady double. Then, with a piercing sound the wild cheering broke out and they were dashing hell-for-leather up the fern slope. The great ten-feet-high war-fence loomed over them but never a Maori to be seen. Not one. The sight and closeness of that fence, its clear strong unbroken length chilled his spine. Somewhere behind that base curtain of thick green flax the muzzles of the Maori guns were poking. Good guns no doubt. New guns. Then, thrusting through the noise and motion and colour came the bullets. Yells, screams, oaths, confusion. The crackle of musketry. Pieces of fiery bullock chain poked down the pah cannon flew through the air and among them like fiery red squirming serpents. And Kenneth was in the middle of the silly hopeless fight, thinking of nothing but England, yelling, hurrahing, hacking with a mounting hysteria the flax withes that bound the palisades with his almost useless sword . . .

His tortured, battle-stimulated eyes saw something wavering and unsteady above his head. A ladder. The only ladder to be seen. A yelling monocled sailor climbed it to be shot and flung spread-eagled and screaming inside the palisade. With bayonets and sailors' cutlasses and their bare hands, in a fury of righteous Cockney spleen, they all went on tearing madly, feverishly, at the inert indomitable unmoving fence, that fence that could not, no matter what they did, be broken. Kenneth's right arm went suddenly limp. His useless hand dropped his sword. His head swam and his eyes danced stupidly. With his other hand he grasped the ladder; under the urgent imperative need for movement, for accomplishment, he crawled desperately up the rungs. A sharpness in his breast. He toppled back.

From a great, vast, almost peaceful distance came the 'retreat', a sweet beckoning to tranquillity. To the dying it was like the gentle wistful music of Paradise.

Ngapuhi war-runners ran through all the north, crying: 'One wing of England is broken and hangs dangling on the ground.' On the pah of Ohaeawai there was shouting and screaming and the wailing of the Tohungas and war-dances and songs of triumph that sounded all through that still, sad night and among the hills like the roll of thunder in the sky. And the taunting challenge of the defiant sentinels: 'Come on soldiers; come on and have your revenge. Your dead are with us; *whai mai, whai mai*.' And the trembling cowering redcoats groaning and blaspheming, or vomiting if they had anything to vomit, as they listened to a captured comrade screaming in his torment to God Almighty for relief as they tortured him to the rhythm of their quivering dances. And in the camp they succoured their wounded and counted their dead.

Ensign Merrill, it was unanimously and solemnly agreed, had died the death of a hero.

PART FOUR

Chapter Eleven

'PUERILE. PUERILE I say . . .' Colonel Clinton shook one eloquent fist in defiance at his wife, and the other at Barbara standing by the window with young Selwyn, 'this weakling drivel of social conscience and suchlike. A man's duties are to his God and his Sovereign, his mission in life to toil industriously in the class into which the Almighty has seen fit to bestow him. And to be cheerful about his misfortunes. A cheerful disposition is indeed a blessing from God.'

Eleanor's lips trembled in silent prayer. Please God keep Barbara quiet. But there . . . the Colonel was leaning forward, shaking a finger at her.

'It is to be hoped, Miss Barbara, that you, trusted as I understand you to be with the shaping of young minds, are protecting them from the taint of Chartist ideas. The lower classes are more easily corrupted than ourselves and it is your sacred duty to shield them from this blight of our time –'

'The only basis I know for education, Colonel Clinton, spiritual or otherwise, is . . . well, the Golden Rule.' Her voice faltered under the barrage of so many eyes, but steadily regained its strength. 'Surely there is nothing more fitting to teach a child?'

'Impossible to associate His teachings with some of the depraved scoundrels who infest His world.'

Godfrey Selwyn cleared his throat. 'Every responsible citizen agrees it is his or her sacred task to guard others as well as himself from much that is to be regretted in this – er – decadent age.'

'Exactly, Mr Selwyn. We must cherish compassion for the ignorant and the foolish.' Charlotte Clinton replaced her scissors in the exact spot from which she had removed them and touched her husband lightly on the arm. 'John dearest, *do* pass Eleanor the pastries.'

Charlotte was pleased with her row of neat little stitches. She was more than pleased with her neat little world. This marriage of her step-grandson's was her most satisfying triumph to date. Hadn't Gil grown up with Anne Huntingdon and, judging by the girl's letters and her eagerness to come out with her brother, didn't she adore her childhood playmate? So, with the reminder that a doting heiress wife could give him his Royal College and his brass plate in Finsbury Square without further arguments with his grandfather over money, Gil appeared to realise the wisdom of the union. Stuff and nonsense, fumed the Colonel, tinkering with pills and potions, when Clinton men always took Army or Church. But the Colonel knew when he was conquered. Gil would be up from Sydney on Wednesday, the wedding was a week from today, and the pair off to England to live out their lives if she, Charlotte, had anything to do with it. And she most certainly would have something to do with it. For she'd had more than enough of Gilbert's sighing over Georgina Merrill. Marriage with the Merrills was impossible. Position they most certainly had, connections that were useful, but no money – indeed it was a mystery how they managed to live respectably at all. And the Clintons always married money. That way they kept their own. The Colonel's voice rose and his wife turned her pale eyes full on him as he wagged a finger at the lion of a youth, all shaggy and reddish like an unclipped setter, lolling awkwardly near Eleanor's couch.

'A continent gasping for labour and all we get are coolies and kanakas. And Irish idolaters. Can't trust foreigners you know. Our lower classes breed quickly enough, don't they? England's gaols are overflowing with the blackguards eating their heads off in idleness.'

'B–but they g–get very little to eat in prison, sir. At l–least I've always heard so.' And Ralph Huntingdon shifted the weight of his large square body from his right foot to his left, his boot scraping the delicate leg of a sofa table. His face reddened painfully.

'Whatever they get it's more than they deserve,' the Colonel boomed. 'Remember that, my boy. More than they deserve.'

Ralph nodded hastily. He was never one for arguments. Particularly with his elders. Old people knew everything. At least they were always telling you so. And in this country everyone argued violently about everything. Unnerving but . . . well, one got used to it in time and finished up doing exactly the same thing. It was – stimulating. Yes, stimulating. But at that moment he would have given most of his inherittance to have escaped from this crowded room, through the slightly open doors to the splash of green lawn and clumped trees in the distance. He was beginning to love this country with an earthy inarticulate passion somehow allied to the girl he saw with a plunge of his great heart running up the verandah steps. He realised he had been staring fixedly at those steps ever since she had gone out with the Werners. His soft eyes followed her as she dropped on to a cushion close to the fire and her mother's couch. A portion of this wide land for his own, a neat little farm well to the south, comfortably remote from – his glance flickered uneasily over Georgina's mother – this entrancing girl for wife, plenty of growing sons, his own safe and indestructible throne of solidity. He knew, he was very sure, he would never go back to England. Not to stay. Home was where the heart was. So, his home was here. He caught his breath with this sudden great illumining.

'Never did hold with weakness.' The Colonel drained his brandy with military precision. 'And coddling the lower classes with this nonsense of sewerage and asylums is weakness. And a sin is a sin –'

'With our duty clearly before us; to save those souls we can,' his wife murmured soothingly.

' – and when a man's mad he's mad. No denying such things. As to felons . . . a drain on all law-abiding Englishmen, our convicts. If they won't let us use 'em here why don't they send 'em to New Zealand and pitch 'em against these demned Maoris, eh? Tell me that.' And his challenging glance came to rest on Barbara once more.

'And kill two birds with one stone as it were.' She placed

239

her cup and saucer on a tray with a sharp clink. 'Quite possibly the Maoris, weary of eating each other, might feel a little more cordial towards a country which added a fresh dish to their daily fare. Is that what you have in mind, Colonel?'

He roared with laughter. The girl had been stewing away up there in her corner – ah, he'd known it! 'You've got wit, girl. I like wit. Giggling idiots most women with hair like glue blobs, castanets of tongues, and showing more above the waist than I've seen since my weaning time. And most of what they show not worth a second glance.'

Anne's nervous giggle died in a bleat. Eleanor fanned her hot face. Shameful, shameful Barbara, encouraging this lecherous old man in his embarrassing talk. Better to have left her at home even if this wedding at the Clinton country home did provide a much-needed opportunity for her to be *seen* with Godfrey Selwyn, as well as one more, if seemingly hopeless, attempt to separate her from the sordid existence she appeared to have made her own. Charlotte's last stitch was crooked. She put down her work and moved the brandy decanter from her right to the small table on her left, deftly, but right under the Colonel's nose, as she did everything.

'John,' she admonished gently but firmly, 'Eleanor is here to forget if she can, even for a short while, her sorrow.'

The Colonel bowed to his guest with faintly tipsy dignity. 'My apologies, ma'am. Shouldn't have mentioned the pagan place. Inexcusable under the circumstances. Quite inexcusable.'

Eleanor dabbed at her eyes with her finest lace-edged handkerchief. '*Dear* Colonel Clinton. My only excuse for my weakness is that it is barely a year since . . . since . . .' Her voice caught, then died away. Moisture trembled on her lashes. Her body rested in an attitude of despair. She knew they were all watching her.

'Since Kenneth died at Ohaeawai beating against the pah with no better protection than a sword and bayonet,' Barbara finished crisply.

The Colonel sat bolt upright. This was *it*! And damn the

squeamish pack of 'em, he would enjoy it. 'There were, I understand, four cannon.'

'And all, I understand, rusty. With useless old balls.'

In the stunned silence Georgina stared from her sister to the Colonel then turned to clasp her mother fiercely about the knees. 'But they wouldn't, they *couldn't* send him knowing . . . knowing . . .'

'Darling.' Eleanor's hands folded over her daughter's. She hadn't the faintest idea what the argument was about but Ralph was staring and no girl looked her best when tearful, no, not even Georgina.

'But is it true, Mama?'

'Perfectly true.' Crisply from Barbara.

The Colonel bent to pat Georgina's arm. 'My dear Miss Georgina, I'm sure your sister's statements were prompted only by her natural sorrow at her brother's untimely death. But it should be comforting to you to be assured that no matter how or why or where it comes, death to a soldier is unimportant. It is his destiny. The glory remains. Remember that, my dear. The glory remains.'

Barbara stirred her tea with a hand she strove to keep steady. It was difficult to go on. It was always difficult. But she must go on. 'Unfortunately,' she said, 'my brother was never a soldier.'

'Fine boy in uniform. Had the figure for it.'

'Ensign Merrill died with great honour.' Godfrey turned his puzzled gaze from Barbara to the Colonel and lowered his pale smooth lids to match his voice. 'He sacrificed his life for his country.'

His betrothed, waving the little maid aside, took his cup and refilled it herself. Godfrey liked a third cup of tea. One sugar lump. Cautious deliberate Godfrey, so wary of this new world riddled with outcasts and seditionists who dared to question the Will of God and the ways of England and her sainted Majesty, Queen Victoria, when one's destiny and duty lay clear and unalterable before one. Loyal, dignified, honourable Godfrey. There were no doubts in Godfrey's life. There was right and there was wrong. So much wrong. She let the sugar slide in carefully and with the tea offered the seedcake. Godfrey liked seedcake.

The Werners came through the garden doors. The room relaxed, then sprang to almost feverish life under the stimulus of Maxim's exuberance. In the surge of talk the Colonel grasped the Madeira and hid it, wondering what had happened to the brandy. The last of the 1800 too . . . odd how his liquor was always disappearing. He must query Charlotte about the maids. He had known the Werners in Kent. Profligate charmers all with prodigious skill – or luck – at cards. This egotistical sprig had made a remunerative marriage, already gloating no doubt over the profits of his rich plum of a pub right at the Barracks gates, a wedding gift from his delighted father-in-law, even if the girl were born to Botany wool and summer prints and seemed nothing more than a smirking little fool. But then, most women men married were fools. Matrimony was more comfortable that way. His eyes blinked doubtfully over Barbara. The making of a matriarch there; a crusader imbued with this newfangled vogue of book learning, floundering in this maudlin stream of penpushers of 'social significance' – whatever that meant. And what was worse, thinking about what she read. All the same, if he had any confidence at all in the Merrill fortunes he might have considered Barbara for Gilbert; if the boy must make a fool of himself she'd help him do it with dignity. She even argued with dignity. Still . . . God alone knew how the girl would finish up.

It was of course that rakehell of an O'Shea who was stuffing her head with mawkish nonsense, using her for what she might be worth to him. And for all his threats Merrill, short of making his daughter a prisoner, seemed unable to cope with her or the situation. Well, who could? Certainly not this young nincompoop they had snared for her. But one did not give advice to Alister Merrill. One complied with the only man to stand up in Council and remind them of the loyalties and traditions that had put them where they were. Not one had an answer to his cold query: 'Might I ask, gentlemen, what you propose to put in the place of convict

242

labour? Wild aborigines?' No, England could not do without Merrill, for Merrill was England, its blessed pride and enough of arrogance to hold his head high while his feet scrabbled on the edge of a dirty pool of financial ruin, living on loans at short terms and high rates. Ainsworth yesterday, today Somerset, tomorrow . . . Merrill? Once in the hands of that bland devil of a Goltby . . . Pshaw, the colony stank with Goltby, but who else was there; the rest were but small fry dealing in pin-money. Yes, Merrill *was* England, God bless it, captain of the world's destiny. But Merrill's elder daughter . . . wrong. All wrong. No woman should use her brain, forming opinions, pondering theories. A woman should be . . . be . . .

His hot old eyes slid hastily over Anne, his grand-daughter-to-be . . . he couldn't stomach plain women. Charlotte's thin nose was pinched . . . he grew sick of her damned puritanism, and her feet that were always as cold as death. The young Georgina was laughing, stuffing herself happily with pastries . . .

Vague, heart-aching ghosts drifted through his mind . . . Indian maids lovely as houris . . . the rounded honey sweet-ness of an officer's child-wife in Madras . . . the sultry Portuguese maidens . . . the buxom, sharp-tongued Orange Girls flaunting themselves about London's theatres . . . the bold and piquant beauty of the Spanish gaditanas – the Ladies of Cadiz – the daring challenge of them as they sat astride their vicious little horses in their short, glowing, provocative dresses weighted with shot and spangles . . . the heart-stopping allure of their dancing . . .

He glanced up just as the young widow passed along the hall. Everyone alluded to her as the widow, doubtless to save embarrassment at mouthing that pagan-sounding name of hers. A quiver ran through his withered frame. Now *there* was a female, a born Cyprian if ever he saw one, flaunting herself even with folded hands and downcast lids in the gaudiest of colours so that a man could do nothing less than look on her, tantalising even when she spoke little, suffering her mother-in-law's orders as a servant might, while deep in those strange eyes mutiny flashed. Ah, he'd seen it! And he'd warrant the Merrill hen resented such a romantic-looking wench bivouacking at Regent Lodge; indeed, her efforts to keep the girl in the background were becoming quite pathetically obvious. He chuckled softly. If it came to a struggle of will he'd back the girl any time. His thin blood raced. What breasts . . . And he remembered – for that and other reasons – the Spanish gipsy women. Languid creatures moving as shadows, quiet and slumberous, yet wild as animals when they danced. They could stir a cool man to madness and were to be shunned as any plague . . . There was something about this girl, this Raunie . . . Could she be . . . But what craziness. Here in his house? At Regent Lodge . . . Major Merrill's own home? Crazy . . .

He sighed. It was always so when he drank too much, this nostalgic confusion, these wild splendid twisting fancies . . . His lids drooped. Wine . . . sickly stuff. Damn it all, where *was* the brandy . . .

Eleanor had stiffened as Raunie passed the door, walking slowly, swishing her skirts, trailing precious négligés from a careless arm along the carpet. As she watched, the girl dropped a froth of lace and muslin and took her time in picking it up. Eleanor seethed; the girl deliberately flaunted the little tasks given her as if to say, 'See how I am treated by my dead husband's family.' If only she weren't included in invitations. But of course she was – and the chit knew it. And if only she'd marry some storeman or bartender and take herself off, but to such hints the slut only smiled and burrowed herself more deeply still into the life of the household. But the expense of her *might* be overlooked if she were less attractive; she was too disturbing by far in a family of dowry-less daughters, encouraged as she was to flaunt herself by Alister's stupid talk of keeping up appearances and their duty towards his son's widow.

She'd long given up trying to understand Alister, the handsome boy husband who had failed her, dragging through life with a shattered leg, casting at her feet nothing but debts and bitterness and a growing lethargy, his only fire the curses he heaped upon upstarts like O'Shea – 'In Sydney or London or Hell the man's up to no good. We'll be getting all the rubbish of the British Isles dumped upon us, see if we don't.' And his railing against Barbara had become merely boring repetition. And now with Council adjourned and Gipps on the high seas he'd gone stamping off in a vague and fretful search for land, officially absent on the inspection of the garrison at Port Macquarie. Alister a farmer? Why, he couldn't grow a weed. And hadn't he dragged her about the world long enough . . . ruined her health . . . as good as killed their son . . . he was a brute . . . a beast . . . But he had stood like a tall uniformed stone against her tears then banged the door on her with the servants listening and all . . . Oh, what had she, his wife, left to her? Barbara was lost, Kenneth gone forever, Gina . . .

There was still Georgina. Her lovely, lovely child. Men were wild about her already. Captain Moore had ridden out from Parramatta three times, while Ralph Huntingdon . . . she beamed upon Ralph. A dullard certainly but the only son of Sir Ambrose Huntingdon, a fine estate, unencumbered, with somewhere around two thousand a year. It had taken time and patience to prise all this from Charlotte – one would think Charlotte had a marriageable daughter – but it was worth the trouble for she had already edged Gina in as maid-of-honour to Ralph's pudding-faced sister, a clever beginning she felt, for all eyes would be on Georgina that day. And she had already invited Ralph to the Lodge. His whim to buy land near the rough new settlement of Melbourne was a disappointment admittedly, but the place must surely improve? Oh Gina was not yet 'out', no, and Roger the key to their security still drew breath, but she could make her plans. And those plans included ridding herself of Raunie, even for a month or so, while Gina's future was assured. She would find a way. She *must*.

Maxim, leaning over his wife's shoulder, found his eyes held by the firelight's glow on Georgina's bracelet. He could not help but recognise it; a coral trinket admired by a magpie of a child and bought on impulse to please her. Did she mean

it to become significant, as she might have meant her sudden
dash indoors just now when Jenny had suggested a stroll to
the summer-house? Surely she hadn't expected him to follow
her, flouting his wife's wishes? But she had. Of course she
had. Her audacity thrilled even while it alarmed him. She
had kissed him for the bracelet that long-ago day, a childish
kiss but a clinging one. And, remembering, he longed with
a sudden hot urge to clasp her white arm, the curve of her
neck . . . there . . . and put his lips to her flesh, again and
again . . . The child had no right to portray so blatantly the
promise of adult fires, particularly now when he was bound
within the cool tense bonds of matrimony. For marriage, as a
perpetual state, had shocked and surprised him. No one told
you that it held you in spite of your chafing, that it bound by
such seemingly trivial ties as concern and compassion, attri-
butes of which he had always considered himself incapable.
No one told you that you grew to accept the frustrations
of wedlock as the price to be paid for its varying but un-
questioned satisfactions. He was surprised, even a little
awed by his newly acquired flexibility. He accepted with
complacency his bourgeois future. And why not? The only
ones who could put their fingers on money were the merchants and publicans, the barons of production and industry.
And between the cycles of her child-bearing Jenny would
make an admirable hostess, a smiling head-of-his-table, even
though – yes, he knew it – there was an underlying strength
and persistency about Jenny that made him at times more
than a little uneasy. He understood the real Jenny very
well and her attitude to the connubial state even better. The
latter was definite and, he suspected, prearranged among
wives of respectability. One submitted one's body to
one's spouse at decently spaced intervals with as much
dignity as possible under the circumstances and bore, at
the end of nine modestly endured months, the fruit of his
passion. Deeper and more complicated lusts were a man's
clandestine and personal problem. They were quite a
problem to Maxim. As he twirled one of his wife's fat curls
she twisted about to smile at him with the confiding glance

Bandol 12th May 1984.

Dear Mr & Mrs Stewart,

First we want to apologise for being late in answering your letter but we were not at home. Secondly friends of Margot are our friends —

on Sunday morning the 16th and spend then a fortnight in Bavaria. Consequently you will be alone and we are grateful for watering the garden and feeding our three cats (of course we'll leave tins of food for them.)

Charge will be £2.5 per each and per day. We don't want any deposit. You will pay at Bandel (In English Pounds please...)

Yours sincerely

that admitted him alone, and for a brief moment, to her secret woman's world of fruitfulness. He patted her cheek. A comfortable soul. He valued comfort. But it was difficult to remain comfortable when Georgina Merrill crossed his path. He was annoyed with himself. And with her. The child was more, much much more, than just a pleasing nuisance.

The ladies were stirring. He handed over his Jenny to Charlotte and heard his wife's voice rising above the others down the hall. He balanced his brandy – no, Madeira, damn the nauseating stuff – and managed to laugh at the Colonel's hoary stories. Blustering old fool. What a pair they were, these Clintons; coarse worldliness and teetering righteousness. A good woman Charlotte Clinton. Maxim sighed. No matter how tired Jenny became her voice never seemed to falter. True, he pondered with a sudden plunge of depression, poor wine and a good woman would always be the most deadly things of life . . .

Barbara strolled with Godfrey in the dusk-filled garden. Godfrey insisted on a stroll each day; toning up the system he called it. But the moment the light faded he would scurry indoors blowing his nose with careful concentration and clearing his throat. He was inclined to be bronchial. Now his voice was fretful and complaining, as it usually was these days. He wore, in spite of his respectably straitened circumstances, a fashionable cravat and a new waistcoat. His side whiskers were coaxed forward to an enviable degree, his moustache well oiled. But no matter how he trained the hairy growth it could not hide his weak, almost flaccid, mouth. He was complaining, politely of course, of her disrespect towards the Colonel. A good Peninsula man . . . family background . . . experience and age . . .

'Other things are important besides age,' she protested. 'At least in this country.'

Something like a snort issued from under the moustache. 'The most dissolute ideas are accorded importance here. But what else can be expected? The very elements are savage. At home it's a gentle sun. You can open your eyes wide to it and it

247

doesn't burn. But here it's all brilliance. I shall never become accustomed to Australia. Never.'

'Some people grow to like it,' she soothed, striving for patience with the fact that he was unhappy, and that she undoubtedly added to his unhappiness – no, not unhappiness exactly, his discomfort. But to Godfrey, personal unease was a calamity. Well, she gave what she could of herself. There was just so little left to give.

'It's barren.' He pursued his grievance with dogged devotion. 'So barren it lays waste my very soul.' He quivered. 'And there's a mystery about it, an antagonism. Europeans are aliens here. It doesn't want us, this land. It just doesn't want us, I tell you.'

'It wants me. I belong here. I know it.'

The eyes he turned on her were outraged. 'I cannot understand you, Barbara. I simply cannot understand you.'

'I suppose not.' Then she was sorry for him. 'But you might be happy enough if you could learn to accept it as it is. If you stop trying to change it.'

His mouth was a thin bitter line. A stubborn line. 'Sometimes I die for the sight of an English valley.'

She looked at him. 'Why yes, you do, don't you.'

'The only way I bear with it at all is to remind myself that my present lamentable situation is but temporary.'

'Isn't there something a little macabre in waiting for someone to die so you might go on living?'

'Why must you always put facts into phrases that sound calculating?'

'I'm sorry.' She gave a contrite little laugh in an attempt to break the tension. 'When you're in England again – '

'When *we* are in England.' He stopped and faced her, very straight and solemn. He cleared his throat carefully. 'Believe me, Barbara, I am reluctant to be at cross-purposes with you at any time but I feel the moment opportune for a serious discussion.'

'Yes, Godfrey?'

'You know that I respect you – one reason of course why I wish to make you my wife – but there are times when I doubt your affection for me, and it . . . well, I find it disturbing.'

'I shall always wish you well and think fondly of you.' It sounded halting and quite inadequate but at that moment she couldn't think of anything else to say. How she wished she could say the things he wanted to hear.

He gave a satisfied nod. All that was right and proper from the lips of a woman. 'Nevertheless I sense, in fact I feel certain, that you do not really wish to return to England with me. Am I not right?'

'As your wife it will be my duty to accompany you wherever you go.'

'Naturally . . . naturally. But when we came to our understanding concerning your philanthropic interests I gave you my word not to constantly refer to them, or complain of them no matter what pain they might cause me. I have tried very hard but lately I find these activities of yours disturbing me almost beyond endurance. Don't mistake me, please; I admire charitable instincts in a woman, but in the name of propriety there must be some restraint even upon philanthropy. You appear to have no concern whatever for your good name, or that of your family. You embarrass your good father in everything you do. You risk your health and your safety, to say nothing of your reputation, which I should not have to tell you is dear to me, mingling with the most abandoned of the lower orders of this city. Worse even than that, you are often seen in the company of a man every decent citizen despises – '

'Mr O'Shea has been abroad almost a year.' She could not prevent the sharpness in her voice.

'That is irrelevant. You are still embroiled in his activities. O'Shea is a man who not only smokes on the racecourse and the street but insults women of gentle birth by continuing the depravity in their presence – '

'He's forgetful, that's all.'

'Ignorant, Barbara. An ignoramus. A person who could never, regardless of what power and wealth he might attain, be accepted as a gentleman. If you respect me, if not love me – yet – you should consider my sensibilities. For instance, that child . . .'

'Jamie?'

'Call him what you please. A brat born of the Lord knows what blood being taken about the city by you, shown this, taught that, spoiled and pampered in the most sickening manner. It's not – not even decent.' And he took out his handkerchief and dabbed at his forehead and his mouth, a little damp now about the bristling indignant hairs.

'Why is it that charity is considered sublime when directed towards the tribes of Africa but shameful when it concerns our own?'

'Felons and papish Irish our own? You insult respectable people. You insult . . . me.' His face was white. He stared at her as if she were mad. Perhaps I am mad, she thought, numbed. He coughed. It was getting cold. But it was she who shivered.

'Why even try to understand my reasons? Isn't it enough to accept me as I am? Is it so very bad, Godfrey, what I am?'

'You either do not understand, or will not. My position . . .'

So, as he talked she nodded and murmured, placating him as best she could while her thoughts, curb them as she would, leaped beyond him, beyond the garden, back to that other world of Sydney she had left, grudgingly, in submission to her mother's demands. Godfrey Selwyn had always been a shadowy arrangement, a future that was obscure while Brick, so far away and for so long, was her close, constant, and vivid companion. Every spare moment was spent in writing to him; long detailed accounts of the school and the crèche, events in the colony, of Jamie – but she was never quite frank about Jamie. She couldn't bring herself to write that if it weren't for the men she would be unable to manage the boy, that twice he had slipped from Margret's care to be hauled back, literally, by Doc Peter after days of searching – he had joined a travelling show as a conjuror's assistant, was quite unrepentant, and threatened to run off again. The men laughed off his threats as childish bravado but she could not help but feel uneasy. Again, she was never certain what restrictions to impose upon him, for Brick had been indulgent and severe in turn. But of one thing she was certain – the child was a rebel, proud, wilful, never giving of himself or his secrets. He simply demanded attention and privileges. He defied them all. Certainly he defied her for it was clear he resented her, indeed at times she felt he hated her. Yet when forced to punish him she felt hypocritical – was she not a rebel too? And there was a delicacy, a charm about the boy that was disarming, as were certain attitudes and expressions that not only intrigued but that she found jaggingly familiar. As she found his young pride and toughness that merged with the delicacy to form a personality unique, impossible to ignore and difficult to resist. She found herself studying him closely on their strolls through the Gardens, or as they climbed the hill so that he could watch the flagstaff through his little telescope, distinguishing the flag-signals with an intelligence that no longer surprised her. He knew more than any of them guessed, did Jamie. It was as if she had seen him before in some other living creature and the identity of that being was there but always just out of her reach. Ridiculous, for of course she had never seen the child's mother.

But other traits disturbed her greatly, creating situations she longed to discuss with Brick – yet did not. One morning she had found the boy wandering the stables when he should have been with Banner – he loved horses, was quite unafraid of them and for a child of his years managed them with aplomb – but, exasperated, she had called for Taffy. The youth had poked his ginger head up from a cellar, supporting himself on the ladder by a hand on the stables floor, to insist he had ordered Jamie out. Quite deliberately Jamie had stamped his strong little boot on the hand, not only from temper but, it was clear, enjoyment of the situation; laughing at Taffy's grunt of pain he had ground his heel round and about the youth's hand, grinding into the back of it with all his young strength. Taffy had freed himself with a wrench that sent the child sprawling but unhurt, to sit shouting oaths and insults blood-curdling in their exactitude. Aghast, she had snatched the boy up and dragged him off but he had pulled behind her still mouthing abuse, his angelic little face contorted, while Taffy had clambered out sucking a raw and bleeding hand to stare after them.

And there were other things . . . Like the time he begged Joey to take him to the Domain to see the dark lady with the necklet, the funny necklet of a little pig . . . the young Mrs Merrill, the one who had talked with Papa. And the way he had glanced sideways at Barbara from his black eyes that were no more at times than sly dark slits. Who else but Raunie could he mean? But it was natural that Brick and Raunie should meet, acknowledge each other, for Raunie had lived, worked perhaps, at Erins Pride – Brick had told her that much himself. Again, there was that slight family connection with the child – Raunie had once been married to Jamie's uncle. Wasn't that what Brick had explained? But at such times, pondering, she felt restless, a little ill-used, and very tired. But then would come his thick long letters and she was again enslaved. Brick's letters were her life. Through the hastily-written sprawling pages she walked every step with him:

'Mothers work from sun-up with but one meal, and a babe put to their breasts three times a day. I could gather a thousand children who have only nicknames, like pups . . . If I ask a dozen men, Where were you last washed? they will laugh and say, When I was last in prison . . . At least we can give them our floods to wash them and our droughts to dry them out . . .'

'No one has an hour or an inclination to decide what to do with the poor who starve from Tipperary to Galway, from Manchester to Birmingham . . .'

But there were lightnesses too: 'The Colonial Office is a place to set tempers ragged. Weeks spent idly pacing the floor and, if one should even clear one's throat or stumble over a chair, swarms of officials shy like frightened livestock. And poor enough sires they'd make as we know our flesh, man and beast. Ah, for the southern sunshine – Australians shrivel here without the sun – and earth where a man can place his feet firmly, insult another, and he'll hit back cleanly.

I've had enough of evasion and smugness and hypocrisy . . .'

But worst of all was the Irish famine: 'They fight over the carcasses of asses and dogs I saw a mother eating the limbs of her dead child, I saw it myself. Seaweed is devoured . . . and diseased cattle . . . and now the plague . . . they die as they hold up their hands for help. And all the time, still, corn goes out in English rent. But what can one do when oceans separate these people from life . . . only money can transport them. And they want as much as two thousand pounds for a ship. So I must get money, and more money . . .'

By such imagery he roused her sympathy. And she knew he did it deliberately. The letters troubled her deeply when she was troubled enough without them. Once she would have scoffed at the things he told, at the most brooded on them for a day but now, even though she steeled herself against sentimentalism, she was unsure, wondering. Could such things really be? If so, why? Who was to blame? Hadn't there always been misery? And hadn't it always been natural, the outcome of sin and indolence, the will and the punishment of the Almighty? There was so much she wanted to ask, a longing to talk to someone who would give her answers. Surely Charlotte the good, the benevolent, the Christian, would have explanations? But Barbara cringed inside herself whenever she remembered her discussion with Aunt Charlotte:

'Can it be true that in England little girls crawl along sewers – '

'My *dear* Barbara!'

'Well, little better than sewers, dragging trucks of coal by chains tied about their waists, above which they are quite naked?'

'Surely you are exaggerating, my dear?'

'And the colliers with whom they work have sometimes nothing at all to cover them. Just think of the dust. And the cold.'

'Naked men and half-naked females? Most indecent. You may rest assured I shall make the fullest enquiries. If these people cannot be kept separate at their labours then the

Society might be induced to provide the girls with shifts.' And she had settled her cap more firmly and returned to her letter-writing while Barbara crept away, baffled.

Her mind went spinning with the discordant didactic phrases from the vast higgledy-piggledy library of books, magazines, clippings and pamphlets Brick sent her by every ship. She grew confused and occasionally a little frightened as she swam clumsily but determinedly along these new vistas of self-examination and torturing analysis. Elizabeth Gaskell . . . the vivid Irish word-pictures of William Carleton . . . Robert Owen . . . Malthus . . . Francis Place – a revolutionist surely? Cobden's speeches, Shelley's poetry – ah, his searing search for spiritual beauty. Carlyle . . . Macaulay . . . Ruskin . . . Rousseau . . . Her feet left her narrow shelf of solidity and she sank, bogged down terribly and maddeningly, in the interlocking swirls of philosophical thought.

But she persisted. The spirit of the Utilitarians; wasn't the sole difference between them and their antecedents – Voltaire, the Rationalists of the French Revolution – one primarily of method? Logic was admirable, yes . . . but Jeremy Bentham's was such a terrible logic, like a . . . a madness of reason. And such teachings, of course, were . . . well, were they not atheistic? Tom Paine was called an atheist. Her own father referred to him as 'that notorious infidel'. Infidel? But she had read his words: 'I believe in one God and one only; the world is my country and to do good is my religion.'

One day she shut her book with a snap and looked up to find Hugh Whaley's eyes on her. Hugh seldom had time these days to sit and talk, for it was he who made the necessary trips inland, but never concealing his dislike of Moll Noakes and the blind adoration she bore her foster-son – Hugh distrusted blind adoration. From time to time he disappeared down into the Rocks on business he didn't choose to explain. And he hustled the almost senile Paddy, the stablemen and the older boys about their duties. But now he was here, yet still she could not seem to voice her questions. It was he who broke the silence.

'Ideas have driven men mad, Miss Merrill. Women too, You can't go mad on such an afternoon.' And he waved his mug of tea laced with rum at the gentle water and the children playing and the little boats riding the tide.

'But which theory does Brick follow?' she persisted, with some hope of him.

'All – yet none. Acquisitiveness makes him hoard this stuff but he's bored before he scans a third of it. It's invariably inactive, always slow, and his grievances are personal and all-embracing. So he digests what he wants of a meal of words and throws the rest to the dogs. To us it seems.' His eyes twinkled briefly. 'As I see it, his creed arises "less from his love of the many than from his hatred of the few".'

Bentham's criticism of James Mill. She shuddered. 'I suppose that is what is meant by love being akin to hate.'

'Possibly. O'Shea can manage without love, I think, but he must hate to exist. Remove one hate and there'll be another, for a man of one large hate usually shows it in many small ones. But hate as he sees it is English authority personified in this country as the gentleman; the military gentleman to be exact. On this symbol he appears to cast the blame for all the injustices, real or imagined, of Australian society.'

'The military gentleman.' Her mind could not leave the phrase alone. 'He hates my father's kind, yes.' She forced the words from her. 'But he hates my father deepest of all.'

'He hates everyone who stands in his path. He can't understand compromise. There are times when he hates me.'

And me. And *me*. She wanted to cry it out.

'My apparent apathy mocks his . . . ecstasy, shall we say. And that, of course, is fatal. But I sleep at night while he wanders the waterfront.' And he stared from the window as if to find the answer out there.

She felt very tired very suddenly. She was so often tired lately. That was not surprising, of course. But there were other things not so easily explained. A weakness that came over her unexpectedly, a lack of appetite, a trembling of her hands and a restlessness of mind and body that roused her at night to wander her room. And the headaches . . . sometimes

255

her head ached so badly she found it difficult to read. She turned wearily from the window. And now there was matron to talk with. And Jamie to take walking. Jamie . . . she would suggest a picnic with some of the other lads. He might like that. She hoped, a little feverishly, he would like it.

Hugh gulped the dregs of his tea then turned to toss the books and pamphlets into a cupboard and lock the door. 'Leave philosophy to those with time on their hands. The brats have been wiping their noses on their jackets long enough. Someone had better see to kerchiefs – a lot cheaper than new coats.' But he paused in the doorway to rest speculative eyes on her. 'It's a long time since you've exercised that wicked looking horse of yours. Too long I'm thinking.' Then briskly he was gone.

Kumara! A longing for Kumara filled her mind and senses. But after a day or two riding the hills even Kumara palled; she had little heart for riding without Brick. She was obsessed with matters of the mind, pondering deeply on tiny unimportant matters. A yearning grew to make sense of the mental confusion in which she was bogging down. A restlessness worse than any pain drove her until she begged Hugh to take her to one of the meetings she knew he attended. 'With your name?' he scoffed. Then she'd change her name for the night – if she must have a name. 'And I'll chance being recognised. Please, I want to go. I *must* go.' Still he refused, sharply now. But she could think of nothing else; she was possessed by a compulsion to meet and mingle with these people to whom he talked, the people with whom Brick breathed the same air, and to try to understand them. She insisted she would find her way there alone if he refused her his protection, and she meant it, though she hadn't the faintest idea how she would carry out her threat. Finally he agreed but she knew reluctantly.

She found herself in a crowded room hazy with smoke in a dingy house off a furtive lane, with men, youths, and even a few women cramming themselves wherever they could prise the space. She was avoided, politely, but not ignored for she caught surreptitious glances at her from under cloth caps.

And there was one pair of eyes that followed her closely, coolly, and unshaded by any cap; young eyes in a young face, she noted, before she turned away. She was glad when Hugh slipped back to her side, reluctant to leave her even for a moment. She wanted him beside her. She was disappointed at how little she understood of the conversation and the speeches – how ignorant she was after all. Depressed, suddenly conscious of her incongruity in such surroundings, a faint sense of distaste impelled her to efface herself in her corner and she drew her cloak about her. But she listened closely to the whispering voices.

'I been to that back room o' Place's. Books all around. And that spot on the mantel – it should be done 'ere. You hand up the pamphlet you want and all that likes it, why they leave their coppers by its side. To print it y' see . . .'

'Shake your chains to earth like dew . . . Ye are many they are few . . .'

Startled, she looked around but could not make out where the soft words had come from. A carpenter, a bricklayer, who knew Shelley? A sense of having stumbled upon a people she could not understand, upon unknown, crouching and, in their obscurity, faintly ominous needs and ambitions, stirred her. What were they planning behind their passionate words? What did they nourish besides a sense of injustice? Quite suddenly she longed for Brick, disregarding the fact that his presence would not ease her confusion but increase it. But, outwardly at least, she was always safe with Brick O'Shea. Physically safe. Her hood slipped from her head. She grasped it then bit back a cry as she felt a hand replacing it.

'Thank you,' she murmured, polite but distant. But it was no street-corner masher who stood before her. She was looking into the same dark eyes that had been levelled on her all evening. Yes, the young man who had been watching her from across the room.

'I am Tom Wells, Miss Merrill.' She could not find words. A man who knew her and was confident in her presence and who evidently had no time for pretence. Sensing his antagonism, she stiffened, and her own dislike grew to match his. She looked about for Hugh, for escape. 'You're scared, aren't you?' he added.

Mastering her panic she met his eyes calmly. 'Do I look frightened?'

'Well . . . you're hiding.'

'I suppose I am. But I – we thought it best as I would scarcely be welcome here. Certainly not as myself.'

'I am surprised Whaley could coax you here at all.'

'I wanted to come.' Her irritation mounted. 'And why shouldn't I be here?'

A faint smile touched his lips. 'For one thing, the place is dirty.'

'I've been in dirtier places, Mr Wells.'

'So I understand. I hear that philanthropists are prepared to suffer greatly for their cause. Or, could it be that you mean to write a book about us? As some comic cult, or below-stairs phenomenon?'

'You seem to be deliberately misunderstanding my motives. I've been associated with Mr O'Shea for a long time –'

'And you can't be far from his old haunts, is that it? I've heard it said he leaves his mark on all he touches . . .' His face darkened and his voice trembled slightly. 'Well, he shall not mark me even if he does as he pleases with you.'

She never knew where Hugh sprang from but heard a crack and saw a spurt of blood. She felt sick. Murmurs swelled to uproar which was being hastily suppressed as she was whisked outside and dragged along the narrow lane.

'Did you kill him?' she panted, trying to keep up with Hugh.

'Tom Wells is hardly worth penal servitude for life. But I think I've stopped his tongue wagging for a while.'

'He seemed . . .' She frowned. 'I couldn't dislike him.'

He laughed shortly. 'He and O'Shea have crossed.'

'Hugh . . .' She eased, breathless from haste and near hysteria. 'What is it they want?'

'The vote.' Then his voice lightened. 'One good thing about it . . . it will keep you away from there in future.'

Her tone matched his. 'Don't be too sure of that. There are worse things than the insults of a fanatic.'

They laughed it all off but she knew that under his casual manner he was angry and worried. She had been wrong in going there, she knew it now. She had intruded. He never mentioned the place again and she never again asked to go with him. Indeed, she could not have gone. She was afraid of that pack or romantic ravenous young dogs lacking Brick's practicality and Hugh's saving humour, dealing in words where they could not employ deeds. But what phrases she had heard! Her head spun and her heart pounded with the challenge of shifting ideas; she understood their precepts if she dared not accept them without reserve. Some were extreme, some shocking, some nothing more terrible than commonsense. But, said Hugh, those indiscreet enough to apply commonsense to old beliefs take their place with heretics and witches. They shock. And so are treasonable. But, for herself, it was becoming difficult to deny all this thought-provoking food Brick O'Shea indirectly set before her. It was not pap, it was strong meat. Her stimulated mind staggered a little drunkenly along such byways. She was so excited and absorbed by this drug of unaccustomed knowledge that the fact that her mother disapproved of her as a social outcast, her acquaintances regarded her as a little odd if not actually queer, her sister laughed at her for an old maid, and her father – ah, even his probing contempt seemed less painful, swamped as it could be by these more immediate incisions – seemed matters of little consequence. She was drowning in quicksand and, exhausted, losing the urge to struggle. She didn't really want to struggle. For Brick had given her all this when she had been encased in a shell of reserve and dull remoteness. He had not broken open that shell – yet – but had prised it loose, chipped it thin and, brittle, it was about to crack. Savouring ecstasy, how could she turn from it, she who had never thought to taste it?

There in the lush cold garden, in a gust of futile compassion, she lifted Godfrey Selwyn's smooth hand and laid her mouth against it. Hard.

Around the roaring fire in Charlotte's lovely room the ladies took off their stays and scratched their skin, massaged their hands and wiggled their cold toes and talked; a clatter-clatter roundabout of flattery and castigation. Charlotte, bolt upright, began to stitch a pincushion and Eleanor, peering from beneath her eye pads, shuddered – the woman made pincushions enough to line her coffin with them! A ruthless woman Charlotte, so spiritually massive. But how exquisitely she managed the Park; the silky smother of her enormous eiderdowns and deep clustered cushions. And her dinners . . . How simplified housekeeping became with a footman and butler and servants galore when all Alister could provide were shoddy flunkeys who got drunk on paraffin oil instead of genteelly on wine. If only he weren't so *mean*. Everyone, simply everyone, borrowed these days. They were forced to, that's what he didn't seem to understand. No one expected to be paid back in a hurry – what were money-lenders for? Well, she refused to go back to the Lodge until the last minute, no matter what her servants were doing – Burdock from Sunvalley always kept an eye on them – for the Lodge was too lonely, particularly now when simply everyone seemed to be up here for this wedding. At the Lodge was creeping poverty and remade gowns and a brave show when company came and stew and oatmeal when they were alone. And nothing left to sell. All her lovely things . . . She could *not* go back to the Lodge. She would not . . . And she huddled into her cushions and wondered uneasily what Barbara was saying out there in the garden to Godfrey.

Georgina clasped Anne's glacé silk about her waist and preened. A London gown. In sheer animal joyousness she hopped and grimaced in the erotic deranged motions of 'The Bobbing Joan'. Ada had taught her the dance but she would never admit that to her perpetually shocked Mama. Their eyes followed her, for Georgina Merrill was – well, flowing gold, the fierce consuming flame of a sacrificial fire . . . Lush and extravagant phrases sprang to mind at the mere sight of the girl. But there was always enough softness about her to temper her noisy dramatics.

All watched her, fascinated. All but Jenny Werner. Jenny, triumphant in her pregnancy, unsatisfied with the solitary whispered questions of the goggle-eyed Anne, folded plump hands over her swollen womb and raised her voice.

'But Doctor Barclay assured Mama that time would tell, and of course it has.' And her little nods of satisfaction rattled her yellow curls liks so many elongated bells.

'It isn't fair, it is *not*,' Georgina pouted, carried away by her own vision in the long mirror, 'that ladies can only bear squ – ea – ling little babes and never wonderful useful things like silk gowns.'

Eleanor twitched an eye pad in reproof but giggled to boot, delighted that Jenny had failed to hold the floor, thankful too that her lovely child's mood these past days was livelier than it had been for a long time. She had been too quiet for too long, had Gina, almost as if intent on some mysterious dream. Ah, the impossible tragic dreams of youth. Kinder that they were shattered before they took root. But she seemed to have emerged from the stricken chrysalis that had wrapped her about since her brother's death. Eleanor shivered, still haunted by the girl's tears hurling themselves against her father's silence that was always worse than his clipped comments. Ah, dearest child, you will waste your tears against him always, don't I know?

> 'When he eats an orange he'll hand you the pips
> They'll grow if you plant 'em says Governor Gipps.'

Georgina, excited, whirled in triumphant gyrations as she chanted the popular couplet to the departed Governor. Pink with determination Jenny loudly and firmly admired Charlotte's black velvet Anne had brought from London. Eleanor studied the dress in silent disgust; if she lived to be

261

eighty which of course was impossible as she would die tragically young – ah, she knew it – she would *never* wear black again. Except for Roger of course. Dear *dear* Roger. For Roger it must be an elegant and expensive black.

'*Distingué*,' she gushed in her crispest French, then decided to grasp the opportunity. 'Darling Charlotte, we dread leaving the Park. All is so tranquil here while at home there's nothing but . . . memories. Sad, sad memories.' Her voice broke.

'Then stay, do,' Charlotte murmured vaguely, occupied with a knot in her cotton.

'Oh Mama, stay. Please *please* stay.' Georgina ran her hands up and down her mother's arms in a childhood caress until Eleanor slapped her in outraged shock.

'Mind your manners, child. Whatever will Aunt Charlotte think? After all, she should be weary of us by now, what with Raunie here and everything.' She paused, hoping Charlotte would deign some unspectacular and civilised solution to the continuing problem of what to do with her daughter-in-law.

'But we love having you all, we do indeed.' Charlotte became more attentive, remembering her third nephew, a notable failure as travelling agent for the Society – dragged ignominiously from the hut of an African belle who balanced a couple of pale babies on her hips – where a fresh climate (and associates) might help the young rascal to forget unsuitable old ones. Alister Merrill exerted influence with governors.

'Dear *dear* Aunt Charlotte.' Georgina flung her arms about the woman's neck before twirling again, her head full of Maxim. Her mother dabbed her neck with cologne. So! That much had been accomplished and one week could always be stretched to two. Now if only Raunie . . .

Oh, drat the girl. A queer little shiver ran up Eleanor's spine. She had seen Godfrey, oh yes she *had*, staring at Raunie only yesterday. The girl's effect on people was almost uncanny. She left an . . . odour, somehow. The very air seemed troubled by her. And there was Ralph . . . Ralph so young and inexperienced. And rich. Dear God, she *must* do something about Raunie.

Stitching a tear in her one decent dress in her box of a room near the servants' quarters, Raunie seethed with anger. She was sick, sick, sick of this scarcely veiled hostility, this keep to your room, stitch this, mend that, do this, don't go there . . . I shall go mad, she fumed and, pricking her finger, flung the dress violently against the wall and paced the room like a caged thing. Kenneth was dead and she was free but if she walked out of the Lodge with nothing where could she go? To a place as housekeeper with some iron-monger's family? To be maid to some squatter's brats? A change of masters, that was all. Oh, Brick . . . Brick . . . But who could tell if Brick O'Shea would ever return? Her only chance in life was to make use of what was to hand. What was . . . to . . . hand. Her eyes darkened, to become different eyes, veiled and inscrutable eyes, there in the dim little room. I must think of something, she breathed. I must. I *must*.

Saturday was fine and mild. St John's, Parramatta, was crowded. They had driven up from Sydney, in from Windsor and far beyond to see the Clinton boy marry. Raunie stood wedged at the end of the row, her eyes aching from the hurried completion of Georgina's dress, her limbs weary from assisting the hairdresser and running with sal volatile from one near-hysterical woman to another. And purges for the children. Bored, she glanced up at the plate set in the wall above her head.

To Ensign Kenneth Merrill of H.M. 99th Regiment who died of wounds received on the assault of Ohaeawai, New Zealand on the 1st. July 1845, aged twenty-four years. This tablet is erected by his brother officers to commemorate the loss of a revered soldier and a warm friend.

Mr Werner had been the instigator of that. How remote now seemed that day the news came. The newly-anchored sloop in the Harbour, a marine closeted with the Major, the tight screaming from behind Eleanor's closed door. At first the tumult had meant nothing, for Eleanor made so many scenes, but when Georgina ran along the hall sobbing and she herself was summoned by a frightened Bess, her heart had missed a beat then settled to a steady expectant throb. Barbara was trying to quieten her sister, while her mother mouthed recriminations against her husband who stood, his back to the door, staring from the window:

'It's all you care about, the Army. The glory of it, the medals, the parades. The . . . honour, as you call it. You won't see the sickness and the death. You're glad Kenneth went. You sent him. You killed him just as surely as if you'd shot him dead yourself. Why wasn't it you? It should have been you.'

So it was over. Her father-in-law turned, his eyes meeting her steady ones with something akin to gratitude, and Eleanor's horrible reproaches sank mumbling into the background.

'Raunie,' he said, 'this concerns you more sharply perhaps than any of us but I feel confident you won't add to the hullabaloo. Your husband gave his life for his country so I feel sure you will accept his loss at least with control. In fact I expect it of you for you have every reason to be proud of him. He is recommended for a decoration. There will of course be . . . but I shall attend to the necessary financial details.' He walked past her to pause at the door. 'I need only say now that what you will receive will be very little so you must continue to look upon the Lodge as your home for as long as you wish it.' His now expressionless eyes travelled over his wife and daughters and his shoulders seemed to droop for an instant before he squared them again. 'A soldier is useless in a woman's world. Do what you can for each other.' And he was gone.

Georgina was gripped by fever for weeks. But it was months before Eleanor considered herself well enough to come downstairs. As for Raunie, her husband was a tablet on a church wall and a wooden tomb in a mission station churchyard. Her pittance would barely keep her in ribbons so she ignored Eleanor's suggestion that she contribute it to the household expenditure. As for the decoration, despite the more than impressive ceremony, she could never quite believe in it. A medal for bravery – Kenneth? To her it was simply a scrap of metal to flaunt on her vivid clothes – she refused to wear black – and for this audacity more than perhaps her many others she felt Eleanor hated her more than ever.

A stir. The bridal party disappeared into the vestry. It all took so long. Her eyes drifted over the guests: Eleanor in satin – how fat she was growing – Barbara in old dull glacé, Mr Selwyn pale and limp with the closeness of the perfumed air; he was given to turns in crowds. She brooded over his stiff back. So often his eyes followed her, self-conscious ashamed eyes though they were, as did the eyes of the wicked old Colonel, and Maxim Werner, and Ralph the awkward country clod so beautifully rich and unused to women – women like herself. She pitted them one against the other caring not a fig for any. But she had no intention of leaving Regent Lodge penniless, or at least without the prospect of collecting money. She must wait, but she was fretting for the world, hungry for it and what it offered. At twenty-one, she had decided, she could hold her own with any lady born. Though she could still read little she listened to everything and forgot nothing. She could add numbers – well, a few – and write somewhat more than her name. She could sew and dance and contrive and entertain. There was much more to know, doubtless, but she had never seen the sense of knowledge that didn't directly pertain to men. Knowing men, Raunie firmly believed, she knew everything.

And in dissecting and discarding men her avidity had finally become centred in Major Alister Merrill. In spite of his abstracted almost patronising air Kenneth's father was conscious of her. She was certain of it. His manner and his remarks to her, though stilted, were never unkind. So she fell into the habit of noting that his decanters were always full, that a fire blazed in his room with his slippers warmed and ready to hand. And she delighted when Eleanor quarrelled with him; disruption gave her a fierce sweet throb of triumph. She was driven to pleasing him, not only by her need of shelter but by an inner excitement, that something in her complex nature which in spite of subtle warnings would never leave her rest, let others rest, or things be. She was dedicated to one specific end – to win Alister Merrill to her side.

The bridal party was returning, Anne almost pretty in her dress of embroidered Indian muslin over satin, a drawn silk bonnet with a fall of lace framing her pallid face. But all eyes were on Georgina, exquisite with a droop of silk scarf over her shoulders and the topaz pendant at her throat, a jewel as brilliant as a diamond. Gilbert had insisted on the topaz. Raunie brooded on Anne's timid glances at her stoical young husband. She, Raunie, had been quite as expectant and doubly as proud when James Lorne had made her his bride that August afternoon some six years ago. Before her hopes and plans for them both had been shattered with his death aboard an immigrant barque. Well, what was love without the hope of it?

Ramsgate Park was gay. The servants had hurried ahead to prepare cake and wine for the bridal party. The guests blessed the warm day as they gathered in the beautiful withdrawing-room gay with flowers from the expansive gardens. The French windows opened on to the verandah that was covered in with flags and hung with lamps for dancing in the evening. The fires were set in every room and would soon be lighted. The bride removed her ring and pieces of cake were passed through it for the maids to dream upon. Bouquets tied with satin ribbon rested on each plate at the long tables. The magnificent cake surrounded by a marvellous array of smaller ones was raised high in the centre. There were hams, chickens, ducks, pies and all conceivable kinds of puddings. There were custards and jellies and creams. Blancmanges and fruits galore. The house, though large, was too small for the distinguished procession of guests.

Roger, the ailing Deputy-Governor, was lamentably missed as was his nephew – but everyone knew Major Merrill was his uncle's right hand and his absence about complex duties was taken for granted. So Eleanor basked beneath the fruity compliments of old Major Normanton and gloated over Gilbert's pointed attentions to Georgina, shameful though it all was. The children, forgetting the scratching of tarlatan frills, clustered about the musicians. Jenny as usual must retire early and obviously, dimpling with importance. The Colonel drank massively of all the right wines and said all the wrong things. Altogether, it was a wonderful wedding.

Later, the gentlemen retired to drink and to talk politics and crops, the older women to rest and the young people to drive, chaperoned by a scattering of young marrieds. They piled in the carriages, the girls with cloaks over their gauzy frocks, a pampered few muffled to the ears in furs. Maxim found himself with an excited bridesmaid and her beau, with a young married pair, aware of their social responsibility, together cosily in the other corner. They persuaded him to drive and as he laughingly flipped the horses Georgina ran, begging to be taken up. He obeyed with mixed feelings. Turning off the Windsor Road they drove towards Rouse Hill while Gina chattered and Maxim wished he hadn't come yet enjoying the sense of her leaning against him. He'd had a good deal of wine, and was experiencing many and varied sensations all connected with the goings and comings, the sound and the sight of this girl at his side. They stopped near the bridge; a small insignificant bridge but picturesque and long adored by lovers. The young couple were primly absorbed in their corner. The maid and her youth went hand in hand across the grass. Watching them, Georgina said softly: 'I'd like to walk too. But the other way. To the stone wall. It's just over the rise. You remember the old wall, don't you, Maxim?'

He'd ridden out with her one day, years ago. She had been staying with the Clintons and his detachment was at Parramatta. No one had known of it, of course – they believed her to be riding with the family of a school friend – and grooms were born to be bribed. He couldn't say why he had bothered with her except that she was an amusing child – but so much more than a child – and was the daughter of a personage and the sister of his best friend. Well . . . she had kept the bracelet. Then what else had she kept? Notes? God, had he ever been gauche enough to write her love letters? And she so foolish as to keep them? Tied up with blue ribbon? Young girls did such things. And wrote in diaries and whispered among themselves.

He helped her from the carriage, confusion making him awkward. Her green cloak with its fur-lined hood made a burning crown of her hair. A man's heart and limbs turned to water with the sight of so much beauty. He had never been afraid to be alone with a woman before and couldn't understand what marriage had to do with it. But it seemed to have everything to do with it. Walking over the damp grass she looked up at him, her feet dragging, perhaps expecting him to carry her over the lush seepage. But he dared not touch her. They paused at last beside the creek and the big tree and leaned on the wall that was black from an old old fire, a place rich with the spirit of its departed owners. A wisp of breeze caught her skirts and coiled them about his loins. His always spontaneous desire surged to become a physical pain. And now, for the first time in his life he couldn't rush to assuage that pain. The last time he had possessed Jenny she had cried herself to sleep. Georgina slid the hood from her hair, slowly, like a lingering caress.

'You'll catch cold,' he said icily. She was silent. Restlessly he added, 'You shouldn't evade your family as you do. It's – well, it's dangerous.'

'Why have you changed?' She flung it at him.

'I haven't changed.'

'Yes. You avoid me.' She put her hand on his arm and he started, his senses sharpened to acute sensitivity. 'When you married Jenny – not long after Kenneth died – I cried for weeks. I wanted to die. I prayed to die. You were all mixed up with Kenneth I suppose, yet it was more you . . . You still like me don't you?'

'Of course I like you.' And he smiled at her in, he hoped, a fatherly fashion. He wished he felt fatherly.

Oh Maxim . . . 'let him kiss me with the kisses of his mouth . . . his left hand is under my head and his right hand doth embrace me . . .' Could the Bible speak such longings if they were sinful? The grass under their feet was like a carpet, a soft and beckoning couch. A yielding couch. How strange her legs felt. Her eyes swam and her fingers groped for him. 'Then why don't you kiss me?' she whispered.

His first reaction towards her for voicing the yearning they both knew was there, was one of anger. Then he was shocked. At her. He drew back slightly, looking away for escape, for time to think.

'You're thinking I'm a hussy,' she pursued. 'Kenneth called me one. Well, if wanting you to kiss me and – and hold me – means I'm a hussy then I just can't help it.' She gulped. 'Look, I'll tell you. At first you were just a wonderful man, someone more wonderful even than Kenneth, someone who made me feel grown up and important. It was all so exciting. Then it was more than that, it was different. It was love. I'd be sure about love wouldn't I? I'm fifteen.'

The tremble of her warm hurried voice mated with the tremble of his heart. He could do nothing else but grasp her and kiss her and go on kissing her. But at last he released her and stood back, his desire soothed enough by the caresses to reason, to master this turbulence. The pounding at his temples was easing. He willed it to die. This was not the pattern he had devised for himself, kissing a child, craving a child in love with love. He, a citizen of substance, soon to be a father, next year perhaps an alderman – so many reasons why he must follow caution. He patted her shaking hands that wouldn't let him go. He was like a father now. Better than any father.

'Fifteen is time to learn restraint, Georgina,' he explained carefully in a voice that was all sane reasonableness. 'You must learn it, you know. We all must.'

The dream in her eyes died as she snatched her hands back and held them tightly to herself. 'They didn't teach me

269

restraint. I've been taught since I could walk to use every power I possess to get what everyone considers I should have – marriage. But not just any marriage. No. Marriage with money. That's the thing. I must watch for it, search for it, grasp it when I see it. And everyone will be there to help me hold it. Horrible, isn't it. Or is it? I don't know. How should I know? But when – when I thought of you I never thought of money.'

'But I thought of it, my dear. I married Jenny.'

'You're not married to Jenny. Not really. Jenny's cold – inside – but she's clever enough to hide it from everyone. Oh much cleverer than I am because she makes you think you're satisfied with her and your life. She's burying you little by little, hour by hour, word by word. No one can be happy that way. Not really. Oh Maxim, I'm so miserable. Sometimes I hate you for not loving me because loving someone is cruel. It hurts. It's wanting . . . wanting so much so terribly, yet not knowing exactly what it is you do want . . .'

He stirred. If he put an end to all this now, here, and quite ruthlessly, there would be no compulsion to think of her, to feel for her any longer, and the absence of the disturbing emotions she roused in him was becoming increasingly important. There was nothing in the world worth undue consideration but comfort, security, solidity. And Georgina Merrill was none of these things.

'Jenny is my wife and you're a precocious child with too much preoccupation with romance. It is a phase of course and will pass. But until it does I do not intend to involve myself in such a situation again. Or you.' He turned and knew he was being pompous. But better that than being a fool. 'We must go.'

His body burned, on fire, but he turned firmly from her eyes that were bright with unshed tears. The breeze was freshening, the sun setting. There was a shout from over the hill. He answered it, then, as she made no move he dragged the hood over her head and her cloak about her shoulders with a quick determined gesture, and did not look at her lips. Anywhere but at her trembling, parted lips. And caught the

glint of gold fire at her throat. It was so like her, the topaz.
She would come back to haunt Gilbert too. Her hand was
clammy yet unyielding as he took it in his and led her from
the old stone wall and the gentle trees and across the wet
green grass to the carriage and home.

'Raunie?'

There was a tremor, something so entreating in the voice that
Raunie turned sharply on her dressing-stool to where Georgina
poised in the doorway, her négligé tied loosely and her hair in
disarray. But it was the girl's eyes, heavy and lifeless, that
prompted Raunie to indicate her one chair, though it was late
and she had thought the girl asleep with the rest of the
wedding-exhausted house. But with one of her childlike
gestures Georgina curled herself on the floor and rested her
head, as if it were too heavy to hold upright, against the other
woman's knee. Frowning, Raunie set her hairbrush aside.

'What *is* it?'

'If only . . . If only Kenneth were here.' So unexpectedly
Raunie withdrew slightly. She did not want to speak of
Kenneth. She did not want to be reminded of him. But the
girl was persisting. 'I think of him often, and I can't think of
him and not speak of him sometimes. And who else is there to
talk to but you?"

There was such desolation in her voice, in her whole body,
that Raunie put out an impulsive hand. Even so, she refused
to reminisce. The girl was in a heightened mood, stirred by
the wedding no doubt. And perhaps by that self-seeking
womaniser, Maxim Werner; the whole house must have seen
them drive off together that afternoon.

'We used to talk, you know.' She was twisting the cord of
her gown around and about her fingers. 'Or perhaps I talked,
not caring if he answered, just so long as he was there. But we
laughed a lot together.' She flung back her head to gaze into
Raunie's face. 'Did you love Kenneth? Really?'

Raunie released her hand abruptly. 'I never thought about
it.'

'I loved my brother very much.'

'I know.' Then a little impatiently. 'But there'll be a different kind of love for you soon. A grownup, lover love – '

'There is.'

'Not *yet*, Gina.'

'*Yes*.' Almost savagely. 'Now. But it must not be, you see . . . And that's what's so awful. You don't know.' She burrowed her head into Raunie's lap and gripped her arms tightly, as if to transfer her need, a schoolgirl's need certainly but none the less urgent for that, into the other, as if she could not bear it alone any longer. 'You don't *know*.'

'I do know. It hurts. It's one half of you off somewhere and you long for that half, to make you a whole person.'

She knew. The ache that was always there for Brick, and only Brick . . . The yearning in the still dark of night . . . The tearing away inside her at unexpected moments over un-expected things . . . Miserable for Georgina but more miser-able for herself, she put an arm about the girl's forlorn and desperate body in an intimacy unusual for her, and rocked her back and forth, back and forth, as one might soothe a child.

'I know, Gina. I know.'

Ralph stood very still for a moment as the tiny ornamental gate click-clicked behind him, then he stumbled on to the path that wound up from the orchard through the kitchen garden, about the neatly bordered flower beds and finally, the Colonel's pride, his lovely morning-bathed rose garden. Most of the blooms had been gathered to decorate the house and only tight buds wet with dew shimmered in the early slivers of sun. His heart was thudding. He strolled these little paths each morning and very early in the hope that even once Georgina might venture downstairs even though he knew she hated early rising – at least he could gaze at her window. Though it was a lovely morning it was frostier than usual so he'd been surprised to see her in the distance weaving her way between the rose beds, slowly, as if waiting for someone.

272

Waiting for . . . him? His pulse began to tingle, his large healthy body stimulated by this unexpected but long-hoped-for delight. But stumbling between his quick eager little runs, his murmur of greeting broke off. The girl's shawl had dropped from her head and he saw it was not Georgina. This girl was . . .

He stood transfixed and awkward as the girl turned to face him, her arms cradling a sheaf of rosebuds, somewhat tentatively he thought. It was the young Mrs Merrill, the widow. He stared dumbly. He didn't know what to do for they had scarcely exchanged two words together. But he was a gentleman, if an awkward one. He stammered his good-mornings. But still he could do no more than stand and stare at her, strangely stirred by the soft warm white négligé wrapping her about – it was that that had deceived him, so much the sort of thing Georgina might wear. His eyes rose to the black hair that was like nothing if not like the earth. Soil slipping through his fingers, rich, thick and silky . . . His hands moved as if to reach out. She smiled at him, a wonderful smile, then held out a hand. He wondered why his throat hurt.

'A thorn.' Her voice quivered at his ears like a bow trembling on strings. 'It always happens when I gather roses. I must be very awkward. Could you remove it . . . please?' And she laughed, softly, gently, not at him but at her own feminine clumsiness.

As he took her hand he was aware, far too aware, of its soft warmth. With a great effort he pulled himself together and began to search her fingers. He could not find the thorn. Even so, he kept looking for it, disturbed by the feel of her flesh and their heads close together, her black head and his sandy one. Through a haze he wondered why her hands should be so warm. Then he became aware of another sound, a bearing down on them, and he looked up in horror. Georgina's mama, wrapped to her ears in wool with flushed cheeks and eyes blazing. Was she angry with him, or the girl? Always shy, he quite suddenly saw a garden full of women and acted on impulse:

273

'The C–Colonel wishes to see me before b–breakfast, so if you w–will excuse me, ma'am . . .' He bowed as best he could, from one to the other, confused. 'Your p–pardon, Mrs Merrill.'

And with a further grotesque patter of excuses he clattered away bowing to them with as much dignity as he could muster while dodging shrubs and tubs. If the house were not awake before it certainly would be now Raunie decided as she prepared to deal with her mother-in-law.

Eleanor's soft white flesh quivered, but she remembered to keep her voice low. 'I was at my window. I saw the whole episode.'

'I was certain you would, ma'am.'

'I . . . heard a noise and glanced down and saw you waiting – waiting deliberately I now see – to intercept Mr Huntingdon as he came up from his walk.'

'Surely I'm permitted to take a stroll in the garden when it pleases me?'

'Stroll? Nonsense. You never get up of a morning till you're forced out of bed. You've been trying to attract Mr Huntingdon's notice since the day we arrived.'

'Could anything but a new compost hold his notice?'

'Don't be insolent. You know that Mr Huntingdon and Georgina – '

'Are they already betrothed?'

Eleanor did not answer. The girl had put her finger on the crux of the matter – nothing spoken, nothing finalised. This fact and her long-pent-up fury against Raunie made her swing her hand in a wild slap at her daughter-in-law's ears. Raunie dodged neatly. Regretting her outburst Eleanor gathered her shattered dignity about her with her shawl, loathing this . . . this man-eater. But the house would be stirring and even now others would be glancing from windows. Moreover, though the sun was strengthening she was still chilled to the bone.

'Have you no pride at all?' she scorned.

Raunie's finger traced the coils of a rosebud. 'In most matters, yes, I believe so.'

'I doubt it. If you had you would have realised long ago

that your connection with my family is over and done with. It is high time you fended for yourself.'

'I have nowhere to go.'

'I do not see that it is any longer my concern.'

'But it seems to be Major Merrill's concern, ma'am. At least, he has always told me so. Of course, if he has changed towards me . . .'

Drat the minx. She couldn't have her go whining to Alister. 'It is not my intention to be harsh, Raunie. Indeed, both Major Merrill and myself deem it a duty to be interested in your future. But I have many problems to contend with, indeed, these little domestic pinpricks trouble us all. So I thought . . . well . . . you might care for a change, perhaps a little holiday?'

'I have no money for holidays.'

Eleanor bit her lip. 'That might be arranged. Ten pounds perhaps?'

'Hardly worth my packing, I think.'

'Fifteen then.' Eleanor fumed. But even a month, surely, would give the tongue-tied young Ralph, free of distractions, time and opportunity to declare himself. So there was nothing else for it, the dressmaker must still wait for her money. But Raunie was still hesitating.

'Twenty then. But not a penny more.'

'If you're sure Major Merrill would not disapprove of my holidaying alone?'

'It will not be necessary for my husband to know anything about it. In any case he is too busy to be bothered by trifles. I shall have you driven in this afternoon to Parramatta.' She brightened. 'You may care to stay there. I understand there are many respectable lodging-houses.'

Raunie met her eyes directly. 'And the twenty pounds?'

Eleanor sighed. 'I shall bring it to your room in good time. Now you'd best go and pack –' she gulped, 'if you will. I shall make what explanations are necessary.'

She was afraid to say more. The girl might change her mind. Let well alone. She turned and walked back to the house, straight upstairs and across to her window. Slam!

What exact noise had made her stir she had no idea, but it was lucky she had awakened earlier than usual. She almost pulled the bell cord from its socket. She would doubtless take a chill. A fire, a warming-pan and her breakfast in bed. And she refused to get up until it was time to send that horrid creature on her way. Twenty pounds. *Twenty!* Oh, what had she done? She couldn't afford twenty pence. And the girl would probably fritter it away in a week and be back on their doorstep to harass their lives once more. She could only pray that she would drown or be run over or that someone would poison her, as some man would sooner or later; poison her and then himself, most likely. Well, the quicker the better. Twenty pounds! She turned over on her pillow and snuggled under the quilts and tried to stifle her groans into her handkerchief.

Raunie dumped the rosebuds on a heap of raked leaves and wrapped her négligé about her as she went inside. It was very cold, but her room would be colder. Well, she'd had enough of being a poor relation. Her little plan had worked, neatly too. What fools people were. She could make them jump to her whims like puppets on strings. How simple it had been – except of course for the early rising – to wait beneath Eleanor's bedroom window and throw a pebble at it when she saw Ralph coming.

She spread her shapely, unmarred fingers wide. Even a thorn in her flesh would have been a small price to pay for this freedom; a sweet freedom of time, and twenty pounds. At least it was a beginning. And she could do quite a lot with twenty pounds. And a few weeks of freedom. Humming softly to herself she went contentedly to her room.

Chapter Twelve

REGENT LODGE had a dissolute air about it; it seemed to sprawl in the thin wintery sunshine like an indolent jade. Raunie found the house in confusion: dust thick on furniture, the big kitchen an odorous shambles, and broken bottles cluttering the scullery and yard. Ada was drunk, while Tilly wandered about, occasionally shoving a greasy gin-spiced bottle into her newborn's twisted mouth. A cupboard had been forced and there was scarcely a drop of wine left; one more day and the cellars would have been beaten in. As it was the kitchen was the background for tipsy brawls, Joey had disappeared, and there was nothing to eat. The well-intentioned Burdock was doubtless back at Sunvalley wringing her hands and wondering what to do. Well, Raunie knew what to do; she hadn't played on their fears of incantations and curses all this time for nothing. After despatching Bess to Sunvalley for the above-stairs keys she made a detailed tour of the house but upstairs all was as it should be – fear of the Major kept the women's most destructive passions within bounds. Ada bawled her insistence that no black-haired baggage was a-coming ordering her about, but so fuddled was she that it required only an expert twist of Raunie's wrist to transfer the keys she had been entrusted with from the woman's waist to her own. And there she meant them to stay. When Joey crept timidly from the bush he was sent to fetch wine from the cellar while, grumbling but obedient, Tilly hurried down to beg fish from the Blacks. So something like order was threatened and coaxed into the slovenly menage. When Bess returned with the keys together with apologies from the defeated Burdock she was set with Tilly to cleaning up the mess. For the present, Raunie determined, Regent Lodge was hers to command. And to use.

But three nights later Alister came home. In an excess of luxuriance she had ordered a fire blazing in the dining-room and dinner to be served there for herself and was lighting the room lavishly with candles – Eleanor refused to have gas, swearing it was hurtful to the eyes and unflattering to the complexion – when she paused to the sound of horses. Then came Alister's distinctive walk and he was standing in the doorway, blinking in the light.

'Exactly what I need – warmth.' He flopped into a chair by the fire oblivious of the mud oozing on to the carpet and rid himself of his boots. His hands moved stiffly. He looked cold and damp. He must have ridden hard and long for in Sydney it had only been drizzling rain for half an hour. 'My wife has retired I suppose?' he added.

'Mrs Merrill is still at Ramsgate Park, sir. She – they decided to stay on a while.'

'I see.' His look was long and thoughtful. He gave a quick little laugh. 'No message, naturally.'

'No. No message. I don't think . . . anyone expected you home. At least, not yet.'

'Didn't expect to be here myself. But an escort sent is an escort sent. One governor recalled and waiting upon another is a ticklish business. But why are you here? Too many woman badgering you at the Park?' She was silent but he persisted. 'Did Eleanor send you down? Out with it now.'

'I wanted to come home. In any case someone had to come. It's never wise to leave the place long.'

He glanced about him when then poked at the already roaring fire. 'Whatever threats you use seem to be effective; the place looks at least habitable. See what you can do about producing a meal, will you.'

'I'll have dinner served immediately.'

'Wait.' The poker clattered down. 'Wine first. And bring it here, I'll see to it.'

She carried the tray to the small table and watched him pour. For two. 'It will warm you,' he said, handing her a brimming glass. He drank quickly, then murmured. 'Don't know why I ever come back, an impulse I invariably regret as soon as I'm inside the door. And yet – have you ever felt as if you must belong somewhere, somehow, to someone that very moment or go mad?'

His eyes rested on her, waiting. He expected an answer. He meant to have an answer. 'Sometimes,' she said.

He moved impatiently. 'You're lying, girl. You're young. The young don't reach out for things because they don't need to. Only the old have reason to beg.'

She didn't want the wine but she sipped it obediently while he drank as he always did now, methodically, hurriedly, as if he couldn't stop, and didn't want to stop even if he could. He spoke quickly. 'That tall-timbered country up there . . . it's different somehow. A world on its own. The Indians are different too. You should see the Marys climb trees. They climb up a vine chopping footholds in the timber as they go higher, and still higher. All in all, it might be easier to tame that world than . . . this,' he finished bitterly.

Chaff upon the wind. She forced polite interest, and waited. 'You've been here a year now, haven't you,' he went on.

Here it was. She sat down and leaned back in her chair, keeping a tight hold on her glass. And on her wits. 'Over a year.'

'It's a wonder you stayed a month. But you seem to have the gift of closing your eyes and ears to petty annoyances as well as dominating ones. Barbara has that ability too. Or failing.'

'Barbara is clever. I'm not.'

'She's too clever. That's her misfortune. A vacillating mind can be trained along paths that are, at the very least, discreet. But Barbara never vacillates. She's as inflexible as . . . as granite.' The decanter tinkled. 'What does she do all the time? Do you know? Does anyone know? What goes on in her mind? What does she want?' A pause. 'And why do you stay on here? Don't pretend it's because you can't bear the thought of leaving us.' He slammed down the decanter and leaned forward with a movement that had something of urgency in it. 'You hate us most of the time, admit it now.'

279

'I stay because I have nowhere else to go,' she answered simply.

His laugh was short. 'I have an idea you married my son for the same reason, eh?'

'Kenneth loved me.'

'Love.' He sneered. 'A cowardly boy, too immature to do anything but disgust and disappoint. He did disappoint you, didn't he now. Didn't he?'

She hesitated. She must be careful. Very careful. 'I never expected much from Kenneth. But I think I must have loved him a little.'

'What could you know of love, either of you? Oh yes, I've heard of your earlier marriage – your mother-in-law boasts of the episode – but what's the truth of it all? Come on, out with it.'

'There isn't much to tell. I was married for a little over three months to Lady Farleigh's eldest son, James Lorne. I thought –'

'He was Farleigh's heir, eh?' He shrugged. 'So now my wife wants rid of you and you don't mean to be cast aside. Not till it pleases you to move on to fresh woods, as it were. That's about the extent of your petty squabbling isn't it, Raunie?'

He rarely addressed her by her name but now she welcomed it. Somehow it softened his unexpected, almost brutal probing that she sensed was not induced only by wine. He was in a strange mood. A state almost of exaltation. This was a fresh situation for them both. They were in close proximity, alone, and free for the first time to talk frankly about anything it pleased them to discuss. These facts, she felt, were intoxicating him faster than anything he was drinking. And she felt the touch of his mood in the heightened sense of warmth from the fire, in the contact of cool smooth glass to her hand. Sounds were sharpened. The wine was sweet and heady to the taste. And her eyes were absorbing clearly and in detail the man before her, a man hitherto a stranger, belonging to that enviable world of wealth and privilege she had only been permitted to view from a distance. Now she was closer to that world – but not yet inside it. Not securely. She could be dislodged . . . Then she must not drink much. He would know nothing she did not choose to tell him. Indeed, here might be the chance to do a little probing for herself.

'You have always told me to look upon myself as a member of your family, sir. Well, apart from your kindness to me I am not – forgive me but it is true – treated as such. I am not even shown ordinary courtesy, for your wife calls me, among other names, a nuisance and a trouble-maker. I have done nothing to deserve her dislike. Not intentionally. Believe me, I ask for no special treatment but, after all, I am a Merrill, am I not?'

'Yes . . . you are a Merrill,' he agreed, if a little coldly. But still, he had admitted it. How well she knew his Achilles heel. 'And if only for that reason I refuse to let this petty victim-isation continue. No one shall say I turned my son's widow into the world penniless and alone. You may stay at the Lodge until I say you're to go. Until I tell you to go. Is that clear?'

'And will you tell me to go?' she asked gently.

'No.' His eyes rested on her, and did not turn away for a long time. 'No. I won't tell you to go.'

Bess broke the long silence to announce dinner. Alister bore her clumsy ministrations in near-silence, abstracted and seemingly lost in his wandering meditations. Raunie humoured him until he was ready to slump again in his fireside seat. Bess finally out of the way he demanded his port. He seemed to want her attention.

'This house has been different of late,' he murmured. 'You've civilised it. No – I can't mean that exactly for you're the most uncivilised chit I've ever laid eyes on. But one knows you are about the place. You have some method, some purpose. You know what you're doing, where you're going, which is more than most of us do. You know too damned well, I'm thinking.' He paused. 'Well? And before Courtney House?'

'I don't remember much before that.'

'Nonsense. You just don't choose to remember; there's no real compulsion. And why should there be? Childhood, no matter what anyone tells you to the contrary, is an inanimate time. You discover that when you try to relive it. It's all a kind of nostalgic sadness, a roundabout of ridiculous sensations over trivialities. Dreams that never come true. You're a little ashamed of those dreams, as you're ashamed of your uneasy emotions. Frightened too. No balance anywhere. You want to die – or live forever. You despise love and crave ecstasy. Old age is an embarrassing outrage before your eyes. And the world is mad, quite mad, and only you can put it right. You wait for the year that is just around the corner because you're certain it will bring the thing you most want, yet you never know, quite, what that thing is. Sixteen – there's a glimmer of sense there. But seventeen – I began life at seventeen. Yes, at seventeen everything was sharply-etched, meaningful. Destiny was in my hands; my destiny, the world's destiny. I was a soldier, and a soldier lived in action. War and all that went with war was doing. *Doing*. Life began for me at Waterloo.'

He must be drunk. She had never heard him talk so volubly, so queerly, almost as strangely as Barbara talked when she deigned to talk at all. He annoyed her. What she could not understand always annoyed her. 'That's where we beat Boney, isn't it?' she observed, politely, stifling a yawn.

'Beat him?' His fist slammed the little table. 'We annihilated that strutting little coxcomb. To most I suppose that day was – well, mud and a weak sun and the rattle of musketry and smoke. A fog of smoke. And rain like water tumbling from tubs; a greater help than Blücher, the rain. But to me that day was a wound that nearly cost me my life yet I didn't care a jot. I didn't feel it. It meant bivouacking in the Bois de Boulogne and the Czar reviewing the Army and a blister on my right heel as big as an egg and a schoolgirl letter from Eleanor in my pocket. I never could get her yellow curls out of my mind.' He jabbed at the fire again, fiercely. 'Then England.' He laughed shortly. 'I expected at least the command of an Indian regiment. I expected everything.' He pulled a small case from an unseen pocket, clicked it open and tossed it on her lap. 'Instead . . . the Waterloo Medal.'

She took out the small disc dangling from its crimson and blue ribbon and stared at it dutifully. A dull scrap of metal. She replaced it carefully and set the case on the table beside him. In many ways Major Alister Merrill was a dull man.

'And a leg that is neither whole nor useless, an impediment that will not kill, merely restrain. A man half alive . . . But you, girl . . . you,' he persisted, a little thickly. Drunk with wine and his memories. She choked back another yawn.

'I was reared by an elderly aunt who kept a haberdashery in Cheapside. Lady Farleigh was a favourite customer and when my relatives died, took me into her household. Then – well I married James and we emigrated for his – his health.'

But he wasn't listening, she was quite certain, to her garble of lies and fact. 'I got India,' he went on. 'Oh yes, India – and fever and grapeshot. My leg was almost finished there. Then a captaincy and the West Indies. A murderous hole, Jamaica, but at least there was power to be had. You weren't forced to hobnob in idleness with the spume of slums and gaols who consider themselves the equal of, if not superior to, any gentleman born. And so here is all that's left to me, the colonies. Banished like a Peninsula deserter to a land I detest when I believed that battle into which I put my life was the beginning.' His voice rose. 'It was the end. The end.'

And in sudden gasping fury he dashed the goblet against the fireplace. The particles scattered, glittering rubies in the dancing flames. He stood up, swayed slightly then, not looking at her and with an immense effort at control, strode from the room yelling for Jeremy. She looked regretfully at the shattered pieces – the last of the set. She could have got quite a neat sum for it. He was mad of course. All the Merrills were a little mad. She rose, stepped carefully over the shattered glass, and poured herself a port. She liked port.

There was no sign, or even word of him, for days. Somewhere in the entrails of the house the baby howled itself sick – it must surely die. Its mother, ill-humoured and tired of helping with meals that were wasted, dressed herself in her garish skirts and, with Bess, disappeared into town to the burlesque, Raunie making sure her child went along with them. Where Ada was she neither knew nor cared. They would all come straggling home in the early morning hours – if they came at all. Only Joey remained in his little room above the stables. Joey was afraid of her and she delighted in scaring him, cuffing his ears when he dared to enquire when Miss Merrill would be home. The only fire that had been set was lighted as usual in Alister's room, otherwise Regent Lodge on this late winter's night was chill, quiet, and deserted, and so, devoid of all resistance and restriction, all restraint. It was a new sensation, this solitude with the cold stars and icy pilgrim of a moon far away and only herself, it seemed, alive in the world and virtually mistress of this beautiful house. She was not afraid of this new isolation. Indeed, she felt exalted in the indulgence of her craving for bodily and emotional freedom that was always the most intense and demanding expression of herself, this freedom that came only with the inviolability of material position. Her mind drifted happily from the possibility of one mischief to another. Her feet took on a new stealth, her eyes a new gleam, as she walked the quiet passages or stood dangling the keys, playing with them, toying with the delicious decision of what to do next. There was so much to do, and the long solitary night in which to do it. She was ecstatically happy.

She decided on Eleanor's room. Its dishevelled prettiness amused her and she enjoyed bouncing on the thick mattress, fondling the lacy spreads and befrilled cushions, and flinging open the huge wardrobe. A mess of clothing fell out and she left it where it lay. Somewhere at the back bottles clinked and she poked among them – all empty, and anyway nothing she would have liked. She brushed her hair with the silver-backed brushes, splashed the French perfumes, tried this rouge and that salve then, losing interest, ran to Georgina's bedroom, a smaller replica of her mother's. Throwing off her dress she tried on one garment after another. They were all loose on her slim body and she discarded them impatiently, not caring if they tore, for in her basically oriental mind her needs were clear and unalterable – it was not this, or this, or *this*. Caught up in the sensual excitement of fingering beautiful things she was careless. She opened trinket boxes and tried on bracelets and pins and brooches, absorbed in the wonderful pursuit of herself. A little breathless she wandered the house again, savouring it, this house she controlled and which, at least for the moment, no one could take from her. She was intoxicated by the thought . . . Why, with one brush of her arm she could sweep those trinkets off that table . . . With one stroke of a knife she could slash those hangings . . . No one could stop her. She laughed aloud. Near-naked and dishevelled she snatched up the keys and turned to Barbara's bedroom. This was the ultimate, this rigid barrier of a door that hid Barbara Merrill's world.

She knew the key – she had brooded over it many times – and turned it firmly in the lock. She had only been inside the room once but she remembered everything about it and knew exactly where to go to light the candle. The light settled gently over the ordered secretiveness of the room. It was a bare room devoid of luxury – well, at least Brick hadn't given her presents. But . . . wouldn't she keep his gifts hidden, even in here? Yes, Barbara would. She opened the wardrobe on a few dull clothes; nothing Barbara wore ever seemed to suit her. But tucked at the back was a gown Raunie had never seen before; a velvet négligé of an old, almost translucent shade of amber. Too dark for Barbara – doubtless that was the reason she never wore it – but Raunie pounced on it. It fitted her to perfection except that, Barbara being taller, it trailed the ground at the back. She loved it. She couldn't bear to part with it. She would not part with it. She wrapped it about her body until it clung like a second skin.

She had been aware for a long time of a trunk, half-covered by a piece of faded brocade, peeping from the end of the bed. It gave the impression of being deliberately concealed. It tantalised her. She swept the cover away – if Barbara had secrets she would hide them here, she was sure of it. There was a key in the shaky lock but it refused to turn. But the trunk must have been unlocked for, dragging irritably at the lid, it opened with a squeak. She sat back heavily on her heels. Pamphlets, a pile of little books – Barbara's 'silly' journals that so provoked her mother – letters tied in neat bundles with twine. No blue ribbon. Just twine. She slipped some letters from a pile and, recognising Brick's handwriting, set herself with a rising excitement to frown over the words. But she could not decipher more than an occasional phrase. Fretting over what these sheets of paper begrudged her she persisted, making sense of it more by instinct than by knowledge, piecing it together slowly and patiently:

'. . . the Irish navvies walk about with the smallpox on them . . .'

She opened another. 'If I'm impatient with this God of yours I'm more impatient with man . . .'

What things to write of to a woman! There *must* be confidences . . . secrets . . . intimacy . . . She ripped open a third letter.

'. . . Dgeralli . . .' Ah, she could not mistake that name, she knew it so well. Dgeralli the native. Inar's husband. Her lips moved with a growing excitement. 'I'll find Dgeralli . . . No one destroys my home or people I value without paying for it . . .'

What Brick O'Shea swore he would do, he carried out. Always. So . . . he had found and had his revenge on the Black for some misdeed, tossed him into a river or left him stretched in the sun for the hawks and native dogs to pick clean. So much for Dgeralli. She read at random.

'If you need advice, monetary or otherwise, go to Bridge Street . . .'

Bored, impatient, she opened one of the blue books. Ladies, she knew, wrote in diaries all the time, and intimately. '. . . I give him all he asks of me because I cannot help myself . . .'

She trembled. Who else could Barbara be referring to but Brick O'Shea? So here it was . . . She loved Brick, while he . . . Well, he was a man, and did any man ever refuse a woman who loved him? Yes. Oh yes. Brick had refused herself, Raunie. He had rejected her. '. . . I give him all he asks of me . . .' A great sob of rage and hurt and despair broke from her and the book twisted between her clenched hands. A schoolmarm, a bluestocking. In her fury she ripped out the

286

page but gripping the crushed paper she grew frightened and tried to hide the damage, smoothing and smoothing the diary . . . There. No one could know, surely, there was a page missing.

The sound of horses. Guests? No, it was Jeremy, cursing and tormenting Joey as usual. 'May the De'il tear ye from the hearse in front of all the funeral.' Now Alister was talking, his voice crisp and urgent. Alister . . . She sprang to her feet, the letters fluttering to the floor and tried to lock the trunk but the key seemed hopeless and she was forced to cover it all hastily and leave it – she would tidy up tomorrow. She screwed the papers into her pocket and glanced about her – yes, the room looked exactly as she had found it. She blew out the candle, closed the door softly behind her and locked it. She paused on the landing to compose herself. Alister calling for Bess. There was no Bess. There was only herself. His slightly halting but now angry tread echoed from one down-stairs room to another coupled with a stream of blasphemy. He was drunk or vile-tempered or both. But she was becoming adept at meeting his anger. She smoothed the amber gown and shook back her hair, wishing she had time to brush it smooth. All the same, there was an illusion, an attraction, in wayward hair. She walked slowly downstairs.

He stood in the hall near the one lighted candelabra, his shirt loose and crumpled. He had not shaved. Well, there were dives about Sydney where even an Alister Merrill could lose himself for days and no questions asked or answered. As she came into the strong light he roared: 'Can't find a servant, blast the pack of 'em. And why is the house so cold? I pay for fuel enough, don't I?'

'There's a fire in your room, sir. But I'll light one down-stairs and bring supper there if you wish.'

'I'm not hungry. I want brandy – no, port. And never mind the fire. And why do you talk of lighting it? Where are the women?'

'I don't know,' she said laconically, anticipating his de-mands by fetching slippers from a closet. 'In town perhaps. They often slip away.' With a gesture of irritation he moved to the withdrawing-room. She fetched decanters and glasses from the consol table and placed them beside his chair. The room seemed suddenly very big and very cold.

'If you hadn't come down I'd have smashed open that cabinet. And every other cupboard in the place.'

He drank thirstily, stretching his now dry-shod feet, his anger soothed as his comfort increased. His eyes followed her as she moved about straightening this, folding that, lingering over her tasks, prolonging her slightest gesture. The silence became intense. 'I woke you I suppose,' he murmured a little thickly.

'I wasn't asleep.'

'Why not? It's late.'

'I don't know.' Deliberately she turned to face him. 'Unless . . . I think I was wondering when you would return. Or if you would return at all.'

A long pause. 'Why?' Then sharply, with a curious intensity. 'Why were you thinking of me?'

She didn't answer. Her silence was deliberate too. She could feel his glance intensifying as he became entirely aware of her and her appearance. She watched his eyes move slowly from her hair to her face, travel down her throat and over her shoulders to flick her body then become so fixed on her hips that she stirred. She could not help it. So often under his intent gaze she had felt . . . shaken, for she knew – even if he did not, yet – she had only to put out a hand to him and he would come. The decanter was at his elbow; he held out his empty glass. Slowly, concentrating on her walk, she crossed and poured for him, keeping her hand steady with a great effort for she was surprised at herself; she had not imagined he could make her feel so, her body trembling and tingling with an excitement that was urgent and quite wonderful. It would be easy, too easy perhaps, to give herself to this handsome, baffled and baffling, hungry – ah, how hungry for the warmth of a woman – unhappy man. He put out his hand in a gesture, fumbling and unsure. But he did not touch her. He seemed to pull himself back, to flop heavily in his chair.

'You disturb me, damn you. *Damn* you!' Savagely, almost as if he resented her.

The decanter was empty. Calmly she picked it up and with the same slow sensuous walk crossed to the consol. And she knew, even without seeing the blur of his hunched figure reflected in the mirror, that he was still watching her; couldn't take his eyes off her. As she bent with studied graceful movements to open the pedestal drawer she risked a glance at him. He was leaning forward, his elbows on his knees, his long thin hands clasping the glass so carelessly tiny globules of dark fluid dripped unheeded on the carpet. He was staring at her directly but he did not seem to notice her glance. There was something predatory and primitive in that still, taut watching; as if the paper-thin veneer of the society that had moulded him so rigorously had quite suddenly cracked to leave him emotionally and physically free. Her hand clenched on the decanter until the knuckles whitened under the stretched skin. He was conscious of her, oh yes, and being conscious of her, desired her. Propinquity, and now opportunity, had sharpened that desire until preliminaries were superfluous. She turned and smiled. Her smile grew into a soft little laugh, a sound utterly alluring and full of promise.

Through Alister's blurred mind her laugh sounded loud and vibrant and young. Hurtfully young. The wine momentarily chilled in his veins and he felt old. Not old with the weight of years but ancient with regrets and lost hopes and disillusionment. Old with loneliness. It was seven years – he realised with sudden painful clarity the astounding but positive fact – since he had possessed a woman. Seven years of twisting his desires back upon himself, of smashing them down relentlessly, viciously, before they could even take root in his starved loins. He thought he had stifled the rack of passion forever until this girl's throat rippled and her thighs moved and his long abstinence was unnecessary and not to be borne. At this moment of all time the past was dead, the future unborn and there was nothing but the urgent exquisite woman's flesh and what it promised before him; nothing but the rapture that looks neither backward nor forward but is

289

of the moment. The feverish needs of youth that he was sure had rotted away were still there, and demanding. They pounded at him, impelled him. He stood and placed his glass on the table, not looking at it. He ceased to think of anything or anyone but himself.

Raunie heard the faint slur of the glass on the polished wood. She watched him straighten and walk across the room towards her. Her narrowed eyes glazed and her thoughts raced and tumbled over each other in a sudden lucid explanation of his actions: You can't help yourself any longer, Alister Merrill. You've fought against me but now it's over, as if quite suddenly all the tiny dragging memories of me had taken place of sense and reason and grasped control of your mind and will. There is nothing you can do about it any longer.

A shutter dropped over her mind at his touch. He pushed up her long sleeves and grasped her arms above the elbows. His fingers were hard and hurtful. His lips moved and she pulled him close – he must not speak or think or hesitate. Her fingers clawed at him as his arms went round her. He held her, their bodies merging, then, moving her to one arm his hand closed about her throat. It trembled under his touch. His hand slipped down inside her gown and closed about one breast. She gasped with the urgency of his hold, and the sweetness of it. She sighed and closed her eyes as she felt herself lifted as he would lift a child and carried up the stairs and along the dark cold corridors. There was no sound anywhere but his quick uneven breathing and the thudding of her heart, so urgent she was sure it could be heard. She felt warmth on her skin and saw a splash of flame and the quiet lazy comfort of his room enveloped her. It lulled her, drowning her in warmth. She refused to think. She could not think. She was thrown roughly on his bed.

She lay trembling, conscious only of the stabs of response coursing through the lower parts of her body. Her hands pressed her breasts back upon themselves. In the hot heavy languor of the room the only urge either of them knew was the swell of their individual desire; fierce and not to be stifled, as if they existed in a doorless shrine of the senses in which it was impossible to ignore or deny the faintest pulsation of each other. With a sob of relief she felt his naked limbs stretching beside her, reaching for her, touching and enfolding her. Ah, the sweetness of desire . . . And this was the sharpest sweetness of it all, this instant before . . . It was true, one could be enamoured of the act of love.

His hands clawed at her gown. The clips were stiff and with an ugly impatience he ripped them apart. The weight of his body was on hers . . . heavy . . . heavier. His hands cupped her breasts, his mouth caressed and nuzzled their tightness. His lips travelled over her, her hips, then her thighs. He buried his head in the yielding flesh at her waist as if his whole body would enter into hers and become a part of it. She sighed and murmured, her yearning mingling with the savage sweetness of his breathing. She clasped him closer . . . closer. His teeth were biting and the pain was a sharp ecstasy. And when he took her at last with a silent frenzied penetration that held something of despair in it, she cried out . . .

She woke, the heat of her soothed to a pleasant warmth, the throbbing in her legs lulled by a purifying and growing relaxation. She remembered and lay still. After a while she turned carefully on her side. Alister slept, one hand tangled in her hair, gripping it. Cautiously she pulled her head free, raised herself on one elbow and stared down at him. Her mind savoured certain very satisfactory details of his love-making. It was difficult to reconcile the Alister Merrill the world knew, a man close on fifty, acidy, precise, sometimes brutal, almost entirely lacking in humour and lightness, his every thought and act premeditated and significant, with this man who was so suddenly her lover. He had, incredibly, swept them both along in a storm of feeling she had not for one moment expected. Not with Alister. James . . . with James there had been no love, only hope. Feli . . . an animal episode best forgotten. She denied it. Kenneth . . . a boy's lusty bursts of passion, a youth's wild orgies of recrimination. Alister was none of these. To Alister she had responded completely, given to him because he had so demanded it, caress for caress, movement for movement until the climax had been complete, an exhausting gushing of the sap from the very root of the tree. Was there more? There was . . . Brick.

But she would not think of Brick O'Shea. Not now. Only of Alister. She stirred restlessly. She wanted him to wake and take her again. She wanted more, again and again. But his heavy satiated breathing mocked her ears. One valuable thing about young men, they didn't fall asleep exhausted. Though the fire was dead the room was cosy and she did not want to leave it, or him. But day would come and people would go about the house watching, seeing. She slid from the bed, wrapped the the torn gown about her and padded across the floor. As soft and sure as a cat she crept along the cold hall and down the small flight of steps to her room. The papers in her pocket rustled. She crunched them into a ball, then hesitated, unsure what to do with them. Perhaps some day she would read them again . . . She snapped open her old carpet-bag and thrust them inside. But useless rubbish after all; now that she meant to have the best the world could offer she could afford to forget trifles. As she flung herself on her bed and drew up the covers she heard a cab coming up the drive and voices singing in tipsy abandon. And Ada's voice shrilled above the others.

The hours dragged till Alister came at night. Then alone with him she felt the house closing about them as a house always closes about a man and a woman who are, in their own minds and secret wishes, its sole inhabitants. She knew and accepted his passion as a physical thing, an appetite to be appeased as he slaked his hunger and exhaustion with food and sleep; forced to accept that desolate role of a woman clasped in male arms intoxicated by male feeling, to be drawn against male lips possessed by male needs and senses. But he did have rare moments of sentiment, bizarre as they were, and because she met passion with her one faith, faith in the value of her favours, she made of herself a pagan creature of avid, almost desperate response.

For here, centred in Alister Merrill, was refuge. She refused to return to hunger. To change – yes. To a wandering existence – yes. But never to that old hunger, that unappeased poverty of the body and the senses; never poverty of any kind whatever. Alister could save her from such deprivation – and in doing so could become her stepping-stone to Brick. If Brick O'Shea despised her for what she was, and had been – gipsy born, a slavey in his house, and in his bordel, the barely tolerated overworked widow woman of Regent Lodge – then she must become what Brick wanted. If he would only look at a blue-blood then through Alister she could assume the life and trappings of one . . .

But in the hours when they managed to be alone he was impatient, often cruel, and demanding enough to spur her to meet him with the same swift absorbed lust, and after it was over and they lay in their blissful release, calmed and lazy, he met her demands with evasion, then irritation. Past a certain point in their relationship she could not for the present lead him. Alone together she might discard humility and he, his secrecy, but about their daily lives he withdrew from any sign of casualness. She felt herself, if subtly, forced back to her old position in the household, and this she refused to accept. Moreover, the Merrill women would soon be home and her influence over her lover further weakened. Their physical contact would most certainly be threatened. This he must know but, possessed by the fleshly satisfaction of the moment, he appeared not to realise it. How to make him face up to the situation and find a solution? The solution she wanted?

And just as she had feared, abruptly, their languorous drifting was over. Leaving Georgina at school Barbara brought her mother down, for the new Governor was expected daily. All Sydney was beating carpets and trimming bonnets; at least the gentry preened and prepared but to the rabble a governor was just a governor after all. Governor or not, Ralph Huntingdon was off on the long journey to Port Phillip, eager for roots, his head spinning with advice – he would need fifteen hundred sheep and many horses and drays, stores and tools and bullocks. So much of everything it seemed when all he really wanted was a neat little farm where he might live the gentle life he knew. But they laughed at that. Long and loudly. They talked loudly too. Large country, large men, large voices. They puzzled him, everything puzzled him, but still they and the land held him, fascinated. Jenny Werner was bearing with cheerful martyrdom her exclusion from festivities while her husband hastened about his absorbing business of crippling all trade that opposed his own. And the young Clintons waited solemnly at Sunvalley for their ship.

Eleanor, after her first hastily covered-up surprise had accepted Raunie's presence with resignation, even, as the crowded weeks went by, with cordiality. She had regretted the undignified scene in the garden, Raunie decided, almost as much as she regretted the twenty pounds. Or perhaps, as was more likely, she realised her daughter-in-law's usefulness. Perhaps Alister had silenced her protests. Whatever the reason, something touching a truce was accepted between them. As for her lover, Raunie's only glimpse of him now was in the presence of others. He was unhappy, she assured herself. He longed for her. But she could do nothing but wait for him, and through him for her life to take a leap forward, waiting and moving through her days as in some hazy underwater world, pausing sometimes to gaze across the Harbour at the fine house springing up among the trees of Neutral Bay. It was rumoured Brick O'Shea had ordered it ready for his return. But when would he return? Nobody seemed to know. Perhaps he would never come back . . . Sometimes she was miserably, achingly, sure of it. Perhaps . . . Perhaps he was dead.

And she would turn from the window brushing a cold hand from her heart. For no matter how she tried to forget him, even if she could not see him or touch him and did not know where he was, or even if he were still alive, he was always with her. Yet . . . even if he did come back to Australia it would not be to her, Raunie. What then could she cling to, believe in day by day? Only what was real, it seemed. Yes, only what you felt, only what was in your hands or pressed against your body, only what you possessed at a precise moment of time and not in some shadowy future world of 'perhaps'. Well then – and she would toss back her beautiful hair and square her shoulders – she, Raunie Lorne or Merrill or whatever name they cared to give her – drew breath, her limbs moved, the blood coursed through her body. She was young and alive and ready for the warmth of a man's arms. And if Alister Merrill's arms were not always warmly tender, they were always strong. Yes, it must be true – there was only now.

Chapter Thirteen

THE *Carysfort* entered the Heads on the second evening of August, 1846. From the resplendent officials weighted with medals and dignified expressions down to the lowliest mopsqueezer, water-carrier and groom, all craned round heads and bunting to watch the arrival of the tall stout Sir Charles Fitzroy already called the 'merry Governor'. And he was indeed a splendid figure with his luxuriant curls and whiskers. Over-critical matrons decided that Lady Mary was 'definitely fading my dear even if she is the daughter of the Duke of Richmond'. Then decided magnanimously to relent – she was of course a semi-invalid, poor lady, and her hands were nice, she had reason to be so proud of them. Eleanor, whirling in the delightful round of social doings – the ladies' levée, soirées, dansantes and all the rest – planned Gina's 'coming-out' at the first ball at Government House (such a dull old pile of a place under Gipps) for surely such a man, with a handsome young son to boot, would plan something splendid? So naturally she must have money – Alister must stop his silly quibbling over the Lodge expenditure, for all were spending beyond their means. She *must* have money. And lots and lots of it.

But she found her husband more elusive than ever. Fitzroy, after addressing the Legislative Council, was off on a tour of his inland counties so, by-passing the ailing Havelock, most of the official duties of the colony fell on Alister's reluctant shoulders. Major Merrill did not greatly approve of the charming, pleasure-loving Sir Charles, and cursed him silently but thoroughly as he snuffed his study candles in the early hours, too tired even to summon Jeremy. But – and his mouth would set as he went heavily upstairs – the Governor of course was the Governor. But still there was work; a light burned in his room many a night to many a small morning hour. And Raunie, prowling, restless and unable to sleep, would see the glow from under the door, or from his window, and pace her room, wanting to pound on his door, hit out at something . . . at him. Then throw herself on her bed to pound her pillow instead and bite back her angry tearing sobs.

Beyond her fury at his rejection was fear. Men forgot so quickly, so easily cast a thing aside if the thing they were accustomed to were not ready to hand – particularly a woman. And she must not lose Alister . . . For beyond her anger and her fear was something else . . . an unexpected, and disturbing, loneliness for the man. She had set out to bind him to her by every breath they drew together, every caress of every nerve in their bodies, and in so doing, it seemed, she had bound herself, even a little. Alister Merrill, the ageing soldier, had touched something in her which she had thought dead, safely subdued so she might make her way through life clear-eyed and so, survive; a naïveté, that innocent eagerness, that *giving* she had first known for the ingratiating, drunken, misfit of a James Lorne, an excitement for him, so soon to be extinguished. The giving had surfaced again for Brick, and would always be there for Brick, but he did not want it. He did not want her. But Alister wanted her, ah yes. Or *had* wanted her. Then she must make it easy for him to want her again . . .

So, as the weeks drifted into months, while they moved as strangers, polite but remote, participants in a game she would not continue to play, she became willing, even eager, to journey into town on trivial errands. She contrived small outings for herself. She had decided what she must do, and more importantly, how she must go about doing it. There was only one way she could be mistress of her days and nights, and so of Alister – her own establishment. She still had her twenty pounds. Little enough, but something.

Christmas. Ralph came overland, riding the dusty tracks like a knight homing from a Crusade, the skin peeling from his sun-baked face and his carroty hair bleached by the sun. Maxim was making an ass of himself over his fat little son while Charlotte was busy foisting an insolvent rake of a grand-nephew on a wary and rake-weary town. The Lodge overflowed with Werners and Clintons and Parkers and, occasionally, the Havelocks whose visits put Eleanor in a pet for days – so many skeletons in the Lodge cupboards to be squeezed into even darker corners. And she hovered anxiously about Ralph when Raunie came near but was relieved to find he had no eyes for any woman but her youngest daughter as Gina scrabbled through her piano pieces and sang in her clear child's voice and swept modest lashes over pink cheeks as she had been told to do as he stuttered his description of the house taking shape in a Gippsland valley. And all the time Barbara, an efficient wraith without whom the household never quite satisfactorily functioned, assisted as hostess, her eyes seeing things others never saw, her heart beating to a rhythm others never knew. For few bothered about Barbara Merrill, an eccentric of a girl left, or bent upon leaving herself, on some far-back and dusty shelf.

Chaperoned picnics and children's teas with a miraculously produced Punch and Judy, carriage drives and riding parties and late suppers and little dinners. Lazy afternoons and long, long evenings in the shelter of yellow jasmine festooned with passion flower, beside the scarlet blooms of the pomegranate, while the small fry sprawled under the loquat tree and made themselves sick on the white flesh, or chased the huge flashing butterflies about the lemon trees. Sometimes a homesick woman would cry, very softly and ashamedly, simply because it was Christmas; such a heavy breathless Christmas, too hot to celebrate in the beloved way or to be '*très gai*', with nary a holly sprig or a snow-tipped branch to soothe one's eyes or lift one's lonely spirits. And on Sunday mornings – decked in new finery Eleanor sometimes chose to remember she was a clergyman's daughter – the Merrill carriage joined the procession of jingling equipages on their proud and splendid way to St James.

Raunie, aside from being admired in her best, was bored by the service and spent the time watching Alister. But even at family gatherings he would not meet her eyes. And he seemed always to be at General Havelock's, where Roger was almost constantly confined to his bed. Eleanor went visiting too with a reticule of clean handkerchiefs to mop up her ready tears, and bouquets for dear brave Janet, and calf's-foot jelly for the invalid prepared by her own hands with Ada grumbling as she cleaned up the mess. Eleanor was determined to see the 'tragedy', as she called it, through to the bitter end even if it drained the last of her strength – as it very well could, she insisted. But dear Roger, so patient, so brave, was looking dreadful, she pronounced to her husband when finally alone with him. Surely the poor dear sufferer could not last much longer?

So the indolent summer passed, the heat shimmering over the waterways, babies crying in their cots and maids slouching barefoot with damp tendrils of hair clinging to their necks, with often the only sounds from the heat-lazy world outside the high unbroken song of the cicadas and the whistle of flocks of tiny green parrots fluttering and whirling over a housetop. And through the languid afternoons while all Sydney waited for the first swirl of the 'southerly buster' Raunie would pause at a window to stare longingly across the Harbour at Brick O'Shea's house . . .

The clang of shutters, with Bess and Tilly rushing to secure them, then to close doors and windows, while the children ran through the bluster of scattering leaves and shivering blooms. The cold violence of the wind was delicious on her hot body as she leaned from the window to watch the children at their play, and to laugh with them . . . Refreshed, she felt a new energy, a deepening resolve.

Brick O'Shea was not dead. Brick O'Shea would return to his land. And when he did she would meet him on his own ground, and he would not refuse her. She must not doubt that for an instant. As she must never doubt that what she had roused in Alister Merrill was there, and waiting.

The highlight of winter's gay 'season', the Birthday Ball. In the ballroom of the beautiful white residence by the water the

299

Court party gathered to do homage to the maidens of Sydney. Georgina Merrill, the youngest and surely the most beautiful there in her gown of billowing white, her golden hair smooth under the circlet of rosebuds, made a perfect curtsy. Ralph could not take his eyes from her – neither floods nor indifferent labour nor the lassitude of his cabbages had kept Ralph away; he had come as a homing pigeon. Mrs Alister Merrill and the Major, their daughters and escorts and their young widowed daughter-in-law attracted the attention due to their importance as they smiled, bowed and curtsied, indicating only by their flushed cheeks and tightened lips the violent scene that had preceded their quite regrettable lateness.

For Eleanor had endured a bitter struggle to have Raunie left out of it all. It was Gina's night and nothing must detract from her younger daughter's triumph. In any case Raunie had nothing to wear; whereupon the girl proudly displayed a transformed evening gown of Gina's. She had sewn resolve as well as embroidery into the dress for she had made up her mind that nothing would keep her from this ball. It was her right to be there. Besides . . . there was her plan. Barbara took no part in the argument but the Major was crisply adamant; the place for his son's widow was with his family. It was for Raunie, and Raunie alone, to decide. Georgina finally clinched the matter with a tearful refusal to go without her so Eleanor was forced to capitulate – a debutante with red eyes? Horrors! Raunie took her time in dressing and descended to join the gentlemen in the shimmering green dress that so heightened the colour of her eyes, knowing full well the men were secretly admiring her. It was Alister who placed her shawl about her shoulders. And as she took his arm she knew that perhaps for the first time in these many months he was completely aware of her. She ignored Eleanor and brushed his hand softly as they all glittered out into the clear winter's night. She had gained Alister's attention, yes. Now she must keep it.

She was, as she had intended to be, a sensation. She was discussed, pointed out, admired. Making the best of the situation Eleanor elaborated upon her daughter-in-law's connections with Lady Farleigh. Certainly no one present would be likely to contradict her, she decided, and drew her skirts carefully aside; for her taste, not enough aristocratic dignity these days, so many yielding provocatively in the waltz and flinging their ankles in the polka. And her own kinswoman behaving like some cheap *demi-mondaine*!

She turned her ashamed face aside to study with growing interest the somewhat grim-faced man who had stood most of the evening in his corner surveying the dancers; a severe but distinguished-looking man in bottle green with fine pomaded whiskers. Perhaps she should join Maggie Parker – busybodies did have their uses. Yes, perhaps the Parkers knew of him . . . She crooked a demanding finger at Barbara to bring her shawl, then brushed her impatiently aside. Why couldn't the girl show even a modicum of feminine animation? What a cross for a mother to bear. She blinked back angry futile tears as she prepared to pump Margaret Parker and her dowager companions.

Raunie's success was sweet to her taste. The Governor was amusing. Elderly Mr Byrnes, who was some kind of veterinary expert, proposed to her – superb little filly. She mastered even the Sir Roger de Coverley with ease and with her exquisite dancing and long-cultivated social graces was the undisputed belle of the ball – a somewhat too obvious one, the women whispered, quite shocking in the fact that she, and not the nubile young maids, was gaining the attention. But the men lost themselves happily in the spell of her voice and the drowsy depths of her eyes. She intoxicated them. As she intoxicated herself with her success.

Driven to distraction by the girl's flirting and flaunting of herself, Eleanor turned with relief to the presentation by the Colonel of the stranger from the far corner, Mr William Aberdeen Blair, lately arrived in the colony and developing a property on the western plains; a widower certainly, but thirty-eight was not really old and his wealth was reported to be great. And here he was beside her, his sombre eyes following Georgina's whirling skirts from under which her shapely young ankles twinkled at tantalising intervals.

Eleanor brushed aside the dark wings of unease; it was woman's destiny to compromise. So she would compromise with the somewhat disturbing tales of his late wife's long and obscure illness – yes, the dowager chitchat had been indeed productive. So she set herself to contriving to have Ralph lead Barbara out – the girl must surely be boring Captain Eustace there and certainly must not be permitted to bore Mr Blair. No one must bore Mr Blair. Mr Blair was then graciously permitted to lead Georgina out in the waltz. Eleanor's body strained with pride. Dared she hope . . . Indeed, it was all she could do to give Mr George her attention as he bubbled over his pet promotion; hunting dingos with a regular pack, everything civilised, ma'am. Yes indeed. Then Eleanor's jaw dropped. At the precise moment Godfrey appeared to place a lemonade in her hand Raunie evaded a partner and with a provocative swirl of the green skirts paused to enquire as to her mother-in-law's comfort, further, if the lemonade were cool enough? Then with a prolonged curve of her fan she flashed an inviting, brazen, and quite irresistible smile at Godfrey.

Raunie began by admiring his dancing. Godfrey Selwyn had never doubted his ability at anything but it was pleasing to be reassured by such a competent judge and he bestowed a look of deeper interest upon his partner. There had been times when he had suspected something approaching a sneer in her now musical voice but tonight she seemed a different person. And she danced exquisitely. His poet's soul expanded. Barbara cared little for dancing, indeed for any social accomplishment. He was very unhappy about Barbara. This young woman melted – Barbara never melted – into his encircling arms, and his arms became distinctly less rigid. He began to feel quite heady with the feel of her. She was asking about England, actually seeming to understand his love of it. She was – what did the French call it? – *sympathique*. Yes, she might even understand how difficult life could be for a sensitive young man. Certainly Barbara made no allowances for sensitive young men. Raunie leaned closer and he sweated a little. What a handsome creature she was. They seemed quite suddenly to be whirling together and alone in a vast high room with the music lilting and fading somewhere into far distant halls. It echoed about them from afar. And he didn't want the music to stop. Now they were following its faroff call together. She was laughing up at him and he didn't want to move his eyes from hers. Not for a moment. He didn't want to let her go. Not now. Not ever.

Eleanor's anxious eyes saw Barbara trip and Ralph steady her with his usual awkward movements. They laughed together. A clumsy, clumsy girl – all those dancing lessons wasted. If it weren't for Godfrey . . . Her fan stilled, frozen in her frozen hand as the music died away with a weird little discord from the fiddle and curious glances about and hesitation among the musicians. For Godfrey Selwyn continued to twirl his partner there in the centre of the room, and in a most abandoned way. And Raunie's head was thrown back as she laughed up at him, laughing long and loudly. Too long and loudly. Eleanor almost fainted. Godfrey must be out of his mind. Both of them mad, quite mad. But no . . . Eleanor blazed. Raunie would know well what she was doing. Was that a laugh? Her horrified eyes darted . . . yes, there a raised eyebrow, there fans fluttering like agitated wings. And was that a smile on the Governor's lips? And still the pair of them went waltzing in the centre of the deserted floor, Raunie too close to Godfrey, her body seeming to melt into his, her hand caressing his shoulder, her mouth parted invitingly.

The slut. The shameless calculating strumpet. First Ralph, now Godfrey. And all the time living under the same roof as her pure and darling Georgina. Oh, would the Merrill name ever live down this degrading, this humiliating, spectacle? Would they ever see Mr Blair again? She swung about, away from Barbara standing there as if she didn't notice a thing – or care – in a desperate search for Alister. Ah, he was moving through the throng to her side, his face expressionless. Well, she too had her pride. Though half-swooning she rose and with all the majesty she could muster gave an imperative flick of her fan to summon her family about her.

Godfrey was deliriously happy. He felt important – Barbara

303

never made him feel important – and was toying with the urge to recite his latest poem there and then when he became aware of his solitude. Of *their* solitude. As he realised where he was embarrassment swamped his elation. Major Merrill was staring at him pointedly and he did not like that. Everyone was staring at him. He proffered an arm to his partner and very straight and white-faced led her to her assembled relations where blessed if strained attempts at conversation enveloped them.

In spite of their invitation to supper with the Governor they must, unfortunately, take their leave. Mrs Merrill was rather too happily affected by her daughter's triumph – nothing serious, oh dear no, a night's rest and all would be well. And, after all, Miss Georgina was very young. His Excellency quite understood; late hours soon faded roses from cheeks, even such beautiful cheeks as Miss Georgina's. In the confusion and strain of their overly-formal farewells Eleanor summoned just strength enough to express the hope that Mr Blair would call? Mr Blair, silent as ever, bowed. She had to be content with it. But Raunie, lingering over her good-byes to an admiring amused circle of young males was forced to spring to the imperative no-nonsense snap of her mother-in-law's fan. And Eleanor's weary but valiant departure surrounded by her solicitous daughters, their escorts, and her tight-lipped husband barely concealed her bitter fury.

So bitter that, gentlemen out of the way and safely inside Regent Lodge, her resentment broke into noisy hysteria. The Governor had been insulted . . . Government House polluted . . . The only life for 'her' kind was fraternising with pavement rakes . . . The girl belonged nowhere else but in the gutter . . .

'Take your mother upstairs,' Alister said sharply. 'I shall attend to this matter.'

He waved Raunie into the withdrawing-room and closed the door firmly behind them. They were alone at last. She turned and waited confidently for him to take her in his arms. But he didn't come to her. He seemed more remote at that moment than he had ever been. Had she gone too far too quickly? She made a desperate little move towards him but he halted her with a gesture. He even took a slight, very slight, step back.

'You cannot stay here any longer, Raunie.' His voice was cold. 'It's an impossible situation.'

'Do you think I want to stay?' she blazed. 'It has always been like this. If I'm merely polite she accuses me of boldness. If I'm natural in my manner I'm flirting. Why does she hate me so? Because I married her precious son? Was it a crime to marry Kenneth?'

'Leave my son out of this.'

'But where can I go if I leave here? Don't you care that I have nowhere to go? Oh, Alister . . .'

She had never used his name quite so beseechingly, so intimately before, but now was not the time to rely on discretion. It was the time to depend on other things, other methods.

'Apart from the fact that it is my duty to see that you are provided for I – care very much.' His voice was rough, jerky. 'It has not been easy for me these months –'

'I've been unhappy too. So very unhappy. How could I be otherwise, being close to you and yet not –' Her voice broke just enough, hung there. 'Sometimes I've wondered if you wanted me to go away, perhaps even to marry again. She's always urging me to marry.'

But as she spoke she knew it was the wrong thing to say. He said a little stiffly. 'I have no doubt there are many men –'

'I don't want other men,' she burst out passionately. 'I only want you.'

She watched the pulse throbbing in his throat. 'It's not possible,' he said at last.

'It is. At least, it would be possible if I had somewhere to live. My own house. Even a tiny house . . .'

His eyes met hers. He was looking at her now, really looking at her, listening in spite of himself. She saw the yearning in his eyes belying his controlled and rigid body. She went to him and placed her hands on his shoulders, her touch urgent and compelling. 'If you would help me find a place of my own, somewhere close to town, no one would

305

know you came to me. How could they know if we were both careful? After all, it's natural for me to set up my own establishment.' Her hands moved to his neck, caressing it. 'I've heard of a house – a small house, but nice. No, wait . . . at least see it.' Her voice was all feeling, all urgency. 'Just see it. *Please* Alister?'

She held his eyes, willing what she wanted from him. Tomorrow she would get the key for they wouldn't hold the house much longer and she just couldn't lose it – she had wanted it from the first. It was perfect. Once he saw it, once they were there together and alone, he would not refuse her. He couldn't refuse. Close to him now, closer, clinging to him, whispering and persuading, her hands resting against his cheeks and her lips moving against his . . . The upsets of the evening were forgotten. At last his arms went round her and tightened and they stood poised and silent, their hearts and their most intimate thoughts racing together as one.

'Say you will, Alister. Say you will.'

She took his hand and laid it against her hip and he felt her body palpitating, to receive him. It was more than he could bear. He put his lips to her throat, to absorb the warm flesh, the curious blindness of passion clouding his eyes. He saw nothing, all his consciousness in his touch. Yes, he murmured . . . yes . . . anything . . . as long as he might have her again. Anything. Anything . . .

Winthrop in Macquarie Street was one of the earliest houses built there. Now that its owner was forced to take his business to Parramatta and more up-to-date residences were springing up all over town, its rent was low as it was small and its offices cramped and old-fashioned. Moreover, it was too close to the Convict Barracks for the squeamish, for it was not so long ago that felons were whipped there daily and carried by four of their fellows like logs, dripping with blood and cursing in their pain and torment, to be dumped at the Rum Hospital close by. New arrivals looking for homes were all squeamish. Raunie was not. She had coveted the little place from first

306

glimpse and suffered agonies of unease that she might lose it. Well, now it was hers, taken on lease, all signed and sealed.

In a triumph of possession she wandered the reception rooms planning how she would decorate about the excellent oil painting in the hall and the golden clock on the creamy mantel. To the attic with the marble urns and the horrible plush sofa. She found holes in the curtains . . . such a dismal colour too. She must have new things. She *would* have new things. Alister would come today. He must come. She had willed him to come. The key was in the door, waiting. Yes, he would come. Her eyes veiled. And when he was here . . . She hurried through her tour of the silent house and went upstairs to the main bedroom. She took off her bonnet, shook her hair loose and undid the clips at her throat.

One thing certain – Abigail would approve of the place. It had just that air of not-too-stuffy elegance that would suit the woman. A housekeeper-companion was essential and she had decided she couldn't let Abigail Luff slip through her fingers; her instinct was rarely wrong and when the neat calm-faced female had faced her at the agency, appraising as she in turn was being appraised, Raunie knew that here was a woman versed in the more sophisticated artistries of the world. The Old World. She felt they would understand each other perfectly for she saw something she defined as anxiety deep in the woman's eyes. She had been on the books a long time, doubtless because of the pretty but sadly indolent daughter she sought to have employed with her. Given a secure place, perhaps the opportunity of a comfortable marriage for her adored Kitty, and Mrs Luff hinted she was prepared to give many favours in return.

'I am widowed for the second time,' Raunie explained smoothly. 'Now I wish to set up my own household. You will understand, I'm sure, that a . . . discreet companion is as essential to me as a housekeeper. I shall also need a housemaid.' She saw the woman's tightly folded hands relax and smiled at her. 'And later a groom when I have a phaeton. But unfortunately I cannot afford high wages as I am dependent on my late husband's family for support. My father-in-law, as perhaps you already know, is Major Merrill.'

As she expected, Abigail Luff was impressed; there were few of these military families left, and so her eagerness for the opportunities service with such connections might furnish was obvious. Might she be permitted a suggestion? She had a nephew of sorts in the colony, a rascal admittedly but a genius at contrivance. If Madam saw fit to employ the boy she promised to keep him in order. So they fell to ways and means and remuneration, both secretly content with their bargain.

As Alister closed the door Raunie called down to him. Her voice seemed to tremble on the still soft air. He stood a moment in the entrance hall savouring the fact of her there alone and waiting. The memory of past intimacy took hold, warming his body, and dwarfing the shock, the angry shock, at the grandiose location she had chosen for herself – did she think he had the income of a factory owner? He had made his way here nursing a tight network of logic as to why this plan of hers must not be allowed to eventuate. He simply couldn't afford it – though everything in him shrank at having to explain that to her. How on earth could he explain it? – that all he had was the Lodge, and if he should lose Regent Lodge . . .

But climbing the narrow stairs his irritation and resolve sublimated itself in desire for her. All these months he had immersed himself in work, avoiding her smothering embrace that meant escape, for when her voice took hold of him, when he looked long and deeply into her eyes, reason was blotted out and he was conscious only of her. Now he had succumbed once again and . . . well . . . to hell with the situation in which he found himself. He was tired of reason – yes, he admitted it. What use to be surprised that he, Alister Merrill, after a youth of discipline and a maturity of self-denial should have taken to himself a clandestine love. Loneliness had begun it. And wine. In his cups. If he had kept his head he would never have touched her. But he hadn't followed his head. He had answered the need of his body. He had been wearied, nay exhausted by his long pretence, and through Raunie was dispelled the terrible nauseating aloneness of body and spirit that had been his bed-fellow for so long. His wife had so recoiled from him over the years that he had come to regard himself as something unclean and incompetent where women were concerned; degrading years of her stooping to ridiculous lengths to keep him at a distance, to explain her tiredness, her vague petty sicknesses as if even now he might possibly want her. Physical desire for her had died long ago though he found himself still actively concerned for her welfare – it was something left. There had been opportunities with women before Raunie, yes, but he had turned from them all until this girl held out her bitter-sweet arms. He had never before known this terrible hunger for a woman that had become centred in Raunie's beautiful and responsive flesh.

He paused in the doorway devouring her with his eyes, enjoying the golden skin of her throat, shining even in the dim light with moist heat. As she flung her arms about him there was no sound but their quickened breathing. She was eager, pulsating with vigour. He wanted her that way. That way she roused him too. Only she could do that to him. Only Raunie.

'Say you'll let me have the house. *Please* Alister. I've been making plans and I'll surprise you how cheaply I can furnish it. We couldn't just leave it as it is, now could we? Alister, do you hear what I'm saying?'

'We'll see,' he murmured, feeling for her.

'No more of waiting.'

'No.' He fumbled at her dress.

'I'll need things for myself too,' she prompted hastily, wriggling a little, postponing his caresses. 'I can't go in and out of here in rags, you know I can't. I must have clothes.'

'Clothes?' His hands rested on her as he made an intense effort to follow what she was saying. She was persisting about something. Women were always persisting. Why couldn't they let things be . . .? But he had cut himself off for so long from women and their needs he had to force himself to understand them. Tolerate them. The young were always

309

wanting things. And she was young, he must not forget that. But . . . He frowned. It was all too easy to lose count of trifling sums that, added up, became substantial – a ball gown, a dinner, a colt to feed, ribbons and laces, and now it seemed, more ribbons and laces. He must put his affairs in order, then perhaps . . . But Roger had been oddly unapproachable of late, almost secretive. Not that he would prejudice his chances there by asking for a loan, even a trifling one. Damn it though, no need for the old man to be apologetic about buying that stud. If he wanted horseflesh he could afford it, even an expensive a stud as this was rumoured to be. Even if he did have horseflesh enough already. It was odd . . . Perhaps his illness was further affecting his judgement where age had already done its damage. But what matter? Three thousand pounds, four thousand, would be a small rock on a large hillside to Roger Havelock.

The room was cloying, spinning a little. Raunie's naked arched body pressed against him. He wanted rid of his clothes too, and quickly. Quite suddenly he loathed anything that bound him as in a vice and he tore at his collar, his tunic. He could not think. But no need to think. Not now. He held her so closely it hurt them both. But the hurt was, as always, exquisite.

'You see,' she whispered, tilting back her head and laughing at him, 'how easy it will be? How very very easy?'

Major Merrill flicked the dust from a chair – a rather decrepit-looking chair – and sat with as much care as reluctance. No neat front office this time, with luxurious furnishings to soothe and console. As the Jew went on scribbling he forced himself to patience – Major Alister Merrill was unaccustomed to waiting for things. Or people. Finally the little man put down his pen, moved his hands together once with a brushing movement as if dispelling fluff or recalcitrant debtors, and remarked what a fine morning it was for September and how convinced he was that His Excellency's arrival would be an excellent thing for the colony. New blood. New festivities. New plans. Even if it did mean that the Forces – with a slight inclination of his head – were burdened with new responsibilities. Was it not so? Alister murmured superfluities – why wouldn't you be pleased about it, you hypocritical little usurer? he fumed inwardly. More silver pawned, more loans, more mortgages, more and more insolvencies.

'Indeed yes, Major Merrill. Sydney has been somewhat in the doldrums, but now – '

'Balls and routs cost money and money is your business. Isn't that what you mean?' Alister could not contain himself longer.

Goltby parted one key from another in his careful ritual of seeking the tiny one that opened his liquor cabinet. It seemed a longer time than usual before he found it. Only then did he smile at his visitor. 'Every man to his trade, eh, Major?'

An inferior wine this time, no doubt of it. Alister sipped it gingerly. But there was nothing he could do but sit there toying with the drink and awaiting the man's pleasure. Making the best of his role as supplicator.

Most unfortunate at such a time, the General's ill-health . . . heart was it not? Ah yes . . . tricky. One never knew there. But in these days of ungrateful relatives and divided family allegiance it was heartening to witness the respect and concern of kinsmen for each other. Er . . . how long did Major Merrill think? A matter of . . . months perhaps? But indeed, yes, who could tell. Sad. Extremely sad. But then again, he might live for years . . .

Well now, to business. He was sure Major Merrill would be one of the first to agree that times were bad. Two thousand pounds? Impossible. Regent Lodge was a most excellent property, agreed, in ordinary times, but these were not ordinary times. If Major Merrill would consider fifteen hundred it might just be possible to accommodate him immediately. Yes, fifteen hundred pounds, with Regent Lodge as security, might be managed . . .

Alister wiped his hands then his mouth and put his

handkerchief away slowly. Exactly when, Goltby, had been ordinary times? The Jew did not seem to hear him. Alister accepted more wine. As to terms . . . Goltby's cough was gentle and prolonged . . . a year? Well then, a year. At twenty per cent. Alister went cold, then a hot rage shook him. He trembled with silent outraged objections. Robbery under the guise of business, that's what it was. Keep your filthy money . . . But he did not say it. He dare not. Marchant was hounding him for settlement. There was his family to provide for. And Raunie . . .

He had expected fifteen at the most. Instead – twenty. He considered feverishly. One had to expect such terms of course, criminal though they were, and he wasn't the only one. But the Lodge. Regent Lodge. Barbara had always loved the Lodge . . . But it was his only asset; the house and the few things of value it contained. In a miserable agony his hand tightened on the far from clean glass, fighting the urge, indeed the need, to smash it into Goltby's face. He needed Goltby. Then, quite suddenly Roger's white face and careful movements were before his eyes and he heard the doctor's words. 'In troubles of the heart one can seldom be definite . . . But these attacks are weakening . . .' His eyes had rested inscrutably on Alister. 'I can only say, Major Merrill, a matter of months.'

He felt calmer. Of course. Roger . . . He drank the dregs of his wine quickly, slammed the glass on the table, and rose. He would bring the deeds tomorrow.

Georgina Merrill was the toast of Sydney Town. As a matter of formality, no more, her mother boasted of, and toyed with, the girl's three proposals of marriage – Captain Moore, Ralph Huntingdon and, most wonderful of all, Mr Blair. But as soon as was proper Georgina Merrill's engagement to William Aberdeen Blair was announced in the *Herald*, with a wedding planned for the spring at St James.

A numbed Ralph drifted disconsolately on the sidelines drinking anything he was offered, and he was heard to remark to Major Merrill apparently apropos of nothing, 'In spite of everything, sir, I beg you to call on me if I can be of help to you or your family.' Alister had glanced at the youth's trembling farmer's hands in surprise then turned from him sharply, almost with embarrassment. 'Marriage is woman's work, Huntingdon, and the sooner you accept the fact the better for yourself.' He, Alister, kept out of the business and away from all land-grabbing settlers. In any case he couldn't abide Blair's clipped Scottish burr. But if Eleanor decided it was to be Blair, it was Blair! Eleanor ignored Ralph – but small fry now – packed away her daughter's sampler which still boasted only, 'our days alas our mortal days are short and wretched too', and set her to crocheting a comforter for her betrothed while her trousseau grew into one of the most lavish ever seen in the colony – the number of petticoats alone kept the ladies a-dither for weeks. Such obliging shop-keepers and trades-people Eleanor enthused, as she ran up accounts with an enthusiasm that refused to be halted by reason. She had waited too long for this. Never, in her whole life, had she been happier.

On a fine November afternoon already warm with summer Georgina Merrill, with the full bosom and rounded hips of her seventeen years, walked from the dim aisle of St James Church on her husband's arm into the sunshine and the 'ohs' and 'ahs' of appreciation, for she was lovely indeed (if a trifle too pale) with the light beauty of a cream and golden lily. No expense had been spared, no one important uninvited. Even Roger was there, heavy on his wife's arm. So dizzy with triumph was Eleanor that she even accepted Raunie's presence with equanimity. In any case she would not have to tolerate the girl much longer, for at last she was taking herself off, leaving the Lodge of her own free will with no explanations given and none asked – Eleanor was only too thankful to leave well alone. With the Blairs off on their journey inland she gave herself up to some contented crying with women callers, but never exhaustedly, for she would be going to her dearest child in the autumn . . . If only Godfrey had been in the position to have made it a double wedding. And Eleanor would cry all over again for the beautiful startling spectacle *that* would have been.

The *Mary Jane* brought London letters. Godfrey's father was dead. Mr Selwyn was a very rich young man indeed. Eleanor wept suitably and publicly over Godfrey's poor papa then dried her eyes briskly and began to plan the next wedding in the family. A difficult bride this time admittedly, but a bride none the less and her relief found outlet in a flood of reckless demands. The Lodge must be repainted. They needed more silver, most certainly fresh curtains. She had even decided upon the bridal head-dresses when Barbara came one evening to tell her parents that she had sent Godfrey away. He was sailing for England, back to the life of a West Country squire. And he was sailing alone.

Through the vocal onslaught that battered her like a south-eastern gale Barbara kept her hand closed over Brick's letters in her pocket. The feel of them gave her strength. He would be home in a few months, perhaps he was already at sea. Two years would be gone as a dream and with them the void they had made in her life, that deep and aching wound in her side. She would be here when he set foot ashore, as he expected her to be. She endured her mother's questions and accusations, her father's ominously controlled fury, with a cool patience, longing for them to be finished with her so she might escape. She craved quiet, to read his letters again and again. Brick had known, had never doubted, that she would not marry Godfrey Selwyn. Her knew her so well. If she'd had doubts before about what she would do she had none now. Here was her life, and here would be her love. It has resolved itself.

Raunie listened to the tumult with a careless ear. So that nincompoop of a Selwyn was off to write poems about gardens and nightingales, a fool blown by any chance wind or flattering woman. But . . . her eyes darkened . . . Barbara was to stay. Barbara . . . But she shook off her mood and turned back to her packing. What was Barbara to her now? What was any Merrill, come to that? Except Alister . . . So when Eleanor flounced in oozing outrage and blame Raunie paused just long enough to fling a shawl over her accumulated treasures and sweep a chair clear for her mother-in-law's quivering bulk. But Eleanor refused to be seated, or to be calm. She stood, scarcely able to speak through her temper. This . . . this catastrophe was the outcome of Raunie's meddling with her daughters' lives . . . Her wicked flirtatious schemes had brought it about . . . No woman was safe, no man proof against her wiles . . . She had snared poor darling Kenneth, oh quite deliberately and wickedly, to say nothing of that episode with Ralph, and now she was the cause of quarrels and misunderstandings between a betrothed couple. Yes, betrothed, to all intents and purposes . . .

With an experienced flick of her wrist Raunie tucked a phial of Eleanor's perfume between her gloves and slammed the lid of the trunk. Yes, she and Alister were safe; Eleanor was incapable of believing her husband could be as other men – if she ever gave thought to his needs at all. She despised Eleanor Merrill, ignoring her, until with a final tirade of hate the woman ran sobbing to her room to sulk.

Raunie followed Jeremy through the now silent house and out into the sunshine – Jeremy was driving her to town. Joey was hiding, the servants, she knew, peeping through the curtains, cringing in case she should turn and put a curse on them, too scared of her to gossip to their mistress even if they had guessed anything to gossip about. It was then she re-membered the carpet-bag. A bedraggled old thing surely to take into a bright new life? All the same it was hers . . . She sent Jeremy back for it

So she turned her unreluctant back on Regent Lodge, disappearing through the sunlit trees. Regent Lodge had served its purpose. She smiled to herself, stroking the bag's shabby brocade; once this had held all she possessed in the world, now it was simply a relic of past struggles. From the back room of a London slum, the hybrid result of an ill-spent hour by a gipsy drab and a wandering Irish spalpeen, to the mistress of one of Australia's most distinguished citizens, was quite a progression, a most enviable one, at twenty-two. Now there was nothing out of her reach. Nothing. Not even Brick

O'Shea . . . The sickness of longing that was always with her, even as she lay in the arms of other men, was for Brick and no other. And no matter who I hold to me, she thought with absolute and final conviction, he is the ultimate, the other part of me, my other self. With Brick O'Shea I'll achieve what the world calls a soul, or eternal damnation, and I don't care which. The only important thing is that now I can meet him on a level with my rivals. On a level with Barbara. No – more than Barbara. Much more than Barbara Merrill.

As the cab drew up before the little house in Macquarie Street the sinewy youth who sprang to assist her down cast a knowledgable and appreciative eye over his new mistress. Real class, this! He preened under her condescending but charming smile. With the bustling Abigail and the blonde Kitty tossing back her curls at Herbert the dandy groom, all following her like the oddly assorted court of a queen, Raunie swept up the freshly scrubbed steps of Winthrop and into another world.

Some three weeks before Christmas, quietly, without any fuss at all, Sir Roger Havelock died at his Sydney residence. The funeral was large and elaborate. Struggling valiantly with her grief his niece Eleanor, exquisite in her new mourning outfit, dried her tears long enough to offer the smelling salts to, and have them refused by, his relict Janet, who seemed actually to be enjoying the ride, quietly watching the crowds lined outside the gates, even smiling occasionally at a child or an old woman. Almost indecent and rather disrespectful Eleanor decided, using the salts lavishly on herself. She gave a delicate little shiver – she simply could not understand chill women – then forgot her relative as she bowed to the Governor, such a charming man with always something delightful and appropriate to say, even at a funeral. She gloried in the day, excited by visions of herself, soon now she was certain, bowling along in a four-in-hand, a shining splendid carriage with perfectly matched bays. Indeed, she grew faint at the very thought of such luxury and reached for the salts again.

Came the reading of the will, a will made a year before, a new will it was explained. The ceremony was remarkably brief. Roger's widow would not be able to do much more than exist – but when had Janet really done anything else? The first surprise. The second . . .

Havelock's nephew, his confidant, his secretary and adviser all these difficult years – to Alister Merrill, Major, was bequeathed the massive mahogany desk before which most of the illustrious of the colony had sat at one time or another and which Alister had once in idle talk admired, together with sundry sentimental but quite valueless personal effects. And the sum of five hundred pounds in cash.

PART FIVE

Chapter Fourteen

THE YEAR 1847 slipped uneasily into 1848. England's southern colony suffered Europe's boil of political violence as a running sore of discontent. Christmas was blighted by Lady Fitzroy's violent death in a carriage accident and the raging influenza, with deaths a'plenty in the coddled suburbs but few, it appeared, among O'Shea's foundlings. The New Year brought Gladstone's hinted revival of transportation to add fuel to the fire and in saloons and clubs and on street corners arguments and fists flew. Granted *someone* must do Australia's work, but felons again? Wasn't it galling enough to watch helplessly as a shipload of Irish – Connaught Irish at that – roared brazenly up harbour with no fever aboard to reduce their numbers? Not the slightest doubt, alarmed Protestant withdrawing-rooms decided, as to O'Shea's hand in it all; he'd made no secret of his crazy dream of a new Ireland peopled by pagan idolators, what else, with himself as its uncrowned king. And wasn't there significance in that four thousand acres on the South Coast awaiting his home-coming, and his proposed settlement of fifty families, while their own sturdy Highlanders were fobbed off with only food and water?

Irish-baiters found ready supporters among the traders, shopkeepers and artisans needing the market of a law-abiding public with money in its pockets – give this dirty rabble the vote? Might as well give it to heathen Blacks. The squat-tocracy bided its time and generally its tongue – better Irish shepherds than none at all. And for all his shortcomings O'Shea was the only one doing anything about their prob-lems, agreed the merchants who would open factories if they could dip their hands into a cheap pool of labour. And the Governor strove to balance protest meeting against

321

deputation, request against request: 'Gentlemen, I am but England's servant' . . . 'But gentlemen, you never cease demanding labour of me. Well, here is labour . . .' And election fever began to engulf the city, now a pompous cluster of villas and gaols and asylums, a refuge of substance aching to stretch its limbs and bare its teeth as a free colony, touchily intent on forgetting, and helping others forget, its conception in a dungheap of felony.

On a fine morning in early autumn the *Marigold* anchored in the Cove, Brick O'Shea aboard along with a horde of volatile youths with Gaelic lilts to their voices to wander about his school and stables or set the sand-hills ringing with the clang of hammers and rasp of saws as they erected flimsy but adequate shelters – was all Ireland on its way? The fretful and fearful complained bitterly of the noise and pollution while watching sourly the unloading of bits and pieces of furniture and farm implements and queer-shaped machinery and boxes of London tailoring – the local bucks could talk of nothing else for days but the gold Albert strung across O'Shea's brilliant-buttoned waistcoat and his signet ring and doeskin gloves, yellow ones at that. Quite the dandy, Mr O'Shea. ' 'Tis the Sultan of Sydney he thinks he is,' had only to yell a 'Black Protestant', and papists and Protestants were at it hammer and tongs. Came too the finest of wines and stacks of books and something that looked suspiciously like a printing press and hot new knowledge and concepts with which to whip growing unease into hysteria. Men loathed O'Shea or eulogised him while their women fell in love with him all over again and sought to entertain him while their menfolk pried what news they could from his suaver-than-ever lips; after all, he had listened to the powerful and the privileged in the Commons, mingled with the Chartists too, perhaps even marched with them.

It was asserted in some quarters that Governor Fitzroy had granted the man audience. Well, O'Shea might have brought letters . . . But who would doubt his money-hungry hands itched to control some of the hundred thousand pounds the Governor had reserved for immigration? Even more

322

alarming, did he actually mean to stand for Council at last, this pro-Irish radical, the native-born son of felons, to argue the country's laws, shape them perhaps, with men of integrity and learning, aristocrats of the professions and the military caste? The nine thousand who held the vote argued uneasily but the rest, the huge politically impotent ninety-one thousand, followed him through parks and lanes and the noisome courts about the wharves, questioning, listening, only half understanding but unwilling to doubt that he could ignore or forsake them. A squatter yes, but no 'exclusive', he was traditionless and single-hearted, belonging to no party. Because he stood alone they trusted him, despite his curly-brimmed beaver and the gold-mounted cane at which they alternately sneered and cowered. They had to trust him. He was all they had.

The last sitting of Council before the General Election dragged itself out, the Governor still absent nursing his grief. Members, bored, were shiftily non-committal. But O'Shea was there, his eyes, as everyone noted, rarely leaving Alister Merrill. The Major, it was whispered, had been silenced rather abruptly by the Governor. 'A citizen is at liberty surely to spend his pounds where he pleases even if the rest of us are scrabbling for pennies?' Would Merrill's rage find expression in caustic explosion? Would the morbid piled-up tensions of years overflow into violence once the two faced each other in Council? The interest of the sensation-seeking slid to the Gallery where the man's widowed daughter-in-law, as well as his . . . But dangerous to linger on *that*. Even so, their eyes clung to Raunie as she flaunted herself through the corridors, a sensuous scatter of silks and laces in a land of seed-stores and stables. The hearts of simple men, indeed all men, beat quicker for the sight of her.

Mid-winter. But Mr Kempt's little bookshop opposite the old Barracks was sheltered, almost warm, as Barbara waited for Brick. A boy had ridden out with a note asking her to be waiting at eleven and sensing urgency she had ordered the carriage for the day though she couldn't imagine what matter he had failed to discuss with her these past weeks. How they had talked! Their first meeting had been exactly as she had hoped; she had simply thrust Jamie forward and Brick had tossed him high willing some answering merriment into the child's face while she stood smiling at them offering up her prayers of thanks that Jamie was alive. It was worth the long struggle to save him. She still shuddered at the memory of the terrible days and nights when he lay gripped by the influenza. Yet perhaps it had not been altogether her personal victory. There was an unsuspected strength in the child's slight form. A tenacity. Brick's delight in the boy was enough to gloss over Jamie's stubborn withdrawal from her, a circumstance which puzzled more than it hurt, for most children liked her, at least trusted her. And Brick's acceptance of them both waiting for him made everything slip back into the old familiar pattern. It was worth being tired, a little lost, and old – yes, old. They called her the old maid now. After all, she was twenty-six.

Riffling the pages of a book she felt his hand on her elbow and such a wave of solace swept over her as he led out into the sunshine, she trembled. 'I'm glad you kept Jeremy,' he was saying, 'though he could scarcely be regarded as the perfect chaperone.'

She laughed. 'You've never bothered about the proprieties before.'

'I'm taking you to see my house.'

'But I know every line of your house. It's been shaping before my eyes – and Papa's – for over a year.'

'And the Major, I don't doubt, has cursed it with his first breath of a morning and his last at night.' They braced for the jerk as Jeremy flicked the horses. 'The workmen have done well considering they had little more than rough plans and my letters to go upon. But now it's time for the furnishings. They must be perfect. So . . . I must have your advice.'

Of course. He wished to show her his home as simply as he showed her the other creations of his mind or hands. She leaned back content. On the Harbour the steamer *Thistle* laboured gently. A brig was slipping out with the tide. It was a lovely morning, a day to be far from Regent Lodge and its domestic wrangling, its air of soggy decay. Enamoured of a new doctor, her mother had retreated with his book *Diseases of Women* and her richly piled trays and her brandy to that dimly shuttered world of her own contriving that was the always disappointing present and quite improbable future. She was toying with the idea of an operation – everyone was having an operation – and demanding Alister take her to visit Gina before their 'blessed angel' of a grandchild was born. If Gina could face *her* ordeal her mama could face the winter roads; indeed she'd heard that the Wellington mails were much improved. Barbara loathed eating at home now, aware that even the food was bought with the small but regular sums her sister sent down; it seemed the Lodge could not function without Georgina's help. But after all, she reflected with some bitterness, wasn't that the purpose of an arranged marriage? The china and silver had dwindled again, and the servants, reduced to only Bess and Tilly, wandered the place in slovenly insolence. She did most of what had been Ada's work herself. As for her father, at their rare meetings she was shocked at the change in him, solitary as she knew him to be in a commercial port shorn of its military glory, ousted by newcomers, obsessed by an O'Shea always before his eyes, and the challenge real or imaginery the man presented to himself as well as to the colonial status quo. Silence was his refuge. He maintained it rigidly before his wife's wailing and complaining over Roger's cruel, *cruel* will – its one consoling factor being that now she *could* ignore Janet. And in the city even the stable-boys whispered of Major Merrill and his son's widow . . . Barbara was grateful for her mother's vanity that shielded her from even suspecting a liaison between her husband and another woman. As for herself . . . she could be resigned to anything if her father were happy. Yes, if Raunie made her father happy the girl could keep her sly mysteries.

Moving out into the sunshine before Parliament House the sun had beat against her eyes and the chatter of women throbbed at her cars while her mind was back with the tensed emotions on the floor of the Council Chamber. Raunie, the centre of her tiny court in the Strangers' Gallery, had inclined her head with her usual mocking smile and Barbara had responded as always, politely but a little absently. The Clintons were in a complacent row. The Parkers . . . the Fletchers . . . Maxim exuding a shining self-satisfaction. Jamie usually watched proceedings obediently enough but this day he was restless. Perhaps it was the weather; it was close for autumn, with a random touch of summer, a tepidness that made them move more slowly, loth even to think.

But moving through the lingering groups outside, Jamie's hand had tugged at hers. His face flushed, he was smiling at Raunie, the centre of her admiring sycophants. Suddenly he broke free and ran to bounce up and down before her. The women laughed, enjoying the childish display. Raunie patted his black head then put her hand deliberately into his – two smooth golden-brown hands merging into one. With her beautiful insolent walk she led the boy back across the court-yard. In Barbara's eyes the two fused to become one being. Out of each face, so wilful and so pagan, gazed the eyes of the barbarian. And the soul of a savage. Her tensed body crumpled a little against the friendly wall. She had not known before because she had not seen them together before. Now she knew. Raunie was Jamie's mother. Then Brick? . . . Quite suddenly she felt tired. Very tired. And very conscious of her heart beating unevenly, strange little sensations that irritated her, adding to her weariness.

The boy clung to Raunie while she laughed down at him indulgently. 'No. *No* Jamie.'

'But I want to stay with you.'

'You can't. You must go with your . . .' Her hand, glittering with rings, made a helpless little gesture, an artificial negation for Raunie was never helpless. 'What do you call Miss Merrill? Nurse? Teacher?'

'It's time to join your father,' Barbara told the boy firmly. 'You know he doesn't like to be kept waiting. Shall we go?'

The amusement in Raunie's eyes gave way to malice and Barbara knew that if she had once been a part of Brick O'Shea's life she was so no longer. For the first time in their lives and perhaps the last the personalities of the two women

326

met and found common ground, burrowed into it. By sheer force Barbara pulled the stubborn boy away and did not murmur when he bent and dug his sharp teeth deep into her hand.

They crossed in the punt to Billy Blue's Point and jolted the rough tracks of the North Shore, cold within their shields of trees, through imposing gates and up a half-completed drive to steps leading to the verandah that enclosed three sides of the house where it rested high overlooking the water. Ladders and beams and stone blocks were piled everywhere. The withdrawing-room was a-clutter with carpets, candelabra, cushions, Nottingham laces. The hall and adjacent rooms were piled with furniture, the finest of mahogany and satinwood and cedar. All about was the smell of paint. Barbara had seen horses near the partly-finished stables. There must be workmen somewhere, certainly a caretaker, but, except for Jeremy's whistle somewhere amid the trees all was quiet and they were alone. She touched this and admired that yet felt no sensual pleasure in these material and expensive things as another woman might. A woman *should* like women's things – yes, she failed in so many ways. Through the verandah columns the sharp blue and green that is the winter brilliance of Sydney was like an exaggerated oil painting. It hurt with colour. The air was still and almost heavy. The peace of it transmitted itself to the two standing close together beside the open doors.

In the tight cocoon of their isolation they were quiet and still. And Brick knew, as he had known but rarely in his life, the blessed balm of repose. Only with Barbara had he ever felt so; it was she who had taught him what a precious thing it could be. He found himself studying her with a critical absorption, comparing her with the girl he had singled out that long-ago night at the theatre – could it actually be seven years? But even before that night, yes, from their first meeting, she had stepped sharply into his life, he into hers. He into hers . . . deliberately. With a purpose. A perversity – for then his vindictiveness against her father could find no other outlet – had drawn him towards her, that first hell-bent

327

mischief growing to a compulsion, some part of his search to satisfy a need that Moll had attempted to fill but that he had sensed finally in the controlled rigidity of an eighteen-year-old debutante. He couldn't define his need then, as he couldn't now, he only knew Barbara was concerned in it and so he had persisted in the relationship, absorbing her until she accepted him utterly and without reserve. Or so he believed . . . But it did not matter. What did matter was that she was the other part of his plans, the missing section of the puzzle. But not yet fitting. Not quite. But now he could and would slide the missing piece tight, making completion. It was as simple as that.

With this new clarity of sight and sense he saw that she had emerged from an angular rather awkward girl into a handsome woman with smooth skin and a tall straight body; a young woman of deliberate movement and thought. He had noticed the beginnings of that years ago. It had intrigued him. But a quivering if resolutely submerged energy that she had then possessed seemed lost. The enthusiasm, the alacrity towards anything that absorbed her interest – gone. Or no longer obvious. Buried still deeper perhaps. She seldom laughed. Even her smile was hesitant. She was too thin. Her movements were subdued, even lethargic. Everything about her was muted, exactly as if she had lived for a long time within a dim shutaway room to which the sun never penetrated. Her brown dress was unrelieved except for the tiny lace collar and amethyst brooch. She should not wear amethysts. Emeralds, opals, yes, to give her colour. But with such obvious fire she would not be Barbara. And yet, what was she exactly, this Barbara beside him? Had she, as Hugh insisted, simply ceased to exist? Here was a woman colourless, even drab, things not to be tolerated, not of Barbara Merrill. Her mind must not slacken and sicken. It was that mind that was his strength and his anchor. He could not let it die, exhaust itself on frivolous nothings. For the first time he could remember Hugh's letter without outrage:

'For three nights she's not slept, tending your brat, but she saved his life. And she bears the filth of gossip flung at her, not only by the scum of the Rocks; the drawing-rooms of the gentry have an indirect but far more vicious aim. She's a saint – emotional statement or not – or the nearest to one you or I will ever see, and I curse you because she won't blame you for making your way over her tired eyes and hands. Scandal, this kind of scandal, can swell to an ugly thing. I could offer her my protection for what it's worth had I not two – or is it three – wives dotted over the face of the globe. But even if I could, and if I dared, she would refuse me, politely as she refuses everything. And rightly. But one thing I am able to do – attend to the dirty mouths that come within range of my fists . . .'

Why had that letter made him so furious? Was it because it dragged into the open, anticipated something that had been formulating in his mind for a long time, years perhaps, and had lain there dormant? That letter had dragged it out and made him look at himself, and at Barbara, the quiet graceful girl he had missed like the soil of his own land once she was not constantly at his side. But here again he had blocked personal probing – Barbara Merrill was one with his plans. He had come home to both. Leave it at that. *Leave* it. He made an impatient movement – he only really understood and enjoyed action – and looked at her again. Her bonnet showed little of her hair. The fact irritated him. His irritation became unbearable. He jerked the bonnet ribbons undone and bared her head. Startled, her hands flew to her loosened hair.

'Leave it,' he ordered impatiently.

But she rolled it tightly, smoothing and patting and tucking in loose ends. Her eyes did not swerve from his. It was unlike her to pointedly flout his whims. As she lowered her arms a shadow seemed to pass across her face and her fingers moved slowly over her forehead. He hesitated, baffled, then turned, skimmed the bonnet on to the dining table and padded restlessly about the room.

'Well, here it is, and pretty much of a mess as you can see. But I must have order soon. By spring I expect all Sydney to be jostling for a place at my table. It is my ambition.' His lips quirked. 'Who knows, perhaps even your father.'

'You seem very sure of your election.'

'Why not? I mean to stand unopposed.'

'And when the time comes to redeem your pledges?'

'I'll redeem them – at a price. A stiff price. All the labour they want but at wages I set, other demands satisfied by bargains made so slowly and carefully there's a possibility, given fools enough, my advantage will not be noticed. And I deal mainly with fools. Once in there I can cling, for those I help indirectly will keep me where I want to be. And there will be nothing I cannot control. Full stomachs and warm bodies mean ears receptive enough to sop up anything put into them. And willing ears mean willing voices. Loud voices too.'

'And when these . . . voices . . . realise they're merely changing one master for another?'

'They'll keep the master who brings gifts. They always have. So – I build my supply.'

He ran his palm slowly, almost sensuously, over the smooth richness of the table. There were few tables of such size in the colony . . . She frowned. And then she saw it, in the corner, its glint dazzling her eyes – the enormous winetray the Somersets had brought from Dublin. There was no mistaking it. Her father had taken her once to the Somerset home . . . She remembered. This table belonged there, along with the tray. Had belonged there . . .

She moved into the small splash of sun but, still cold, flexed her fingers. He stood there, as he had always stood somewhere, flinging his arrogant schemes in her face, mocking her father, mocking her. She should not be here. She was Alister Merrill's daughter and she should run from this man, hating him. Instead she stayed and hated herself. All too often this sickness of self-loathing possessed her. And the restlessness that came after and was even harder to bear. He was sorting a pile of boxes. The rigidity of his back told her he resented her questions, or was bored by them. But for once she refused to heed his silent reprimand.

'And to bring enough of these voices?'

'The only bridge that spans oceans – money. And it must

330

be my money, to use as I please.' He turned. 'I took time to shop in Paris.' He put a box into her hands, a large box of lilac and blue embossed with scrolls and fat gently-folded rosebuds, and cupids – or were they nymphs – in gold and silver. Such delicate colour and design. 'Open it,' he added with amusement as she studied the fragile thing, fascinated by such pale and elaborate delicacy. When she still didn't move he wrenched off the lid, scattering filmy paper in clouds.

She had never seen such a beautiful dress. Rich magnolia satin, stiff with embroidery. Her finger traced the swollen curves of it. Paris . . . Her shining eyes rose to his. A ripple of her nerves startled her as she saw warmth – yes, warmth – in his eyes.

'And one of those new hoops they call a crinoline,' he explained. 'Women are bouncing all over Europe in the things, or soon will be I'm told.'

But her fingers snagged on the cool smoothness of the material. Her hands looked rough against the silk. It was quite suddenly all . . . wrong. She felt more awkward than usual. Gauche. Her eyes clouded. 'It's beautiful but I – I've no use for it.'

'A perfect wedding dress, I think.'

She sighed. 'I wrote you about Godfrey –'

'Damn that helpless dude to perdition. I took Selwyn no more seriously than you did yourself. You're marrying me.' Then, with no softness at all, only urgency. 'Well, aren't you, Barbara?'

Her eyes widened slowly in her white face as she stared at him. He frowned. He ran his hands through his hair then flung his arms wide in a gesture of helplessness. 'I shouldn't have put it so – badly – I suppose. Ladies, I understand, have . . . ideas about proposals. Well, I've never made a proposal –' He smiled faintly. 'At least, not of this kind. It's not easy to say what's in my mind but you're a part of this . . . this life, and must stay a part of it. It just had to come. You know that as well as I do.' He paused, then as she said nothing, 'Damn it all, Jamie needs you.'

'Jamie doesn't like me,' she said flatly.

'Why shouldn't he like you? Aren't you the only mother he's ever had?'

'You're foolish about that child,' she burst out, then bit her lip, shocked at her recklessness.

'Perhaps.' He must have been dwelling on her words. 'A man must be a fool about something. Well then, aside from Jamie . . . this house needs a mistress. The right mistress. You are, I can well believe, an admirable hostess, with the right answer to the wrong question, and there'll be plenty of those.' He paused and she was amazed to see – could it actually be fear? – in his eyes. 'All this can so easily get out of hand. It must not get out of hand. You'll keep a kind of . . . stability is the word I think. Again, you can do so much for me inland; all these new settlements, the Pride – you've never even seen Erins Pride yet. And naturally, in return for all this you shall have everything you want. There must be many things you want – clothes, books, money?'

She was silent, reluctant even to look at him, so insistent, rather flippant, even a little spiteful. He had not said it. Only a fool would expect him to say it. She licked her lips.

'When do you wish me to marry you?'

She hadn't meant it to sound so ridiculously stilted. But she could not help it. He was not even looking at her. He was staring out across the water, one part of him even now lost to her. 'As soon as possible,' he said at last. 'My South Coast farms will have to wait. To avoid trouble here I must settle my folk along the Edward River this summer, a settlement I've been planning a long time. Difficult or not I mean it to be done.' His voice quickened. 'I'll show them. Seven years ago no one wanted the land, too flat and arid they said and passed it by searching for their trail to Gippsland. But I bought part of an old grant for one hundred pounds. Thousands wouldn't get it from me now. Or all the Land Commissioners in Sydney. The best sheep country in Australia. All this will of course take months but I have till Council sits next year. After the elections Moll can take this over, Jamie along with it, and leave you free to come with me. So! Five . . . six weeks? And offer up your prayers for an early spring and a dry one.'

332

She stirred. Riding across country few white men had yet traversed, her husband at her side. Yes, that was the way. Brick needed her. The women needed her. They were all afraid, these immigrant women, tumbled across the world into a hardship that held a deeper bitterness because it was unfamiliar, seeking clumsily for advice, for help, for some other woman who *knew*. There was so much she didn't know – but she could learn. She could read and watch and try to understand. She'd given Brick O'Shea almost every hour of her life, certainly every beat of her heart. Now, as his wife, she must give him more.

'It's but a fortnight to polling day so I leave for Goulburn tomorrow.' He waved a hand at the confusion around them. 'I leave this in your hands.'

'I'll need help,' she protested, struggling with a feeling of desperation.

'Get it where you can till I bring Moll down.' He paused. 'You understand about my foster-mother, don't you?'

She nodded. 'I understand that she loves you very much.' She struggled for words. 'You said I might have anything I wanted . . .'

'A piano? I'll get you the best. Import one if necessary. Or is it a curricle? You shall have that too. I know where – '

'Nothing like that. It's just that . . . a woman likes to bring at least a trousseau to her marriage.'

'Good heavens!' He laughed, enjoying her discomfiture. 'Choose what you want at any store in town, at every store if you like.'

'But I don't want gifts. I only want the . . . money you say I earned with you. I was once quite sure I'd not touch it but – well, I've calculated as best I can and I believe it would amount to something like two hundred pounds. I know it is a great deal – '

'Are you still quibbling over that?' He was angry. He scribbled on a sheet of paper and clapped it in her hand. 'An Order on the Bank of Australia.'

She gasped. 'Three hundred pounds? It's too much.'

'If you don't use it I'll scatter it in guineas in the Domain and every Jacky in town will be drunk because of your thrift. Waste it. It's yours.'

'Yes,' she agreed. 'It's mine.'

But it seemed to burn her ungloved hand as she placed it carefully in her reticule. It had been a difficult thing to do. Her head was throbbing as she folded the dress and replaced it in the box. All else necessary came with it – gloves and flowers and a most exquisite fan – but she didn't examine them more closely. Not now. She didn't know quite what he expected her to do with the things so she left them where they were.

'Now,' he said briskly, 'as to details . . .'

'Please understand I'll have no secret ceremony. Not unless . . . every other way fails.'

A long pause. She was afraid to meet his eyes. 'In that case,' he said at last, slowly, 'I shall call on your father the moment I return to Sydney.'

'He will never receive you at the Lodge.'

'Elsewhere then.'

'He won't receive you at all.'

'But he must receive me.'

'I – ' Her eyes met his. They implored him. 'I wish to tell my father in my own way and in my own time.'

'Good heavens, girl . . .' he exploded, then stopped and she heard his nails tap-tapping the table. His precious, most valuable table. Was she being childish? If only she knew how to approach him in this, what to do . . . And this was the man she had just promised to marry. Marriage . . . An odd little fear shook her body. What was marriage, really? What exactly did he expect of her? She had no way of knowing – yet. She was very ignorant. He turned abruptly. 'There's very little time. As you know there are plans for an election banquet but I must leave immediately it is over, with or without you. I can delay no longer.'

'I promise to tell my father soon.'

His shrug made her feel more helpless than ever. 'Meanwhile I am to remain mutely in the background, is that what you want?'

'It will be best for us all. Believe me, I know.'

'As you wish then.'

How formal they were. And, it seemed, ill-at-ease. She was annoying him yet seemed powerless to help it. But as she turned to him in an attempt to end the tension between them but not knowing at all what she was going to do he folded her hand in his, gripping her fingers, as if to reassure. It was a deliberate contact and her heart, her hungry and very foolish heart, thudded. She felt light-headed and happy in a way she had never known before. What demanding thing was there inside her crying out, greedy and still unsatisfied? The happiness of love is the security of love. I am beloved. I love in return. Yes, that was it, the knowledge that you can safely give all of yourself because the loved one gives all. She had never pondered on love. It was something that happened to other people, wonderful gay people, not dull plain women like herself. Yet love had been within her so long, growing there, but suppressed to become fortitude. Well, now she could expend love, express it. She could learn to express it. For if she loved him all would come right, would it not? Love would teach her all she had to know.

Brick opened her slim hand and placed his mouth on her palm. The unexpected tenderness of him shook her. She ached to place her own mouth, her lips that had not yet touched any man but her father in affection, deep into his black hair. It did not matter what he was or what he had done. This is the meaning of my life, she thought, of my breathing and praying and walking and the things I say. This is the meaning of everything. It all starts and ends with him.

'You are the greatest lady I have ever known.' His voice was gentle as she had never heard it before, and warmer even than when he talked with Jamie. 'I swear I will treat you as such. Always, Barbara.'

'I know,' she whispered. Somehow she did know. She could not doubt it. Their eyes met and they stood there strangely poised. This is the first time I have seen his eyes exactly like this, she thought, close, at ease. The first time I have felt, even briefly, entirely outside the tremendous urgency of thinking and doing. She seemed to be seeing everything, each object in the room and through the doorways and windows, sharply separated, clearly in focus, a little larger than life. It was wonderful. Her eyes moved lazily from the faint smudge of sweat across Brick's forehead to his glistening hair, downwards to the dark hairs on the back of his hand. She noticed how strong his hands were. But suddenly, there she was, back with the penetrating taste of fear, of uncertainty, all the queer fuzziness, the blurring. And it was, could only be, because of him. She wanted to touch him, to smooth dry his forehead with her palm. But she wanted to cry out to him too – don't frighten me. Don't be so much . . . yourself. Be as other men. And because she knew she couldn't do any of this; because she knew she wouldn't be loving him so terribly if he were otherwise; because she wanted to do so many unaccustomed things she moved irrationally, in a panic. She snatched up her bonnet and hurried out and down the steps and did not look back. But as she ran her lips shaped the words she had longed to cry out to him above all else:

'My love . . . my dear strange love . . . my only love . . .'

In the carriage she sat very still, glad of the concealment for she was shaking, her teeth chattering. Was it excitement? Fear? What *was* it? To you, Brick O'Shea, it's so very simple. To me nothing has ever been simple. For you it's reasonable, a practical expediency to marry a lady born, from the upper echelons as they say, because she has refinement and sense and a certain taste, is acceptable and rational and always at your right hand. Such a 'right' mother for sons of your own, no doubt, while you keep passion, the extension of your desires, for the trollops of the streets. More than that – for Raunie. You didn't kiss Raunie softly. She felt such rage it alarmed her for she believed she had learned to stifle resentment, to compromise, a deference to life itself. She trembled, consumed by emotion that no amount of control could kill. She felt weary and futile, back with the despair of reality. So many years of waiting and longing yet holding fast to anchoring ties against a man she had been conditioned to

336

despise yet eternally adored. Her head ached. How it ached. She must lie down, sleep perhaps. Yes, sleep would be a wonderful thing.

Moving through the silent house she remembered and turned to her father's study. It was empty. But she knew, even if her father had been there she would not have found the courage to speak to him. Not yet. She needed time. Could he, oh *could* he stop her marriage? No. No, he could do nothing. For, whatever reasons Brick had in marrying her, marry her he would.

She closed her door behind her. Sobbing quietly in her exhaustion she sank heavily on her bed.

'. . . contrived from the equipment at hand. Direct fire from an angular point cannot be severe. Make use of this fact . . .'

Alister put down his quill and threw another log on the fire then stood frowning at the pile of correspondence on his desk – though his world and Regent Lodge were toppling about him despatches must be written. He moved restlessly about the small study. Why did the loss of beloved horseflesh seem like the loss of one's blood? His stud was no more. He still had Donna of course, but the mare seemed to eat more than the rest put together so, despite Jeremy's pleadings and his own regrets, Donna must go. Bergson had long been interested in her, with his latest offer too attractive to refuse. And sooner Bergson than O'Shea. Anyone but O'Shea.

He turned to the window, racked by a choking sensation, long endured, but heightened the last few days. There was still Kumara of course . . . But Kumara belonged to Barbara, he had given her the horse himself. He thrust open the window with awkward fingers. So . . . even though he had kept his stud from Goltby, he had lost it in the end. At least Marchant was out of the picture, along with most of his small creditors. Now there was only Goltby. But time was his enemy; even if granted the extension he had been literally begging for could he, even now, save the Lodge? He had tried everyone . . . everything. He was exhausted, and the lethargy

337

of hopelessness, of resignation, was gripping hard. It was now but a matter of weeks. And Eleanor was still to be told, Eleanor his wife who was upstairs writing to Gina, oblivious of his despair, determined on this visit to her daughter, for her grandchild was soon to be born. His grandchild. Blair's child. A son perhaps?

His lips felt dry. Blair? No. *No.* But hadn't he swallowed his pride so often of late that it might just be possible to swallow it again? Strange that he had not considered his son-in-law before this – and knew that he had and had resolutely blocked off the idea. But even if nothing else came of it, two weeks, even one, spent out of Sydney and away from Goltby's cat-and-mouse torment, might help in other ways. The point was, his request for an extension had not been refused, not in so many words; the creature of course was inhuman, amusing himself with polite ambiguities before he pounced on him, dangling him on the rope before he chose to tighten the knot. But he dared not lose his temper with the Jew again . . . Safest to get away from the man. From everyone. Yes, even from Raunie.

Raunie . . . With a savage gesture he screwed wastepaper into a ball and tossed it in the basket. Another torment, and one as equally difficult to resolve. He had tried losing himself in Raunie almost with ferocity for in the sexual act, uncomplicated and always definite, was a dispersion of restlessness and longing, an appeasement of nameless and unspecified hungers. Physical release from needs that were deep and terrible had come with Raunie – and with his wineglass. In unity they had offered – and given – escape. But an escape that was only momentary. One had to return. And now even that escape had failed, leaving at best, disappointment, at worst, a bitter despair.

The room, despite the slit of open window, was suddenly stifling while his mind struggled to avoid the terrifying vista of frosty unanswered letters, accounts, bills and deeds. There was no escape from any of it . . . Forcing himself, under a sudden stimulus he took up his pen again.

'. . . also of the fact that the pahs are not flanked . . .'

The knock was a gentle one but he looked up impatiently. Barbara closed the door quietly behind her. Though his pen was ink-laden he dipped it carefully and precisely in the fine brass inkpot, intent on the act, taking his time, while she rested her hands on the desk, lightly, but enough to brace her body.

'I must speak with you, Papa.'

He stood slowly, one part of him not noting that 'Papa'. So he had driven her back much further than he had imagined; strange that such a trivial word could mean such finality. The fire spurted.

'Surely there's been enough useless talk between us?'

'But this is important. You see, I've known for a long time that you were worrying over . . . money.'

'I don't doubt it,' he snapped. 'You've always meddled in matters not normally the concern of women.'

'But I feel this is my concern – and it surely is, Papa – for I can help you.'

'Indeed? In what way?'

'I have money, not a great deal, but my own.' She thrust a sheet of paper into his unresponsive hands. 'It will make me very happy if you use this. I beg you to take it, Papa. I *beg* you.' She watched in agony as he bent his head slowly to read. Oh God, let him understand. Please let him understand.

The paper trembled in his hand. 'It would be kinder,' he said at last, throwing back his head, his eyes colder than she had ever seen them, 'if you were to tell me the reason for this . . . surprising . . . gift, instead of leaving my powers of deduction, or imagination, to work as they may.'

'It was not a gift to me, Papa. I earned it.'

'You earned *this*? Three hundred pounds? Really Barbara, I am sick and tired of being taken for a fool. I am sick of this creature O'Shea buying you with his filthy money. I am tired of you and your shameless impertinent escapades.'

'Papa . . . no. *No*.' Her voice choked helplessly as he ripped the paper and threw the pieces in the fire. 'Papa . . .' She forced the word from her. 'Sometimes it is difficult for me not to . . . hate you.'

'I've long been aware of your feelings towards me. We need not dwell on them. You may go.'

She turned blindly and fumbled for the doorknob, praying her limbs would carry her, at least with dignity. She stumbled outside. Her throat burning, her eyes stinging, she wandered down the narrow rambling path to the Bay and sat staring through the trees, watching the water lose itself in the little channels between the rocks. She folded her arms and with her palms on her elbows rocked slowly and rhythmically in an anguish of humiliation and remorse. I told him I hated him. I told him that. What is wrong with me? I told my father, my dearly loved father, that I hated him. Please God, forgive me for telling my father that I hated him. *Forgive* me. Oh God and Papa, forgive me . . .

Alister stood at the window for a long time, staring at the trees beyond the little patch of garden. He turned abruptly and riffled through the papers on his desk. He paused, drew one out and read it through slowly. He knew every phrase, indeed every word for he had read it through many times. But still his eyes lingered. Another tavern theft . . . An insolent Irish-brogued youth wounded as he fled towards the sand-hills . . . O'Shea's sand-hills . . . Another scurfy peasant in hiding . . . O'Shea's peasant . . .

O'Shea.

He sat and pulled a fresh sheet of paper towards him. Dipping his quill in the ink in his careful precise way, he began to write.

> 'Policeman, policeman, don't take me
> I've got a wife and family
> How many children have you got?
> Twenty-four and that's the lot.'

At the final chant the lieutenant's horse shied in a cloud of sand and dirt and the scarlet-cheeked children, screaming with excitement and fright, ran scattering about the huts of the sleazy sprawling settlement that was Irishtown.

The redcoats, all picked men, formed up quietly behind their officer. And the crowd that seemed to have come to-gether out of the dust, or simply out of the air, stood watching just as quietly, the Spanish-eyed women drawing their children close against their skirts and the Paddys nodding in awed admiration at so many fine steeds. With the bland vigilance of the trained soldier the lieutenant looked about him. Somewhere here surely . . .

Yes. Down the hill to the left, far down in the hollow, too far for the voice of authority to carry, was the Father surrounded by his flock. But the path was blocked by stacks of timber and heaps of rubble and stores of all kinds. The lieutenant turned back to the waiting watching crowd.

'You are suspected of hiding a fugitive from justice on these hills. As you well know, this is a grave offence. We mean to find this man. If we don't find him today we will return tomorrow, then the day after, and keep returning until we do find him –'

Tipsy voices over the little hill. He stiffened and though there was no perceptible movement from his men he sensed them take a firmer grip on their weapons. But only a pair of drunken old cronies came stumbling through the sand to go their way in happy and oblivious argument. But a third, a wizened gnome of a creature with tufts of grey hair dotting his large head, paused as his eyes lighted on the soldiers. He swayed, blinking at them, reeling no doubt from poteen as much as from a crippled leg.

'Another thing.' The lieutenant's voice was crisp and distinct as if he were speaking to children – ignorant, dirty, rebel children. 'There are complaints concerning your dis-order and repeated brawling, due in part no doubt to your success in brewing your whiskey. Steps will also be taken against this. Now bring water for the horses.'

Silence. No movement but a hound dog snuffling in the rubbish and the scuttle of an urchin round a hut corner. The

341

lieutenant jerked his head at a strong-looking man with russet hair leaning against a wall. 'You there . . .'

The man straightened slowly. 'We have little water,' he said.

'Bring what you have then.'

'An' divil a drop for the English "red".'

The officer went scarlet. 'You'll pay for that.' At a murmur from the crowd he swung his arm in an imperative arc. 'Clear the way down the path there or tell your priest to come up. We wish to question him.'

No one moved. The lieutenant's arm shot out, finger pointing at a wide-eyed, tousle-haired lad. 'Bring your priest here. Now.'

The youth turned to obey but the russet-haired man's great hand gripped and held him while he defied the officer. 'We be doin' nought to be badgered. Father Hamill neither.'

The lieutenant stared over the man's head at the trembling youth. 'Bring the priest here, I say.'

'An' do not be troublin' the good Father I say,' the russet-haired man insisted. 'Let the "red" be goin' to him if he can.'

The youth's eyes were wild. But he struggled vainly against the iron grip on his shoulder. ''Tis a new land in which to forget old hates,' he spluttered, near tears. 'Father says so. Meself I be hatin' no man, soldier or no.'

'Then ye're a disgrace to ould Oireland.'

The crippled little man with the odd tufts of hair flung himself forward almost spinning himself off his unsteady feet with the violence with which he swung at the lad, sending him into the sand. He stood looking about him, hands clenching and unclenching, his whiskey-shined face working. So many soldiers. Too many soldiers. Soldiers . . . soldiers ranked and gleaming in the bright winter sunshine. His twisted hands went out, groping like a blind man. They closed about a hunk of wood.

An instant of suspension, of massed shock. Then motion, like a wave, as the crowd, feverishly yet with a mute determination, followed suit.

342

'Stand back there.' The lieutenant's hands tightened on the reins. A drunken and truculent mob fast getting out of hand, spoiling for a fight . . .

The man with the russet hair picked up a spade.

Orders were orders. The lieutenant waited no longer. His men moved swiftly in disarming the crowd. They did not resist, at least not until the crippled one they called Paddy. For the years, the long, long years had dropped suddenly from Paddy Harrigan's shoulders and the scarlet tunics of the hated 'red' blazed before his fuddled eyes and the sky was an Irish sky and these about him were his allies all in love with the woman, Erin, confronting her enemies as one. And in his hands a weapon, a strong hard weapon. Paddy felt strong again. And young.

With a cry, cracked and old but resolute, he lunged. A horse, catching the end of the blow, screamed and reared. Paddy stumbled. The soldier grasped the awkward lump of wood. Paddy went down. The crowd blundered in. Out of control the horse began to kick. The lieutenant barked his orders . . .

It was then that Father Hamill, panting, breasted the little hill. For an instant he paused, in his dusty cassock and dirt-caked farmer's boots. Then he ran forward, hands beseeching.

'Mither o' God . . .'

Nominations were slow. When the candidates did trickle in the *Herald* warned 'no man of notoriously immoral reputation ought to be returned as a member or even listened to as a candidate', intended, many insisted, to dispose of that upstart O'Shea once and for all. But everyone, suspicious or otherwise, listened to Brick O'Shea if they listened to no one else. In the city the old factions moved to the crosscurrents of old grudges and injustices . . . They'd had enough of the stigma of being a penal colony, stormed the expansionists. But what of the work waiting to be done? Take coloured labour, take anything that could be harnessed to work, argued the hardy perennials. A demagogue might be permitted, if grudgingly, to lack principles, but he must never lack charm. And, to satisfy, he must exhibit a sense of drama, the more stirring the better. City and country alike hung on the words of Brick O'Shea, that unacceptable but undeniably charming and most dramatic of opportunists.

On the twenty-fifth day of July all manner of got-together bunting flew from Goulburn pubs and stores as Brick O'Shea was escorted into town by a chorus of weird instruments blown, plucked or thumped amid the cheers of his rabble army. He stood unopposed, and over this whispers exploded into brawls between his supporters and those led by Murchison's men pledged to trouble, the Irish settling the question to their satisfaction with palings and stones, boots if they had any, helped along by a stolen pistol or two. The most anyone could be definite about at the finish was that O'Shea had found scab in Murchison's sheep, had personally forced their dipping and beaten Clark for his carelessness to the extent of a broken nose and a couple of shattered ribs leaving him sprawled on a cot incapable of anything but abuse. And that put Murchison and his machinations out of the way. There seemed nothing anyone could do short of shooting O'Shea to prevent him carrying the day.

In any case no one seemed to want to try. Feeling had grown steadily for O'Shea, and in the end there seemed more for him than against him. Old Paddy had been popular around Goulburn and it was strange to think of him as dead. O'Shea had been his master and, as masters went, a good one, no denying that. And Jasper Morton for one had plenty to say about the young officers who'd galloped to extinction two of his favourite mounts for the sheer sport of it – half-pay loungers the lot of 'em, far too free with their whips and muskets. So the solid citizens of Argyle drifted with the prevailing tide until O'Shea was elected, if at times uneasily, to serve for Argyle in the Legislative Council. But his electors pushed their lingering doubts with their hats behind the

Arms of England and New South Wales that festooned the hotel dining-room and fell to on fish brought incredibly from the coast, oysters and the rarest of wines provided by the new Member himself. There seemed no end at least to the wine and as bumper after bumper was called for and everything reasonable and unreasonable toasted in voices thick and with bands discordant they fell to cursing as always all land laws new and old – squatters to *buy* their grazing land, waste land at that, at a pound an acre? Where did England think they could get such money? O'Shea would do something about it. O'Shea *must* do something about it. O'Shea . . .

They brightened. Get drunk and leave all in the lap of the gods – or with O'Shea. Why not with both? The wine flowed. Altogether, it was a rip-roaring day.

And a crisp windless night. The fires blazed, roasting the sheep for the station hands and their families, the settlers and visitors, the fat smooth rumps of the beasts sizzling and dripping, permeating the still cold air with mouth-watering vapours. Ringing the Pride the Blacks made carrobbery to celebrate the master's return as well as his elevation to some vague importance in the white man's scheme of things. The new Erins Pride showed no fire scars, only fine lamps and carpets with even curtains at the windows, a little lopsided but the best Moll could do in spite of the elegant magazines Brick provided. Moll Noakes did as well as she intended to do. She knew her place. The new mistress would know about curtains and such for Miss Merrill was one of the finest born in the colony. Ladies were trained to such decorations. Gladly, most definitely, Moll washed her hands of frills and fripperies.

The great wagon stood still unloaded but Moll's complaints had gone unheeded. With such excitement to distract, the boxes and crates stayed where they were, enough bonnets and bonbons given to the women and children to keep them happy until the festivities were over. And Moll had to be content preening about the kitchen steps in a new shawl and a bonnet topped with outsized plumes. Brick aimed a bone still heavy with flesh at the topmost feather and as the native women fought over this prize from their master's hands Moll folded her arms with her new primness of manner that amused her contemporaries or drove them almost insane.

'Time you mended your manners now you be wedding a lady born. Miss Merrill be not used to the ways o' Indians.' She stamped on the Jens' hands as they crept up to feel her new finery. 'Greedy grasping sluts.'

'Easy with your new airs and graces, though I'll own you look as grand in that headpiece as any lady.' He laughed softly. 'It reminded me a little of the one you admired on Raunie years ago.'

She dragged it violently from her head and tossed it aside but it fell, he noticed, on a patch of grass, and, furthermore, that her foot shot out to shield it. 'I'll not be wearing a thing that reminds me o' that jade.'

'Time has a way of altering things and people – even jades. Raunie's edges have smoothed somewhat since she began queening it in her house in Macquarie Street,' he teased.

'Guvment House couldn't change such a baggage born. An' the pity you will not see what I see, like mother like son.'

'Enough of that,' he snapped. 'I said my last on Jamie long ago, to you and to Raunie both. And I'll cut out the tongue of anyone – yes, even yours, Moll Noakes – who blabs of his birth. He's mine and none shall say otherwise. I'm to do the shaping of him.'

'You can try.' She sniffed.

'As for the polish, that's for my wife to give; to Jamie and to other matters in my life.'

'Do you think she'll be bothering about another's bratling when she has her own?'

She picked up the bonnet, dusted it off and set it carefully on her head. "A boarnt's a boarnt, though you've spoiled me pleasure in this bit o' nonsense.' But she came to sit beside him on the steps, settling her newly corseted buttocks into a familiar groove. She'd taken to washing herself of late but in the glow from the indoor lights her face shone with something more than soap.

'Down in Parliament hobnobbing with the best of 'em – an'

346

the worst. Hobnobbing with the Guvner too . . . The finest house in the colony t'boot . . . An' a lady for wife.' She gave a long sigh of satisfaction. 'When I remember the years I've hoped for such things yet all the time been afeard . . . Not even for an hour have I not been afeard.'

'When were you ever afraid of anything?' he scoffed.

'Many's the time. Not afeard o' beast or bird or fowl, but . . .'

'Of what then?'

She wrapped the shawl tightly about her as if the cold had given a sudden snap. 'Of men an' the things men do. But even more afeard o' the things women do to men.'

He stirred impatiently. 'Women are nothing to me –'

'They're all to all men though none see it till too late. I know. I see. When I thought I was rid o' one pestilence another turned up. But I never fear'd for you with any like I fear'd with Raunie. Those witch's eyes –'

His laugh drowned her words. Her hands twisted in her lap while her eyes clung to his shadowed face. 'An' I be never quite certain you speak true about the other one.'

He swore at her. 'Will you never give me peace as to Inar? She's an idiot with a knife scar cutting her face. She looked right through me, I tell you. Exactly as she'd look through you. She knows nothing, remembers nothing.'

'I always said McPhee'd do for the gal.' But there was veiled enquiry in the statement.

'And I told you his end. I've accounted for them both. As I account for Raunie. So leave them be. Leave us all be.'

'An' . . . Dgeralli?'

He stood slowly stretching and easing his limbs. He had expected her questions and had told her all he meant her to know. 'It seems we've seen the last of that runaway nigger,' he said at least, evenly, lightly. 'And wherever he is, he'd best stay, out of my way.'

Forever holding back – ah, she knew. So far and no farther. The old helpless anger against him flared. So much of himself and his life he refused to explain, or to reveal, kept hidden behind a wall of reserve before which, no matter what gifts of heart and mind, of loyalty and devotion she laid at his feet, he forced her to a halt. He turned from her questions with the subtlety of long practice, separating his one existence from another, silent as to the deeper machinations she knew were there. Even to Paddy's death . . . 'That debt will be settled, never fear.' And what of his marriage . . . his wife-to-be? Must she, Moll Noakes, his mother in all but blood, be forever the outsider, only permitted to reach him with her careless ribald laughter?

Horses galloping up the road. He turned sharply. He had been waiting for them. Rob Witherstone back from Sydney with news of the town. And with a new son to toast . . . Brick took the final steps down then paused. 'There's a dress for you in the wagon. A dress fit for a dowager queen.'

'An' what might I be doing in a dress fit for a queen?'

'Wearing it to the Sydney banquet.'

'I'll not be attending this feast. 'Tis not me place,' she said firmly, even a little primly.

'Do you mean to desert me at my marriage too?'

'*Desert* you?' she shrilled. But her heart glowed. 'That be a different matter. When you wed I must be there in Maddy's place for your mother longed for the world at your feet, as I've done all your life. But neither of us dared hope you'd be wedding in such − ' She paused then plunged recklessly, 'happiness.' Silence. A long silence. She grew afraid; had she finally dared too much?

'I am marrying Miss Merrill because it is important in my scheme of things that I do so. She must be with me always.' He began to pace the dusty strip by the steps. His voice had been calm and unhurried but now it took on a sharpness. 'What has happiness, love then − which is what you meant, didn't you, you old humbug − to do with me or my life? Love is something I have never known, which I suppose is appropriate as it also happens to be something I have never wanted. I want other things far too urgently and have concentrated on those things I do want. This . . . love people talk of, and seem to wallow in, is unnecessary to my plans. I have no use for it, or need of it − from my future wife or from anyone else.

348

Certainly I have none to give. And that is best. I move easier – and farther – without such shackles. Do you understand?'

He paused beside a Jen stripping meat from bones and storing all in her net. He balanced the greasy net cords lightly across his palm. 'All I want now – all I need – ' he added softly, 'is to draw the final cord over the others and . . . tighten.' He pulled, knotted the bulging net and threw it back into the woman's lap. With one of his quick changes of mood he cupped his hands to send a series of cooees to where the men were dismounting. Muted, the answers came back.

'Be ready to leave at dawn,' he called to her as he strode into the inky black slashed only by distant roaring fires and the milky glow of stars. She looked up . . . there, the Southern Cross. She knew that much, if she knew little else. She sat hunched on the step, in her ridiculous precious bonnet, staring into the darkness long after he was lost in distance, growing as cold as the cold night. But it did not matter.

'Do you understand?' he had asked. She trembled. No, she did not understand. She would never understand. How could she understand his explanations, his arguments, that were of the world outside and the unknowns who peopled it; she who knew nothing else in life but her own personal abiding loves.

Chapter Fifteen

ABIGAIL LUFF parted the folds of the new gown and with deft and experienced movements slipped it over Raunie's head. As she stood bearing the intricate process of hooking up, the girl studied herself in the long mirror, and knew she had never looked lovelier. The dress was the red of the garment in which she had first set foot on Australian soil but there the resemblance ended. In all Sydney there was not another dress like this. Respectable widows did not wear scarlet velvet, scarlet anything for that matter. But Raunie not only wore it, she flaunted it. She pushed two beautifully wrought combs over her ears leaving her hair to fall into snakelike coils on her neck. The combs were unpaid for and she owed Mademoiselle fifty pounds, without the dress, while the cost of the dinner tonight would be enormous, but she refused to dwell on any of it. She would arrange another card evening soon and her luck would hold. It always did. Besides, she was clever at scrounging money, a little here, some there. Usually she managed very well. Other times, well . . . somehow or other they lived. Abby looped a lace scarf over her shoulders, nodded with approval then, scolding Kitty and the hired maid peeping round the door, went bustling downstairs shooing the excited girls before her.

Raunie anointed herself lavishly with perfume, anticipation lending a warm flush to her skin. Brick's card of acceptance had been the last to arrive but it *had* come; a triumph, surely, now that all Sydney was rushing to entertain him, particularly the Sydney that had formerly professed to despise him. She had waited long and patiently for this opportunity, raising no objection when Alister had taken his wife away; she even made a great show of shopping for a gift for Georgina's child. Indeed, her lover's absence came as a welcome respite, for since his uncle's death Alister Merrill was noticeably changed; given to violent rages and bitter criticism, and so paltry in his meannesses she grew exasperated, as if she were not making herself increasingly independent of him. She was weary of his hates, the reasons for which she cared not a jot. True, there were moments when he seemed to want to talk to her, hesitated over a few words, but invariably walked out banging the door behind him. Abby, who had her own sources of information, insisted he was gambling heavily. Well, his horses must be a poor lot. And he must be an even sadder hand at cards. She shrugged her shoulders at his moods and forgot him for as long as she could. In his arms she yielded hurriedly, anxious for it to be over for she found him maudlin and often fumbling, an old man. She could seldom be bothered stimulating him. In any case, since Brick's return she had been unaware of any other men, driven by excitement now that he must see her as he saw other women, all the cosseted beauties of the world's great cities, the indulged and petted of the colonies, a lady as Barbara Merrill was a lady, nay more than that, a pampered young widow with a house and servants and a carriage, the result of careful if sometimes tedious preparation, for she had set herself deliberately to acquire a background of enviable gentility. And had done so, oh yes she had, despite Abby's occasional murmurs of 'superficial' and 'scrappy' – Abigail Luff didn't know everything! She, Raunie, was the darling of a circle of charming dilettantes: a Parisian couple, a Monsieur who sang and a Madame who plucked a harp on the Victoria stage, the Robsons who kept an extravagant salon and gave discreet little card evenings, and a string of raw young officers of the North Devons who rode in from their spanking new Barracks out on the sand-hills to beg her to applaud their dramatics at the Barracks Theatre and become the belle of their after-performance suppers. She shone at these affairs, chaperoned steadily by Abigail. Despite her critical moods, which Raunie felt were inspired more by Kitty or Herbert than by her mistress's enthusiasms, Abby was invaluable. As was the groom, Herbert Wickler.

In spite of his vagabond ways. Or perhaps because of them.

On the racetracks and about the 'ring', swaggering in a glory of tight trousers and glaring waistcoats, Herbert Wickler shone. Prize-fighting, bull-baiting, cocking, were all twisted to his advantage, and there was not a foot-race or another of the crazy contests upon which sporting gents loved to gamble that didn't set him up (and Winthrop) very nicely for a week or two. He made a tidy income as the darling of the saloons, earning his ten shillings swallowing a quart of melted bacon fat or basinful of mustard with a bottle o' gin to wash down the mess, all under the half-hour set, then offering to do it over again right then and there. When trouble loomed he took cover as groom at a favourite hostelry where he was well paid for his tips, and a box of tea or bag of sugar could be filched and resold at a nice little profit. Herbert had once made the mistake of pawning 'Aunt' Abigail's silver pin and ever since had been forced to entertain a grudging respect for her wishes. His present duties were made endurable only by the handsome worldliness of the mistress he deigned to put in the way of a certainty in return for time off – and Kitty's heady charms. Herbert Wickler was not included in Abby's plans for her child but Herbert consoled himself – there were always ways. And 'she' would be on his side. Herbert knew 'her' kind. 'She' wouldn't be bothering her handsome black head about a husband for anyone but herself. In this Herbert was correct: Raunie had washed her hands of her housemaid the first time she had caught the girl slapping a careless duster over the bric-à-brac and peeping through the window at her suitor attempting to flirt with her from the yard.

'He'll put you to work you know,' she teased, rescuing a china figure teetering on the edge of the shelf.

The girl sighed. 'But such dandy manners he has, ma'am. Such a fine elegant way with him.'

And Raunie laughed, gave her a box of candies she had no taste for, a necklace she'd tired of, and the afternoon off to go walking. Abby or no Abby, the problem of Kitty would most certainly resolve itself.

So, when the band played on the Barracks green a deliberately gay and carefree Raunie bowled along in her low light phaeton behind her beautifully matched ponies, an impeccably garbed Herbert on his seat; she had turned up a definite nose at the smartest gig or curricle and, driving Alister almost to distraction, had had her way as to her equipage. She flirted with the officers and petted her lap-dog, a creature she detested but endured solely for the air of distinction it gave her. She was adept at the polka, she knew a few phrases of French grammar, and was taking singing lessons, learning to accompany herself on the elaborately carved Eavestaff for which Alister had paid a hundred guineas at Christmas. Her likeness was preserved for posterity – and Alister's birthday – at a shocking fee on the new and fashionable daguerreotype. She won at cards – coached by a wizardly expert Abby – often enough to pay pressing debts or buy herself a coveted parasol, lucky indeed as the Robsons played for high stakes. And when she lost, well . . . a Merrill could still get credit. She had credit all over town caring nothing for her lover's protests. A born gambler, she loved above all else the excitement of the game. Any game. Sometimes she drove out to Homebush races and winning, they revelled in luxury, losing, they dined on potatoes and cabbage broth for a fortnight. She developed a taste for champagne as the symbol of her new status, and in a spasmodic way kept a diary of superficial jottings and laboured over little notes for the satisfaction of posting them off in the fashionable new envelopes. Altogether she frittered away her time in the witless pursuits and fancy trappings she firmly believed made a lady of fashion. She shopped and danced and entertained as extravagantly as her allowance and Abby's miraculous management would allow, was complimented on her flower arrangements and her little supper trays and the sherry with hot water sweetened and highly spiced that was her speciality. Her social accomplishments were as varied as they were trivial, her conversation daring, and when conventions became unbearable she dispensed with them despite Abby's scoldings. Intoxicated by her success

353

she was heedless of anything but her own needs and desires.

Alister's chill refusal to be seen with her about the city spurred her to excesses of extravagance – a desire to hurt, to pay back. The clothes she accumulated became a by-word: velvets and laces, the exciting frou-frou of new silks, négligés, ball gowns, bonnets and caps galore, shawls and scarves and flowers. Trinkets and ornaments and all manner of adornments spilled from every drawer – if a bauble glittered she must have it. And somehow or other she got it. No belle in Sydney boasted more petticoats or tighter jackets or revealed more of her bosom when the occasion demanded – and quite often when it didn't. When she tired of a thing she flung it to Kitty which kept Abby's allegiance. Poring over *World of Fashion* with Mademoiselle, they evolved bizarre but always arresting creations to dazzle her admirers. She was, Raunie firmly believed, the city's scandal, though how much gossip was born of the liaison between herself and Alister and how much from the notorious independence of the widowed Mrs Merrill she didn't know or care. Women whispered and men stared, but men had always stared. And as for their wives – when had any woman been of willing use to her in her life? When a weary Alister complained of her latest escapade or remark she laughed at him then taunted him into making love. As he always did. He simply became hers again. She gloried in making him dance to her tune, teasing, goading, so that maddened beyond civilised endurance by her moods he sometimes struck her. Then she made a business of forgiving him, of winning him back. She became more audacious, more assured, more demanding, and always irresistible. Life in the crowded little house in Macquarie Street was an egregious, hedonistic existence, with a future so promising as to appear limitless, and the past, except when it suited her, dead and resolutely forgotten.

Or so she had intended, and believed, until the day she was jolted into associations she had determined to deny to her last breath. Captain Cook's River, weaving towards its mouth, was choked and blackened with refuse from the limekilns, shanties and rotting lean-tos that sheltered itinerant fisherfolk and tinkers, throwing itself finally through odorous swamps to be cleansed by the tides of Botany Bay. Amid this litter, foul with disease and apathy, huddled half-breeds, quadroons, beggars and vagrants, a veritable thieves' kitchen of the living dead.

Because of the isolation, and the superb view – provided one looked out and never down – Alister occasionally took his mistress driving over the rolling little hills about this region. On one such afternoon, bored with him but more sharply with herself, she had strolled away from the phaeton to find herself staring at a woman, a young woman she could see despite her shapeless rags and the withered hands that gathered wood so painfully stick by little stick. But it was at the woman's face Raunie continued to stare, stupefied, unable to turn away. That horrible scar marring the dark skin could mean only one creature – Inar. And Inar it was behind the eaten-in grime and the dull shifting gaze that lighted on everything yet saw nothing. The woman's eyes met Raunie's with vacancy – without sense or memory. Someone had left her here for dead, no doubt of that. The Duchess? Who else would be interested in what happened to Inar? Except . . . Brick perhaps? Well Inar, though breathing, could never tell. Raunie watched the woman with eyes now chill and detached; the past was dead, as dead as if Inar had disappeared in the ashes of the Hulk fire. She took a deep shuddering breath of relief, swung her silk parasol in a sheltering arc and turned back confidently to life.

And now, to complete her triumph, Brick O'Shea was home, even though as yet elusive. From the morning the *Marigold* anchored she had sought his eyes over her fan at the theatre or from under her bonnet brim in the Domain but if she did happen to catch his quizzical glance he would only bow, murmur some nicety and move on. It maddened her. She was one of so many, for women were making fools of themselves over him. He didn't seek her out even if he didn't actually avoid her and, jealousy gnawing with a deeper pain than ever, she would rave and kick her dog, scream or break whatever breakable lay to hand. Bored, she sat through the dullest debates. She went to election meetings (losing count of the times she was rescued from the inevitable free-for-alls by the adroit Herbert) purely to devour with greedy eyes the figure dominating the crowd by his very presence and whose most casual phrase stirred the upturned faces like a summer wind, hating Barbara for being there and closer to him than she could edge herself and holding Jamie – *her* Jamie – by a proprietary hand. Well, let Barbara think what she liked about Jamie, about Brick, about herself . . . she, Raunie, had scored over Barbara, and could any time she wished – she had gloried in her power over her child that day outside Parliament House. She lay awake night after night plotting . . . planning . . . Finally, a note had accompanied Brick's invitation to dinner – nothing begging this time, she was done with humility – a decisive, entirely practical letter. Did he know Jamie was beginning to seek her out? Exactly what was she expected to say and do when she met the child about the city, as she must? Surely he could see, as she did, the necessity to discuss such matters? Her invitation was accepted. Now, he would soon be here.

The clock below struck a ponderous seven. She picked up the fine gold chain dangling her little bunch of charms and clasped it round her throat letting the baubles rest between her breasts. Let them see and wonder if they must for tonight it was her fancy to wear the trinkets proudly, as a gipsy. She laughed at her bold reflection and hurried down. The house was lavish with light, heavy with flower scents, and warm from the blazing fires. In the kitchen the tables groaned while Kitty and the hired girl preened, proud of their starched caps and frilled aprons. As usual, Abby would watch Herbert when he handled the gentlemen's coats. Raunie hastened to check the wines, hoping Brick at least would appreciate the continental gesture of after-dinner cognac for the gentlemen. If only there were more champagne . . . Even so, she demanded a bottle opened for herself and brought in, and of course, once opened it must not be wasted. In her excitement she held her glass high in a salute. Tonight, Brick O'Shea, we stand side by side. If you have dragged yourself up to the

356

world of the élite, then so have I. And if I tell you how much I need and want you, you will not turn away. You cannot . . .

The table looked wonderful. What Abby and her nephew had not borrowed they had hired to match the Wedgwood, the double damask cloth, and the napkins intricately folded and standing up like stiff lilies in the red glasses with the delicate stems. Low bowls of full-blown red roses. Slim yellow candles, not too many – men were affected by the mystery of subdued rooms. The epergne towered writhing as some eastern temple. She made certain the hothouse fruits lay on top, the wax ones well underneath – Abby usually agreed with her on what constituted a 'front'. She placed the cards with care. Brick . . . The virginally plain Miss Dulcey . . . Valetta Robson's new fiancé (the smugness of the girl was out of all proportion to a mere lieutenant) . . . Valetta herself since she had more or less demanded it . . . The two amiable pekinese of Misses Bellaw interspersed with subalterns brash and ponderously witty . . . Two newly married couples to whom she owed dinners (thank heavens honeymooners left early) interspersed with the Chercherons. Now Captain Aubrey, big and hairy with a lion's voice, on her left. She sipped her champagne wondering what the Captain would say if she told him she had folded the napkins herself. Perhaps she would tell him. Tell them all . . . She giggled. Then hiccuped. She put down her glass. Giggling women were talkative women. Well then . . . sixteen in all. Dull, dull women and ogling men. Except Brick. Brick never ogled. He came straight to the point. But tonight he would be late. She felt it. She drank more champagne. And went on drinking it.

Brick O'Shea was very late. Monsieur was repeating his favourite story for the third time and for the third time they laughed without understanding a word, Abby was making despairing signs about spoiled soufflés and overcooked beef, and Raunie was taking another sherry, to the Captain's delight, when Brick was announced, unhurried and unruffled. His dress clothes were impeccable, his hair smoothed as much as it could ever be subdued. Raunie's heart seemed to

357

stop dead then thump along at an accelerated pace – it had been so *long*. There was a flurry among the women, meaningful glances between the men. They were all insulted of course, yet highly intrigued; it meant they were, to put it one way, *in* on things. Brick was jovial to the ensigns and attentive to the women – too attentive, Raunie fumed, for after an extravagant flourish over her hand he'd scarcely glanced her way. Difficult to tell whether he was serious or sardonic when it came to the European niceties, to him it might be merely a convenient way to spend an idle evening instead of a night she had longed for for years. In a nervousness alien to her she dropped her fork. Then she knocked over her wine and it splashed on his clothes. Barely pausing in his talk he mopped it up calmly. She wanted to hit him. Then she wanted to cry. Instead she drank champagne till she was fuddled and hated them all. In particular, Brick O'Shea.

Madame Chercheron's voice soared above her husband's, no mean feat at any time. '. . . and such a relief to find English ladies different from what we had been led to expect.'

'And what exactly had you been led to expect?' Miss Violet Bellaw's skirts rustled.

'Why – a countryman of ours who was, er – detained at Plymouth during the War –'

'Imprisoned, ma'am. Imprisoned,' the Captain growled. He loathed the Froggies.

But Madame never permitted any Saxon boor, any boor for that matter, to interrupt Gallic reminiscence; the Chercherons gloried in the *ancien régime*. ' – assured us that English ladies dressed in short woolsey petticoats and blasphemed shockingly.'

The Captain roared. 'Fishwives, ma'am. Plymouth fishwives. Ah . . . England!' He shook his head, but indulgently, at his personal and England's collective foibles. 'We billet our foreign prisoners who, though barbarians, certainly have eyes, about our docks and quays and ship Tommy Atkins across the seven seas to be our most widely known ambassador.'

Brick cracked a nut. 'Who better? A decent enough fellow,

358

invariably enlisting through hunger, the best almost as good as the finest soldier anywhere – the Irish peasant.'

'Bah!' The Captain despised the Irish almost as much as the French. 'Tell any rabble it's heroic and it will insist on proving it.'

'Exactly, Captain. There's nothing good or bad but mass thinking makes it so.'

Captain Aubrey frowned. Mass thinking? The fellow was crazy. Dangerous too. The masses didn't think, they felt. And bred. He gave a delicate imperceptible little shiver. God, how they bred. 'Unfortunately – or perhaps fortunately for myself – I do not have your experience of the masses.'

'A pity.'

Miss Valetta patted her back curls. 'We long to hear you tell of the Continent, Mr O'Shea. Poor exiles as we are, we must exist on crumbs from Europe's table. But you won't dwell on the fighting, will you. Violence is so horrible. Such a dreadful thing to imagine the desecration of the world's great cultural centres.' She sighed prettily and patted her hair again.

'For my part, Miss Robson, I found Europe a bare enough table, with what's left on it reeking of decay.' He smiled at her. 'I suppose, after all, one can scarcely blame the privileged for clinging to their wealth, it does help them avoid the more unpleasant smells of living.'

Captain Aubrey pushed his plate aside. The fellow's conversation was not only barbaric, it was indecent. If he'd known he'd be sitting across the table from him tonight he wouldn't have come. Still, what more boring duty than convict guarding? With nothing to do otherwise but seek another wanton, and when you'd worked your way round to where you'd begun – what then? He yawned behind his hand and, heavy-eyed, brooded on Raunie's shoulders glowing under the candlelight, wishing he could prise her away, even once, from that damned duenna of hers. She was as enchanting as rumoured . . . and discreet it seemed. And shrewd enough to be safely rid of Merrill before she flirted in earnest with the rank and file. A touchy prig, the Major, where his womenfolk were concerned. Close as an oyster to boot. Typical of the man to close his eyes to the fact that all Sydney knew he was heading for ruin. Not simply a fool, but a proud one. Such dedication was madness. You used your head where the Army was concerned – more fun to be had that way – whereas Merrill would lose his shirt before he sold out. Army was a religion with him.

Raunie's laugh, deep-throated and arresting, skimmed the talk. This grandam Madame here had put a neat finger on it . . . a *gamine*, she had called the girl, indulgently, but with a subtle curl to her mouth. Irish, was she not? With a dash somewhere of the Spanish perhaps? And something more . . . But he felt too lazy, too satisfied with the excellent table she kept, to decide what it might be. And it didn't really matter what she was apart from being a woman to rouse a man to unheard of feats . . . He visualised her hips, the long gentle curve from hipbone in . . . Jehovah! O'Shea's voice shattered his musing.

O'Shea. The little widow hadn't taken her cat's eyes from the man all night – there, she was staring at him again. Well then, let her burn her fingers at that flame, like all her sex, and be damned to her. He yawned again, not too regretfully. Who should know better than he that all women were the same when you snuffed out the candles . . .

O'Shea. He shifted uneasily on his seat. Trouble was, men as well as women must bear with the bastard, the laws of this outpost being what they were. As if England's laws were not good enough, too damned good sometimes for colonial up-starts. Why, he'd just as like put up for the Australian Club next and damned well be accepted!

'Mr O'Shea . . . I have heard . . .' Newlywed Flora Bradley was as pink as her frock, but determined; she supposed it was quite shocking how determined she felt. She made a fresh start, a firm start. 'It it true, Mr O'Shea, that chloroform is being used in childbirth?'

'Flora!' Her husband folded his napkin with careful precision and placed it firmly on the table while the ladies stared at the scraps on their plates. All ladies except Raunie.

She stared at Milton Bradley. Hypocrite, she thought, playing the prude when you owe me twelve pounds for that card game at the Robsons'. Ah, wouldn't this earnest bright-eyed bride of yours be interested in listening to a few things about her new husband. Well, Milton Bradley, this won't be the last dinner party of mine you'll be expected to attend. She picked up her glass, felt a sudden distaste for its contents, and replaced it. She shook her head to clear it. She was tired of them all, of the dinner, of this wearying trifling talk. All Brick had done was flirt with a pack of boring simpering women. 'We cannot deny Genesis you know,' Milton was saying coldly. 'Women must suffer for their share in original sin.'

'I don't care a fig for Genesis. And I can't see what I had to do with original sin.'

'*Flora* —'

'Well I don't, so there.' Her mouth trembled. She was very young. But she was also very angry. She lifted her glass and caught Brick O'Shea's eyes. Why, his eyes were . . . kind. Yes, *kind*. Who would have thought it? This ravisher of native women, this go-getter, this . . . Could that dreadful story of him laughing while his drunken men bet on the darts thrown at the Queen's portrait actually be true? *Could* it? With all eyes on her she sipped her drink, slowly, savouring it. She drank it all even though she knew she was likely to be sick.

'I have heard, Mrs Bradley,' O'Shea put in, 'that a growing number at Court give chloroform parties.'

'But doesn't it — kill?'

'Sometimes. But so do other things. The only difference really between the effects of chloroform and boredom is that the former sends us more hurriedly to extinction. Certainly more mercifully. Most humans it seems can bear with a vicious companion but never for long a stupid one.'

Raunie sat fuming. It seemed an age before the ladies showed any willingness to retire, another age before the gentlemen joined them. The Misses Bellaw tortured German songs, Monsieur warbled with exciting gesticulation, but Raunie refused point-blank to sing, furious at Brick as he argued over the finer points of kangaroo hunting with his fawning ensigns. If *he* begged her to sing . . . But he seemed oblivious of the fact that she had even been asked. Her eyes glimmered, there was a flounce to her hips that drove the Captain wild, and her words stung: 'I shall never hear the bird again without being reminded of you, Lieutenant,' she purred over Lieutenant Hartland's imitation of a laughing jackass. And she broke into a discussion on fox shooting. 'Have you not noticed, ladies, that those men over-concerned for domestic animals – and children – are the keenest at hunting wild ones? Both beasts and children.'

At last she had gained his attention. He was watching her. But still she could not have him alone, for the supper table was brought in and the talk dawdled until she felt she would go mad. Mr Bradley did make a move; he decided his wife must have a megrim she was so flushed and bore her off, both of them overly polite to their fellow guests and hostess, and rather sickeningly so, Raunie thought, to each other. But still the talk and laughter and directionless pointless joking went on. Winthrop's order and elegance seemed to have taken on a wilted, even faintly decadent look before the last clip-clop of carriage horses died to silence and she was able to slam the withdrawing-room door behind her and lock it.

Brick turned sharply from the fire, brandy in hand. She tossed her head in defiance and dropped the key cleanly between her breasts.

'You'll not keep me here longer than I want by such cheap tricks, Raunie. Don't let my plumage fool you. I'm no more the gentleman when it comes to women than I ever was.'

'But you don't really want to go, do you,' she taunted, sure of herself again.

'No.' He looked about him. 'I'll admit I'm interested in the *décor* – ' He broke off to laugh at her look of amazement. 'Oh yes, I've picked up enough French to dazzle the wives and keep the husbands on their toes with suspicion.'

Except for the crackling of the fire the room was quiet. Very quiet and very warm. His eyes resting on her were black and moist. But he looked at many women that way, she reminded herself hastily. It could mean everything – yet nothing. 'You look damned handsome in red,' he said at last, slowly. 'You look like . . . a tinker girl.'

'What's a tinker girl?' she asked suspiciously.

'Tinkers are wanderers along the little roads of Ireland, despised, but free as the wind – and usually very lovely. They're not gipsies but . . . in you there's the blend of both. No,' as her eyes, startled, met his, 'I've kept my promise. I've left them to guess your breed if they can.'

'Well, they don't guess it.'

'Not even your proud and suspicious Major?'

She ignored this and flung herself on the couch, leaning against a gold cushion, watching him stroll about the room fingering this, examining that, for all the world as if he were . . . well . . . assessing. He was intent on the room, not her. She moved restlessly.

'Why have you ignored me all evening?'

'Impossible to ignore you, my dear Raunie, when you were wriggling at my elbow all through that impossible dinner. No wonder you only attract half-starved sycophants when you're so clumsy with your guests.' He indicated the damp spots on his jacket. 'Cost a deuce of a lot too.'

'Other men don't ignore me,' she persisted.

'I don't ignore you either. I couldn't. I just don't make love to you. And because I don't you want me to.'

'That's not it. Not really.' She gulped, baffled. She tried again, a little sulkily. 'Why did you come then?'

'First of all, to discover your reasons for asking me.'

She wavered. 'Jamie –'

'You already know everything there is to know about Jamie,' he interrupted sharply.

'He hates Barbara. I know that.' She delighted in flinging it in his face.

'If that were true – and I doubt it – I'd blame you if I weren't quite sure you're more determined than ever to keep your precious secret.'

'What makes you so sure?'

'You would never flaunt a seven-year-old offspring before the Major – or anyone else. Admit it.' But she noticed that even though they were behind closed doors he kept his voice down.

'Why do you keep on so about Alister? What has Alister to do with me – us – here and now?'

'And why do you keep play-acting? I'm scarcely an appreciative audience. I know only too well that you glory in the fact that your *mésalliance* – oh yes, my new lingo covers almost every situation, legal and otherwise – with my enemy is the talk of the town.'

It was then that she decided to abandon her role of innocence and ignorance. She flung up to face him. 'And why not? Why shouldn't I make the most of it, take everything I can get? Alister considers I'm worth this house, these clothes, worth anything. I'm more valuable to him than his most important friends, his wife, yes, even that precious daughter of his. Far more valuable than Barbara.'

'Leave your jealousy of Barbara out of this.'

'Jealousy? Why should I be jealous of Barbara? I've more than she has. Oh yes I have. I *have*.' Her eyes smarted and she stopped, panting and confused. It was a lie. She, Raunie, had not yet possessed this man, while Barbara . . . She had to *know*.

'As to the Major, you may be right,' he was saying smoothly. 'From all I see here he's evidently a generous, even a reckless patron. But then I've never underestimated your powers, Raunie. Indeed I've staked everything on them, taken a risk on them, and that's something I seldom do. But I know only too well that if there is one woman in this world who can seduce a man to scatter his own – and other people's – money to the four winds of heaven, you're that woman.'

He always irritated her when he talked in riddles, and now his riddles held a suggestiveness that aggravated. 'Well, he doesn't give me money to throw away,' she said sullenly. 'Not any more. He's driving me crazy with his meanness.'

'And why would Major Merrill be mean to you?' he asked, leaning against the mantel, tracing the outline of an ivory figurine with his fingertip. She envied the ornament. She envied it so much that with a swift feline movement she swept

364

it against the wall. It finished under the couch. She wished it could have splintered to fragments. 'After all,' he went on calmly, ignoring her action, 'he was Havelock's heir.'

'He swears he got nothing – well almost nothing – from his uncle. I think he's lying.' Her eyes narrowed. 'But why should you be concerned about his affairs?'

'Not concerned exactly, just interested.'

And he drank slowly, watching her with a steady compelling gaze that caused all caution, all reason to leave her. Like a thirsty beggar she held his eyes, determined to hold his attention. 'Why?' she persisted.

He put down his glass. 'Isn't it reasonable that if I'm interested in – you – I must be interested in his activities? Particularly, at the present time, his whereabouts?' He moved towards her. 'After all . . .'

She held out eager responsive hands. He took them in his and drew her against him. 'I take it he's out of town?' he murmured.

'Of course he's out of town.' Her heart was racing. 'Do you take me for a complete fool?' She pressed herself against him, maddened by her impatience. 'Why do you want him out of the way? Tell me why. *Tell* me.' She wanted to hear him say it.

His arms slid round her waist and tightened. She pressed her body against his. They rocked together slowly and gently. Her eyes closed. Enjoying him, she heard him murmur, 'Do you take me for the complete fool? Because I do not want my visits here, to you, to clash with his.'

Her arms moved up and about his neck. Her long urgency, her damned-up need exploded in little love murmurs, a wild gushing forth of her love for him. 'All these years I've wanted you but I would get tired of waiting and make myself hate you so I could forget you. But each time I saw you I knew it was useless. I've never been able to forget you, not for one minute. You're here in my brain all the time driving me mad, mad. The little shell you gave me, remember?' She held it against his mouth. 'I've wished every night on it, whispered spells over it, kissed it –' She pressed it against her own eager quivering mouth, 'when what I really wanted was to be kissing you.' And with a fervour that was childlike, or simply primitive, she pressed her lips against his throat, hard. 'You despised me for being unwanted and alone, oh yes you did, but now see me. Look at me. *Look*.' She strained back in his arms, laughing up at him. 'Alister was the way to get you, you see. He doesn't know it but he's helped me to be what you want. But I care nothing for Alister – '

'All the same,' he said evenly, 'neither of us can push him aside so easily.' He kissed her ear. His lips were in her hair. He was bemusing her. 'He might return suddenly.'

'Why should he?' Her words tumbled in her eagerness to reassure him. 'He was so anxious to get away – oh, I could see it. Besides, in his letter yesterday he said it might be weeks before Gina's child is born.'

'So that's where he is – Blair's. I should never have imagined Merrill sentimental over a grandchild. Could it be he went hoping for a loan?'

'From that skinflint?' She laughed her scorn. Then stirred restlessly in his arms. 'Oh, why bother about Alister?'

Begrudging his questions she caressed him, entreating, aware only of herself, a self roused and excited by the force of her desire. It was with dismay she felt his faint . . . yes, his withdrawal from her. Astonished, she clutched at him with a growing fear of the thing that was happening and that she could not comprehend.

'You don't have to marry me, you know.'

He laughed indulgently. 'I have never had the slightest intention of marrying you, Raunie.'

'Well, I don't think much of marriage either. All I care about is that you love me.'

'And what has this to do with love?' Now there was something more; a harshness of manner, the old edge to his words, a resistance of his body. It terrified her.

'I don't care what you call it. I just don't care. Not as long as you want me. Say you'll always want me. Say that. *Say* it.'

She caught her breath as his lips clung to her throat in a long kiss. But just as suddenly he clasped her hands together and held her away from him. His eyes were cool and determined.

'Listen, Raunie, and listen carefully. From the first moment I looked on you, yes, awkward and tired and angry, working in my kitchen at the Pride, I saw you as the loveliest thing ever created to satisfy a man – at the same time depriving him of his senses. But my reasons for coming tonight were not your reasons for inviting me. Understand this, you shall never get your claws into me this way; no, or in any other way you might try. I vowed that years ago and I meant it then and by everything I have ever sworn by, I mean it now. You shall not bend me to your will through your body any more than you shall through that scheming self-centred mind of yours. Never.'

But she clung to him, refusing to understand, refusing even to listen. 'I'm your kind, you know I'm your kind. How can you be bothered making love to that prim school-teacher with her white gloves and her prayer book and her patting my child on the head. *My* child –'

'Enough of Barbara.'

'*My* child, hypocrite that she is. What does she care about Jamie? She despises him. And she despises you. Oh yes she does. Why wouldn't she despise you? She'd never do anything but amuse herself with such as you. Her kind is proud without admitting it, without even knowing it.'

He thrust her away. 'There are things between Barbara Merrill and myself that you could never understand.'

'What things?' she scorned. 'What is there to understand but the one thing, the thing everyone understands? Don't . . .' she wailed as he clasped her wrist.

'Just what is it you – and everyone – understand about myself and Barbara? Tell me.'

'That she's your woman. *Woman*. Some could give her worse names. I could myself.'

She expected him to strike her; indeed she wanted him to hit her, to resume contact, but instead he let her go. She rubbed her wrist where the skin was raw. His voice was icy.

'Then you may inform – everyone – that very shortly Miss Merrill will no longer be in the unfortunate position to be called such names. Give me the key.'

'Key?' she gasped, his demand and its significance wiping all else from her mind. 'Why?'

'Give me the key, Raunie.'

'No. *No*. You're not going. I won't let you go. I can't let you go. I can't.'

She flung herself against him, wailing, near tears in her despair. With relief she felt his hands on her, but they were not the hands of love, or even of desire. His fingers hurt her arms, her throat, her shoulders. He wanted the key. He meant to have the key. She realised this and fought him, dragging at his wrists, biting, kicking, maddened by her disappointment and her throbbing need of him. He wasted no more time. Ripping her dress, pulling and tearing at it until he found the key, he threw her aside. She slithered along the floor and grasped him about the knees. Holding her off with one hand he managed to unlock the door. She clasped his ankle. He tore himself free with an oath. But he did not kick her. She would not have felt it if he had. She was beyond articulate thinking, any thinking at all. Squirming, scream-ing, blaspheming, she began to throw things; ornaments, goblets, anything to her grasp. She tore off her shoes and flung them too.

'You'll come begging for me some day,' she screamed. 'I'll make you beg. I *make* you beg.'

But he was gone. She was choking. She stumbled to her feet and thrust herself after him, half-naked, demented, screaming hoarsely, ribald gipsy curses that some unbidden knowledge and memory thrust through her lips. They saved her from going mad. As she stumbled into the open she heard rather than saw his horse at a gallop and was too weak to do more than collapse into Abby's arms. With Herbert support-ing her she was half-dragged, half carried inside and the door slammed on the, as yet, mercifully deserted street. Even then she fought them, moaning her despair, sinking on to the floor, drumming her fists into the carpet like some insane creature enslaved by her hysterical body. Unaware of anything but herself and her deep and thwarted needs she wallowed in self-pity, surrendering herself with an almost masochistic savagery to her misery. And her demons.

For days she scarcely knew what she did. She must have eaten, slept, at least moved about her bedroom, but time was a murky effortless twilight. In her muted world she thought Abby had talked to her, even shaken her, but she wanted only to be left alone in the hushed house, to lose herself in the blessed lethargy that was all that was left after emotion had drained away. She was wrapped in weakness. Brick . . . Barbara . . . Their names worried at her like the small dog at her heels until she kicked the little creature and it fled, whining, beneath the bed.

When Alister came she was sitting half-dressed at her dressing-table pondering with only half awareness on a pile of bills. All she had in the world was six pounds ten shillings. She had counted it three times yet could not make it more. Neither, for all her cleverness, could Abby. Mr Solom had called the previous afternoon and Abby had spent a difficult half-hour getting rid of him, Raunie aware of their raised voices from behind her locked door. Mr Solom had never called before, indeed had always been obliging over small accounts. But it seemed small accounts could suddenly become large ones. And this morning there were letters, four letters. Unpleasant letters, Abby said. There was even something different about Abby. She was brusque, almost bullying. Well, Raunie sighed, she supposed she had better be pleasant to Alister. And thinking of Alister made her push back her hair and study herself a little anxiously in the mirror. It was time surely he was back in Sydney. And as the morning wore on she even began to wish he would hurry.

With fitful little spurts of energy she was making a choice of garments when she heard his voice below and Abby's in answer. They talked a long time but she was glad of the respite. She drew her mussed négligé about her, attempting

369

to tie the ribbons but her fingers were unsteady. His footsteps. She slipped before her mirror to smooth her hair. Quick now, where had he been? Some place called . . . Wellington? Yes, Wellington. He'd been staying with Georgina. Then it must be days, perhaps even a week since Brick . . .

She turned for her lover's kiss but Alister did not touch her. He stood looking about him and she was shocked into awareness of the untidy room, her own careless toilette, her tiredness. She picked up her hair brush as she held out a hand in welcome. But still he did not come to her. He moved slowly and heavily to the window.

'I arrived yesterday.' His voice was curiously lifeless.

She began to brush her hair with as much vigour as she could manage. 'Then you took your time in coming to me.'

'I had matters to attend to. This for one.' He spread a newspaper before her, his finger jabbing the page. 'That . . . woman of yours tells me you haven't seen it yet.'

'TO BE SOLD BY PUBLIC AUCTION . . . BY ORDER OF THE MORTGAGEE . . . REGENT LODGE . . .'

Their eyes met in the mirror. 'There'll be nothing left, you know,' he said. 'Nothing. So you'd better get used to the idea.'

She put down the brush and swivelled about on the stool. 'What do you mean, nothing left?'

Her bewilderment seemed to amuse him for, incredibly, his lips quirked in a tiny smile. 'No money, Raunie, that's what I mean.'

'Money?' she repeated dully. She had never really understood about money, the legitimate sources of it or how it was managed. In the world of the gentry one was not required to know about money. Certainly no woman was expected to ponder over the mundane collection of it. Money was there as the gentry was there. She had simply cultivated the fashionable art of spending it. She picked up her brush and drew it a little abstractedly through her hair. He reached out, snatched the thing from her hand, and flung it on the dressing-table.

'Yes, money. It's time to face up to things. Playing the lady is over. Where do you think this came from? And this?' He snatched up garment after garment, then threw them all down in a colourful heap. 'More clothes than you can wear, all the other useless trappings you've wheedled out of me. Have you ever asked how much the bays cost? And all that stuff downstairs? It wasn't all bought with lucky wagers.'

'You're mad. You must be mad.' But she knew he wasn't mad. She was just beginning to understand. Abby had tried to tell her about the Sale. 'You . . . but your uncle was a rich man. I thought – everyone thought –'

'And there was the mistake, the fatal mistake, forgetting that a rich man can become a poor one. And quickly. Oh, I knew Roger dabbled in horseflesh but I didn't know his brood mares were from O'Shea's stud – at the highest prices. I certainly didn't know of a useless property he never even bothered to inspect, sold him by a minion of O'Shea's. And the refurnishing he did last year, the new carriage . . . But all that is small stuff. I knew of his charities but not of his commitments – personal commitments – expensive ones. And of course . . . cards. Money goes, you see. The spending of it is a contagious disease. Usually a fatal one. Most who catch it rarely get over it. Paisley succumbed early. Somerset . . . As for myself – well, I managed to stave off the crisis a little longer than most, but I can't congratulate myself on any particular astuteness there; it almost seems as if I were put aside to vegetate. To be dangled on a string . . .' There was a deep bitterness in his voice. 'But it's not your function, is it, to understand a word of what I'm saying.' He paused, watching her shake back her hair and pat it into place. 'So you see,' he went on, 'after the mopping up the most I can hope for is enough to send Barbara to England.'

She swung about. 'Barbara? But what am I to do?'

'You?'

'Of course. What shall I do?'

'I suppose . . . a room.'

She sprang up. 'I'll have no poky cell in a back street. And these . . . I can't pay these.' She scooped up the bills and letters and flung them at him. 'You must do something.'

'What do you think I've been doing these past weeks – shearing sheep?' Better not to dwell on his son-in-law's rebuff. *Difficult, sir, I might even say impossible to raise so much so quickly.* And the rest of it Blair had left hanging in the air . . . *Even if I wished to do so.* 'The Sale's next month,' he finished. 'With Goltby determined to get his pound of flesh – cut to the bone at that.'

Goltby? She concentrated on what he was saying. She no longer felt tired. 'You mean . . . Isaac Goltby?'

But he was wandering the room, pausing now and then to stare from the window, distracted, detached, unreasonable. But her mind was working, and clearly. Goltby . . . Isaac Goltby. So the cause of this turmoil, this upheaval in their lives, was that fawning secretive little man safe behind the shades of his secretive little house in Bridge Street. How could she possibly forget Goltby – or the house. She knew that house as she knew her own hand. And wasn't it there before his house that she had first seen the young Jamie? – Jamie with Brick. And Brick talking so confidentially to the Jew that neither man appeared conscious of anyone else. Brick O'Shea strolling with Isaac Goltby as friends might stroll. More than friends. As conspirators . . .

Her eyes widened. She stood staring at Alister. Then she began to tremble, but it was not a frightening sensation, more a pleasurable anticipatory ripple of the nerves. An expectation. She sensed, she knew the importance of it. It was tremendously important, this coupling of O'Shea and Goltby, the smooth ex-barker who held most of fashionable Sydney in his hands.

'Goltby . . . And what does Isaac Goltby do with all the money he's supposed to be making? Has Goltby built a house on the North Shore? Has Goltby imported fine furniture or immigrants at his own expense to ensure paid supporters? Has Goltby bought his way into Council?' Alister had turned to her and was listening. She crossed to him quickly. 'All Goltby has to show are the teapots and tureens and bedroom clocks. Where are all the lost grants, the houses, the carriages? Where is all the money? Don't you see? It is not Goltby's money, not the bulk of it. It goes past him. It must go past him.' She grasped him and shook him, trying to rouse him to awareness. 'Goltby's a tool, that's all. A creature. O'Shea's creature. I know all about fronts and Goltby is the perfect front. For O'Shea. Brick O'Shea's the one you should be fighting instead of wailing against Goltby, letting yourself be sucked dry, banished into the bush to rot. Are you going to let him do this to you, and to me, without hitting back some way? *Are* you?'

Alister let out his breath heavily. 'What you say is . . . fantastic.'

'But true.'

'But the man's been abroad – '

'What does that matter?'

'Besides, how could *you* know? You . . . a girl . . .'

'By taking your pieces of family junk to Bridge Street and coaxing what I could get for them.'

'How could you – how could anyone – be certain?' His eyes clung to hers.

'I know it's true, Alister. I know it.'

'Instinct, is that what you mean?' he mocked.

'Not altogether. I hear things. Abby hears things.'

'That . . . creature.'

'She's a useful creature.'

'Granted. But what is a harridan's tongue worth? Where is the proof?'

'Proof?' She frowned. 'What would be proof?'

'Oh . . . eye-witness accounts, statements of a victim, letters . . .'

'Letters?' She pondered. 'Would a letter in O'Shea's hand – '

'How would you come by a letter from O'Shea?' he broke in.

She hesitated only slightly. 'He writes to your daughter, doesn't he?'

'So! You've been tampering with Barbara's correspondence.'

'No.' Her chin rose. 'I found the letter in the passage by her

373

door – I couldn't help reading a line or so of it – and then of course I had to keep it; if I'd returned it both Barbara and her mother would have accused me of stealing it. Oh yes they would. Even you might have believed such a thing of me – then.' She waited.

'Show me the letter.'

In her mind was only a suggestion of what she was seeking, those few words, a sentence or so, but she was driven by a deep certainty. She was sure, very sure. She dragged open drawers and closet doors, flinging clothes aside, seeking the important letter. Or rather, page of a letter. She paused. There had been more than one letter. Yes. Odd pages screwed into a bundle. For the love of God where had she put them? Then she remembered – the carpet-bag. James's carpet-bag where she had always stuffed her treasures; her apparently worthless treasures. She dragged the bag from the back of the wardrobe, ripped open the rusty clip, tipped it upside down and shook the contents on to the bed to slide over to the floor. She scraped about amid the bits of silk, beads, forgotten trinkets – ah, the papers. She smoothed them out and spread a sheet before him. 'There – see?' Her lips followed his as he read.

'. . . should you need advice, monetary or otherwise, go to Bridge Street . . .'

'Monetary means money, doesn't it?' she prompted, excited, a little dizzy with her triumph. But he was intent on the letter. *The mention of my name will be enough. Have the utmost confidence in this party* . . . He looked up. 'Hardly conclusive all the same. Others conduct business in Bridge Street, you know.'

'But it *is* Goltby. I know it. You said something just now about – about eye-witnesses. Well, I saw Isaac Goltby coming out of his house with Brick O'Shea. I saw them together with my own eyes.'

He got to his feet. There was a sharp crunch. His foot had struck a small sandalwood box and smashed it. With military tidiness he scooped up the rubbish and dumped all on the bed. He bent for a wayward scrap of paper but, about to toss

374

it on the heap, he paused, staring at it. His silence was so long and absorbed she grew impatient.

'Alister.'

He was smoothing dust from the paper – no, not paper. It was thicker than paper. It was some kind of pasteboard, grimy with congealed food, dirt, and perhaps age. It was filthy. But he was examining it, turning it over and over, even . . . reading it? She watched him, curious.

'Do you know a woman by the name of Moll?' he asked.

For some unaccountable reason her heart began thudding. Her mouth felt dry. 'Moll?'

He looked up sharply. 'I want the truth, mind. Do you know any woman by that name?'

'Only – Moll Noakes.'

'Noakes?' He frowned. 'And who is Moll Noakes?'

'Brick O'Shea's foster-mother, housekeeper – oh, whatever you like to call her.'

'Ah . . . yes. Tell me what you know of her.'

'She lives on his station, Erins Pride. She watches him like a hawk, hates any woman who as much as goes near him –'

'And how did you learn all this?'

She bridled. 'It's no more than others know. You must have heard of her. Everyone's heard of her.'

'But vaguely.' He tapped the pasteboard. 'How did you come by this?'

She shrugged. 'Whatever it is it must always have been in the box you just smashed, and the box was in the red purse – that one there – when it was given to me.' The purse, of course, was Inar's, forgotten for years, the bedraggled bulging old thing she had snatched from the Duchess's room as she fled the Thames Hulk. Inar's rubbish. Alister was turning it over with a fastidious finger.

'Then where did you get the purse? Tell me, girl. It's important.'

She was wary; she hesitated. She couldn't understand his persistent questions any more than she understood his interest in a dirty scrap of pasteboard.

375

'I'll make you tell me sooner or later, you know,' he added coldly.

'Tell you what?' She almost spat it at him. 'What are you talking about?'

'This.' He flicked the pasteboard. 'I must know how you came by it.'

'All I know is that a – a girl gave me the purse years ago and it was old even then. Nothing but rubbish inside it. Ah –'

For he had grasped her wrist and pulled her down beside him on the bed. He held her fast.

'Who gave it to you, Raunie?'

'A native girl.'

'Tell me everything you remember of her.'

'She was only a bit of a half-breed Indian, hanging about the place where I – worked. You know I had to work when I first came out. I've never tried to hide it –'

'Never mind yourself. This half-breed . . . where is she now?'

'Dead.' Without the slightest hesitation.

'Is that the truth?' He shook her. 'Is that the truth?'

In sudden anger she hit out at him and tore herself free. 'Why should I lie? She was nothing to me. I hated her. And why should you care about her?'

'Because there are words here, words that have obviously been part of a sentence. A message.'

'What kind of message?'

Searching her bewildered face, close to his own, he must have believed her ignorance. He placed the pasteboard in her hand. 'Read it for yourself.'

She stared suspiciously at the scrawled words; it was difficult to make sense of any of it for the ink had long faded under the grime. And yet . . . Her eyes clung to a word, devouring it. Yes, it did look like . . . Suddenly disturbed, even a little frightened, she threw it back to him.

'I don't care what it says. I don't care.'

He read it aloud. ' "Moll . . . never . . . Brick . . ." '

Then she had been right. Brick . . . She stared at Alister.

' "know he . . . Black . . ." '

Her mouth slackened and her hands clutched at the lacy spread. She was almost afraid to breathe. 'Black?'

'It's clear enough. What else could it mean but: "Moll, never let Brick know he is Black."?'

'You mean . . . Brick O'Shea is an . . . Indian?'

'A quadroon most likely.' His voice strengthened. 'I knew. I was always sure there was . . . something.'

Their eyes met and held. And even in the grip of his excitement, his growing sense of power, the confirmation of old nagging suspicions, he could not help but watch the change in her, fascinated by her as always but now in a different, more elusive way. Her face was transformed. It held an emotional exaltation so vivid it surpassed anything he had ever seen and experienced of her moods of mischief and delight. He felt something new stir in him, an intense consciousness of her, now, as she was at this precise moment. And the room, the litter about them, was part of it. Carefully, critically, his eyes wandered from her to the piled pathetic mess on the bed, the bright trashy gewgaws hoarded because they were symbols perhaps of her needs and desires; of creatures she had wanted or loved or hated or envied. A shabby, shoddy world. An alien world to his own, unrelated even to the world they had contrived and shared together. And he felt a repugnance sharp and unsavoury, a deep nausea, that sickness always sensed but sharply, insistently, crushed; crushed so hastily he had scarcely been troubled by it. But now for the first time he faced it, even welcomed it . . .

His eyes came back to Raunie. Her fingers were wandering over the scrap of pasteboard, lingering on it. Brown fingers. He had not noticed before how dark her skin was. But there were many things he had not noticed about her. A myriad tiny fleeting details pricked at him. The strange, sometimes slanting eyes of her . . . They slanted now. Yes, they did. And the lilting beguiling cadences of her voice that still hung in the room, trembling on his ears. He hadn't wanted to acknowledge these things. But he acknowledged them now. He wanted to. He had to. Out of what existence had she come, caught hold of his body and his life and twisted both?

Recklessly. Savagely. A savage . . . He snatched the pasteboard from her hand, got quickly to his feet, and stood on the far side of the bed. Away from her.

'What . . . what are you going to do?' she asked, but distantly, as in a dream, watching him place the board carefully in his pocket.

'Thursday is the Banquet –'

'I have my card. You can't stop me –'

'Oh, go where you please. It doesn't matter.'

Let her show off her finery if she must; he had more important things to do now than linger to quieten her storms and hysterics. Even so he stood looking at her, unable to drag his eyes from the trinkets dangling at her throat, baubles he had noted with indulgence at one time or another and ignored as playthings, whims of a fanciful luxury-loving woman. Now he saw clearly that they were talismans of some kind. Charms . . . Pagan charms. He dragged her to him, gripped them in a bunch and shook them in her face.

'These are pagan things. In heaven's name, Raunie, who are you? What are you?'

'Leave them alone.' She fought him, scratching and clawing. 'Leave me alone.' In a final paroxysm of rage she bit into the flesh of his wrist.

With an oath his hands loosened but slid to her neck. He felt her throat beneath his fingers, soft and quivering, and he shook with fury, a terrible mastering fury. And, as always, behind the worst of his fury was the fury centred in Brick O'Shea. In his mind, then, the man and this woman came together, merged to assume the contours of a genie, an hermaphroditic genie, enormous, grotesque and malevolent, the selfsame breed of monstrosity that had always meant Brick and Barbara. Raunie and Brick. Barbara and Brick. O'Shea, O'Shea, O'Shea . . . It was more than he could bear. His hands tightened on her neck. 'O'Shea,' he gasped. 'Always O'Shea . . .'

With a frantic painful twist of her head she freed her throat. Panting, she struggled to escape entirely from his hands that still restrained her. 'You know his secret. Well, I know it too. We both know he's part-aborigine, a nigger, a Black. Then let everyone else know. Tell them all. Tell the whole world. For if you don't I shall. I'll make him squirm for every time he's despised me for being what I am.'

'What are you?' His eyes clung to her face. 'What *are* you, Raunie?'

'A gipsy. Yes, a gipsy. And I don't care. Not any more. I'm glad of it now – do you hear? *Glad.*'

His hands slipped from her. She sank back on the bed. Her throat was marked. She smoothed and smoothed the skin, soothing it. Then she seemed to become conscious of him again and braced herself on her hands, watching him warily. But he did not touch her. Only his eyes followed the contours of her beautifully loose body, her golden half-naked limbs. The gold and the black . . . A gipsy. He shuddered. He had not probed before because he had not wished to do so. He had put up a block against understanding, against knowing; the block of her lips and hair and soft sensual loins. God, he might have had children by her. A gipsy. A savage. Yet even now he could not but feel the strong urgent tug of her. Such a deep and terrible need it had been, an obsession of the flesh that had finalised itself in this idiotic futility. He could not help a slight move towards her, as he could not help the reluctant hesitant cry of yearning that came from him.

'Raunie . . .'

But she curled herself away from him. And he knew that even if she had not, despite his body's need of her, nothing on earth would let him touch her again. For now there was revulsion in his need, a disgust that would, at the final instant, conquer his desire. It was all over. Dead. As he was dead. He turned and his feet brushed scattered papers – the bills she had thrown at him. He pulled a handful of coins from his pocket, a few sovereigns among them. He threw them at her. The door slammed behind him.

But Raunie did not even see the gold. Not then. She turned slowly on to her back and her laboured breathing eased and she let herself lie limp and still, only her breasts rising and falling gently, giving herself up wholly to this wonderful new elation that widened her nostrils and parted her lips and made a strange voluptuous she-animal of her. 'She will not have you,' she breathed. 'Not now.' Then aloud to the room, to the world. 'She will not have you, Brick O'Shea.' It had a wonderful ring to it! She hugged her thoughts, savouring them. Nor can you hope to have her, for they will not let you; the blue-bloods of Australia do not ally themselves with the Black. But I will have you . . . wanting to cry it to the winds. I will have you, for we are each the half of the other. I am Irish pedlars grubbing potatoes from the grudging soil of Ireland, wrenching a crust and a bone from the London of thieves' dens and sewers. I am black-eyed women glinting beads and bangles round gipsy fires. You are beaten stricken convict men. And you are black-brown bodies forever hunting, scratching grubs and berries where you can . . .

And she stretched her arms to the emptiness, holding them out to him. I will have you, Brick O'Shea, for we are both outcasts from a world we covet. We belong together.

Chapter Sixteen

THROUGH THE nostalgic eyes of those who had savoured its gay, even tinselly past, Regent Lodge presented an impersonal and somehow rootless air now that most of the curtains were drawn and there was little sign of habitation even about the service quarters. In the kitchen there was only Tilly cleaning fish and slopping tea while her latest offspring's cries permeated the house like the persistent wailing of a wake. No one wanted the Tillys of the colony or their colicky brats so Barbara counted on Doc Peter there. Bess was already installed at the Werners' while Joey – she knew she could never part with Joey. Jeremy was her father's problem – or his own. As for her mother, Eleanor's hastily penned letter waited on the Major's desk; she had no intention of returning to scandal and poverty or even continuing to correspond directly with her husband – one thing, poor dear Kenneth had been spared at least this shame. Thank heaven her youngest daughter knew her duty towards her mother. And her grandson was a precious tie even if William seldom allowed him to be fondled. Such a cruel man, to deprive a grandmother of her own flesh and blood. Georgina cried too often and long – weakness of course – and would need a mother's comfort, for William talked of more sons . . .

For this respite, brief though it might be, Barbara gave up her thanks, leaving as it did only herself and her father to go to Sunvalley when it pleased them – the Colonel's doing, *that*. His note coupled with Charlotte's waited on Major Merrill's desk. Barbara shrank at the very idea of Charlotte but it would only be till this horrible business was over and her father settled. Settled . . . but how? Where? Some lodging-house? A hut at Port Macquarie? When she attempted to make plans, to work out some form of future living that might appeal to him, she was troubled. If only he would come home and talk with her. All she could do was bury the shock and depression of the past weeks in hard work, avoiding the town with its dual topics – the plunging Merrill fortunes and the Election Banquet – while waiting as patiently as she could for her father. She had not even seen him for days and there were times when she was afraid . . . But Jeremy would never leave him. Jeremy was still Jeremy, thank God.

There had been, quite literally, no time for more than a hurried meeting with Brick after a boy had arrived with the dress – the wedding dress she had left behind. She, who was so sensitive to and receptive of Brick's slightest variance of mood sensed an intensification of his leashed energy, a bodily drive that was at any time seemingly inexhaustible. As they strolled the path near the water she was acutely aware of him tearing leaves from a branch, the impatient tap-tap of his gloves against his thigh and she knew he was suppressing deep emotions, a suppression unusual in him, for generally he let his angers loose upon her head. He was angry with her no doubt for her procrastination. But she suspected, uneasily, that his deeper and longer silences concerned her father. Well – and her chin rose – there was now nothing more for her, or her family, to hide. And Brick most probably knew more about her father's affairs, even his present whereabouts, than anyone else in the colony. He knew everything. But if she were to question him about her father he would shrug or brush her questions aside with sarcasm – or lie. And he had told her nothing of the school, of Hugh, of Doc Peter; he was holding them back from her too when he must know she missed them. Even his remark as she expressed sympathy for Paddy Harrigan's death was abrupt and cold. 'That search on the sand-hills was carried out on your father's orders, did you know?'

He was not being fair. Surely he knew that such unpleasant duties were part of her father's life? But she felt too weary to pursue the subject, too sick-at-heart to argue it out with him and she experienced one of those queer familiar instances

382

where her love for him extended to hate. Then pride came to take the place of both. She vouchsafed nothing and asked nothing. She only explained, briefly, that for the present her father needed her. After all, their marriage could be quite easily and quickly arranged, could it not? But Moll was waiting to welcome her to her new home. The house was ready to the last bell-pull. Didn't she want to see the results of her own planning? Jamie was getting out of hand, lording it over the idle colleens waiting to do the bidding of their new mistress. And time was running out; the Banquet was at the end of this week. He must make their plans now, his plans at least. A twig snapped between his fingers.

She looked at him standing beside her, thin-lipped and rigid, and ached to touch him, to soften him if she could. And could she not? Soon now she would have the opportunity and, she hoped, the power. The dusty sunburnt plains across which she would ride with this man as her husband seemed very close, and precious because of their solitude, luring her, as he lured her by his nearness. One word, a gesture of response and his arms would be strong, his will stronger, strong enough to shut out all else. She caught her breath, startled by the strength of her feelings. There would be no one else, nothing else but Brick. But now, at this moment, she had no choice; because of his great need her lonely harassed father was dragging her back in the old familiar pattern of allegiance. Of loyalty. Of love too. Her father . . .

She buttoned her gloves firmly and detached her skirts from the twigs and brambles with the retort that she had no more time to spare for him. Not today. Not tomorrow. Indeed, she could not be ready for some weeks. He must leave without her if necessary. It was unfortunate but she could not help it. In spite of his angry frown as he handed her into the carriage she turned from him resolutely and went home to sort and fold and tabulate, and take leave of a beloved home, a severance expected with her marriage of course but with memories of it secure and always there. This was a bitter parting. She had tried to write what she must say to her father, believing it to be the easiest way for him – for them

383

both. But through the long still afternoons she tore up sheet after sheet of paper, closed her writing case, opened it again to make yet another attempt.

'. . . and though I have tried to do what you and Mama and everyone else expected of me, I am a sad disappointment. I know it. But there is something I cannot deny, my need of Brick O'Shea. How can I explain this to you when I cannot understand it myself. If it is wrong I cannot help it. I will marry him. But I hope with your consent. And only when this horrible time in our lives is over. For I love you most dearly Papa and will only be completely happy if you will love me again as I think you used to love me.'

It was a pitiful, almost childish effort but she felt better now that it was written down for them both to see and accept. She would leave it on his desk. But . . . a coward's way? Surely a coward's way. The way of those other letters waiting for him, letters from those too embarrassed or too full of their importance to confront him in his humiliation. Ah . . . how confused and weary she was. Her fingers smoothed her forehead. Her hand on the quill trembled. There was a . . . discomfort about her head. The beginning of a headache. The last few days her headaches had been more persistent, sharper. As she sat restlessly smoothing the hair from her temples, massaging her forehead gently, she heard familiar sounds – a scurry, Jeremy's distinctive commands to the horses. Relief spurred her to her feet. There . . . her father was in the house calling to her. No more putting off. She could tell him now, *now*. She picked up the letter and went out. He was below in the hall twisting his crop round and round, round and round; her eyes could not help settling on the sinuous coiling thing.

'Still slinking up there in your hole, eh? Well, come down where I can see you.' He gestured sharply with the crop. 'Come down I say.'

'Of course, Papa.' She hurried down, adding a little breathlessly. 'There is something I must tell you.'

'And there's a great deal I have to tell you.' He nodded towards his study. 'In there.'

She obeyed him silently. But as he closed the door sharply behind them she turned and held out the note. 'It will explain – '

'More money?' he sneered, tossing down the whip. 'I'm in no mood to be tormented. I'm tired, body and soul. Tired, tired, *tired*. Weary of being treated like some common vagabond. And as if that isn't enough it seems I'm expected to beg for my own liquor. Damn the lot of you, I'll beg for nothing.'

He picked up the poker and before she could find the key had shattered the cupboard lock. Part of the delicate veneer scraped away As he scratched about for wine she studied him anxiously Yes, he was exhausted. But where had he been? Raunie? But Raunie wouldn't want him now. She felt the urge to speak of Raunie, to tell him she understood about Raunie, yet was silent, knowing he would resent mention of her name. She felt a swift pity for her father – now he wouldn't even have the partial escape of Raunie. She winced as he dragged the decanters across his desk; their assets were so few and she had polished the furniture till her arms rebelled. Would he let her pour, she enquired, anxious about the goblets and glasses. He brushed her hands aside. She felt helpless and wished her limbs would not shake so. She massaged the back of her neck with one finger. There . . . *There* was the worst of the pain, there in the hollow, the soft little hollow at the base of the skull. The room was dark and stuffy. Her skin was warm, much too warm. She pulled at a curtain but he stopped her.

'Leave it. Leave everything. The place is dead, so let it be. It's like ourselves. We've died slowly, somewhere along the way.' But he straightened to face her. 'But for you, Barbara, I wanted much.' Did she fancy his eyes and voice had softened? 'You never knew that, did you? I suppose not. We've left so many things unsaid . . . But what matter now. I hoped the things for you that are the important things – position, deference, respect. They are yours by right. Instead – ' Goblet and decanter jarred against each other in his irritation. 'Can't you stop that brat squawling?'

'The baby will be gone tomorrow. I've made arrangements.'

'Naturally.' The bitterness was in his voice again. He drank with concentration then filled up his glass. It was cognac. She wished he would not keep drinking so, just as she had wished it for years. He dropped heavily into his favourite chair. 'You're like all the rest, deciding how best to dispose of me with the minimum of embarrassment. It's absorbing Sydney, this question of what to do with the Merrills. Whipper-snappers toss advice, oh politely veiled, I'll grant, but still advice. Pink-skinned youths bestow charity – "Because of my affection for your family sir I would regard it as an honour if you would make use of some forty acres" – Huntingdon. Why should a stammering boy called Huntingdon patronise me?'

'Ralph would never patronise. He loves Gina.'

If he heard he gave no sign. Under the liquor flush the look of exhaustion was disappearing. But she did not like the colour that was taking its place.

'So there you are – forty acres of bush bestowed by a pink-faced boy. Your only legacy.'

She grasped her opportunity. 'You must not concern yourself over my future, Papa. I assure you I shall be well provided for. You see I – I have promised to marry Brick – Mr O'Shea.'

Though she had prepared herself for any reaction, even the most violent one, she was frightened. The colour drained from his face. But she was even more disturbed by the way the blood rushed back suffusing him. He stood up slowly, levering himself with his hands on the chair arms, but he grasped the table quickly and she noticed his knuckles were dead white. He straightened to his full height. 'So that's the way of it.' His voice was deadly. 'Once I'm out of the way, buried too as it were, you plan to scuttle off and marry this man, furtively, sinfully.'

'Not sinfully, Papa. Or furtively if you will only consent.'

'Sinfully I say. Are you out of your mind expecting me to consent to such a sin before God, marrying this –' He gulped, making a great effort at control. He moved closer. 'Somehow

I must make you understand and judge this rogue. I must make you *see*.' His voice was hoarse with strain.

'Couldn't you . . . bear with him? Just bear with him. For my sake.'

'It's for your sake I refuse to let you go through with this travesty of a marriage. My daughter could never be joined to a liar, a cheat, a man of one degrading love affair after another. Don't you know – '

'I know. I do know.'

'But there are things about this man you couldn't know, that I prefer to believe you don't know. I have discovered things about him even I find difficult to accept. But there can be no doubt. Listen to me, Barbara . . . For years O'Shea has been ruining citizens of this colony by ruthless foreclosures, colossal interest, other noisome tricks you couldn't be expected to understand. So he has ruined me. Deliberately.'

'We've ruined ourselves, Papa.'

'O'Shea's money is behind Goltby the Jew, behind others too I have no doubt, but principally Isaac Goltby. It's a cunningly screened, vicious business – '

'Goltby?'

'Did you know of this association?'

She closed her eyes for a moment, then blinked, trying to clear her head, trying to think. She had had little occasion to meet Brick's business associates. Yet . . . yes, she remembered now. Brick had given her Goltby's name and address in case of emergency. She said a little wildly. 'But you – we – were glad enough to take his money, to spend it.'

'Paisley, Somerset, even your Uncle Roger to some extent, were broken to his pattern. Well, now it's my turn. Oh, it's all clear enough now. O'Shea has waited a long time to spring the trap, not only for the paltry thousand or so he might squeeze from me but for the salving of his vindictiveness and hate. It has long been his plan to destroy me and my family. All these years that man has seeped between me and everything I've ever loved and wanted. He'll take nothing less than submission. Annihilation if you like. But my helplessness is not the final degradation. He wants your helplessness, your dependence on him. So his marriage to you, my daughter, before the world, is to be the ultimate insult.'

'Papa . . . no. He needs me.'

'He is not in love with you.'

'I –'

'Has he told you he loves you?'

'No.' Her eyes were fixed on him, as if mesmerised. Only her lips moved.

'Or done anything at all, ever, to show you that he cares for you? Has he?'

She had no answer. He moved swiftly, gripped her shoulders and shook her. His hands hurt but she was more sharply conscious of her head. It ached, yet felt strangely light. Detached. 'You know what a quadroon is, don't you?'

'A – what?' Stupidly, ignorantly, like a small child. With an immense effort she concentrated on what he was saying.

'Quadroon. A quarter-caste. A man tainted with the aboriginal, a savage at heart who wanders as his fellows wander from one settlement to another, despised as those abandoned creatures out there on your precious hills. An outcast and a nomad. All with him nomads. Then . . . O'Shea is a quadroon. At the very least. Is that what you choose to father your children?'

Her eyes widened into his. Then her face convulsed . . . with horror? Revulsion, yes. Most certainly disgust. But against him. Yes, against him, for she put up a hand and took a step back. Fascinated, with an intensity he could not help, he watched her transfiguration. She was different. She was crumbling. So it could be done.

'It's . . . impossible. He's white. He *is*. Oh, I shan't listen to your horrible lies. I refuse to listen.'

'There's no doubt of it, I tell you. His mother was no convict woman, she was a native. A half-caste most probably, but the degree doesn't matter. Now . . . O'Shea's foster-mother, housekeeper or whatever she calls herself . . . Her name?' He shook her again. 'Her *name*, Barbara.'

'Moll.' Her voice still faltered. 'Moll Noakes.'

'Exactly. Now read this . . . words written to this woman Noakes by someone desperate, someone ill or dying perhaps, but someone intimately concerned for O'Shea and his future. Who else but his natural mother? Read it I say.'

She brought her eyes on to the scrap of paper, no, not paper, pasteboard of an old faded blue, pale as the blue of the box Brick had brought her from Paris. A line or two of spidery handwriting, a word obliterated here and there. That word there . . . The shape of the blurred letters burned in her brain.

'*Read* it,' her father repeated, commanding her. Oh dear God, her head. And something, it was her heart, thumping, thumping till she felt she would choke. Do what he demands and escape. Escape from him, from it all.

' "Moll . . . never . . ." ' She hesitated but there was no doubt of it and she forced herself to say the word. ' "Brick know he . . . Black . . ." '

'Now do you understand?' He was triumphant. But she was stubborn.

'There are other Molls.'

'But no other Brick.'

'No.' Her eyes burned. 'Where did you get this?'

'Does that matter?'

'It matters to me.' But as she searched his face she knew. Raunie. The one woman who would not only know the secret places of Brick's heart and soul but use them against him when it suited her. 'Raunie,' she told him. 'Raunie.'

His gesture was impatient, defiant. 'Ask her. Ask this woman Noakes. Ask O'Shea himself. Yes, ask O'Shea, and let him prepare his lying defence if he can.'

'He doesn't know – this. He couldn't know it.'

'Because he ignores it? Because he knows that pointing fingers could only have been uncertain fingers? Because he's taken full advantage of the fact that he looks as European as anyone else?'

That was true, she thought wildly. There are quadroons out on the sand-hills with red hair and whiter skin than mine. Much whiter. I've seen them myself. Oh dear God.

'Wouldn't any man hide such a thing, deny it with his last breath?' The pasteboard had slipped to the floor. He bent swiftly and picked it up. She had forgotten it. Involuntarily her hands reached out for it, then dropped uselessly. 'But if he does not know,' he went on slowly, 'so much the better.'

Panic took hold of her. 'What are you going to do?'

'Tomorrow evening at the Banquet O'Shea will be strutting before the Governor and the colonial best. Well, he'll enjoy his triumph just as long as I allow him to enjoy it. When I choose I can bring his secret into the open for the whole world to know. Then . . .' His fist struck the desk.

'No. Oh *no*, Papa.'

'Yes.' Savagely. 'This scrap of paper is enough to damn him forever in the eyes of his fellows, of all Australia, to push him back to his beginning where he belongs.'

'You . . . you wouldn't do it,' she whispered. 'Not even to O'Shea would you do that. You couldn't do it.'

'Couldn't? It is my duty as an Englishman. But I waste such words on you; you've long forgotten what duty means.' She caught her breath at his scorn and pressed her fist against her mouth to still the shaking of her lips. 'That is why I'm sending you home,' he added stiffly.

'Home?'

'You will sail for England as soon as possible. You are no longer to be trusted and have shamed me before the colony long enough. Don't imagine you will marry this man even if you are shameless enough to still wish to do so. I swear I am prepared to go to any lengths to prevent you becoming his wife. Meanwhile . . . in spite of our present – predicament – I will not allow my family to provide further food for gossip in this colony. I have arranged for you to attend the Banquet in Mrs Clinton's care.'

'I cannot go to the Banquet, Papa. I cannot.'

'You will not only be present, you will conduct yourself with dignity. I insist upon it.'

Her hands dropped to her sides. They clenched and un-clenched while she faced him squarely. 'Papa, what you do to me doesn't matter now. But I shall never let you harm Brick. Never.'

A terrifying fury drove him. He lifted the crop and swung it. It struck her with a stinging blow. A shocked scream was torn from her and, as if the sound stimulated him to new madnesses, he struck her again and then again, blow following blow about her arms and shoulders, viciously and persistently. She bent over, crouched almost on her knees, quivering at each cruel slash but not murmuring until from sheer tiredness he ceased and leaned against the desk, panting, sweat pouring from him. There was a trickle of blood down her neck staining her white collar. Breathing painfully, his eyes fixed on it. Her eyes, big and swollen, wavered. He flung one hand across his face.

'Get out. Go to your room and stay there, damn you. *Damn* you.'

She rose stiffly and with a queer little run was gone. He thrust the whip violently aside, kicked the door shut then gripped the desk, gasping for breath. The wailing of the baby was the only sound to be heard. It went on and on . . .

Joey huddled on the stairtop, poised to scurry at the first sound or sight of Jeremy or the master, even of Tilly, stupid as she was, but no one had come near since he had crept up to keep vigil at his mistress's closed door. The almost unrelieved silence of this day was even worse than the macabre sounds of the night before. After he and Jeremy had helped the master up to bed, more in his cups than usual, they had gone to the stables. And had watched Miss Barbara's shadow against the blind as she walked up and down, up and down, up and down. Jeremy had sprawled, picking at a mutton bone, poking it dolefully at her window.

'Be the Holy, 'tis a pity now she don't sleep. 'Tis a well-known thing in the ould country she'd drop off aisy over a bubbling tide sweeping up and down, up and down. Somethin' to the mind it does . . .'

He had almost hit Jeremy. Jeremy and his bubbling

tides . . . the great overgrown gossoon. Later he had crept up stairs and listened to her tread – up and down, up and down. Towards morning he could stand it no longer and wanted to fetch Mrs Clinton, or Mr O'Shea – she would surely want Mr O'Shea? He could ride in now . . . But Jeremy, roused from sleep by his fretting, had hissed at him then kicked him quiet – was he a mad thing and all, wanting to interfere in the affairs of his betters? There were bad doings about and they'd be wise to keep their noses out of them. Wasn't the master in a dark enough mood already? And didn't Miss Barbara always wish to be left alone when she was bothered or poorly? That of course was true but . . . oh, he wished he could be certain he had not heard that scream. Scream? Who now would be screaming? A head full o' foolish fancies, mumbled Jeremy as he turned his face drowsily to the wall; fancies caught from kitchen slatterns, though it was quite true – here Jeremy's eyes blinked open and rounded while he blessed himself hastily – the evil eye could be found in upstairs quarters where it had no business to be, mentioning no names past or present. So Joey had no choice but to subside, whimpering, into a kind of half sleep. But this morning his mistress had sent down her breakfast untouched. Then the master had gone up but, though he had listened intently, there had been no quarrel, no sound at all unusual. Certainly no scream. Only the master's voice. Then the master had come down and, finally, gone out, riding down the drive like some fiend with alien fiends in crazy hot pursuit. Tilly, grumbling at the unlikelihood of her brat being taken off her hands this day with Miss Merrill looking like a ghost, and herself with orders to press and arrange the clothes for the flash 'do' tonight, as if even that fine dress upstairs – a hoop and all – could hide the fact that the poor thing was surely going into a decline. She remembered a flower girl in Lunnon . . . a month before they carried her out in her coffin she'd looked exactly like Miss Merrill . . . Ah, but a fine funeral the girl had had, such flowers too, all the throwouts from Covent Garden.

Joey had slunk about the house loathing Tilly and the baby

who cried and never stopped – chock full o' wind and gas like all males, Tilly would shrug. Well, he'd kill the brat if it bothered his mistress, vowed Joey, slamming the door on its yells. And so the terrible day wore itself out until the Major, resplendent in regimental dress, had ridden off with Jeremy – no carriage needed tonight – to Tilly's farewell bobs and curtseys. Yes sir, she quite understood sir . . . Mrs Clinton would be here to assist Miss Merrill with her toilette. On no account was Miss Merrill to be late. Oh *no* sir.

Joey started and gripped the stair-rail. There . . . footsteps, the same steps, the same deliberate rhythmic tread as last night. He listened carefully, holding his breath as long as he could. Yes, there now, up and down, up and down. He stared miserably at her door. Dared he? Oh, dared he? He saw the knob turn one way then the other. He waited, his heart thudding. The door opened slowly and she stood facing him. He was on his feet and on the landing in a flash. She was looking towards him yet didn't seem to see him – at least she made no recognition. It was very queer. His little peaked face grew whiter, his eyes desperate under the fringe of lank hair. He crept closer. Then he saw the thin streak of dried blood – yes, blood – from a cut on her neck there beneath her left ear. She moved awkwardly but she smiled at him. Ah . . . she smiled at him. He trembled with relief. Then she must be well enough.

'Joey . . .'

But her voice trailed off. Her face looked strange and her hair, always neat, was untidy. He put up an awkward finger and dared to tuck a loose tendril behind a comb, timidity lost in his concern for her. There, she looked almost like Miss Barbara again. Then his eyes, wavering past her, glued themselves to the dress spread on the bed, the dress and all the other lovely almost unbelievable things piled beside it. His jaw dropped. Never had he seen anything as absolutely beautiful as that dress. Certainly never on Miss Barbara. And he knew a fierce boyish pride that it was hers. She seemed to understand perfectly, smiling at his astonishment.

'It is beautiful isn't it? I shall wear it tonight even if I never wear . . . Papa must be proud of me. Papa as well as . . .' She passed a hand across her eyes. 'I need water.' She followed his surprised glance at the pitcher. 'It's empty and my head's burning, my throat too. I want to dampen this.' She held out a cloth.

He ran down with the pitcher then stumbled up again with it, brimming. He poured water in the basin, careful not to slop it and watched her wet the cloth and hold it to her forehead, wipe back her dry hair, then press the cloth to the back of her head. He wanted very badly that she should wipe the blood away but she seemed half asleep or far off somewhere where he could not travel, and dared not. She was breathing quickly, very flushed. He didn't know what to do. So he stood there, his small young-old face puckered, trying not to cry. But finally his anxiety spilled over.

'Shall I fetch the doctor?'

She shook her head. He remembered she did not like Dr Barclay.

'Mr O'Shea then?'

'No.' Her eyes held his. She was very much aware of what he had said. 'He must never come here. You know that.'

'Then . . .' He bit his lip. 'I know you like fish fresh out o' the Bay. I could get some for your dinner.'

She said nothing but he was sure she must be hungry. Nothing to eat all day. It was terrible. He became obsessed with the idea of coaxing her to eat; it was something he could do. She was walking up and down again, pausing only to dampen the cloth and hold it to her head. He could not just stand there watching her do that. It bothered him to watch her walking up and down, up and down. He turned and ran, a long-legged streak, down and out into the wild afternoon.

Barbara felt her way downstairs, one hand sliding cautiously down the bannister, the other holding a cloak about her carelessly donned riding habit. She tried to fasten the cloak at her throat with one hand but fumbled and her fingers slid indolently away. She moved with a peculiar heavy intensity.

The house was silent, except . . . was that the cry of a baby? The cry seemed to have been there, around her, for a long time. Nurses were careless and she was weary of reprimanding them. Nurses? But this was Regent Lodge, the *Lodge*. She shook her head. How stupidly she was behaving. She stood still for a moment. Then she moved down again, slowly.

It had been so warm, stifling really, up there in her room that when the rising wind creaked through the trees and shivered the curtains and she felt the coolness on her face and neck, she craved more of it, more chill agitated air to caress her burning body, to soothe her. She must have it. And this ache deep, deep in her head where she could not touch it – a relentless stinging wind would surely get rid of *that*. Useless to lie up there thinking, losing reality in imagination. The long inward but feverish conversations she held with her father, with Brick, with her mother, made the ache worse, she'd noticed that. The pain went right through to the back of her head. It was there in the hollow; the soft, soft little hollow which she was afraid to press yet did so, bearing with all her summoned strength the almost exquisite agony her own muscle and bone provoked. Did one grow to be lonely without pain, a familiar pain that enveloped even while it was dreaded? She was – yes – actually concentrating on pain. Stupid of her. She must not do it. Pain must be left behind . . . cast off . . . given up. Thrown to the winds – that was it. The winds would scatter the pain finally and irrevocably as they scattered everything else.

Kumara's nostrils twitched and he whinnied restlessly. She patted his black neck. It took her a long time to saddle him. Joey did it all so quickly. She realised how much she had depended on Joey of late. But now there was no Joey. She had called for Joey – hadn't she? Perhaps she had not called loudly enough. She half turned to summon him but, in-decisive, then reluctant, turned back to her task. She tossed back her cloak and it slipped from her shoulders and she was cold so she put it on again and managed to tie the strings, feeling tired out even by the simple movements of her fingers. Somehow she completed the saddling and, in spite of her increasing weariness, savoured the stallion's impatience, his throbbing urge to be off. His longing matched her own. This was unity of a kind. A good kind. But . . . there was something wrong with Kumara; *had* been wrong . . . what was it? The foreleg? She wished she could remember. But it seemed so long ago and far away the thing that had happened to Kumara. Her arms were like lead. Her cloak brushed across the horse and she put up her hood – she had forgotten her hat but it didn't matter for she would not have been able to bear it on her hair. The excited stallion reared and she steadied him, her hands stinging – she had forgotten her gloves too. Too late now.

She turned him on to the drive and then, with a flurry, on to the road. Here the wind surged and the cloak swung mischievously about her body. She tried to tuck it in neatly but it would not stay and so, weary of it, she left it alone, tried to ignore it. She did not want to think about it. She did not want to think about anything. Considering anything closely tired her. Everything tired her. She swayed as a person half asleep, bemused by the fine cutting breeze on her face. She wrapped the reins tightly around her hands. There, now they were as one, Kumara and his mistress. As of old. She could forget about her mount now and think of herself if she so wished. Think of the pain – she couldn't seem to stop thinking of *that*. But concentrate on spiriting it away. The coolness would do it, the coolness and the softness. Nothing in the world but this softness . . . coolness . . . A wonderful cool embracing world . . .

The Barracks were away to her left, lines of stone cut by neat window eyes. From now on little that was human. A phantasm of road and then – as they rode farther out and she gave the horse his head – tracks. And everywhere the little hills; hills cut by these meandering tracks that some day would become roads leading to somewhere. Somewhere important. But now they were only deserted tracks wandering the hilly wastelands. Lost tracks. She felt suddenly elated. No one in all this waste with cold accusing eyes and *this* is right . . . you *must* do that . . . you *should* do this . . . you *shall not* do that. She steadied Kumara to a canter. She would gallop again when the ground was smooth enough. Gallop and gallop and gallop; there was nothing so wonderful in all the world as galloping these hills on Kumara. Ah, she had forgotten how wonderful Kumara was! Slabs of grey, some crooked in the dirty sand, embraced uncertainly or pushed aside by green shrubs, reared here, now there. Gravestones. How people shivered and stared when they heard that Barbara Merrill rode at such strange lonely times to stranger lonelier places on hills that belonged to cemeteries and wasters – the dead and the living dead. Why did they shudder? She was no longer afraid of misfits. Or burial grounds. How could one be afraid of the helpless? Oh, they could never understand, these safe, careful, contented people, what she had come to understand; that graves were an end, a rest. Perhaps a beginning too.

It was blustery here in the open, a hard harsh buffer against her easy progress. But there was a challenge in bracing herself and her steed in united force against the elements, for she had no craving here and now for warm sweet zephyrs. She summoned more of her strength, and still more, till she was conscious only of her will. The will was all; Brick had said so. Kumara shied and reared slightly. She steadied him. But he eased of his own accord and walked a while then paused, quivering, nuzzling the bushes.

She was on the brink of a gentle slope leading down to the farflung open ground spread about the Bay, gloomy under the wash of sun struggling with the shifting clouds. Tiny scampering waves ruffled the expanse of water before her, shimmered, chased each other and spread out again, wild and directionless. She shivered. It was very cold. An immense and terrible sadness enveloped her. She slid from the stallion, her feet stumbling. She steadied herself with difficulty. She was within a clump of bushes, out of the worst of the wind, a quiet abrupt retreat, a cave of greenery. The encircling bushes were a shield and quite suddenly she could not bear to leave them. Not yet. She needed them. They were like friends; friends who asked no questions, friends who did not demand confidences, friends who held out an uncritical wordless protection. Friends who offered her sanctuary, most blessed.

She crouched in their shelter, turned from the world and buried her face in her arms under the folds of her cloak. The wind was still fierce, but now far away, exactly when as a child she had banished the frightening turbulence of her life by cuddling her head under her quilt. Quiet now . . . be still . . . and all else will be still. Don't think. Peace. An endless void. A bottomless limitless marvellous void. Nothing . . .

The Victoria Theatre was a triumph of walled-in stage and boarded-over pit, a giant frame and support for the closely packed tables wellnigh swamped beneath their lavish bowls of flowers and fruits. Flags and banners drooped and curved, the theatre pillars writhed in evergreens and native flowers, while the brilliancy of lighting shimmered over the peacock men, and set their women a-glitter as they followed each other upstairs to endure as cheerfully as they might the long hours watching the male élite of the colony gorge itself on the finest of food and wine if not conversation. Tiresome or not it was unthinkable that they should not be present as pampered background to this daguerreotype of the colony's industry, wealth and position. Colonial Society was growing up even if, with one thing and another, it appeared to be growing lamentably hump-backed. There was not a woman worth her salt who would not put in an appearance some time during the evening, or a man who had not given days of thought to his haircut, his evening clothes, and his address, if such was required of him.

The ladies amused themselves by criticism of toilettes and the excited quizzing of new arrivals. The Chairman there – the Governor would be at his right and the Chief Justice on his left, would they not? They pointed out the Judges, the Speaker, and the Ministers to a man wearing a smooth mask of urbanity. Bright eyes and faded searched for Brick O'Shea but were not over-surprised when they failed to locate him, for O'Shea would make an entrance, late and probably alone, and their sense of the dramatic thrilled even if their sense of the orthodox rebelled – but without the outrage of former days. Mr O'Shea could almost be regarded as respectable could he not with his fabulous new house everyone was longing to inspect, a seat in Parliament, and all that *money*. Why, even the most uncompromising of mamas . . .

Gossip simmered. The soft laughter swelled and died then swelled once more. The warmth of the place soothed and beguiled since the weather had turned cold again, the wind blowing straight off the snowfields irritating, flicking nerve ends like pumice on a sensitive skin. The procession of guests – the intelligentsia, the social and political cream of the colony – found their places or clustered in affable pose, to see and be seen; that way they kept the illusion of London or, more likely these days, the stucco pillared pomposity of Manchester or Birmingham. But they glanced surreptitiously at their watches and fussed a little and flicked their cravats, remarking that the theatre was really *too* warm – after all, one expected to be cold in September. Or moved from group to group, openly hearty and expansive but secretly uneasy, gnawed by the canker of insult, not only to themselves but to their Governor, the representative of Her Gracious Majesty. O'Shea was very late. Indeed, too late.

A sudden stir to fan the theatre. Women fluttered and shimmered as so many blooms before a spring breeze. Murmurs gained strength and floated down from the crowded boxes. Below, the clink of glasses, the shuffling of anxious nervous feet, the scrape of chairs. A moment of silence, then the talk and laughter resumed with an air of determined gaiety.

Brick O'Shea had arrived at last.

As Barbara lifted her head she shivered with one of those unearthly spasms of the nerves that cannot be self-controlled or terminated at will. She sat up slowly and stared about her, bewildered. It was dusk, a windy dusk, not cold but with a grey slaty film pressing down from the sunken sky upon the world. She could not tell how long she had lain under the sheltering bushes for she had fallen asleep, or rather somewhere between waking and sleeping, vague but disturbing visions still there at the back of her mind. She was not refreshed. A terrible disappointment, a desolation, pricked at her eyelids. Her head . . . that demon thing that was the ache in her head was still there, possessing her. She could stand it no longer. She could not bear it . . . Her heavy head dropped into her hands and she swayed in her agonising despair. But where was help? One was taught to go to God in supplication . . . 'come unto me all ye that labour and are heavy laden . . .' Matthew. She liked reading Matthew. She liked these words . . . 'and I will give you rest . . .' Oh God . . . dear God . . . I need rest. I need it so terribly. She tried hard to be still, crouching there in the sand, but her head went on aching. She raised her head at last and looked about her with dull eyes. Nothing had changed, nothing. But one thing did soothe her a little; Kumara's dear familiar presence. And the bushes; there was something familiar about these shrubs around her . . . She must have been here many times with . . . Brick. Kumara had known. She stirred. Brick . . . they'd been happy here together, before . . . she began to remember things, too many things. Jamie. Jamie and Raunie and Brick. Brick . . .

She struggled to rise. The Banquet . . . it was . . . it must be very late, and her father . . . Something was to happen at this Banquet, something to do with a scrap of pasteboard scrawled with words. Smudged words. But smudged or not the words proved something. They were damning words. Raunie . . . there was something more about Raunie struggling in her head. Raunie and Brick . . . they belonged. It hurt her. It was an actual pain in her breast. But that same pain could mean, of course, that there was something wrong with her heart. Raunie — yes, Raunie was beautiful and desirable while she, Barbara Merrill, was but useful like a kitchen chair. And she belonged . . . where? Exactly where did she belong? There was something terrible and very sad in this – this not belonging . . .

400

A sickness – a nausea – came from somewhere deep inside her. But she scrambled up, swaying a little with vertigo. Kumara . . . she must take hold of Kumara. She staggered and slipped. The horse pawed the shifting sand. With a great effort she reached him, held him, and paused to get her breath. A lone figure moved across the path and for an instant a face turned towards her. Dark eyes met hers then slid away. Her head cleared slightly. A native woman, horribly scarred about the face. A native. As Brick was a native; a Black, one of these subhuman rejected creatures who disgusted her as they disgusted everyone. Her heart pounded. There must be some dreadful mistake. Brick could not be as this. There was nothing in him to show . . . was there? One of the saturnine O'Sheas . . . she had heard the phrase many times. A sun-burned, silky-haired Irish-Australian. What else? She'd never looked for anything else. But her father had. And found it. It was true then . . .

Her head – ah, her head. She rested her forehead against the saddle striving for clarity of thought. So Brick was damned. Yes. Her father would destroy Brick O'Shea as Brick O'Shea had destroyed him. In destroying each other they destroyed themselves. Her father and Brick O'Shea. She felt she was choking. In her despair, without realising she was doing so, she slashed Kumara with the reins. Startled, the stallion reared and, shocked at herself, she hastened to soothe him. She took a long time to mount. Everything, even the slightest movement was difficult. Her eyes watered. But somewhere in her mind was the compulsion, that motivation. Her father had ordered her to dress for the Banquet. Then she must dress. That beautiful wonderful gown . . . She must dress with the greatest care, for they must be proud of her . . . the two men she loved beyond all beings in the world.

Her heart pounded. She tried to wrap the cloak about her. She was perspiring so greatly her clothes felt damp and clinging. And there was a pulse in her ear; a thud-thud, a strong jagged sensation that bothered her deeply. There must be something wrong with her heart. Yes. She knew it. Her mother would insist that such inward suffering was punishment for sins . . . She turned the horse but didn't know which way to head him for she could see little in front of her and the wind whipped the cloak across her throat and face. The cloak was impeding her. She wanted to be rid of it yet clung to it. The path . . . where was the path? She couldn't seem to find it. And where was she going? Where? The sand whipped about her, stinging her as they moved off jerkily, indecisively. Kumara, still startled, disobedient, tugged against her hands and she couldn't fight him. The reins loosened around her cold fingers and the horse took his head. He broke into a furious gallop. Then she forgot the horse as she forgot all else but the pain. Pain engulfed her. She was sobbing quietly but persistently. She must find help; a doctor, a clergyman. The Reverend Westman. Yes, oh yes, she did like the Reverend Westman. But where was he at this terrible moment? Could she find him? She didn't know, she simply didn't know where to start . . .

This terrible, this evil pain. Bentham was right. Pain is evil and so must be cast out. But was that what Bentham really meant? Her mind slid from the query . . . She could not wonder longer what people meant. It did not matter. She knew only one thing, she must toss pain to the wind. She must separate herself from pain, leave it behind, run from it, no matter how far or how fast she had to run. Somehow, she must have done with it. She must leave it here, out on these sand-hills, and find peace . . .

Jenny seated herself with a plop – heavens, with each pregnancy she grew heavier and now only three months gone; not that she minded her third in so many years for it did prove *she* knew her duty even if there were others who didn't. Not that she supposed Anne, with that big empty English nursery, could exactly help it. Still . . .

She settled herself with a small grunt of satisfaction and concentrated on what was taking place below. But nothing of any importance seemed to be happening. A small lake of bald heads. She yawned prettily behind her fan and composed herself again. Through all the fluctuations of Jenny's bodily contours her face remained unchanged; childish, unlined by any emotional storm either of ecstasy or sorrow. Her eyes slid from Mr O'Shea – one could never mistake that thick hair – to her husband's active and rhythmic jaws. She hoped he wouldn't be bilious in the morning. Being bilious herself was quite enough. Maxim, as always, looked distinguished and most commendably proper though she wished he wouldn't go about mystifying all these nice people with his talk of *enceinte* mouthed with such stolid Saxon enthusiasm. Or laugh so heartily at his own mystifying jokes. Or bring home such mystifying friends. Well – she moved her buttocks in their protective layers to even more comfortable grooves – what cannot be cured must be endured. True, but she could never see the sense of enduring one little thing that might possibly be altered in the smallest degree.

No sign of Mrs Clinton. No sign of Barbara. For all the time it was taking Barbara to arrive she'd still look no better than an old peg-bag. A delicious little shiver ran up Jenny's spine. Queer really that anyone as dull-looking as Barbara Merrill could be bad. For she was bad. Mama said so. So it was little wonder that Mr Selwyn had jilted her. And even though she'd known Barbara for such a long time she, Jenny Werner, was in the respectable and agreeable position of being able to cut her dead when and if she wished to do so. But Barbara was very strange; she didn't seem to notice. She seemed oblivious of so many things. And people. Well, at least Gina wouldn't be sweeping in preening and prancing; somehow it was comforting to remember Georgina out in the middle of wind-swept nothingness with rough hands and undressed curls.

There! Mrs Havelock had just crept – no other word could possibly describe her almost apologetic entrance – into her box in that dreadful old puce clashing with the lime green of that odd companion-secretary she'd employed in the last few weeks. All that money too. Though there were those strange stories about Georgina's Uncle Roger. No one knew what to think. She must try pumping Max, though for all his wise

403

glances she doubted he knew much about it either. Not that Mrs Havelock had ever been anything but a frump; she'd had that velvet for years and was so funnily content with slipping from one dim parlour to the next, sipping her pale half-cold cups of tea . . . Bored, Jenny spread her plump fingers to show her rings – Maxim liked her to display her gems just as he liked her to show her children born or unborn – wriggled her shoulders to set her new brooch gleaming under the lights, and stared about her. The Clintons were late indeed . . . The Merrill box still empty . . . Then Jenny coloured to the roots of her bright yellow hair.

Raunie was smiling at her. Quite deliberately smiling at her. Jenny's fan fluttered as she tried to fix her attention elsewhere, on anything at all but that outrageous woman looking more outrageous than she remembered having seen her before. She wore red. Shameless. What a *creature*! And even if men did call her 'a luscious cocotte' she was far too thin. In any case, why shouldn't she look luscious? Women like Raunie thought of little else but decorating their bodies. Adornment and frippery. Behind the camouflage of her fan Jenny patted her scarlet cheeks. She was upset and she *never* allowed herself to be upset. She would not look at Raunie. She simply would *not*. She tilted her smooth plump chin and turned her back as deliberately as she comfortably could, devoting herself to the task of conveying to Mrs Simon Blodge that it was an honour, Blodges being chapel, to be permitted to sell their public-house to the Werners who were most decidedly church.

Raunie laughed to herself. Silly provincial Jenny. Weary of teasing the girl she bowed to Ralph Huntingdon, taking a delight in watching him colour. Her mood of reckless gaiety, flushed by so many eyes on her – hostile eyes, jealous eyes, but admiring eyes too – as she had swept to her seat sprang from the singing excitement that had driven her the past few days to exclude all but the perfection of her gown and coiffure, her choice of perfumes and flowers. For this was her night of triumph. She was here in her own right, a woman of consequence . . .

Colonel Clinton was quizzing her through his eyeglass. She smiled at him over her fan, flirting a little. She caught the Governor's glance – an eye for a pretty woman there – and bowed with all her graces. He remembered her. Why would he not? Didn't she put all these wishy-washy English posies to shame? With a fine condescension she turned to the woman on her left, an eager common little creature whose husband was the one decent tailor in the place and who had political aspirations and was willing to pay in deference or in gold – or both – for their fulfilment. If they could not reach Major Merrill they could reach his mistress they reasoned – ah, she knew. She had come to expect this kind of homage and not only deal with it but make use of it. To revel in it, a power sweet to her taste.

And she would keep that power. Alister was hers as long as she wanted him. She could win him back any time she wished; the bond between them was too strong to be easily broken. She brooded on Alister. But he was looking up to the Merrill box. Now the Clinton box. Impatient, her mind merely skimming the fact of Barbara's absence, her eyes moved to Brick and lingered. Her triumph was not yet complete. He had not met her eyes. Look at me, she willed, watching him. But he did not look her way. He too was watching the Merrill box.

Kumara was possessed. The ground rang, the sand flew. Barbara's hair whipped about her face and her eyes blurred before the sharp wind. But she saw and felt nothing but her hands tight on the reins and the pulsing flanks beneath her. Now the strain on her hands was too great; she could not hold to these beloved sensations, they were growing remote . . . It was almost dark and she must hurry; hurry from this pain and towards Brick . . . towards her father. But she could not find them until she was free of pain. A half-sob tore itself from her hot dry lips and she swayed. Her throat ached . . . Her throat burned . . . She was thirsty and the thirst grew until it was an agony. She needed water. The need of water became an obsession. Sound intensified and beat at her ears, hurting them. They tremulated with the thud-thud of Kumara's flying hoofs. Now the trees were thicker – even the bushes seemed to be closing in. She whipped Kumara and his whinnying that became a harsh screaming filled her head as he lurched with a terrible violence. A flash of heavy heaving trunk, branches rushing at her face. Ti-tree and scrub and flying sand. A horse convulsed . . . plunging.

No pain . . . Nothing . . .

Joey fell from the mare and staggered to the dark twisted shape. The man with him, the Clinton coachman, knelt too, then thrust out an arm to push the boy away. But Joey had seen her eyes and nose filled with sand and the trickle of blood from her mouth. The man groped for her pulse.

'A doctor . . .' He looked vaguely about him. Joey, sobbing, stumbled through the sand seeking his mount. People were beginning to appear, ghostly as wraiths conjured from the elements; cottage women with shawls over their heads, boys, an old man with a lantern. They clustered, peering in the wavering light. An old crone pressed her hands over her heart.

' 'Tis her, 'tis her. An' I seen it beside her the last time she rode this way, an' heard it wailin' too, a goldy-haired banshee 'twas . . .'

'Be ye a surgeon?' The old man with the lantern was suspicious of the crouching man pressing on the limp wrist.

'No, but I can tell death when I see it.'

'Death?' Joey trembled. 'Death . . .'

The old one turned to the poised assembly. 'She's dead. May the gates of Paradise be open to receive her. May the gates of Paradise . . .'

The lantern went dancing over the dunes. The news passed from one to the other, flung back to those running to see. They took the words and passed them on, bandied them about and dwelt on them. And the Irish among them – and there were many – blessed themselves and sank on their knees and raised quivering arms to heaven for this soul delivered in violent death on a violent night. Such prayers and entreaties, such a howling and calling and lamenting from their devout suspicious hearts merging with the sighing and singing wind and the tormented creaking of trees. Their eyes, staring and fearful, peered through the mist of whisking sand and whirling leaves seeking whatever was out there, and waiting.

To the high sharp chorus of tinkling glasses Brick O'Shea, M.C., rose to his feet. A murmur from the boxes died to expectant silence as all eyes rested on him, taking in the expensive black and frosty white of his dress-clothes, the glitter of a ring, the shine of his hair; large, dark and awesomely assured, he was a man, now more than ever, not to be ignored. A theatre of eyes followed his every movement, or that of the equally impressive man seated opposite twisting the fine stem of his glass in jerky but rhythmic little movements. Major Merrill, it was noted, did not raise his eyes, to O'Shea or to anyone else, absorbed as he appeared to be in the wine shimmering in his goblet. The clapping dwindled away.

'Gentlemen. I have the honour of proposing a toast, one I know will be responded to with the keenest enthusiasm. A toast gentlemen, that is always the most popular at any gathering – the ladies!' In the burst of applause the colonial wives, daughters, and female kin of all ages flushed, rustled a little, then settled once more to wait.

'But tonight there is something more. I would ask you to drink to one lady in particular, a great lady, a lady who has honoured me with the promise of becoming my wife. Gentlemen, I give you my future bride, Miss Barbara Merrill.'

In the abrupt and painful stillness Raunie's fan clattered to her feet, unnoticed as she stared at Brick. Marriage? But it was ridiculous. Fantastic. He was mad . . . insane. The Barbara Merrills of this world did not marry the Brick O'Sheas. They might amuse themselves with them, even love them, but they did not marry the sons of convicts. Even less did they marry natives; not even one drop of savage blood. Did he actually believe he could keep his secret from her? Or . . . her heart began to pound . . . could it be that he did not know? Her feverish eyes sought Alister. What was he doing – going to do? She made a movement to rise but stilled, catching her breath, as Alister Merrill rose to his feet, picked up his glass and flung the wine in Brick O'Shea's face.

A woman screamed thinly, someone began to chatter without meaning. The diners sat as if stunned. Then a wave of hysteria swept the women as O'Shea reached across, scattering the table fittings and, grasping his antagonist's collar, shook him as a dog might shake a rat. The Governor's big body came alive. As his hands fell on the two O'Shea was the first to let go. It had all happened so swiftly the upstairs audience were looking at each other, whispering about the uneasy tableau below. No one seemed to know clearly what was happening, but one could not help but grasp the general effect. Trouble.

Governor Fitzroy spoke softly but definitely. 'Such behaviour, gentlemen, demands instant apology.'

'No insult was intended towards yourself, Your Excellency,' Alister said quickly, his eyes on O'Shea. 'At least, not on my part. I simply find myself in a situation that is intolerable.' He felt in his pocket. 'No gentleman here, most particularly myself as the father of the lady concerned, could be expected to permit his daughter to be coupled even verbally with an aborigine.'

A long stillness. The Governor, very stiff and rather pale, managed to speak. 'I hope, sir, you realise the seriousness of such an extraordinary accusation?'

'I would not have made such a statement, Your Excellency, without foundation. You will understand if you will be so good as to read this.' He placed something in the Governor's hand. 'Mr O'Shea,' he went on, 'should be only too ready to deny it – if he can.'

The Governor bent his head. The theatre waited. Fitzroy looked up sharply and with raised eyebrows handed O'Shea what appeared to be a small slip of pasteboard. It was a long time before Brick O'Shea raised his eyes from it. The men stared at each other.

> 'But what avails it now to whine
> And crying eyes to jelly,
> The clock has struck, it's time to dine,
> Love will not fill the belly.'

Choking over the words in a gastronomic ecstasy the hot apple of the tart dripped down Jeremy's chin. Startled by his robust singing the kitchen girl threw a porter pot. It landed on his bunion.

'Chhrist!' He wailed, gulped and chewed hastily to salvage his mouthful. 'That's scared away me appetite.' He rubbed his bunion, smacking his lips. 'If a touch of the quince gives such a fine flavour what would an apple pie taste like made all of quinces?'

The girl kicked at his backside spread comfortably on her top step. He ignored her. Maddened, she slammed the half-door, pinching his flesh. 'If ye've lost your appetite I hope a gintleman finds it for 'twould ruin a poor man in a week, it would.'

He grabbed her apron end dangling over the door and pulled. 'But I niver lose me appetite for kisses. Ould Jeremy can still throw as eager a leg over a goil as he can over a horse, come see if he can't.'

She jabbed at his fingers with another porter pot till he let go to suck his stinging flesh. 'If me eyes light on ye agin tonight,' she hissed, 'I'll break yer impenetrable head and let the brains run out o' your empty skull. Git from me door, ye ould humbug.'

With the pot after him, Jeremy got. He wandered unsteadily along the lane then sprawled in the gutter to get his breath. But he scrambled to his feet as the sweating little mare came to a standstill and the thin dishevelled figure tumbled to the ground. Jeremy's eyes popped.

'Here, where ye be goin'?'

Joey gasped for breath. 'To find Mr O'Shea.'

'Are ye mad?' Jeremy stumbled across the road to grasp the boy's collar. 'None but toffs in there with the Guvner.'

'I must tell him now.' Joey's eyes streamed. 'About her. About Miss Merrill.'

'Miss Merrill?' Jeremy was sobering up by the minute. 'What ye blatherin' about Miss Merrill for?'

'She's dead.'

Jeremy's hands loosened with shock. 'By the – Holy – Cross . . .' He turned and ran towards the lights after the frantic speeding boy.

The already astounded diners swung as one towards the stage door, ears pricked to the brogue shrill above the commotion. It was again the Governor who moved. With an angry gesture he motioned the outraged stewards and waiters aside.

'What *is* all this?'

Brick started forward. 'Joey!'

'She's dead.' The distracted young voice rose in terror, a terror less of this alien world into which an entry had been forced than of the force of his inner agony. 'Miss Barbara's dead.'

PART SIX

Chapter Seventeen

BY THAT spring of 1848 Brick O'Shea's newly completed harbourside house was the showplace of Sydney and the pinpoint of the colony's folklore, basking as it did in the reflected glory of its owner and host. O'Shea's success, fantastic but fact, was the supreme example – what the 'cornstalk' offspring of convicts had done others could surely do – and the native-born swaggered so these days that gentlemen did well to avoid the city's backwaters. Wherever men gathered, speculation ran rife concerning O'Shea and his future which, like it or not, appeared to be the future of the colony. But to Moll Noakes, rustling through the luxurious rooms in her stiff new skirts, houskeeping keys importantly at her waist, such homage to her foster-son was simply the realisation of old dreams. Her eyes devoured, her hands sensed, and her mind lingered on the dinners and routs and drawing-rooms planned for this unbuilt house long ago. She nourished herself by her own images so thoroughly there were times when she could not tell clearly where imagination ended and reality began. It had all become one.

It was almost two o'clock of the chill windy morning when she heard hoofbeats. Relief slackened her limbs but she shivered, suddenly aware of the icy room; she had let the fire go out when the girls had gone to bed. She seemed to have been pacing for hours, pausing only occasionally to peer beyond the branches flickering at the windows for she had been more listening for him than watching. Now at last he was coming, and alone by the sound of it. That was good. It was orderly. This unfamiliar regulation of life was becoming a passion with her; a deliberate dedication, with the outer forms of convention and tradition rigorously, almost feverishly, maintained – the silver tray for his letters, the dinner gong sounding precisely on the hour, the maids' caps and aprons stiffened with the precise amount of starch. For the first time in her life she was conscious of the importance of minor things and the abundance of such little things astounded her. Brick laughed at her affectations but it was for his sake she flaunted her newfound respectability even though she suffered much in the doing. Her dress scratched, her stays pricked, and so did her hairpins. She couldn't abide soap. And her country idioms raised eyebrows even in the kitchen – ah, the sharpest stab of all there – the sluts resented her even entering her own domain.

Restless, she swung about – and met her eyes in the large Italian mirror. It was so glitteringly ornate, this mirror, that it seemed to her to fill the room with repetitive reflections. She stood in much awe of the magnificent thing. It was Venetian, Brick had explained, and its pattern of intricate engraving had been done by a diamond. But no matter how wonderful or how valuable it was, she hated it, throwing back as it did her every disturbance, nay, magnifying it – her striding back and forth, the hasty jerk at her keys, the tucking in of hair ends beneath her overstarched cap – expressions of her anxiety in seemingly never-ending succession each time she entered the room or raised her head from the floor. But there was an irritation beyond that – the mirror reflected her incongruity in her surroundings. Gazing on herself she gazed on an outsider, an interloper in this delicate, privileged, almost hot-house world of her contriving.

She turned aside and straightened her respectably garbed shoulders. Late as it was she meant to talk with Brick, goad him to confidences. Paddy . . . it was bad that he still refused to talk of Paddy. And she must know when the marriage was to take place – surely it would be but a matter of weeks despite this trouble over Major Merrill? The Merrill home was to be sold – kitchen women were expert at milking gossip. Well, Major Merrill might be a ruined man but his daughter would remain what she was; this other woman, this young, proud, knowledgeable woman who would complete the human being she, Moll Noakes, had moulded to the best of her peasant ability, the wife who would smooth Brick O'Shea's harsh edges – and there were still many – and bridge the clefts between all their alien worlds.

It was all she had hoped for, this marriage. Towards the girl whom she had met but once she held neither suspicion nor resentment, only deference, trust, and hope. A lady, the ultimate, bringing Brick O'Shea the one thing he could not otherwise gain for himself and his – prestige. It simply did not occur to her that Barbara Merrill might sever old loyalties, such as existed between Brick and herself, only that something in the man, that something that had always held her at bay, would be tempered, perhaps even dissipated. Once married to this woman, she firmly believed, Brick would be content, therefore different, and no longer hold back in the old baffling ways from Moll Noakes, his foster-mother. And her position, if different, would be as unassailable as ever. Certainly the old familiar pattern of life had gone, but with it, happily, facets of that life she had hated and long rejected – Inar. Raunie. There still remained the boy, Raunie's brat – but Brick halted her there, as he had always halted her. There was, there must be, something in Raunie's child Brick wanted and would fight to keep in spite of her, in spite of the child, even in spite of himself. She could only wait until his wife, and time, changed everything.

Confident in her place, Moll patted the luxurious curtains back into their folds – Brick was home and all was as it should be. She walked with a tread that had not weakened over the years into the wide entrance hall to admit him and lock up, any lingering anxiety firmly controlled. She did not even cry out at his arm supported in the rough sling of his cravat. She simply moved to help him. But he halted her.

'No bones broken so leave it. And luckily we found a good boatman.' He indicated the shivering boy at his heels. 'Joey here needs attention.' He placed a reassuring hand on the lad's shoulder. 'You're safe now. Sleep as long as you want.' Supporting himself against the door he refused to move until the lad went off with Kate, whimpering a little, wiping his nose on his torn sleeve.

'You be near dead yourself,' Moll accused him when they were alone. 'Brawling afore the Governor himself now is it?'

He brushed past her into the room and let himself heavily on to a couch, his eyes half-closed in his tired face, his body twisted awkwardly. Uneasy, she stood looking down on him. She had not seen him so for many years, never perhaps quite like this and she did not like it. It did not so much worry her as anger her, as his silence and so his retreat had always angered her. She moved, as was her wont when disturbed or irritated, to action, to take off his boots perhaps, but he motioned her away with his sound hand. She stood a moment, baffled. Then concern over-rode caution and she tried to prop a cushion behind the injured shoulder. But even the slight physical response required of him seemed too much. He was exhausted. 'You be poorly.' Her voice was sharp with concern. 'What's to do?'

'The doors at Regent Lodge are solid.' He gave a wry little smile. 'Plenty of good cedar there. I can vouch for it.'

She stiffened. 'You mean you went . . . there? When you swore – '

'I went to make sure she was dead. Nothing could have stopped me from seeing it for myself. Nothing did.'

Her face went a deathly white and she gripped her hands tightly together, but that was all. She stood waiting for him to go on.

'They'd just brought her in, half the hills gawping through the gates, so there were plenty to batter down the doors they tried to bar against me. I think I half killed the sawbones mopping up the blood – too late for that, the fool. I suppose I went mad for a while and . . . well . . . a madman must be shackled, mustn't he? They tried.' There was an infinite weariness in his voice but the little table beside the couch bounced under his fist. 'The boy swears she was dead when he found her and I must believe that.'

'How . . . how did it happen?' Very quietly and carefully.

'No sense from Merrill. A lunatic too far gone to even do much about my presence. And the servant girl is hysterical. There's only Joey to tell . . . He came up from the Bay this afternoon to find his mistress gone, along with her stallion.'

'Bad time of a bad day for a lady to be riding.'

'No woman in the colony sat a horse easier, even a stallion with a weak foreleg.'

'Then . . .' She was dreadfully afraid of her thoughts, even more terrified of her questions. 'Why?'

He stirred, his inner voice echoing: Why Barbara? Why? His inner eye saw her limp hands, her mud-caked hair, her empty bloody face . . . His inner ear heard Merrill's raging as the man was held in the strong hands of his friends . . . His own voice persisting. 'She knew, didn't she?' And Merrill's final triumphant. 'It saved her from you.'

Forget it. Forget it all or go mad. But he knew that he would never quite forget it. Always, down the years, as part of him it would stay, as Barbara would stay. It took what remained of his strength to control his voice.

'She was in her room all day refusing to eat. She wouldn't let Joey fetch me. He thinks there had been a quarrel. With her father.'

Barbara couldn't have known of his close association with Goltby. No one knew of it. They might ponder, they might surmise, but they could not know. He had taken good care of that. Wasn't he an old hand at the game of bribery, threats, persuasion, without having to step outside the law far enough to be nabbed? And hadn't he been expert enough to contrive within those same laws circumstances in which a man might destroy himself? From the beginning, of course, Goltby had had his price. But from the beginning he, O'Shea, had met it, knowing the man's worth to him – if only in silence. And the Jew had proved invaluable. He'd expected to wait a long time for Merrill but Goltby had seen and seized the opportunity. The day the Jew's letter arrived stating he'd taken up the mortgage on Regent Lodge he, O'Shea, had got roaring drunk and finished up in a London gin palace with a vile head and his pockets picked. But triumph had made it worth while. And in the triumph somewhere was Paddy, avenged. So the long contriving, the careful secrecy, had paid off. An ageing ailing Havelock fumbling with dwindling capital, toying with bequests and legacies at a stray suggestion or a mood – a Havelock lazily compliant. While for Alister Merrill – Raunie. Corruption of flesh by flesh; no odorous loathsome erosion, only a corroding sweetness to temper her demands. Yet . . . even if by some chance Barbara had guessed his part in her father's affairs it would not have mattered. Not to Barbara. He was very sure of that. Barbara was – had been – incapable of withstanding him, Brick O'Shea. Barbara had always been his. Until . . . He took a small piece of pasteboard from his pocket and placed it on the table.

'I think . . . this is why. One reason why.'

Moll stared at it obediently. He seemed to be attaching great importance to the thing, fingering it, smoothing it. What was it? There were marks on the faded blue. Handwriting? She frowned.

'Fancy, isn't it? Or it was once. A long time ago.' He tapped it sharply with his forefinger. 'Recognise it?'

'No.' Then some faint inner tremor of . . . warning? . . . made her stiffen. 'I don't –'

'You should remember it. There is a message written here. A message for you.'

'For me?'

'For you, yes. A message from my mother.'

'Maddy?' Her jaw slackened. Then she drew back indignantly. 'You *are* lushy. Or crazy.'

'Neither,' he said sharply. 'Just determined to get to the bottom of the whole confounded riddle. Read the thing and refresh your memory.'

'I be never the one for reading –'

His mocking laugh cut off her protest. 'I've known you to figure out words when you wanted to. And figure them very well. Listen then.' He snatched up the scrap of board. "Moll . . . never let Brick know he is Black . . ." His eyes rose to hers. He watched her thin mouth, her whole body tremble.

' 'Tis a lie,' she breathed. 'A *lie*.'

'If these words are a lie then my mother lied for neither you nor I can deny her handwriting, faded though it is.' He gave

418

a tired gesture. 'For that reason alone I suspect the colony, from Fitzroy down, isn't in the least concerned that I made off with his proof.' He reached for a book from the bookcase at his left, opened it at the flyleaf and held the pasteboard against it. 'Look.' As she stood staring from him to the book his voice grew hoarse with rage. 'Come here and look or by God . . .' Slowly she came to stand beside him. 'The same backhand – see?' His finger moved slowly and carefully. 'The same M and the R . . . No one else ever made their letters so. They could not.'

They were silent, staring at the matching letters, dim with time but still decisive, definite. He snapped the book shut and flung it aside. 'So let's have an end to lying once and for all.'

'I never lied to you. Never.'

He ran a distracted hand through his hair. 'No . . . in a way that's true. But you didn't lie to me because you had no need to lie. I never probed, perhaps because I sensed . . . something . . . I don't know. But you plotted. From the beginning you and my mother must have plotted to hide the truth from me and from everyone else, to let me live out my life, marry, breed . . . You wanted that of me, didn't you, both of you? – you wanting it perhaps even more than she.'

' 'Twas no lie. 'Twas but pushing aside a thing we learned was bad for you. Maddy ached to give you the chance your forebears never had. Why do you think she planned to wed Bellamy, hating him as she did?'

'That swine?'

'But she would have wed him because she loved the Pride, as you loved it. 'Twas your home. 'Twas your chance. Don't you *see*? All she did was for you.'

He winced with a twinge of pain. She paced restlessly, yearning and wondering over these damning words come back from the grave to destroy. From Maddy's grave. But how? Primitive and still superstitious as she was, Moll Noakes had learned enough not to embrace ghosts. Maddy's words could only have returned by the agency of hands that were alive and malevolent. Damning hands.

'And how . . .' Hesitant in her bewilderment she pointed to the damning piece of pasteboard, 'did you come by . . . that?'

'My arch-enemy Merrill set it before the Governor's eyes tonight. Proudly. Fitzroy in turn set it before mine, not so proudly. There's no mistaking its meaning, to myself or to anyone else. *Black* . . . A native. An Indian. And God knows how long Merrill has been nursing the thing, saving it for the precise moment. Well, he had his moment.'

'But how could Major Merrill come by words wrote to me, a convict woman, by your mother who died thirty, nay more, years ago, words I never knowed were wrote?'

'That is for you to explain.'

'How can I explain it when I don't know't? I swear by your mother's name I don't know. I never set my eyes on these words afore. If I had I would have destroyed 'em – don't you see that? Never would I have let your eyes, other eyes, see what the poor soul begs me I must not let 'em see.'

In spite of his deep and smouldering anger, his bafflement, he could not but believe her. Moll Noakes saw it in his eyes and felt it in his silence, but knew he would still have her speak. His remoteness told her, his harshness told her, his unyielding body was command enough. So at last it had come, the moment she had dreaded all her life. Gone were the years of cutting off awkward questions before they had clearly begun, of avoiding the curious glance and the murmur of doubt, of the deliberate diversion of talk when it became dangerous in those warm hours of reminiscence at the fireside. So had been her life. Deceit. But the deceit of necessity. And now, because of a few words on a scrap of pasteboard, all had been made useless.

'Then my mother would only have set down such words if she were desperate, or ill – or afraid,' he persisted.

'Maddy were never afeared.'

'She died without you at her side; you told me that much of her death.' She paused in her pacing, but a wave of his arm blocked any interruption. 'You couldn't know how she died, not entirely. She might have been delirious . . . raving . . . there at the end. She must have been. She knew only that she

420

was dying and – well – fear for me drove her as a need, a final desperate need, to talk to you. So she spoke to you in the only way she could.' He shifted in his corner, straightening his body. 'But never mind the end now.' His voice altered, grew brisk. 'Go back to the beginning.'

'Thirty years?'

'Longer if you must.'

' 'Tis long ago. An' such a web.'

'Unravel it.'

'One . . . forgets.'

'You forget nothing; nothing that is of any value to you.' Then his patience snapped. 'I'll have no more pap to soothe me, cheat me, is that understood? Can't you see that there's no longer need for secrecy? For God's sake, woman, it's written down for all to read. Half the world knows it by now. Anyway, all Sydney. It's finished, all finished, can't you see that?'

No need for her to hide it longer . . . It was true. And her despair found its outlet in a bitter rage against him, against the world, even against the dead Maddy. For Maddy had betrayed her work of a lifetime in one impulsive frantic sentence. Sick at heart she sat heavily on a Chippendale chair, one of the set she had arranged so carefully and dusted with such reverence; a suddenly old woman whose forlorn, slumped body pleaded with her adored for compassion and understanding if not forgiveness in what he would have her say. She leaned back and with a gesture of resignation folded her hands together.

'I first knowed her, the child Maddy who was to be your mother, when the new century was a few years old – eight I think. I was twenty or so, an' newly transported. Most of us then were sent to the Female Factory at Parramatta to be hired out or wed off but I'd been too much wed already for me own good. No need to dwell on the Factory except that I held me own there, fought for others too if need be. Well . . . I was a good washerwoman so the place I got was not so bad. An' Maddy made it better.

'A perky child with knowing dark eyes an' a quick way

with her. She laughed even when they thrashed her, but then it was not a merry laugh, it was a laugh full o' pride. That was Maddy, you see – pride. I . . . well, I loved her then as I loved her always, perhaps because I had no kin, no child, an' she trusted me. Many's the time I took a thrashing for her, an' gladly. Ah, but I was used to it – you've seen the marks upon me – naught.' She preened, but baulked by his unresponsiveness let fall her squared shoulders, sighed and went on.

' 'Twas a big place we were at, but all was wilderness then an' one place was much as the next – work an' bastin' with perhaps a journey to town if we were lucky. I went to Sydney once an' never forgot it. Well . . . we had many lags there, an' so many Indians they were a part o' the place an' our living. So it seemed naught that one o' them – ' She broke off and stared at her hands as if she were seeing them for the first time.

'Well?' he prompted. 'One of them?'

'Maddy but suffered that mother o' hers,' she said violently. 'A native mother bothered her no more at that time than it bothered us all. At worst she suffered her. There was even a sort o' comfort in it when so many were born so. It was . . . ordinary, y' see.'

'So my grandmother was the full-blood.'

'Dirty culch.' With a savage gesture Moll disposed of her. ' 'Tis your grandfather, Maddy's father, you must remember, the one she spoke of when she was at ease, or lonely, an' even with me she was often lonely. Maddy *was* that father o' hers, that I knowed. She longed to speak of him to you many times but we were afeared that, young though you were, you'd ask too many questions. Well . . . Maddy adored that big black-haired Irish felon for his wisdom an' his learnin' an' followed him where she could for he was given some freedom about the place when the master's liver were easy. An' I knowed he trusted me as he trusted few though he spoke of it but once when he had been basted an' I tended him. "A man can sink so low in suffering that a woman, any woman, can help. But it is to the child the cruel thing has been done. See she gets a chance; herself an' the innocents who come after her. Others

422

will forget with time. Help them to forget, help her to forget, then there will be only yourself to remember what blood is in my child." So I promised, an' I kept the promise so well that in time even Maddy herself forgot.'

'Not completely.'

She shifted about in her unease, spreading her hands and staring at them. Then resolutely she folded them in her lap and began again.

'We had little pleasure then but the tales we heard, an' Mickeen – so they called your grandfather – told stranger tales than any; fine stories of old Erin, of kings who fought great battles, of Cuchullain of Ulster, of the men of Leinster, of journeys to Scotland, all the queer fine tales Maddy told you at her knee an' I've told you since, an' between us never let you forget. For there, y'see, was all Maddy could safely do to learn you of her father an' the country she loved because it was his. Well . . . all this time I'd see Maddy's Black Jen mother watching us an' I'd feel poorly – ah, what use now to wonder over the spite an' jealousy in that savage? She betrayed Mickeen to the redcoats; he had books y' see, an' some o' those books the "lobsters" were seeking. I could never see why they wanted such smeary old things, they seemed just books he brought out from somewhere to learn Maddy to read – with meself pickin' out a word here an' there – but when he would not say if he had books hidden away like it was whispered, they basted him. But he made no sound. An' they forced Maddy to watch him basted an' she made no sound neither . . . But I cussed 'em.' She touched the scar at her lower lip. 'I cussed 'em till they struck me. Then they took Mickeen away as good as dead an' we never saw him agin nor heard o' him . . .'

The ormolu clock chimed into the silence. Brick, eyes closed, appeared to be asleep but he lifted a hand in a sign for her to continue.

'One master gave place to another, then managers come an' overseers for the heirs that were in England, then the place was sold an' who was born o' who was lost in time an' none to care. Only Maddy an' meself were left with the books a new man dug up wrapped in linen near the convict shed – how your grandfather hid 'em I can't tell though even lags minded their business when it suited 'em. So – as he'd died for those books we cherished 'em. An' neither of us knowed nor cared what had happened to the woman who had given Maddy birth. We forgot her very name . . .

'When Maddy met your father she still had the soft child's flesh on her – she was barely fifteen years old. She loved him perhaps for the things in him that were her own father – or the things she believed were there. Or she loved him for Ireland's sake. Who knows? But for your sake she wished to wed him so I found a churchman – an' the devil of a time I had doing it – but 'twas all done right an' proper in the end, to that I can swear. But your father was off agin as he was off for the rest of his life. No need to tell agin of *his* end for every street urchin does that; ah, a wild and wilful wanderer, Shawn O'Shea, just as the story-tellers say. Then at last I was a free woman an' could go where I chose, an' Maddy heard o' your father's death an' her only tie were broke, so I chose to work for Bellamy if he'd take Maddy as well. She'd taken to watching you close for signs of her blood, but we found none; even so we come to passing you off as mine. A convict mother had some chance where a half-breed had naught. We had learned much y'see. We were learning too to bide our time. So the three of us crossed the country to a new world.

'I kept Bellamy's greedy claws off your mother me own way. That it was a worrisome way at times matters not now – I did it – for Maddy would have the dirty rapscallion only as husband. At first he sneered at the idea but we knowed he came to thinking on it for she was, indeed, a fine-looking woman. With your mother, y'see, a body had to *know* about her. So she went on making her plans, quiet plans they were, for even to me she said little. But I knowed. Ah, I knowed. Yes, the past years were dead, an' could have stayed that way, but for . . .'

'Well?'

'In the early days a cousin to Maddy worked about the kitchen beside her. You were close to four years old when she turned up at the Pride; not so strange a thing when you know how the Indians can track others. Well . . . the woman had brought her pickaninny, a gal a few years older than yourself – '

'Inar?' His eyes flickered open to rest on her. But she avoided his eyes. She nodded briefly.

' 'Twas then I was afeared, why I couldn't really tell for they were but two more Indians about the place – an' there were many. But I knowed your mother was uneasy too, though she said naught an' refused to send 'em away; the woman was close to labour y' see. But I bellared like a ninny for joy when she an' the new babe died. Ah, I did. All would be right agin I thought. But . . . there was the other bratling. Inar.'

'I prayed. Yes, prayed, so y' can see how uneasy I were when I did *that*, an' me never understanding why or to what anyone prayed. I'd beg to have Inar die too or run off but she lived an' stayed, a reminder, a link. Always a link . . . For though none could have knowed a thing of you, that was the one thing we were never quite certain of an' never dared put to a question. The most I could do was frighten Inar. But even when Maddy sent her to the Mission, back she come – she doted on you, y' see. So . . . she stayed to plague us, a sly little trapesy thing, always listening at doors, always teasing, lying, creeping into Maddy's own room to thieve what was bright an' a-shimmering – '

Her voice broke. Her hands gripped the chair arms tightly as she struggled to rise. He pushed himself straighter too, steadying himself with difficulty. He was still in pain, it was clear.

'My mother,' he prompted sharply, urgently. 'Her death . . . finish that. Finish it all.'

She gave a great shuddering breath and sank back with an air of resignation. 'The winter she died were a time o' storms an' floodings.' She spoke rapidly and breathlessly, as if now she could not tell it fast enough. 'Naught in the stores, an' the Pride trembling because Bellamy was without his grog. With a dray an' two men I reached Goulburn but, homing, we were bogged for two days an' nights. When we limped into the Pride at last it was to find Maddy . . . dead. A Jen had found her by the river pinned by a fallen tree, even then a-dying. She could only have been taking vittles to a runaway; they knowed where to come for vittles, y'see, for Maddy had been doing such things for years. So . . . she died without me, alone but for scared lags an' a stupid Bellamy an' you running about with the pickaninnies, all unknowing.'

'The Jens?'

Moll's eyes were haunted. Her hands twisted together in agony. 'Too afeared for sense, them that had not run off . . . an' her poor broken body scarce cold in her bed . . . Only there in her room, in a corner, that bratling Inar a-singing to a scrap o' doll Maddy herself had made her – '

'And the room? Think now. *Think*.'

'Muddled. Ah, such a muddle. An' ink . . . ink spilled about – '

'So Inar stole this bit of pasteboard from her pillow, from her clothes, from wherever my mother tried to hide it for you to find and read – she knew you were the only one who could read at all. And you would have found it only . . . Inar stole it because it was gay. Because it had colour. She couldn't read but she loved to hoard. And she carried it with her until . . . it was lost – or stolen . . .'

Moll was on her feet, her eyes wild. Gripping the little table to steady himself he was on his feet too, facing her. They hung like that a moment then she stumbled forward to sink against his shoulder, half supporting him, half supported.

'Raunie.' She choked, clutching him. 'Raunie . . . If I could get m' mawleys on that slut I'd twist her neck like I'd twist a chicken's – ' She broke off, choking and suddenly helpless.

'Listen to me. Listen.' He straightened, freeing himself firmly from her grasp. 'If you or I were to keep her in torment all the days of our lives what can it alter now?' He pushed her aside but his hands were gentle. Then he did not hate her. Calmer now, her eyes followed him.

The mirror. He was staring into the mirror. The ornate Italian mirror. He moved close to it. And though she

426

hated the mirror her eyes remained on his reflected face, fascinated. For something – a trick of the light, his movements perhaps – accentuated his features, casting dark shadows across them, deepening his eyes in their sockets, causing the hair to curl even more blackly and stiffly about his suddenly wider forehead, even flattening the nose a little. Was it illusion? Or was this, by some odd reflection of the mirror, or what was there burning in their minds . . . truth?

His breath quickened. He knew. Here at last was truth; the truth that would seek him out wherever he went and whatever he did, the truth to confront and hold him. A truth that he could never escape. The truth that, no matter if he should cut his skin and tear out his hair and his eyes from their sockets would remain with him and with others for the rest of his life. And he knew one thing more: this truth had been with him unrecognised as he banished a half-breed aboriginal girl, as he hunted and throttled a full-blood. Inar. Dgeralli. His own long-ago words came back to haunt him. 'A half-breed's a half-breed.'

With a curse that strangled with the violence of it his hands gripped a statuette of the finest Italian marble, small but heavy. The mirror cracked in a miscellany of sound and their reflections danced and blurred. As did all else about them. He snatched up another ornament, then another, his curled strained fingers groping with the feverishness of a madman. And like a madman he hurled his treasures at the mirror until it shattered to the carpet and there were only a few tiny splinters clinging to the opulent frame. But as any madman he could not stop. He grasped the curtains and brought the mass of velvet and all else that was near and breakable and moveable tumbling to the floor. And when it was all done he and Moll stood in the shambles of the beautiful room, in the ruin of his own making, with no sound but his despairing, shattering, exhausted breathing. Finally he placed his clenched fist against the wall. He rested his head against it and his body trembled and his voice broke loose in terrible gasping sobs. It was the end of Brick O'Shea, the hero. It was the end of a world.

427

Chapter Eighteen

ABIGAIL LUFF puffed up the stairs of Winthrop with what was definitely a waddle; Abby was getting fat. But as she entered Raunie's bedroom she shivered. The tiny burned-out fire of the night before taunted the chilly air. Raunie struggled upright from the tumbled pillows rubbing her eyes.

'No wonder they ache, stitching till one in the morning,' Abby scolded.

'I want to see the sun. You know I'm not alive without the sun.'

'None to speak of today.' But Abby obediently drew back the faded curtains. The fitful light of that May morning of the year 1851 played over a changed room. The floor was bare, the one chair sadly frayed, the dressing-table devoid of its fancy fitments.

Raunie shivered. 'I'm hungry.'

Abby threw a wisp of threadbare négligé about her mistress's shoulders. 'There's an egg. And cheese. And tea enough if you drink it weak.'

'We'll not stop eating for days on end when the Archer bill's settled.'

'It was paid long ago and you know it; despite her well-padded hips that Belancon creature will wriggle out of the smallest debt. You're a fool not to marry Dover and live on the colonial best. A well-stocked general store is better than needle-pushing any day.'

'But I hate being married.'

'You've managed to live through two marriages.'

'And I hate the smell of soap and oatmeal, and that snivelling Dover girl and the dragon of a housekeeper and her silly crocheted mats.'

'Easy enough to get rid of the mats. The housekeeper too.

428

And the child could be packed off to school. As for Mr William Dover . . .'

'*Could* I bear with him? Could I, Abby?'

Her eyes filmed. Abby knew that look. She unfolded the morning paper hurriedly.

'Real news today. Gold.' She laughed. 'When you're settled I might take a chance on it myself. Many's the time I've dug potatoes and I can't see much difference between potato scrubbing and gold washing. Both dirty.'

Raunie was scrambling out of bed. 'I've forgotten the hooks at the throat. Bring my tea to the workroom.' But she remembered to take the paper with her.

The old guest-room across the hall was changed too. With the precious mirror placed to catch the sparse light there was a scarred table, a dummy, a chair, and a pile of fashion magazines. Mademoiselle – or Madame Renay as she now was – occasionally sent customers for fittings – the difficult least important customers. Raunie unfolded the heavy garment but, loathing the sight of it, pushed it aside and opened the paper.

'DISCOVERY OF AN EXTENSIVE GOLDFIELD'

Gold . . . The thrill of being caught in the whirlpool of events, making them exciting personal happenings, surged through her, warning her as of old, yet, as of old, stimulating her to a prodigality of imagination. And longing. Gold . . . She remembered Paddy's shimmering guineas dripping through her fingers, the scatter of yellow light from an old red purse – how long ago it all was – and possibilities of which she had not dared think for a long time began to torment her. She stared from the window over the rooftops of the city, this city that was her constraint yet her very life because it held so much of that life. So many crowding memories. So much of hope. Brick . . . Yearning over him, dwelling on the little remembered things of him that she could never forget . . . the smell of his hair, the odour of his man's body, the desire she knew when she was near him to press her face against his neck . . . She twisted the talismans she wore heedlessly now because there were so few to notice, nuzzling the cowrie shell about her lips and throat, holding it between her breasts, caressing the baubles with hungry lonely fingers till the sense of them against her flesh warmed her, soothed her even a little, bringing him for an instant close to her.

Two years. A kind of madness it had been, a pressing from within that had not faltered till it had run its course, worn itself out. It had been inevitable because she was inevitable; she could not, it seemed, even love as others. She belonged to the world of drifters and adventurers, the vagabonds, the driftwood, the lost curling spiral of a campfire, unconfined and untamed . . . the brotherhood whose agitated fingers clutched at nothing as much as they clutched at survival. And Brick O'Shea was all this too. Brick O'Shea was herself; both of us, she thought, clinging to the life of it while the sheltered, the weak, and the vulnerable are conquered by this country and its demanding future, all of them gone or going. The riches of this land belong to me, she thought, with a deep and wonderful conviction. As they belong to Brick. They belong to us together. But Brick had refused to take her along with him; he fought her stubbornly and silently. But even so, all the while, he belonged to her and sooner or later must acknowledge it. Brick O'Shea might bar the fusion of their bodies but she would never accept it as final. She would never let him go.

This fixation, coupled with hope that would never quite be extinguished made her hold on even while the shaky façade of her existence grew dingy, even sleazy. Abby took her ring with the fine blue diamond, her garnets and the pieces of coral and brought home enough to settle her immediate debts. The phaeton brought a fair price, the piano a better, and the lease was extended. The Robsons, ostensibly packing for Europe, were seen about town but never near Macquarie Street. Madame Chercheron pleaded ill-health . . . *ah, désolée, chère Madame Merrill*. Invitations ceased, then calls, and her sole attentions came from sensation-seeking dudes dazzled as much by her reputation as by her looks. She met them with a carelessness that sprang from indifference. Abby, finding Kitty in the family way, beat her till she was blue and marched her off with the protesting Herbert to see them safely married and the reluctant bridegroom installed at a Kent Street hotel as porter, with orders to visit his aunt weekly with a bag of coal or some tea – anything at all that might be of use. But even with his help there were times when they were hungry and Raunie would have put herself under the protection of the most generous of her admirers if Abby hadn't violently protested.

Abby had plans for her. Respectable plans. Abby encouraged Mr William Dover who was in trade and very respectable, fanning Raunie's disinterest to a bleak acceptance of his courtship so that he drove in most afternoons from his store to sip their precious tea and munch Abby's scones with a great licking of fingers and click-clacking of new teeth of which he gave detailed descriptions as to price and contour. But still Raunie parried, selling her ornaments and toilette effects till the house was indecent in its shorn glory and the big wardrobe had to be flung open and her clothes parcelled out to Madame Renay. The woman cheated her but, even so, discovering Abby's small savings almost gone she begged Madame for work and received the dark colours and the rows of hooks and the long, long seams. And so she existed, only occasionally jolted from this strange embracing lethargy by the crowding of other women. There were many women in the colony now. Younger women. She could not help but notice that. One did get old, it seemed. Moments of panic would send her running to a mirror but Abby would be there with her dabs of rouge and her warm drinks and her reassurance. And her William Dover. Yes, though almost twenty-seven, with hair uncombed and face unpainted under the cruel morning light, Raunie knew that she was still beautiful; lovely enough for a man to want. For a man to marry. But not Brick, it seemed. Never Brick O'Shea.

Two years. Slipping by they had scarcely touched her in their stark outer changes. All she knew of the family whose life had been so intimately tangled with her own was what she heard through Abby and Herbert. Regent Lodge was a school run by Roman Catholic Brothers, its grounds

431

encroached upon by ugly monuments to the solidity of colonial trade. And the Merrills were no more than a legend – or a warning – according to those who told their tale. Alister in particular was remote, clinging pathetically to his military status and his uniform, creeping as a shadow of an old man about a few tall-timbered acres at Port Macquarie, dependent upon the still faithful Jeremy . . . So there was Alister. And there he could rot, Raunie insisted. And yet . . . in lonely drifting moments he would come to mind, trailing threads of that sweet savage secret life they had fashioned – if from different reasons – out of their need of each other. She would thrust nostalgia aside. The conflict, the hatred between Alister and Brick O'Shea, the two men who had most urgently shaped her life, had resolved itself, scattering lives. There was no going back. From Ada Jollopy, gossiping over a pot of ale with Bess, Abby brought news of Georgina; always heavy with child, she churned her own butter, addressed her husband as Mr Blair, and ran at the bidding of her imperious young sons and her dominating mama. Maxim Werner was an alderman with a chain of pubs and stores; hadn't Abby been forced only yesterday to scurry from the big-stepping horses of his massive mail-phaeton? And the Clintons and Janet Havelock and all the rest were flashes of silk behind parasols and flourishing carriage whips about the better thoroughfares of the city. As for Brick O'Shea . . .

Still a squatter of apparent wealth, a merchant, a manufacturer, and many other things beside no doubt, to the world Brick O'Shea was the quadroon. The Indian. The nigger. Women who had craved him shuddered delicately, men who had drunk with him wiped their mouths clean and brushed down their garments, while women who had slept with him lost caste with everyone but themselves. On that stunned morning of Barbara Merrill's death a bewildered city roused itself to find O'Shea gone from sight. With the carelessness of the ignorant they passed judgement: the scurrying off of a coward, said some; a retreat no gentleman – or outcast – could have managed with more delicacy, said others. There were angry murmurs and whispers and rumours and shocked faces. O'Shea was seen riding north, someone had seen him riding west – wherever his destination, he was gone from his old haunts. Another week or so and it was as if he had never been – the respectable refused even to mention his name. Only those who couldn't afford to care what blood flowed in their veins openly bothered about him. But many bothered, and covertly all were curious. His movements were traced from time to time and it was said that in his face was fanaticism, in his hands and body fury, for he had either lost the art of concealing these traits or they possessed him to a reckless degree. He never attempted to hide what he was; indeed he let you know it. The 'quadroon', the 'savage', he would laugh, his self-mockery and laceration as ferocious and consistent as that of any flagellant.

But his power over others seemed to have increased instead of diminished. Though walking away from Government his imprint was to be seen, more often felt, as a fresh and vigorous graft on a restricted colonial tree. His farm colonies were dotted from Port Phillip to north of Moreton Bay. A new crèche in new premises, an immigrant ship through the Heads, crates of machinery needed to open factories for woollen goods – all this and more testified to his silent but still potent direction. His recently opened City Store was the heart of the city's commercial life. And he planned, it was said, stores all over the country; a countryside stirring its strengthening limbs, growing in stature, putting out feelers, making plans, digging and hacking tracks then roads beyond horizons never seen before.

But the seething growth around her was meaningless and unimportant to Raunie except where it brought Brick into focus. He could castigate her, beat her, anything, if only he would confront her. The notes she persuaded Abby to write and deliver to his house were ignored; in vain did Abby explain that the place was bolted and deserted, the grounds overgrown. She had even taken the ferry across one day to see for herself, to run off, desolate, to the scuttle of lizards and the mocking laugh of a kookaburra, with not even a Moll in residence to hint of his return. That day was like the house – like her life in many ways – barren and bitter. Her search for Brick, her hunger for even a snippet of news of him, was an obsession. Yet she could never find him. He was never rumoured seen about Sydney; not even at the crèche or at his school. Sometimes she dreamed the old, old dream . . . the mountain of black rock with the honeycomb of dark caves through which she wandered, searching, always searching . . . And the dream brought memories of Jamie. Her thoughts often went beyond Brick to her son. Where was Jamie Lorne? Was he wandering the country with Brick? Where, in God's name, was the centre of her life, her world, Brick O'Shea?

Now, her fingers pulled the chain about her throat till the skin was marked. Bored and miserable she picked up the black dress and smoothed it out. She began to stitch with fingers of long habit. But, suddenly, her hands stilled. Brick had not only been the core of movement, he had directed it. If the world were on the move, would he not move with it? More, would he not direct it?

And the world was indeed on the move. Ships landed a stream of fortune-hunters to peddle firearms to the highest bidder while outgoing barques sailed almost empty. Stages west rolled off, packed solid, even at three pounds or more a seat with the final ride to the fields in open rickety spring-carts. The town of Sofala burst its boundaries. The Flats of the Turon River swarmed with human ants. And by the end of May two thousand men clustered about the raucous rowdy town of Ophir.

Madame Renay was off to become hostess at her husband's store at Mt Alexander – a shilling a glass for rum was easier come by than stitching for the carriage trade. In any case, ladies had scant use these days for fashionable new gowns. Abby scolded the gold-hungry Herbert – they needed the tidbits he brought to the house – but Abby herself grew restless. They were irritable with one another and blamed the baby's wailing for their moods. And Raunie took to wandering down into the town alone to see who was riding off. Or riding in.

For Sydney Town was a Fair, a city gone mad. No one

it seemed went to bed. Carts, drays, wheelbarrows bumped over the pot-holed streets from one dawn to the next. Bigger and yet bigger nuggets blazed in the displays of the jewellery shops. Prices went up, and up again. Gaudily saddled horses galloped abreast down George Street scattering terrified women and children before their flying hoofs. But behind the glittering feverish façade Sydney meant scared invalids battened into their mansions for safety, servants slipping out of back doors to join the spendthrift beckoning diggers, abandoned children wandering empty abandoned houses. And through it all Raunie wandered, scanning the shops and the passing traffic and the rows of faces, seeking . . . always seeking . . .

Mid-June saw an almost deserted Victoria, with loaded vessels due in Port Jackson from Adelaide and Hobart Town by the first winds from the south . . .

With the rich fields of Ballarat discovered, what was left of Melbourne became hysterical with greed, even to small boys armed only with tins and hope tramping the long hard roads to try their luck . . .

Bendigo!

Fitzroy, swamped by mounting demands and one crisis after another, sent his Commissioners to scamper about after unpaid licences and warring diggers. In Victoria, La Trobe followed suit. And the sober citizens who remained in their homes and about their businesses or simply marked time, wrote frantic letters to any paper that would print them. A leader . . . a leader, they were begging in effect. And the cry was taken up, whipped about, inflated till it became a demand. This ignorant, grasping, often violent migration needed direction. And it needed protection. Certainly it needed discipline. And pamphlets began to drift about the dusty streets, into cottage doorways, or to cling on sodden winter nights to damp ankles.

'. . . English Chartists and Irish Repealers, Poles and Spaniards, Italian Nationalists, visionary idealists, exponents of Utopian theories, saints, charlatans, fools, sinners; they drift with the tide of excitement, wasting the enthusiasm and

435

energy that could be our life's blood on the road and along the streams, drinking themselves to satiation for the gain only of grog-sellers . . .'

'. . . the wind of circumstance has blown him to our shores – the freeman, with hands and the voice certain quarters have been clamouring for for years past . . .'

Raunie frowned over the phrase 'certain quarters'. There was something familiar about it. Other phrases haunted her too. '. . . for here is unmoulded flesh, wandering the land, lying ignored and exhausted, leaving what is left of it to nurture our as yet unnurtured earth. Better that such men be kept alive to turn the earth with a spade. Let us be moulding them to the shape we need, our own way . . .'

And she knew, even before Abby discovered his name, who was writing the mocking tirades. Tom Wells. A young adherent of Causes and Creeds, an anarchist most probably, said Abby, fiercely respectable as she screwed a bunch of his pamphlets into the stove as fire fodder. But as each new pamphlet appeared Raunie made the woman read it to her; read over and over the boasts Wells was now throwing back in O'Shea's teeth:

'. . . if these men are worn hopeless their children need not be . . .'

'These are beings with whom one at least of you insists you have understanding and persuasion. But that one, who so ardently and arrogantly assumed the garments of the Almighty, does none of His work . . .'

There was more, always more; hinting, suggesting, damning. And taunting. It was the talk of what was left of Sydney. Over their haphazard dinners at often servantless tables, citizens argued whether a wolf could be so tormented from its lair, for how could such phrases be directed at anyone but the silent O'Shea? It took riff-raff to manage riff-raff, did it not? So Sydney waited. And with impatience, yet some measure of hope, Raunie waited, for if nothing else could lure Brick from behind the siege wall he was erecting about himself might not the mockery of a Tom Wells do it?

Herbert disappeared. Abby finally ran him to earth running

a kind of 'dolly' shop, literally sitting on a pile of stolen goods. He refused to leave his hideaway until he'd made a nest-egg; a pick and a blanket and toiling his way to the fields was not good enough for Herbert Wickler. Abby threatened him home, but Kitty complained of his resolve to go digging, come what may. And Raunie sensed Abby's abstraction, certain that if it weren't for her mistress the woman would also be off, Kitty and the baby and all. And as the days hastened by, her own fever, like the fever of the city, mounted. Each morning she woke restless and dissatisfied. All life was passing her by. The whole world seemed off to the fields. Everyone except herself. And, as Abby persisted in reminding her, Mr William Dover.

Serving him tea one afternoon she turned impatiently to the withdrawing-room window away from his bald head and shrewd eyes that followed her every movement, away from his nasty child jabbing pins into her kitten in a dark corner. But she started as he clattered his cup into his saucer. He knew she was not listening to him. He raised his voice.

'So . . . seeing as 'ow I was dealing with O'Shea I didn't come out too bad. He needs the stuff but even if he wasn't needing it he knows he can't afford to act up these days. Thought he showed proper – er – humility. So I didn't fleece – er – didn't ask what I might've.'

Her hand tightened on the threadbare curtain. At last. Brick was here – or he had been here. She stirred to a wave of excitement. But . . . Brick humble? She watched with scorn the self-satisfied greedy William chomping away to the last crumb. What Brick O'Shea could not accomplish one way he would manage another. And for some reason he was stocking up on provisions.

'Didn't do too bad with the drays neither. Wish I had half a dozen to sell him – needs all the drays he can get too. Well now, I'm in the happy position to be doing a little quiet looking about; must make the most of the times y'see for they won't last forever. Too unnatural. Mark my words, the disappointed ones'll be back and by next summer I reckon I can ask six guineas for a couple o' rooms, no cooking neither, in some neat little boarding place. And then perhaps a villa with a shop attached out Erskineville way, even some of this new plush that's all the rage back 'ome. Nothing but the best for Willy Dover and his wife, eh, m'pretty? Now what do you think of me plans?' And he beamed, showing his new teeth, and selected another scone.

The cat squealed in its corner and the child bawled as it scratched at her. Raunie turned. 'Before you order plush – or anything else – you'd best understand that I have no intention of becoming your wife, now or ever.'

William Dover dropped the scone butter-side down on to what was left of the carpet. 'But my dear young lady –'

'I am not your dear young lady. In any case I am not as young as I pretend to be.' She laughed softly. 'You're the only man to whom I've admitted that and I don't care. Indeed I care for nothing at this moment but that you go away and take your child with you. And the cat. Whatever you do don't forget the cat.'

William Dover struggled to his feet. 'And I thought . . . I thought . . .' Quivering, he knocked the sugar basin off the tray. His starched napkin floated into his teacup. He gave up at last and flicked a shaking finger at his whimpering off-spring. Finally he bundled up the cat, took his child by the ear, and marched to the door.

'Just one thing more . . .' she said clearly.

He turned stiffly.

'Why should Mr O'Shea be needing so many drays and stores?'

His face livid, his nose twitching, he forgot his manners and his language. 'Some demned fool trek to the goldfields by the sound of it. What else does anyone think of these days but gold?' His daughter slyly kicked his shin. He spluttered. 'But I am not interested in the goings-on of that disreputable native –'

'Only interested in doing business with him. A bit of sharp business at that. I understand perfectly. Good day.' And she slammed the door after them. For a long time she paced the dim cool room, pressing her hands ecstatically to her mouth, her hot cheeks, her eyes. Trembling and longing. Loving . . .

At last one morning in October a veritable storm of pamphlets pelted the Sydney streets. Tom Wells's barbs had struck home. O'Shea had taken up the challenge.

'Three weeks from today I, Brick O'Shea, will lead to the Bendigo diggings as many as are sober and in possession of at least a month's ration for themselves and dependents, or coin to purchase same. Lacking money a man – or woman – may labour at work I choose, when I choose. Drones and thugs and drunkards are known to me and will be weeded out. I am setting up canvas towns with shelter and provisions along the route; the same at Bendigo. Transport will be furnished at small extra cost for those who need it. Order and justice are available, my order and justice, in the absence of any other, so I hold the right to refuse escort to anyone I please. A committee is in formation and men are needed now, so those wishing to work off a grubstake in advance apply to my store. Information – and rules – available . . .'

O'Shea's big open-fronted store next to the Post Office had become the focal point of Sydney, the core of the city's energy and activity. The place was dim and musty, redolent with the pungent odours of paint and tar and spices warring with the smells from the gutters and the fly-covered dung of tethered beasts. About the store front the pavements were littered with picks and shovels and cradles, pots and pans balancing in great shining piles. On this sunny spring morning with something undeniably heady in the clear air it was the only place that mattered. Barely more than an inch of George Street was to be seen. So far as the eye could reach all manner of vehicles, even pushcarts and perambulators loaded to the hilt – goods tied to the sides and trailing off to the roadway – vied with each other for the best positions, their owners fighting for their rights with fists and clubs and knives. What police there were had given up long ago – this was O'Shea's picnic, wasn't it? Let him take on the world if he must, but he'd need all his men and his whips and his money before he was out ten miles. Particularly his money. But being O'Shea he'd no doubt manage to show a profit on it all even if it were only in sweat. And in the midst of the dusty activity children squatted to shoot their marbles and spin their tops and scream as they were trampled upon yet still refuse to budge. The women let fly at each other as they ran to rescue their offspring. Men laughed and swore and ogled the girls, as they stood idly or crowded over cards or drank themselves into an early morning oblivion. Or made love as if they hadn't a moment to lose.

But like ants scurrying from an ant-hill the crowd sifted and shifted as O'Shea's men appeared, ranks of them, mounted and on foot, to give orders, pass information, and exact penalties. Colours jarred and shimmered in the sparkling air. There were those in spanking blue and red serge shirts, in Californian sombreros, and flashy gold-digging gloves. There were gay woollen shirts and blankets scarlet and white already dingy with dust and use. There were knitted comforters. There were foppish shirts and dandy coats, and rags. Many rags. And there were, it seemed, all the women of the town, some already spoken for and aboard, others wheedling to be taken. And so they waited, every Jack and Jill of them, for the order and determination, for the decision, for the very presence of O'Shea.

Over the garbage and the spittle, past the shuffling horses and between cursing bystanders, Raunie picked her careful way, bent on avoiding the neat green wagon Abby had forced Herbert to buy. In the almost empty carpet-bag the few salvaged possessions of her lifetime rattled against the two sovereigns that, despite her desperate bargaining, was all she had been paid for her one decent dress at the Rag Fair down on the wharves – gold-miners' women needed working clothes not fripperies and everyone wanted rid of excess baggage. So she wore the only thing she possessed not worth selling, the red dress, covered by a shawl as sensible as she could bear. Old and discoloured as the dress was she wore it as a gesture; as the one visible link remaining between her past life and the one to come.

It was difficult to designate exactly where the cavalcade began and the store precincts ended, so great was the crush. And this was only part of it – other pilgrims would fall in along the route. Raunie watched the scene with mingled excitement and dismay. Never in her life had she willingly left the familiar trappings of a town and its creature comforts, spasmodic and grudging as they might be; those amenities that pandered to her vanity and her flesh. But today she had simply walked out of Winthrop – the lease was almost expired – and had not even glanced behind her. There was nothing to keep anyone there longer. Her network of lies had finally soothed Abby and sent the woman off at her ease, outwardly at least . . . Of *course* Abby must go with her folk if only to see Kitty and the baby safely settled. When it pleased her she could return to keep house for Mrs William Dover, for of course she would marry the man sooner or later; after all, what else was there for her to do? Raunie was not really surprised at Abby's almost casual farewells. In spite of the woman's years of devotion, Kitty was her primary passion; if Abby believed her mistress's lies it was because the woman longed to believe them. Sooner or later Raunie must meet up with them on the road – but not yet. Not, she hoped, for days to come. She planned to make at least her start alone and unhindered.

'Where are your smiles, you scraggy bawds? 'Pon me sammy but you're a puny lot. Wake up there or you'll be left to rot along the way. No loss neither.'

Raunie stopped dead. How could she ever forget that voice . . . She climbed on a pile of boxes and, shielded by another pile, took a cautious peep. Yes, there in all her dingy glory was the Duchess. With a wagon as stage a fellow in yokel's garb was bawling a comic song to the vague harp strumming of a girl with dirty yellow hair. At the other end of the vehicle a couple indulged in clowning and repartee that brought guffaws and hoots and an occasional coin from the crowd. Marshalling a group of music-hall girls waiting their turn was the Duchess, tweaking their bonnets and sticky curls, exchanging witticisms and obscenities with the mob and inviting the collection. So tightly laced was she into an outsize in crinolines her words issued in blasts and her face glowed red under the powder. Raunie noted her bloodshot eyes, blotched veins in her cheeks, and her sweating restless hands – yes, for all her bravado, the Duchess looked very much down on her luck. And by the looks of her jaded, half-starved women she would be glad of a dancer, a young attractive dancer. Raunie went her way with a new confidence. With the Duchess along to provide her with some kind of shelter Brick would have little excuse to send her back, even if he wished to. And the Duchess had better be willing to take her under her wing for she, Raunie, knew things about the Duchess the woman would do much to keep hidden. She swung along humming a tune to herself, well satisfied. The Duchess would keep.

She did not know just how or where it began, that zephyr of a murmur, infinitesimal but persistent and gaining in strength: O'Shea. The name was all about her. And it was still a magical name; not only to herself but to all there. She trembled, stirred by the wind of talk, buffeted by the gale of excitement. Necks craned, people shoved, climbed on the sides of wagons, were lifted high on each other's shoulders to see what they could of him. Raunie clung to the side of a brightly-painted little cart. There . . . yes . . . on one of his greys, surrounded by his henchmen. Now she could see him clearly. She did not know what she had expected after two years but it was Brick, and only Brick, country hat tilted back, his wide smile that could, when he chose, soften his most imperious and aggressive mood. He had not changed. Not to the eye. And she stared her fill of him until pushed aside and her energy became directed towards keeping her feet against the surge of human bodies.

The sun was warm now, piercing the dark cold corners of the city. Slowly, but very surely, under O'Shea's orders and the organised manoeuvrings of his men those off to the fields were assembling in some kind of formation and beginning to move forward. The good-byes began and the tears and the shouts and the excited laughter. Slowly at first, so slowly there seemed no order or direction, the human snake moved along George Street lined with the only ones to be left in the city, the helpless drunks, the maimed, the old, the mothers of babes, and the fearful – and those without money or ambition or impulse. Raunie, coughing in the rising dust, studied the little cart bumping beside her. Its pony was driven by a lad of about twelve while a woman, probably his mother, lay back feeding a baby. Yes, it would do. She proffered some coins and the boy's eyes glittered as he helped her in. The woman glanced at her, gave a lazy smile, then turned back to her babe. They were crowded but Raunie curled down, hiding herself as best she could from wandering, too curious eyes.

The boy, excited, insisted on chattering. His papa was already at the diggings and they were off to join him. Way ahead Mr O'Shea was moving but he would be riding back to direct the placing of children and their mothers on the long line of waiting drays and carts. And to keep his eye on the store-wagons and spare horses. Raunie pulled her shawl more closely about her. They turned into Parramatta Street and the crowd sorted itself out to plod past well-kept fields and stores and stately houses in their parks and gardens. The sun grew warmer and she was feeling pleasantly drowsy resting back in her corner when the reining up of a horse crowding the cart and a boy's clear voice roused her. She looked up, startled. A thin spare lad of about ten years of age was staring at her. His eyes shone.

Raunie looked up into Jamie's black eyes and she liked what she saw. He sat his horse well, a lithe young lad with a set to his head and a swing to his body that was herself, only a petulance about his mouth reminding her of the man who had fathered him. Jamie was no one in all the world but his mother. She knew that. Her son. They stared at each other with an understanding that was instant, an awareness and a knowledge of each other that had always been there groping and unspoken and that always would be there, she felt, in spite of everyone and everything that came between them.

She was not aware of any rush of affection for the boy, only a pleasant sense of possession. She sat up, uncaring now of the notice of others, and laughed at him. 'Hello, Jamie.'

His glance moved from her to the boy then the woman and baby, curiously. 'How are you getting back to the city?' Though the question was offhand enough she knew he hung on her answer. So she made him wait a little, wriggling closer to his horse's flank so she might speak more intimately.

'I'm not going back. I'm off to the fields.'

'You're not,' he derided.

'Oh, but I am.'

He tossed his head. 'That's a poor thing to be riding in then. I can find you better.'

'It will do,' she said quickly. 'At least for the moment.'

His face lighted up. 'You could ride with me a while.'

'I'm not clever at horse riding.'

'But it's easy. I'll hold you steady. Teach you to ride too when we're out a bit.'

'Do you ride up front?'

'When I can. It's where I like to ride. A kind of leading the way – you know?'

'I know.'

'Papa is up front. He'll be riding in advance most of the time. You want to see him, don't you?'

'Do you think he wants to see me?'

'Why not?' He was indignant. 'I want to see you.'

She laughed. 'But you're *you*, Jamie. He doesn't have to feel the same about people and things as yourself, does he?'

'Well, I suppose not. But he'll do most anything I want,' he boasted. 'You'll see.'

She smiled at him. 'That's hard to believe.'

'It's true,' he flashed. 'I can make him do a lot of things.'

'How, Jamie?' she teased. 'By the use of magic?'

'Magic?' He laughed joyously. Clearly he thought it a wonderful joke. And it was a wonderful laugh, she decided, lighting up his smooth handsome young face. A confident, head-turning laugh, and she sank back a little in the cart. Grinning, he looked down on her through half-closed lids.

444

'He does what I want because he sort of dotes on me – though sometimes it's in a funny way. He wants to send me to Ireland, through Europe too, but I don't want to go. So I won't. Not ever. I want to stay here and be with the Indians and dig for gold and make a lot of money and spend it and buy land and hire lots of people to work it for me. You know, be somebody, like a king, so that everyone will know who I am and talk about me. Do *you* see what I mean?'

'I do indeed.' They smiled at each other companionably. 'But you've a battle on your hands if you cross your father,' she warned.

He smirked. 'I don't care. I rather like . . . battling. I like winning too. I think I like winning a fight better than anything else in the whole world.'

'I like winning a fight too.'

'Do you?' He swept his finely shaped hand in a boyish extravagant gesture. 'I have plenty of land. I mean, I'll have it some day. He says so. But he'll never make me do anything with it I don't want to do. Never.' He tossed his head again with that distinctive gesture. 'He's not my real father, you know. He just makes me call him Papa. But when I'm grown-up I won't. And even if he were my real father, I'd still do what I like.'

'I can see that.' A long pause. 'What's he like now, Jamie?'

'Like? How do you mean?'

'Well . . . hasn't he been rather different this last year or so?'

'No. Well, I don't think he's different. He just does things differently.' He bent over to pull roughly at her dress. 'Is this all you've got?'

'About all.'

'And that's a silly looking shawl. You'll freeze. I'd better tell Papa.'

'Not yet.'

'But why not?' He was fretful, itching to have his way.

'Not for a long time yet. Not till I say so.'

The boy stiffened. His mouth set. 'I'll tell him about you when I want to.'

'Oh no you won't,' she said softly. They looked into each other's eyes. At last her face softened into a smile and she watched the hostility in his dissolve a little. Her voice was soft too. 'You won't, will you, Jamie? I want to surprise him. I think he'd like that.'

He fidgeted with the reins, considering the matter. 'Oh . . . all right. I don't care anyway. Why should I care?' He flicked his horse but, as he melted into the crowd, with one of his abrupt changes of mood he called gaily over his shoulder, his white teeth flashing in his suntanned face. 'I'll be back. But I won't tell you when – I'll surprise *you*!' She heard his laugh and his chant bubbling away down the line. 'I'll be back. I'll be back.' And she knew that he would.

An hour went by: another. They were well out now; there was little to see but scrub and trees and the rough dusty road. The woman dozed while her baby slept. The boy gave Raunie water, then bread and cheese and sharp little onions that made her eyes sting. She ate ravenously, contentedly, uncaring where they would camp the night or how, heedless of the difficult weeks of travel ahead. Luck would stay with her – not once had she been halted or questioned. Abby was here, the Duchess was here. And now there was Jamie.

Jamie would do nothing, say nothing, to displease her. She was quite sure of Jamie. Already she knew how to handle him. And already he felt a tie with her, yes he felt it, even though he did not know the reason for it. One day he would know of course. When it suited her to tell him. She leaned back, musing, visualising the power she might have over Brick through Jamie. A great deal of power. But she would bide her time with her son. For the moment his admiring homage was sufficient, to be actually preferred, a relationship without ties, without responsibility. A relationship of camaraderie, of pleasure. And she anticipated the moment when he would come riding back for her, tomorrow perhaps, or the day after, and he would urge his horse carrying the two of them through the people and they would move aside for him. O'Shea's son; his heir. Though they would not all give him smiles they would give him deference. They would doff

446

their caps to him, most of them, and he would like that. She would like it too. And then . . . when they were far out, far from the city, so far that he could not send her back even in spite, out there in nothingness she would face Brick . . .

For she was, as she had always been, a wanderer over the earth. A gipsy. An outcast. Wild no doubt, but free . . . with singing heart. Both she and Brick O'Shea, as one. In her mind, her eyes and her heart, they belonged together. She would have it so. Where he went she would follow him always, caring nothing of the world but the sweet savour of drawing breath, of eating and drinking, of loving him. It was enough. It was everything.

She stirred under the caress of the sun. Something new had entered the rhythmic medley of sound and movement. She turned her head slowly, to listen, then smiled a little and with an almost sensuous wriggle of contentment settled herself more comfortably, more securely, into her corner. From far behind now came a new sound rising above the chatter, the shouts, the squeaking of many wheels, the neighing of beasts, the crack of whips, the grind and crunch of overloaded vehicles on a dirt highway, the swinging kegs, the clank of piled baggage, and the tired cries of little children. The sound that came to her was the long slow swell of voices, many voices. And the song, or the mingling of songs, grew and overwhelmed until it was one great song; a hymn, a prayer, a paean of thanks and praise and entreaty and hope. And Raunie's lips moved too though she did not know or care what they were singing or why, but mingling her voice and her heart and her soul with the half sad, half joyful chorus, as the long long line stretched over the dusty road, on to its Eldorado.

Raunie gripped Jamie about the waist. The horse reared in a swirl of dust, steadied under determined hands and broke into a gallop.

Brick O'Shea turned in his saddle . . .

447

Glossary

Aborigine, Aboriginal
Both in common usage but often applied incorrectly. Aborigine is the noun and Aboriginal the adjective. Correctly, the Australian native is the Australian Aborigine.

Botany Bay
Early name for the Colony of New South Wales

canary
Convict, because of the yellow in his uniform

carrobbery
Aboriginal celebration, nowadays spelt *corroboree*

Caroline Chisholm
The pioneer philanthropist who began her work among the destitute female immigrants of Sydney in the early 1840s. Born into a farming family of Wootton, near Northampton, England in 1808, she died at Fulham, London, in 1877 and is buried in Northampton's Billing Road Cemetery, her grave marked 'The Emigrants Friend'. Her portrait is on the Australian five-dollar note.

cornstalk
Nickname originally for people of New South Wales, later for all Australians

currency
Term covering whites – particularly young whites – born in Australia, distinguishing them from immigrants:
One of the many names for a convict:
Term used for a wide variety of notes and coins, as distinct from English gold pieces called 'sterling'.

diddikai (Romany)
Half-caste

emancipist
Ex-convict

Female Factory

Establishment housing women convicts at Parramatta, where they worked at various tasks until selected as servants, wives or mistresses

First Fleeters

Those who arrived at Sydney Cove with the First Fleet under Captain Arthur Phillip on 26 January, 1788

gitano (Spanish)

Gipsy

gorgio (Romany)

A native of the country; from Raunie's viewpoint as a part-gipsy, the English and other whites

gunyah

Native shelter of sheets of bark supported by pronged sticks

hog

A shilling

Homebush

Homebush Racecourse, Sydney

Indian, Nigger, Black

Terms used by early settlers for the Australian Aborigine

jen

Aboriginal woman – strictly, a wife. Nowadays spelt '*gin*'

lobsters

Soldiers – from their red jackets; also 'redcoats'

Old Stringy

A colonial home-brewed beer

new chum

A newly-landed inexperienced immigrant

New Holland

An early name for Australia

Norfolk Island

A convict settlement off the east coast of Australia, at first a branch of the New South Wales penal settlement, later for convicts who committed crimes in the colony. Known as 'the Ocean Hell'.

old lag

Ex-convict or ticket-of-leave man

Riverside

A Thames-side area comprising Wapping, Limehouse and Billingsgate, frequented by sailors and their women. A Riverside woman was invariably a prostitute.

The Rocks

The crowded squalid district of old Dawes Point, likened to London's St Giles

shammack

A slattern

slops

The ill-fitting rough clothing issued to convicts

squatter

Originally, the derogatory term for stockholders who wandered the inland seeking fresh grazing for their stock and who 'squatted' on Crown land where and how they pleased. The term has evolved as one for the long-established, affluent, landowning class of rural Australia.

station or run

A sheep and/or cattle property in Australia

sterling and pure merinos

The 'upper crust' of the free settlers

tester

Twenty-five lashes

ticket-o'-leaver

A convict of good behaviour who having served part of his sentence was issued with a certificate, a 'ticket', giving him greater freedom of movement and the right to seek employment outside government service and become self-supporting

ti-tree or tea-tree

In Australia a shrub from whose leaves bushmen brewed a substitute for tea

traps

Mounted police

NEL BESTSELLERS

Even Chance	*Elizabeth Bennett*	£1.50
The Marriage Bed	*Constance Beresford Howe*	£1.75
Lights, Laughter and a Lady	*Barbara Cartland*	£1.25
Forefathers	*Nancy Cato*	£2.50
Maura's Dream	*Joel Gross*	£2.25
Memory and Desire	*Justine Harlowe*	£2.50
Only Perfect	*Rochelle Larkin*	£1.75
Sisters	*Linda Lauren*	£1.50
Almonds and Raisins	*Maisie Mosco*	£1.95
The Enticers	*Natasha Peters*	£1.95
Believing in Giants	*Charlotte Vale Allen*	£1.75

All these books are available at your local bookshop or newsagent, or can be ordered direct from the publisher. Just tick the titles you want and fill in the form below.

NEL P.O. BOX 11, FALMOUTH TR10 9EN, CORNWALL

Postage Charge:

U.K. Customers 45p for the first book plus 20p for the second book and 14p for each additional book ordered to a maximum charge of £1.63.

B.F.P.O. & EIRE Customers 45p for the first book plus 20p for the second book and 14p for the next 7 books; thereafter 8p per book.

Overseas Customers 75p for the first book and 21p per copy for each additional book.

Please send cheque or postal order (no currency).

Name ....

Address ....

....

Title, ...

While every effort is made to keep prices steady, it is sometimes necessary to increase prices at short notice. New English Library reserve the right to show on covers and charge new retail prices which may differ from those advertised in the text or elsewhere. (C)